Praise for Kristin Hannah's *New York Times* bestseller, *On Mystic Lake*

"[Hannah] writes of love with compassion and conviction, her characters so alive and dear you can't bear to see the novel end."
—LUANNE RICE

"Superb . . . I'll heartily recommend *On Mystic Lake* to any woman . . . who demands that a story leave her in a satisfied glow."
—*The Washington Post Book World*

"Marvelous . . . A touching love story . . . You know a book is a winner when you devour it in one evening and hope there's a sequel. . . . This page-turner has enough twists and turns to keep the reader up until the wee hours of the morning."
—*USA Today*

"Excellent . . . An emotional experience you won't soon forget."
—*Rocky Mountain News*

"A big, beautiful story of love, family, and second chances . . . Kristin Hannah has written the Must-Read Book of the Year!"
—SUSAN ELIZABETH PHILLIPS
Author of *Dream a Little Dream*

By Kristin Hannah
Published by Ballantine Books

A HANDFUL OF HEAVEN
THE ENCHANTMENT
ONCE IN EVERY LIFE
IF YOU BELIEVE
WHEN LIGHTNING STRIKES
WAITING FOR THE MOON
HOME AGAIN
ON MYSTIC LAKE
ANGEL FALLS
SUMMER ISLAND
DISTANT SHORES
BETWEEN SISTERS
THE THINGS WE DO FOR LOVE

Books published by The Random House Publishing Group
are available at quantity discounts on bulk purchases for
premium, educational, fund-raising, and special sales use.
For details, please call 1-800-733-3000.

ANGEL
FALLS

Kristin Hannah

BALLANTINE BOOKS • NEW YORK

This is a work of fiction. Names, characters, places, and incidents are the products of the author's imagination or are used fictitiously. Any resemblance to actual events, locales, or persons, living or dead, is entirely coincidental.

A Ballantine Book
Published by The Random House Publishing Group

Copyright © 2000 by Kristin Hannah
This book contains an excerpt from *The Things We Do for Love* by Kristin Hannah, published by The Random House Publishing Group. Copyright © 2004 by Kristin Hannah

All rights reserved under International and Pan-American Copyright Conventions. Published in the United States by Ballantine Books, an imprint of The Random House Publishing Group, a division of Random House, Inc., New York, and simultaneously in Canada by Random House of Canada Limited, Toronto.

Ballantine and colophon are registered trademarks of Random House, Inc.

www.ballantinebooks.com

ISBN 0-345-47894-0

Manufactured in the United States of America

First Mass Market Edition: February 2001
First Mass Market Special Edition: June 2004

OPM   9   8   7   6   5   4   3   2   1

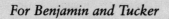

For Benjamin and Tucker

Acknowledgments

To Ann Patty and Elisa Wares—thanks for your boundless enthusiasm, your insightful editing, and your friendship. It has been a pleasure and an honor to work with such outstanding editors.

To Dr. Barbara Snyder and Katherine Stone, thanks—again—for your immeasurable help in medical matters.

To my good friends Ruth Hargiss, Trish Bey, and Lori Adams, thanks for so many wonderful memories.

Part One

What might have been and what has been
Point to one end, which is always present.
Footfalls echo in the memory
Down the passage which we did not take
Towards the door we never opened . . .

T. S. ELIOT, FROM "BURNT NORTON"

Chapter One

In northwest Washington state, jagged granite mountains reach for the misty sky, their peaks inaccessible even in this age of helicopters and high-tech adventurers. The trees in this part of the country grow thick as an old man's beard and block out all but the hardiest rays of the sun. Only in the brightest months of summer can hikers find their way back to the cars they park along the sides of the road.

Deep in the black-and-green darkness of this old-growth forest lies the tiny town of Last Bend. To visitors—there are no strangers here—it is the kind of place they'd thought to encounter only in the winding tracks of their own imaginations. When they first walk down the streets, folks swear they hear a noise that can only be described as laughter. Then come the memories, some real, some manufactured images from old movies and *Life* magazine. They recall how their grandmother's lemonade tasted . . . or the creaky sound of a porch swing gliding quietly back and forth, back and forth, on the tail end of a muggy summer's night.

Last Bend was founded fifty years ago, when a big, broad-shouldered Scotsman named Ian Campbell gave up his crumbling ancestral home in Edinburgh and set off in search of adventure. Somewhere along the way—family legend attributed it to Wyoming—he took up rock climbing, and spent the next ten years wandering from mountain to mountain, looking for two things: the ultimate climb and a place to leave his mark.

He found what he was looking for in Washington's North Cascade mountain range. In this place where Sasquatches were more than a campfire myth and glaciers flowed year round in ice-blue rivers, he staked his claim. He drove as close to the mighty Mt. Baker as he could and bought a hundred acres of prime pastureland, then he bought a corner lot on a gravel road that would someday mature into the Mount Baker Highway. He built his town along the pebbly, pristine shores of Angel Lake and christened it Last Bend, because he thought the only home worth having was worth searching for, and he'd found his at the last turn in the road.

It took him some time to find a woman willing to live in a moss-chinked log cabin without electricity or running water, but find her he did—a fiery Irish lass with dreams that matched his own. Together they fashioned the town of their combined imagination; she planted Japanese maple saplings along Main Street and started a dozen traditions—Glacier Days, the

Sasquatch race, and the Halloween haunted house on the corner of Cascade and Main.

In the same year the Righteous Brothers lost that lovin' feeling, Ian and Fiona began to build their dream home, a huge, semicircular log house that sat on a small rise in the middle of their property. On some days, when the sky was steel blue, the glaciered mountain peaks seemed close enough to touch. Towering Douglas firs and cedars rimmed the carefully mowed lawn, protected the orchard from winter's frozen breath. Bordering the west end of their land was Angel Creek, a torrent in the still gloaming of the year, a quiet gurgling creek when the sun shone high and hot in the summer months. In the wintertime, they could step onto their front porch and hear the echo of Angel Falls, only a few miles away.

Now the third generation of Campbells lived in that house. Tucked tightly under the sharply sloped roofline was a young boy's bedroom. It was not unlike other little boys' rooms in this media-driven age—Corvette bed, Batman posters tacked to the uneven log walls, *Goosebumps* books strewn across the shag-carpeted floor, piles of plastic dinosaurs and fake snakes and *Star Wars* action figures.

Nine-year-old Bret Campbell lay quietly in his bed, watching the digital clock by his bed flick red numbers into the darkness. Five-thirty. Five thirty-one. Five thirty-two.

Halloween morning.

He had wanted to set the alarm for this special Saturday morning, but he didn't know how, and if he'd asked for help, his surprise would have been ruined. And so he snuggled under the Mr. Freeze comforter, waiting.

At precisely 5:45, he flipped the covers back and climbed out of bed. Careful not to make any noise, he pulled the grocery sack from underneath his bed and unpacked it.

There was no light on, but he didn't need one. He'd stared at these clothes every night for a week. His Halloween costume. A sparkly pair of hand-me-down cowboy boots that they'd picked up at the Emperor's New Clothes used-clothing shop, a fake leather vest from the Dollar-Saver thrift shop, a pair of felt chaps his mom had made, a plaid flannel shirt and brand-new Wrangler jeans from Zeke's Feed and Seed, and best of all, a shiny sheriff's star and gun belt from the toy store. His daddy had even made him a kid-sized lariat that could be strapped to the gun belt.

He stripped off his pj's and slipped into the outfit, leaving behind the gun belt, guns, chaps, lariat, and ten-gallon hat. Those he wouldn't need now.

He *felt* like a real cowboy. He grabbed the index card with the instructions on it—just in case—and went to his bedroom door, peeking out into the shadowy hallway.

He peered down at the other two bedrooms. Both doors were closed and no light slid out from underneath. Of course his sixteen-year-old sister, Jacey, was asleep. It was Saturday, and on the day after a high-school football game, she always slept until noon. Dad had been at the hospital all night with a patient, so he'd be tired this morning, too. Only Mom would be getting up early—and she'd be in the barn, ready to go, at six o'clock.

He pushed the flash button on his Darth Maul watch. Five forty-nine.

"Yikes." He flicked up the collar on his flannel shirt and bounded down the last set of stairs. Feeling his way through the darkened kitchen, he hit the "on" button on the coffeepot (another surprise) and headed for the front door, opening it slowly.

On the porch, he was spooked by the black shape of a man beside him, but in the second after he saw the outline, he remembered. It was the pumpkin-headed farmer he and Mom had made last night. The smell of fresh straw was strong—even a day later.

Bret picked his way past the decorations and jumped off the porch, then he ran up the driveway. At the empty guest cottage, he zagged to the right and slithered between the fence's second and third rail. Breathing hard, he clambered up the slippery grass pasture.

A single floodlight lit up the huge, two-storied barn his granddad had built. Bret had always been in awe of the famous grandfather he'd never met, the man who'd left his name on streets and buildings and mountains, the man who'd somehow known that Last Bend belonged right here.

The stories of granddad's adventures had been told and retold for as long as Bret could remember, and he wanted to be just like him. That's why he was up so early on this Halloween morning. He was going to convince his overprotective mother that he was ready to go on the Angel Falls overnight trail ride.

He grabbed the cold iron latch on the barn door and swung it open. He loved the smell of this old barn; it always made him think of his mom. Sometimes, when he was away from home, he'd smell something—hay or leather or neat's-foot oil—and he'd think of her.

Horses nickered softly and moved around in their stalls, thinking it was feeding time. He flicked on the lights and hurried down the wide cement aisle toward the tack room. He struggled to pull his mom's jumping saddle off the wooden tree. He dropped it twice before he figured out how to balance it on his arm. With the girth dragging and clanging behind him, he headed to Silver Bullet's stall.

There he stopped. Jeez, Bullet looked bigger this morning . . .

Granddad would never *chicken out.*

Bret took a deep breath and opened the stall door.

It took him lots of tries—*lots* of tries—but he finally got the saddle up on the horse's high back. He even managed to tighten the girth. Not enough, maybe, but at least he'd buckled the strap.

He led Bullet to the center of the arena. He couldn't see his boots—they were buried in the soft dirt. The lights overhead cast weird shadows on him and Bullet, but he liked those slithering black lines. They reminded him that it was Halloween.

Bullet dropped her head and snorted, pawing at the ground.

Bret tightened his hold on the lead rope. "Whoa, girl," he said softly, trying not to be afraid. That was the way his mom always talked to animals. She said you could talk down the craziest animal if you were patient and quiet.

The barn door shuddered, then let out a long, slow creaking sound. Wood scraped on cement, and the door opened.

Mom stood in the doorway. Behind her, the rising sun was a beautiful purplish color and it seemed to set her hair on pink fire. He couldn't quite see her face, but he could see her silhouette, black against the brightness, and he could hear the steady *click-click-click* of her boot heels on the concrete. Then she paused, tented one hand across her eyes. "Bret? Honey, is that you?"

Bret led Bullet toward Mom, who stood at the edge of the arena with her hands planted on her hips. She was wearing a long brown sweater and black riding pants; her boots were already dusty. She was staring at him—one of those Mommy looks—and he sure wished she'd smile.

He yanked hard on the rope and brought the mare to a sudden stop, just the way they'd taught him in 4-H. "I saddled her myself, Mom." He stroked Bullet's velvet-soft muzzle. "I couldn't get her to take the bit, but I cinched up the saddle just like I'm s'posed to."

"You got up early—on Halloween, your third favorite holiday—and saddled my horse for me. Well, well." She bent down and tousled his hair. "Hate to let me be alone for too long, eh, Bretster?"

"I know how lonely you get."

She laughed, then knelt down in the dirt. She was like that, his mom, she never worried about getting dirty—and she liked to look her kids in the eyes. At least that's what she said. She pulled the worn, black leather glove off her right hand and let it fall. It landed on her thigh, but she didn't seem to notice as she reached out and smoothed the hair from Bret's face. "So, young Mr. Horseman, what's on your mind?"

That was another thing about his mom. You could *never* fool her. It was sorta like she had X-ray vision. "I want to go on the overnight ride to Angel Falls with you this year. Last year you said maybe later, when I was older. Well, now I'm a whole year older, and I did really good at the fair this year—I mean, hardly *any* nine-year-olds got blue ribbons—and I kept my stall clean and kept Scotty brushed all down. And now I can saddle a big old Thoroughbred by myself. If I was at Disneyland, I would *definitely* reach Mickey's hand."

Mom sat back on her heels. Some dirt must have gotten in her face, because her eyes were watering. "You're not my baby boy anymore, are you?"

He plopped onto her bent legs, pretending that he was little enough to still be held in her arms. She gently took the lead rope from him, and he wrapped his arms around her neck.

She kissed his forehead and held him tightly. It was his favorite kind of kiss, the kind she gave him every morning at the breakfast table.

He loved it when she held him like this. Lately

(since he'd started fourth grade) he'd had to become a big boy. Like he couldn't let Mom hold his hand as they walked down the school corridors . . . and she definitely couldn't kiss him good-bye. So now they only had times like this when he could be a little boy.

"Well, I guess any kid big enough to saddle this horse is ready to go on an overnight ride. I'm proud of you, kiddo."

He let out a loud *Whoopee!* and hugged her. "Thanks, Mom."

"No problema." She gently eased away from him and got to her feet. As they stood there together, she let her gloved hand sort of hang there in the space between them, and Bret slipped his hand in hers.

She squeezed his hand. "Now I've got to work Bullet for an hour or so before Jeanine gets here to worm the horses. I've got a zillion things to do today before trick-or-treating."

"Is she giving any shots?"

"Not this time." She ruffled his hair again, then reached down for her glove.

"Can I stay and watch you ride?"

"You remember the rules?"

"Gee, no, Mom."

"Okay, but no talking and no getting off the fence."

He grinned. "You just *have* to tell me the rules again, don't you?"

She laughed. "Sit down, Jim Carrey." Turning her back to him, she tightened the girth and bridled the mare. "Go and get me my helmet, will you, Bretster?"

He ran to the tack room. At the chest marked

Mike's stuff, he bent down and lifted the lid, rummaging through the fly sprays, brushes, lead ropes, buckets, and hoof picks until he found the dusty black velvet-covered helmet. Tucking it under his arm, he let the lid drop shut and ran back into the arena.

Mom was on Bullet now, her gloved hands resting lightly on the horse's withers. "Thanks, sweetie." She leaned down and took the helmet.

By the time Bret reached his favorite spot on the arena fence, Mom was easing Bullet toward the path that ran along the wall. He climbed up the slats and sat on the top rail.

He watched as she went 'round and 'round. She pushed Bullet through her paces as a warm-up: walk, trot, extended trot, and then to a rocking-horse canter. Bret watched as horse and rider became a blur of motion.

He knew instantly when Mom had decided it was time to jump. He'd watched so many times, he knew the signs, although he couldn't have said what they were. He just *knew* that she was going to head for the first two-foot jump.

Just like he knew something was wrong.

He leaned forward. "Wait, Mommy. The jump is in the wrong place. Someone musta moved it . . ."

But she didn't hear him. Bullet was fighting her, lunging and bucking as Mommy tried to rein the mare down to a controlled canter.

"Whoa, girl, slow down. Calm down . . ."

Bret heard the words as Mom flew past him. He wanted to scramble down from his perch, but he wasn't allowed to—not when she was working a horse over jumps.

It was too late to yell anyway. Mom was already at the fence. Bret's heart was hammering in his chest.

Somethingiswrong. The words jammed together in his mind, growing bigger and uglier with every breath. He wanted to say them out loud, to yell, but he couldn't make his mouth work.

Silver Bullet bunched up and jumped over the fake brick siding with ease.

Bret heard his mom's whoop of triumph and her laugh.

He had a split second of relief.

Then Silver Bullet stopped dead.

One second Mom was laughing, and the next, she was flying off the horse. Her head cracked into the barn post so hard the whole fence shook. And then she was just lying there in the dirt, her body crumpled like an old piece of paper.

There was no sound in the big, covered arena except his own heavy breathing. Even the horse was silent, standing beside her rider as if nothing had happened.

Bret slid down the fence and ran to his mom. He dropped to his knees beside her. Blood trickled down from underneath her helmet, smearing in her short black hair.

He touched her shoulder, gave her a little shove. "Mommy?"

The bloodied hair slid away from her face. That's when he saw that her left eye was open.

* * *

Bret's sister, Jacey, was the first to hear his scream. She came running into the arena, holding Dad's big down coat around her. "Bretster—" Then she saw Mommy, lying there. "Oh my God! *Don't touch her!*" she yelled at Bret. "I'll get Dad."

Bret couldn't have moved if he'd wanted to. He just sat there, staring down at his broken mommy, praying and praying for her to wake up, but the prayers had no voice; he couldn't make himself make any sound at all.

Finally Daddy ran into the barn.

Bret popped to his feet and held his arms out, but Daddy ran right past him. Bret stumbled backward so fast, he hit the fence wall. He couldn't breathe enough to cry. He just stood there, watching the red, red blood slither down his mommy's face. Jacey came and stood beside him.

Daddy knelt beside her, dropping his black medical bag into the dirt. "Hang on, Mikaela," he whispered. Gently he removed her helmet—should Bret have done that?—then Daddy opened her mouth and poked his fingers between her teeth. She coughed and sputtered, and Bret saw blood gush across his daddy's fingers.

Daddy's hands that were always so clean . . . now Mommy's blood was everywhere, even on the sleeves of Daddy's flannel pajamas.

"Hang on, Mike," his dad kept saying, over and over again, "hang on. We're all here . . . stay with us. . . ."

Stay with us. That meant don't die . . . which meant she *could* die.

Dad looked up at Jacey. "Call nine-one-one *now*."

It felt like hours they all stood there, frozen and silent. Finally red lights cartwheeled through the dim barn, sirens screamed; an ambulance skidded through the loose gravel alongside the horse trailer.

Blue-uniformed paramedics came running into the barn, dragging a bumping, clanking bed on wheels behind them. Bret's heart started beating so loud he couldn't hear.

He tried to scream *Save her!* but when he opened his mouth, all that came out was a thick black cloud. He watched the smoke turn into a bunch of tiny spiders and float away.

He clamped his mouth shut and backed away, hitting the fence so hard it knocked him dizzy. He covered his ears and shut his eyes and prayed as hard as he could.

She is dying.

Memories rush through her mind in no particular order, some tinged with the sweet scent of roses after a spring rain, some smelling of the sand at the lake where she tasted the first kiss that mattered. Some—too many—come wrapped in the iridescent, sticky web of regret.

They are moving her now, strapping her body to a strange bed. The lights are so bright that she cannot open her eyes. An engine starts and the movement hurts. Oh, God, it hurts . . .

She can hear her husband's voice, the soft, whispering love sounds that have guided her through the last ten years of her life, and though she can hear nothing from her children, her babies, she knows they are here, watching her. More than anything in the world, she wants a chance to say something to them, even if only a sound, a sigh, something . . .

Warm tears leak from the corners of her eyes, slide behind her ears, and dampen the stiff, unpleasantly scented pillow behind her head. She wishes she could hold them back, swallow them, so that her children won't see, but such control is gone, as distant and impossible as the ability to lift her hand for a final wave.

Then again, maybe she isn't crying at all, maybe it is her soul, leaking from her body in droplets that no one will ever see.

Chapter Two

When he was young, Liam Campbell hadn't been able to get out of Last Bend fast enough. The town had seemed so small and constrained, squeezed as it was inside his famous father's fist. Everywhere Liam went, he was compared to his larger-than-life dad, and he fell short. Even at home, he felt invisible. His parents were so in love . . . there simply wasn't much room left over for a boy who read books and longed to be a concert pianist.

To his utter astonishment, he had been accepted at Harvard. By the time he'd finished his undergraduate studies, he'd learned that he wasn't good enough to be a concert pianist. The best player at Last Bend, even the best at Harvard, wasn't good enough. He could be a music teacher at an expensive private school, maybe, but his talent didn't include the power or the anger or the desperate passion of the best of the best. So he'd quietly tucked that youthful dream aside and turned his attention to medicine. If he wasn't talented enough to entertain people with his hands, he believed he was caring enough to heal them.

He studied day and night, knowing that a quiet man like him, so reserved and ordinary, needed to be better than the competition.

He graduated at the top of his class and took a job that stunned and appalled his Ivy League classmates—at an AIDS clinic in the Bronx. It was the early days of the epidemic and people were terrified of the disease. But Liam believed that there, amidst true suffering, he would discover the man he was meant to be.

In hallways that smelled of death and despair, he made a difference in patients' lives, but he never once got to say "You'll be fine. You're cured."

Instead, he dispensed medicines that didn't work and held hands that got weaker and weaker. He held newborn babies who would never have the chance to dream of living in Paris. He wrote out death certificates until he could no longer hold a pen without horror.

When his mother died of a sudden heart attack, he came home and tended to the father who, for the first time, needed his only son. Liam had always meant to leave again, but then he'd met Mikaela . . .

Mike.

With her, at last, he had found his place in the world.

Now he was in the hospital, waiting to hear whether she would live . . .

They had been here for only a few hours, but it felt like forever. His children were in the waiting room— he could picture them, huddled together, weeping, Jacey drying her little brother's tears—and though he longed to be with them, he knew that if he looked at his children now, he would break, and the tears that fell from his eyes would scald them all.

"Liam?"

He spun toward the voice. His hip cracked into a crash cart and set the supplies rattling. He reached out and steadied them.

Dr. Stephen Penn, the chief of neurology, stood before him. Though he was Liam's age—just turned fifty—Stephen looked old now, and tired. They had played golf together for years, he and Stephen, but nothing in their relationship had prepared them for this moment.

He touched Liam's shoulder. "Come with me."

They walked side by side down the austere corridor and turned into the ICU. Liam noticed the way the trauma nurses wouldn't look at him. It was humbling to know how it felt to be the "next of kin."

At last they entered a glass-walled private room, where Mikaela lay in a narrow bed, behind a pale privacy curtain. She looked like a broken doll, hooked up to machines—ventilators, IVs, monitors that tracked everything from her heart rate to her intracranial pressure. The ventilator breathed for her, every breath a rhythmic *thwop-whoosh-clunk* in the quiet room.

"The . . . *her* brain is functioning, but we don't know at what level because of the meds." Stephen produced a straight pin and poked Mikaela's small, bare feet, saying nothing when she failed to respond. He conducted a few more tests, which he knew Liam could assess along with him. Quietly he said, "The neurosurgeon is on board and up to speed, just in case, but we haven't identified anything surgical. We're hyperventilating her, controlling her pressure and temperature. Barring development of any bleeding . . . well, you know we're doing everything we can."

Liam closed his eyes. For the first time in his life, he wished he weren't a doctor. He didn't want to understand the reality of her condition. They had a state-of-the-art medical center and some of the best doctors north of San Francisco, all drawn here by the quality of life. But the truth was, there wasn't a damn thing that could be done for her right now.

He didn't mean to speak, but he couldn't seem to hold it all inside. "I don't know how to live without her . . ."

When Stephen turned to Liam, a sad, knowing expression filled his eyes. For a split second, he wasn't a specialist, but just a man, a husband, and he understood. "We'll know more tomorrow, if . . ." He didn't finish the sentence; it wasn't necessary.

If she makes it through the night.

"Thanks, Steve," Liam said, his voice barely audible above the whirring of the machines and the steady *drip-drip-drip* of the IVs.

Stephen started to leave but paused at the doorway and turned back. "I'm sorry, Liam." Without waiting for a response, he left the room. When he came back, there were several nurses with him. Together they wheeled Mikaela out of the room for more tests.

Courage, Liam thought to himself, wasn't a hot, blistering emotion held only in the hands of men who joined the special forces and jumped out of airplanes and scaled unnamed mountains. It was a quiet thing, ice-cold more often than not; the last tiny piece you found when you thought that everything was gone. It was facing your children at a time like this, holding their hands and brushing their tears away when you were certain you hadn't the strength to do it. It was swallowing your own grief and going on, one shallow, bitter breath at a time.

He put away his own fear. Where, he couldn't have said, but somehow he boxed and buried it. He focused on the things that had to be done. Tragedy, he'd learned, came wrapped in details—insurance forms that had to be filled out, suitcases that had to be packed *in case*, schedules that needed to be altered. All of this he managed to do without breaking; if he did it without making eye contact with another human being, well, that was the way it had to be. He called Rosa Luna—Mike's mother, who lived on the eastern side of the state—and left an urgent "Call me" message on her answering machine. Then, unable to put it off any longer, he walked down the busy corridor to the hospital's lobby.

Jacey was sitting in one of the red vinyl chairs by the gift shop, reading a magazine. Bret was on the floor, idly playing with the toys the hospital staff kept in a plastic box.

Liam's hands started to shake. He crossed his arms tightly and stood there, swaying a little. *Help me, God,* he prayed, then he forced his arms to his sides and strode into the area. "Hi, guys," he said softly.

Jacey lurched to her feet. The magazine she'd been reading fluttered to the floor. Her eyes were swollen and red-rimmed; her mouth was drawn into a tremulous line. She was wearing a wrinkled pink sweatshirt and baggy jeans. "Daddy?"

Bret didn't stand. He pushed the toys away and wiped his moist eyes, tilting his little chin upward. "She's dead, isn't she?" he said in a voice so dull and defeated that Liam felt the grief well up inside him again.

"She's not dead, Bretster," he said, feeling the hot sting of tears. *Damn.* He'd promised himself that he wouldn't cry, not in front of them. They needed his strength now; the fear was his alone to bear. He forced his eyes to open wide and pinched the bridge of his nose for a second, then he knelt down beside his son and scooped him into his arms, holding him tightly. He wished to God there was something he could say, some magical bit of verbal wizardry that would banish their fear. But there was nothing save "wait and see," and that was a cold comfort.

Jacey knelt beside Liam and pressed her cheek against his shoulder. He slipped an arm around her, too.

"She's in bad shape right now," he said slowly, searching for each word. How could you tell your children that their mother could die? "She's suffered a pretty severe head injury. She needs our prayers."

Bret wiggled closer to Liam. His body started to shudder; tears dampened Liam's lab coat. When Bret looked up, he was sucking his thumb.

Liam didn't know what to do. Bret had stopped sucking his thumb years ago, and here he was, huddled against his dad like a boy half his age, trying desperately to comfort himself.

Liam knew that from now on his children would know that dark and terrifying truth, the one that he and Mike had tried so hard to keep from them: The world could be a frightening place. Sometimes a single moment could change everything, and people—no matter how much you loved them—could die.

The hours of their vigil dripped into one another and formed a day.

Finally it was evening. Liam sat in the waiting room with his children, each of them watching the slow, methodical pirouette of the wall clock's black hands. It had been hours since anyone had spoken. Words, he'd learned, had the density of lead. Each one seemed to weigh you down. And so they sat, together and yet alone.

At eight o'clock they heard footsteps coming down the hallway toward them. Liam tensed instantly and leaned forward. *Please, don't let it be bad news . . .*

Jacey's boyfriend, Mark Montgomery, swept into the quiet room, bringing with him a swell of energy. "Jace?" he said, his voice too loud. He stood in the doorway, wearing a red-and-white letterman's sweater and baggy black sweatpants. "I just heard . . ."

Jacey ran into his arms, sobbing against his chest. Finally she drew back and looked up at him. "We . . . haven't gotten to see her yet." Mark kept his arm around her and led her to the sofa. Together they sat down. Jacey leaned against him. The quiet flutter of their whispery voices floated through the room.

Liam went to Bret and hugged him, cradling his son in his arms, carrying him back to the chair. And still they watched the clock.

Just before nine o'clock, Stephen came into the room.

Liam eased Bret onto the floor. Then he stood up and went to Stephen.

"The same," Stephen said softly. "There's nothing more we can do for her tonight. We just have to wait and see." He lowered his voice then, speaking with a friend's concern. "Take your children home, Liam. Try to get some sleep. We'll talk again in the morning. If anything . . . happens, I'll call you."

Liam knew that Stephen was right. He should take his children home, but the thought of walking into that empty, empty house . . .

"Take them home, Liam," Stephen said again.

Liam sighed. "Okay."

Stephen patted him on the shoulder, then turned and left.

Liam took a deep breath. "Come on, kids. It's time to go home. We'll come back in the morning."

Jacey stood up. "Home?" She looked terrified. Liam knew that she didn't want to walk into that house, either.

Mark glanced at her, then at Liam. "A bunch of us were going to go to the haunted house. Maybe . . . maybe you want to come?"

Jacey shook her head. "No, I need to stay—"

"Go, Jace," Liam said softly. "Just take your beeper. I'll call you if anything happens."

She moved toward him. "No, Dad—"

He pulled her into his arms and held her tightly, whispering, "Go, Jace. Think of something else for an hour or two. We can't help her this way."

She drew back. He could see the war going on within her; she wanted to go and she wanted to stay. Finally she turned to Mark. "Okay. Maybe just for a few minutes."

Mark came over, took Jacey's hand in his, and led her out of the room.

"Daddy?" Bret said after she'd left. "I'm hungry."

"Jesus, Bretster, I'm sorry. Let's go home."

Bret popped his thumb back in his mouth and got to his feet. He looked small and pathetic. For the first time, Liam noticed the clothes his son was wearing. Plaid flannel shirt, fake leather vest with a tin sheriff's star pinned on the chest, crisp Wrangler jeans, and cowboy boots. A costume. The haunted house.

Shit.

It was almost nine-fifteen. For the last few hours, all over town, kids dressed as astronauts and aliens and princesses had been piling in and out of minivans. Their parents, already tired and headachy before it began, would crank the music up—mostly comfort rock and roll from their youth—and drive to the single housing development in Last Bend. In a town where your nearest neighbor was often half a mile away, trick-or-treating had to be carefully planned.

Liam glanced down at his son. He had a sudden flash of memory—Mike staying up late at night to finish the chaps that went with the costume. "You want to drive over to Angel Glen and go trick-or-treating?"

Bret's cheeks bunched up as he sucked his thumb, then slowly he shook his head.

Liam understood. It was Mommy who always organized Halloween. "Okay, kiddo. Let's go."

Together they walked outside, into the cold, crisp October night. The air smelled of dying leaves and rich, black earth.

They climbed into the car and drove home. The garage door, when it opened, cut a whining, scraping hole in their silent cocoon.

Liam took his son's hand and led him into the house. They talked in fits and starts—about what, Liam couldn't have said. He turned on the interior lights, all of them, until the house was awash in false brightness.

If only it weren't so damned quiet.

Make Bret dinner.

There, focus on that.

The phone rang. Mumbling something to Bret, Liam stumbled into the kitchen and answered it.

"Hi, Liam. It's Carol. I just heard . . . really sorry . . ."

And so it began.

Liam sagged against the log wall, hearing but not listening. He watched as Bret went into the living room and lay on the sofa. There was the *hm-click* of the television as it came on. *The Rugrats.* Screamingly loud. Bret stared dry-eyed at his least favorite cartoon, one that only last week he'd said was "for babies." He curled into a ball and sucked his thumb.

Liam hung up. He realized a second too late that Carol had still been talking, and he made a mental note to apologize.

Then he stood in the empty kitchen, wondering what in the hell to fix Bret for dinner. He opened the refrigerator and stared at a confusing jumble of jars and cartons. He found a plastic container of leftover spaghetti sauce but had no idea how old it was. In the freezer, he found dozens of similar containers, each marked with a date and contents, but no instructions for cooking.

The phone rang again. This time it was Marion from the local 4-H chapter. He tossed out a jumbled explanation, thanked her for her prayers, and hung up.

He didn't make it five feet before the phone rang again. This time he ignored it and went into the living room, where he knelt beside his son. "What do you say we order pizza?"

Bret popped the thumb out of his mouth. "Jerry doesn't deliver on Halloween. Not after the Monroes tee-peed his truck last year."

"Oh."

"It's stir-fry night, anyway. Mommy and me put the chicken in its sauce last night. It's marinatin'."

"Stir-fry." Chicken and veggies. How hard could it be? "You want to help me cook it?"

"You don't know how."

"I can slice open a man's abdomen, remove his appendix, and sew him back up. I'm sure I can cook one little boy's dinner."

Bret frowned. "I don't think you need to know all that for stir-fry."

"Why don't you climb up onto one of the kitchen stools? We'll do it together."

"But *I* don't know how, either."

"We'll figure it out. It'll be fun. Come on." He helped Bret off the sofa and followed him into the kitchen. When Bret was settled on the stool, Liam went to the fridge and got out the plastic bags full of veggies and the marinated chicken. After some searching, he found the cutting board and a big knife.

He started with the mushrooms.

"Mommy doesn't put 'shrooms in it. I don't like 'em."

"Oh." Liam put the mushrooms back in the bag and reached for the cauliflower.

"Nope." Bret was starting to look scared. "I tole you you don't know how to do it . . ."

Liam grabbed the broccoli. "This okay?"

"Uh-huh. *Lots* of trees."

He started to chop it up.

"Littler!" Bret shouted.

Liam didn't look up. He sliced the broccoli in small pieces, but the contours made it difficult.

"You gotta put oil in the wok."

The phone rang. Liam reluctantly picked it up. It was Mike's friend Shaela, from the Saddle Club, wondering if there was anything she could do.

Liam found the electric wok. "Thanks, Shaela," he said in the middle of her sentence—*God, I can't believe it*—or something close, and hung up. Then he plugged in the wok and poured a cup of oil into it.

"That's a lot of oil," Bret said with a frown as the phone started ringing again.

"I like it crispy." Liam answered the phone—Mabel from the horse rescue program—and repeated what he'd told everyone else. By the time Mabel said "I'm sorry" for the fourth time, Liam almost screamed. He appreciated the calls—truly—but they made it all too real. And now the damn oil was popping and smoking.

"Daddy—"

He hung up on Mabel in the middle of a word. "Sorry, Bretster. Sorry." He tossed the chicken and marinade into the oil. It splattered everywhere. Tiny drops of scalding oil hit his cheeks and stung.

Swearing, he went back to the broccoli.

The phone rang again, and he cut his finger. Blood squirted across the vegetables and dotted the countertop.

Bret screamed, "Daddy, you're bleeding!"

Riiiiing . . . riiiiing . . .

The smoke detector went off, *buzzzzzz*. Liam reached for the phone and knocked the wok with his hip. Greasy chicken and burning oil and smoke flew everywhere.

It was Myrna from Lou's Bowl-O-Rama, wondering if there was anything she could do.

When Liam hung up, he was breathing so hard he felt dizzy. He saw Bret, backed against the cold fridge, his whole body shaking, his thumb in his mouth.

Liam didn't know if he wanted to scream or cry or run. Instead, he knelt in front of Bret. The smoke alarm was still bleating, blood was still dripping from Liam's forefinger. "I'm sorry, Bretster. But it's okay."

"That's not how Mommy cooks."

"I know."

"We'll starve."

He put his hands behind Bret's head and stared into his son's eyes, as if by pure will he could make Bret feel safe. "We won't starve. Now, how about we go to town for dinner?"

Bret looked up at him. "I'm gonna go change my clothes, okay?"

Liam hugged him again. It was the only thing he could think of to do.

Bret was crying, softly now, silently, and Liam felt as if his own heart would break at the pathetic silence of those tears.

Chapter Three

Jacey came home earlier than Liam expected, looking wan and tired. She hardly said a word; instead, she kissed his cheek and headed up to her room.

When he was pretty sure that both kids were asleep, Liam went into Mikaela's office. He opened the door and flicked on the light.

The first thing he noticed was her fragrance, soft and sweet as newfallen rain. Her desk was scattered with piles of haphazardly stacked papers. If he closed his eyes, he could imagine her sitting at that desk, a cup of steaming French Roast coffee in her hand, her gaze glued to the computer screen as she wrote letter after letter on behalf of animals that were being neglected.

On an ordinary day, she would have looked up at him, her mouth turned downward, her beautiful eyes filled with compassion. *There's a mare in Skykomish so starved she can't stand up . . . Can we take in one more?*

He went to her desk and pushed a pile of newspapers

off the chair. They hit the wooden floor with a *thwack*. He turned on the computer and maneuvered himself onto the Internet, where he ran a search for "Head injury."

For the next hour, he read about other people's pain. He filled up almost an entire yellow legal pad with scribbled bits of information—books, specialists, medications. Anything and everything that might make a difference. But in the end, he knew only what he'd known at the beginning. There was nothing to do but wait . . .

He clicked the machine off without even bothering to close out of the program and left the room.

Downstairs, he poured himself a double shot of tequila—something he hadn't done since the Tex-Mex hoedown at the Legion Hall two summers ago. He drank it in one swallow. Disappointed that the world still seemed remarkably stable, he poured and drank another. This, at last, lent his mind a soft dullness, and finally the knot in his throat eased.

He went to the big picture window that framed the darkened pastures below. The horses couldn't be seen now on this black night, but they were out there. A dozen horses that Mikaela had saved; they'd come from all over the western half of the state, from groups and individuals and bankrupt farms. They arrived, broken and starved and untended, but Mike healed them, one by one, then gave them away to good homes. She had such a tender heart. It was one of the things he loved most about her.

But when was the last time he'd told her that? He couldn't remember, that was the hell of it.

He'd never been good with words. He *showed* his love, over and over again, but he knew that words mattered, too.

He wished to hell he could remember the last time he'd told her that she was his sun and his moon, his whole world.

He poured another shot and slumped on the over-stuffed down sofa.

She could die . . .

No. He wouldn't let his mind wander down that road. Mike would wake up soon, any minute now, and they would laugh together about how afraid he'd been.

But the road beckoned him anyway; he could smell despair burned into the asphalt, hear the fear rustling treelike along the shoulders.

He closed his eyes, remembering everything about her, and when he opened his eyes, she was there, beside him on the couch. She was wearing the ratty, torn old Levi's that he was always threatening to throw away, and a black chenille boat-neck sweater that could have fit a woman twice her size. She leaned back and looked at him.

He wished he could reach for her, touch the softness of her favorite sweater, kiss the fullness of her lower lip, but he knew she wasn't really there. She was inside him, filling him so full that she'd spilled out. "You would have laughed if you'd seen me in the kitchen tonight, babe."

He couldn't hold the grief inside him anymore; he couldn't be strong. At last, he leaned back on the sofa, and he cried.

"Daddy?" The small, hesitant voice floated down the stairs. "Who are you talking to?"

Mike vanished.

"I'm not talking to anyone." He wiped his eyes and rose unsteadily to his feet. He crossed the room and climbed the stairs.

Bret stood at the top in his makeshift pj's—a purple glow-in-the-dark triceratops T-shirt and flannel boxers. Somewhere in his jumbled chest of drawers were several sets of real pajamas, but only Mike could find anything in that mess.

"I couldn't sleep, Daddy."

Liam scooped Bret into his arms and carried him up to the master bedroom, tucking him into the bed that was too big without Mike in it. He curled against his son.

"She was lookin' at me, Dad."

Liam tightened his hold on Bret. It was funny, but only last week, Liam had thought that Bret was growing up too fast. Now the boy in his arms seemed impossibly young, and since this morning, he had been regressing. It was something that would have to be dealt with . . . later.

"When you saw Mommy, her eyes were open. Is that what you mean?"

"She was lookin' right at me, but . . . she wasn't there. It wasn't Mommy."

"She was just too hurt to close her eyes and now she's too hurt to open them."

"Can I see her tomorrow?"

Liam thought about how she looked—her face battered and swollen and discolored, a nasogastric tube snaking up one nostril, all those needles tucked into her veins, the machines . . . It would terrify a child. Liam knew what those memories were like—he had them of his father. Some things, once seen, could never be forgotten, and they could taint an image forever.

"No, kiddo, I don't think so. It's against hospital policy to let a child into Intensive Care. You can see her . . . as soon as she gets moved to the regular ward."

Bret said quietly, "That's how dead looks in the movies."

"She's *not* dead. She's just . . . resting for a little while. Like Sleeping Beauty."

"Did you try kissin' her?"

It took Liam a long time to answer. He knew he would remember this moment forever, and that's how long it would hurt. "Yeah, Bretster. I tried that."

Liam stayed in bed until Bret fell asleep, then he cautiously extricated himself and went downstairs. This time he made himself a cup of tea. God knew the tequila hadn't worked.

Did you try kissing her?

Liam glanced up at the slanted wooden ceiling. "Did you hear that, babe? He wanted to know if I'd tried kissing you."

The phone rang.

He ignored it. On the fourth ring, the answering machine clicked on. He wasn't ready to hear Mike's soft, throaty voice. He squeezed his eyes shut. *You have reached the Campbell residence, and the winter office of Whatcom County's horse rescue program. No one is available right now . . .*

When the message clicked off, another voice came on. "*Hola,* Dr. Liam. This is Rosa. I am returning—"

Liam picked up the phone. "Hello, Rosa."

"Dr. Liam. This is you? I am sorry not to call earlier, but I was working the dinner shift this ni—"

"Mike's had an accident," he said quickly, while he still had the nerve to form the words. Then, taking a deep breath, he told his mother-in-law everything.

A pause slid through the lines. "I will be there tomorrow."

"Thank you," he said, not realizing until that moment how very much he needed her help in this. "I'll arrange for a plane ticket."

"No. It will be quicker if I drive. I will leave first thing in the morning. Will she . . ."

Make it through the night.

"We hope so," he answered the unfinished question. "The morning should be . . . fine. Thanks, Rosa."

"Dr. Liam?" Another pause, then a soft "Pray for her. More than medicines and machines, she will need God now. You pray for her."

"Every minute, Rosa. Every minute."

When he hung up the phone, he went to his bedroom. It took all his strength to merely cross the threshold. When he'd come in here earlier, he'd had Bret with him, and the child in his arms had acted as a talisman. Now, Liam felt acutely vulnerable and alone. *This* was where Mikaela belonged; in this room, theirs, the one she'd once painted fire-engine red just for fun; the one that now had gold moons and stars and suns stenciled on its smooth eggshell-white walls and a chiffon-draped canopy bed that she said made her feel like Candice Bergen in *The Wind and the Lion.* Unfortunately, it made him feel like Candice Bergen, too, but so what? She loved their room, and so he'd crawled into their bed every night and thanked God that she wanted him there. Him, an ordinary man whose only claim to the extraordinary was the depth of his love for a woman.

Rosa Elena Luna walked toward the small altar in her living room and carefully lit two votive candles. Thin spots of light glowed reassuringly within the pebbled red glass.

She sank to her knees on the cracked linoleum floor and clasped her hands, staring at the figurine of the Virgin Mary as she began to pray. First, the Lord's Prayer.

But the familiar words didn't ease this ache spreading through her chest. Tears blurred her eyes but didn't fall. She'd learned long ago that tears were just bits of water that had no power to heal.

She grabbed the rickety table leg and pulled herself

to a stand. After a long night at the diner, her knees made a sound like popping corn.

For the first time in many years, she wanted to call William Brownlow. She glanced longingly at the phone on the wall.

He would be no help, of course. She hadn't seen him in several years. Sunville was a small town, but even in so small a place, they traveled in different circles. He owned a modest apple orchard—not a powerful, wealthy man by anyone's standards, but compared to Rosa, he might as well have been a Kennedy. Though he had fathered Mikaela, he had never been a father to her. He had another family, a lily-white one. He had spent fifteen years in Rosa's bed, but every moment had been stolen from his wife and legitimate children.

He would not come to the rescue of his bastard daughter.

Rosa stood in the darkened living room. Here and there, watery moonlight peeked through the worn, tattered curtains, illuminating the garage-sale sofa, the wood-grained plastic end tables, the religious paintings on the walls. Mikaela and Liam had often tried to get Rosa to move from this house, or to accept money to repair it, but she always refused them. She was afraid that if she left, she would forget the mistakes God wanted her to remember.

It had all started here, in this house she never should have accepted. It had seemed safe enough at the time, a present from a man who loved her. In those days, she had still believed he would leave his wife.

Candlelight illuminated the streaks of condensation that slid down the too-thin glass windows.

When Mikaela was young, she used to love that condensation. She would shout to Rosa, *Look, Mama, it's raining inside the house.*

Rosa wondered now if Mikaela had ever understood why her mother never came to stand beside her at the window. Rosa had seen tears instead of raindrops, had always known that this old house wept at the sadness it had seen.

Bad love.

It was the heart of this house; it had purchased every nail and paid most of the bills. It was mixed into the paint. Bad love had planted the hedge and made it grow tall; it had crafted the gravel walkway that led to a front door designed to conceal that love from all who would recognize it; it was woven into the fabric of the curtains that hid the windowpanes.

She had always known that she would pay for these sins. No amount of confession could cleanse her soul, but this . . . she'd never imagined this.

"Please God," she said, "save *mi hija* . . ."

Again, silence. She knew that if she stepped outside, she would hear the rustling of the bare willow tree, and that it would sound like an old woman weeping.

With a tired sigh, she walked into her small bedroom, pulled her only suitcase out of the closet, and began to pack.

Chapter Four

The bedside phone rang at six o'clock the next morning. Liam had been dreaming—a good dream in which he and Mikaela were sitting on the porch swing, listening to the children's distant laughter. For a second, he could feel the warmth of her hand in his . . . then he noticed the boy sleeping quietly beside him and it all came rushing back.

His heart was clattering like a secondhand lawn mower as he reached for the phone.

It was Sarah, a nurse from the hospital. Mikaela had made it through the night.

Liam leaned carefully over Bret and hung up the phone. He crawled out of bed, showered—not realizing until he'd gotten out that he forgot to use soap or shampoo—then went to wake his children.

Within an hour, the three of them drove to the hospital. Liam settled the kids in the waiting room, then went to the ICU.

He went to Mikaela's bedside, hoping—absurdly—to find her sitting up, smiling . . .

But the room was deathly still; she hadn't moved.

She looked worse. The right side of her face was swollen almost beyond recognition. Both eyes were hidden beneath puffy discolored flesh.

Clear plastic tubing invaded her left nostril, and her mouth was completely slack. A tiny silver trail of spittle snaked down her discolored cheek, collected in a moist gray blotch on the pillow. The flimsy blanket was drawn up high on her chest; it had been folded with methodical precision and tucked in tight to her body in a way that made Liam think of death.

The team of specialists arrived. They examined her, tested her, and talked among themselves. Liam waited silently beside them, watching as his beloved wife failed one test after another.

Truth is, Liam, we don't know why she's not waking up.

Some of the best doctors in the country, and that was all they could say. They didn't know why she wasn't waking up.

Just wait and hope. Pray she lives another day, then another day after that. Pray she wakes up on her own . . .

Although Liam hadn't really expected a medical miracle, he'd certainly hoped for one. Even a radical surgery would be better than this . . . nothing.

*   *   *

The next time Liam glanced at his watch, it was eleven A.M. Through a sliver opening in the curtains, he saw a rosy line of morning sunlight.

It was time to tell his children . . . something.

He walked slowly toward the waiting room.

What a joke. As if expectation would sit only in that particular space. From now on, he knew, every room would be a waiting room. They would bring it with them, him and the children. At home they would see the empty spaces as clearly as their own hands. A vacant chair at the dinner table, an empty place on the sofa.

He allowed himself a moment's pause before he turned into the alcove beyond the nurses' station.

The room was good sized—big enough for large families to gather in grief or celebration. It was antiseptic white, with brown Naugahyde chairs and fake wood-grain tables that held scattered magazines and a few carefully placed Bibles. Like all such rooms, it seemed to amplify the ticking of the clock on the wall.

Jacey stood at the window, with her back to him. She appeared to be intently studying the parking lot, but he doubted that she saw anything except the image of her mother, broken and bleeding on the arena's dirt floor.

Bret was on the gold sofa, his small body curled into the fetal position, his eyes squeezed shut. God knew what *he* was seeing. Again today he was sucking his thumb.

Liam found just enough strength to remain where he was. Maybe that's how it would be from now on; he would make it through on "just enough."

"Hi, guys," he said at last, his voice so soft he wasn't sure for a second that he'd spoken aloud at all.

Jacey spun to face him. Her long black hair—normally manicured to teenaged perfection—hung limply along her arms. She was wearing a pair of baggy flannel drawstring pants and an oversized knit sweater. Silver tear marks streaked her pale cheeks. Her eyes were red and swollen, and in them he saw the agonizing question.

"She's still alive," he said.

Jacey brought a shaking hand to her mouth. He could see how hard she was trying not to cry in front of her younger brother. "Thank God."

Liam went to the sofa and scooped Bret onto his lap. The little boy was so still he seemed to have stopped breathing. "Sit down, Jace," he said.

She sat down on the chair beside them, reaching out for Liam's hand.

Bret snuggled closer and opened his eyes. Tears rolled down the boy's pink cheeks. "Can we see her today?"

Liam drew in a deep breath. "Not yet. Yesterday I told you that her head was hurt, but there's . . . a little more to it than that. She's in a very deep sleep. It's called a coma, and it's the body's way of healing itself. You know how when you have a really bad case of the flu, you sleep all the time to get better? It's like that."

Jacey's colorless lips trembled. "Will she wake up?"

Liam flinched. Any answer—every answer—felt like a lie. "We hope so."

He looked at Jacey and saw the sad, desperate knowing in her eyes. She was a doctor's kid; she knew that not everyone woke up from a coma.

God help him, Liam couldn't say anything to save her from the truth. Hope was something he could offer, but it wasn't a prescription he could fill. "She needs us to believe in her," he said, "to keep our hope fresh and strong. When she's ready, she'll wake up."

Bret wiped his eyes. "Fix her, Daddy."

"The docs are doing everything they can right now, Bretster, but she's asleep . . ."

"Like Sleeping Beauty," Jacey said to her little brother.

Bret burst into tears. "Sleeping Beauty was asleep for a hundred years!"

Liam pulled Bret into his arms and held on to his son tightly. Jacey scooted closer and hugged them both.

When Liam felt Bret's tiny shudder, and the warm, wet rush of his daughter's tears, he buried his face in his son's coarse, red hair.

And he prayed.

There were too many cars in the hospital parking lot. Absurdly, that was Rosa's first thought as she drove into the Ian Campbell Medical Center that afternoon. It took her several minutes to find a vacant parking space. Finally, she pulled in between a battered Ford pickup truck and an old Impala, and turned off the engine.

She took a deep breath and released her grip on the

steering wheel, one finger at a time. When she finished, she found that she was sweating, though the heater hadn't worked in years and it couldn't be more than forty degrees outside.

She gazed at the small figurine of the Virgin Mary anchored to the beige plastic dashboard. Then she got out of the car and walked toward the hospital.

The electronic doors whooshed open; the bitter, astringent smell of stale, medicated air assaulted her.

Rosa's step faltered. She tucked her black vinyl purse against her narrow body and focused on the floor at her feet. It was an old habit, one she'd never been able to break. When she was nervous, she counted every step between where she was and where she wanted to be.

At the front desk, she stopped, barely looking up when the receptionist greeted her.

"I am here to see Dr. Liam Campbell," she said.

"I'll page him," the girl answered. "Please have a seat."

Rosa nodded and turned away. She kept her head down and counted the steps back to the collection of gray plastic chairs. Fourteen, to be exact.

She heard her son-in-law's name echo through the halls. A few minutes later, she watched him walk toward her.

He looked as she would have expected, tired and beaten. He was a tall man, her son-in-law, although you didn't notice that most of the time. There had been several occasions over the years when Rosa had turned to speak to Liam, or hand him something, and had been startled by his height. Ordinarily, he just didn't seem to take up that much space. But he had the heart of a lion. Rosa had never known anyone who loved as completely as her son-in-law.

"*Hola,* Dr. Liam," she said, pushing to her feet.

"Hello, Rosa."

For an awkward moment, she waited for him to say something. She stared up at him. In his green eyes, she saw a harrowing sadness that told her everything she needed to know.

"Is she still alive?" Her voice was barely a whisper. He nodded.

"Ah . . . thank God. You will take me to see her now?" she said, her fingers toying nervously with the brass closure on her purse.

Liam looked away. His sandy blond hair was clumpy and tousled, as if he'd forgotten to wash it. "I wish . . ."

His voice, always quiet and carefully modulated, was now as thin as a strand of silk thread. The whispery tenor of it sent a chill down her back.

"I wish I could spare you this, Rosa," he finished, and when he was done, he tried to smile. It was a desperate failure that frightened Rosa more than his words.

"Let us go," was all she could say.

They walked down one hallway after another. All the way, Rosa kept her head down, counting every step. Liam's body beside her was like a guardrail, keeping her on course.

Finally Liam stopped at a closed door.

Then he did the most remarkable thing—he touched her shoulder. It was a brief, comforting touch, and it surprised her. They were not that free with each other. She couldn't remember him *ever* touching her.

That he wanted to comfort her now, in the midst of his own pain, moved her deeply.

She wanted to smile up at him, or better yet, touch him in return, but her fingers were trembling and her throat was dry.

"She doesn't look good, Rosa. Do you want to go in alone?"

She meant to say yes, *thought* she'd said yes, but she heard herself say no. Liam nodded in understanding and followed her into the room.

When she saw her daughter, Rosa stopped and drew in a sharp breath. *"Dios mio."*

Mikaela lay in a narrow bed—a child's bed, with silver railings. All around her, machines hissed and beeped. The room was dim; thank God. Rosa didn't know if she could stand to see this under harsh fluorescent lighting.

Nine steps. That's how many it took to get to her daughter's bedside.

Mikaela's beautiful face was scratched and bruised and swollen, her eyes hidden beneath puffy black folds of flesh.

Rosa leaned over the railing and touched her daughter's cheek. The skin felt bloated, hard to the touch, like a balloon overfilled with air. She was silent for many minutes. "My little girl," she said at last, "I have seen you looking better, *sí*? That must have been quite a fall you took." She drew back. Her hand was shaking so badly, she was afraid Mikaela would hear the rattling of her fingers against the bed rail.

"We don't know how much she can hear . . . or if she can hear at all," Liam said. "We don't know . . . if she'll wake up."

Rosa looked up at him. At first she was stung by his words, but then she realized it was the doctor in him speaking. He couldn't change himself any more than she could. He was a man of science; he believed in evidence. Rosa was a woman of faith, and a long, hard life had taught her that truth almost never revealed itself to the human eye. "Do you remember when you all went to Hawaii last summer?"

He frowned. "Of course."

"When you got home, Jacey called me. She had been surfing, *sí?*"

"Yes."

"And she got into trouble. The board, it hit her on the head, and when she was underwater, she was scared. She did not know up from down." She noticed the way Liam's fingers tightened around the bed rail, and she understood. "Do not be afraid, Dr. Liam. Mikaela is like Jacey. She is lost in a place she cannot understand. She will need us to guide her home. All we have is our voices, our memories. We must use these as . . . flashlights to show her the way."

Liam's gaze softened. "I'm glad you're here, Rosa."

"*Sí.* It is hard to be alone for something like this."

He flinched at the word *alone,* and she knew what he was thinking, that without his wife, there would be a lifetime of alone. He had his children, *sí,* whom he loved, but still there was a kind of loneliness that only a lover could ease. This, Rosa knew too well.

And one thing Rosa knew about Liam—she'd known it from the first time she saw him, almost twelve years ago—he loved his Mikaela. Loved her in the bone-deep way that most women long for and only a handful ever find.

Rosa couldn't help wondering if Mikaela knew this, if she understood her good fortune. Or if, in some dark, forbidden corner of her heart, there grew the untamed remains of an old, bad love.

Rosa knew how deep the roots of that love had gone into her daughter's heart, and she knew, too, that sometimes a first love went to seed, growing in wild disarray until there was no room for anything—or anyone—else.

Rosa spent almost an hour with her daughter, then she left Liam at Mikaela's bedside and went in search of her grandchildren.

Jacey and Bret were in the waiting room, sitting together on the sofa, their arms wrapped around each other.

It took her a moment to find her voice. "Children?"

With a cry, Jacey pulled out of her brother's arms and hurled herself at Rosa.

"It will be all right, *niña,*" Rosa said over and over again, holding her granddaughter.

Bret sat quietly on the couch, sucking his thumb.

Rosa eased away from Jacey and went to the sofa. In front of Bret, she knelt. "*Hola,* my little man."

Bret's red-rimmed eyes looked huge in the tear-streaked pallor of his face. "She's dead, Grandma."

"She is alive, Bret, and she needs us now." Slowly Rosa took hold of Bret's right hand, tugging gently until the thumb popped out of his mouth. Then she pressed her hands against his in prayer. "These hands of ours, they are for praying."

Jacey layered her hands on top of theirs.

Rosa bowed her head and began to pray: "Our Father, Who art in Heaven . . ." She let the words fill her aching heart. It was the prayer she'd offered to God every day since her First Communion more than five decades before.

At last Bret and Jacey joined their voices to the prayer.

The house was quiet now, not like it should be at nine-thirty in the evening, but the way it had become.

Jacey was in Mike's office, surfing the Internet for a school report. Liam came up behind her.

"How's it going?" he asked, squeezing her shoulder gently.

She looked up. Her eyes were still a little puffy; he knew she was like all of them, prone to sudden, unexpected tears. "Okay, I guess."

"We could move the computer into the living room if—"

"No. I . . . like being in her office. I can feel her in here. Sometimes I forget and think she'll poke her head in here and say, 'That's enough, kiddo, I need to use the computer.' " Jacey tried to smile. "It's better than the quiet."

Liam knew what she meant. "Well, don't stay up too late."

"Okay."

He left her there, in that room that held Mike's presence like a favorite scent, and headed to Bret's room.

He knocked on his son's door. There was a scuffling noise from inside, then a quiet "Come in."

He opened the door. The room was dark except for a small Batman night-light that tossed a triangle of golden light toward the bed, and a skylight cut into the sharply angled ceiling that revealed the starry night sky, making the room seem almost like an astronaut's capsule.

"Heya, kiddo."

"Hi, Daddy."

It was a baby's voice that came out of the darkness, not at all the voice of a nine-year-old boy who'd hit his first home run last spring, and the sound of it brought Liam to a halt.

When he realized he wasn't moving, he forced a watered-down laugh. "Sorry. I think I just stepped on Han Solo."

"His legs were missing awready. Joe Lipsky bit 'em off last summer."

Liam folded himself awkwardly onto the narrow bed. He brushed a lock of red hair from Bret's eyes.

"You know you can sleep with me anytime you want."

Bret nodded but said nothing.

"You used to come into our bed whenever you had a nightmare. You can still do that . . . even if you haven't had a nightmare and you just feel like being with me."

"I know."

This wasn't getting them anywhere. It had always been Mike who could get the kids to talk about anything; Liam wasn't quite sure how to go about it.

"Mommy's not there."

Of course. The king-sized bed seemed as big and empty to Bret as it did to Liam. "I'm still here, Bret, and you know what?"

"What?"

"It's a secret. Will you promise not to tell anyone?"

Bret's blue eyes looked impossibly big in his small face. "I promise."

"Sometimes I get really scared . . . especially at night when I'm alone. It would help me an awful lot to be cuddled up with you. So, you come on in, anytime you want to. Okay?"

Bret laid his head on Liam's shoulder and burrowed close.

They lay there a long time, so long the stars twinkled and faded one by one. Liam started to pull away, thinking that Bret had fallen asleep, but the moment he moved, his son said, "Don't go, Daddy . . ."

Liam stilled. "I wasn't going anywhere." He twisted to the right and pulled a slim paperback book out of his back jeans pocket. "I thought I could start reading to you every night, the way Mo—Mommy and I used to. I know you're big enough to read your own books, but I thought you might like it. Might help you sleep."

"It would help."

"I brought one of your mom's favorite books. *The Lion, the Witch, and the Wardrobe*."

"Is it scary?"

"No." Liam positioned himself against the bed's headboard and pulled Bret up beside him. Opening the book, he flipped to the first page and began to read aloud. "Once there were four children whose names were Peter, Susan, Edmund, and Lucy . . ."

The words gently bound father and son, and transported them to a world where children could step into an armoire and discover a magical land.

Finally Liam came to the end of a chapter and closed the book. The bedside clock read ten-thirty, well past time for Bret to go to sleep. "That seems like a good enough place to stop for tonight. We'll pick up where we left off tomorrow."

Bret looked at him. "Do you believe in magic, Daddy?"

He smiled. "Every time I look at you or Jacey or Mommy, I *know* there's magic."

"Tell me about when I was born again."

It was a well-worn legend, a quilt of often-told stories that could warm them on the coldest night. "She cried," Liam said. "She cried and said you were the most perfect, most beautiful baby she'd ever seen."

Bret smiled. "And you said I looked like I wasn't done cookin' yet."

Liam touched his son's soft, soft cheek. "You were so little . . ."

"But I had big lungs, and when I got hungry, I cried so loud the windows rattled."

"And the nurses had to cover their ears."

Bret's genuine smile warmed Liam's heart.

"Daddy, the kids that went through that . . . armwar. Do they come back?"

Liam wasn't surprised that Bret wanted a guaranteed happy ending. "Yes, they do. Sometimes they get lost, but sooner or later, they always come back to the real world."

"Will you read me more tomorrow night? Promise?"

"You bet." He leaned down and kissed Bret's forehead. As he did it, he remembered the "Mommy Kiss." Mike had invented it when Bret was three years old. A magical kiss that prevented nightmares. "Should we start a daddy kiss? I have a bit of magic myself, you know."

"Nope."

Liam understood. Bret wanted to save that kiss for his mom. Trading it would make it feel as if she wasn't ever coming home.

Bret looked up. Tears flooded his blue eyes. "I think about her all the time."

"I know, honey," he said, pulling Bret close. "I know."

For a moment, perhaps no more than a heartbeat, life settled into a comfortable place. Liam smelled the sweet scent of his little boy's hair, felt the soft twining of arms around his neck, and it was enough. A dozen treasured images came back to him, memories he'd collected over the years of their lives together. And in remembering what had been, he found the strength to pray for what could be.

Chapter Five

Rosa moved into the small cottage beside the main house, set her few personal items in the pink-tiled bathroom, and stocked the refrigerator with iced tea and a loaf of wheat bread. There was no point in doing more; she planned on spending all of her time with the children or Mikaela.

The next morning, after Liam left for the hospital, Rosa made the children a hot breakfast and tried to take them to school.

Not yet, Grandma, please . . .

She had not the heart to deny them. She granted their wish for one more day at the hospital—but after that, she said, they must go to school. The waiting room was no place for children, not hour upon hour, day upon day.

They drove the few miles to the medical center, and then Rosa settled the kids in the waiting room.

She hurried through the busy corridor, head down,

purse tucked against her body, counting the three hundred and eleven steps to Mikaela's room in the ICU.

The small, curtained room still frightened her—there were so many unfamiliar noises and machines. At the bedside, she gazed down at her beautiful, broken child. "I guess it does not matter how old we get, or that you have children of your own, you will always be my little girl, *sí, mi hija*?" She gently stroked Mikaela's unbruised cheek. The skin was swollen and taut, but Rosa thought she could feel a little more softness in the flesh than had been there yesterday.

She picked up the brush from the bedside table and began brushing Mikaela's short hair. "I will wash your hair today, *hija*."

She forced her lips into a smile and kept talking. "I am still not used to this short hair of yours, even though it has been many years like this. When I close my eyes, I still see my *niña* with hair streaming like spilled ink down her back."

Rosa's thoughts turned to the bleak days when her daughter had been so unhappy that she'd chopped off her own hair with a pair of drugstore scissors. Mikaela had been waiting for *him*. Waiting and waiting for a man who never showed up, and when she realized that he had no intention of returning, she'd cut off her lovely hair. The thing he liked best about her.

You cannot make yourself ugly—that's what Rosa had said when she'd seen what Mikaela had done, but what she'd meant was, *He isn't worth this broken heart of yours.* She hadn't said that; she was the last person in the world to devalue a woman's love for the wrong man.

She had thought that Mikaela would get over him, and that when she got over him, she would one day grow her hair long again.

Yet still, Mikaela's hair was as short as a boy's.

"No," Rosa said aloud, "I will not think about him. He was not worth our thoughts then and he is not worth my words now. I will think instead about my little girl. You were so bright and beautiful and funny. Always you make me laugh.

"You had such big dreams. Remember? You used to pin all those *fotografías* up on your bedroom wall, pictures of faraway places. You dreamed of going to London and France and China. I used to say to you, 'Where do you get such big dreams, Mikita?' And do you remember your answer?"

She stroked her daughter's hair gently. "You told me, 'I have to have big dreams, Mama . . . I have them for both of us.'

"It broke my heart when you said that." Rosa's hand stilled. She couldn't help remembering how her daughter's swollen dreams had shriveled beneath the hot California sun.

It had happened years ago, so many that the scent should not remain in the air, and yet here it was.

"I am the one with big dreams now, *querida.* I dream that you will sit up in this bed and open your eyes . . . that you will come back to us." Her voice cracked, fell to a throaty whisper. "I have a dream now. Just like you always wanted. I am the carrier of my dreams now . . . and yours, too, Mikita. I am dreaming for both of us."

Later that afternoon, Stephen called Liam and Rosa into his office.

"The good news is, she has stabilized. She's off the ventilator and breathing on her own. We didn't need to do a tracheotomy. She's being fed intravenously. We've moved her out of the ICU—to a private room on Two West."

Liam barely heard the words. He knew that whenever a doctor started a sentence with "The good news is," there was a hell of a right hook coming.

Rosa stood near the door. "She is breathing. This is life, *sí*?"

Stephen nodded. "Yes. The problem is, we don't know why she isn't waking up. She's healthy, stable. Her brain activity is good. By all measures, she should be conscious."

Rosa asked, "How long can a person sleep like this?"

Stephen hesitated. "Some people wake up in a few days, and some . . . stay in a coma for years and never wake up. I wish I could tell you more."

"Thanks, Steve."

Stephen didn't smile. "She's in Two forty-six."

Liam rose to his feet and went to Rosa, gently taking her arm. "Let's go see her."

Rosa nodded. Together they left Stephen's office and headed for Mikaela's new room.

Once inside, Liam went to the window and shoved it open, sticking his head out into the cold afternoon air. Turning, he went to his wife's bedside and gently touched her swollen cheek. "It's winter, baby. You went to sleep in the fall, and already it's winter. How can that be, in only three days?" He swallowed hard. His life flashed before him, an endless collection of busy days and empty, empty nights. A calendar of weeks without her. Thanksgiving, Christmas, Easter.

Rosa came up beside him. "You must not give up hope, Dr. Liam. She will be one of the lucky ones who wake up."

Liam had given his mother-in-law the gift of ignorance. He'd told her that a bad outcome was possible, but he'd made it sound improbable. Now he didn't have the strength for subterfuge. Brain damage, paralysis, even a lifetime of coma; these were the possibilities. He knew that tomorrow morning he would be stronger, better able to hang on to his wobbling faith. That's what the last few days had been—long stretches of hope punctuated by moments of severe, numbing fear.

He stood perfectly still, trying not to imagine how it would feel to wait for Mike to wake up, day after day, week after week. He drew in a deep, calming breath and exhaled slowly. "I won't *ever* give up, Rosa. But I need . . . something to pin my faith on, and right now my colleagues aren't giving me much to work with."

"Faith in God will be your floor, Dr. Liam. Do not be afraid to stand on it."

He held a hand up. "Not now, Rosa. Please . . ."

"If you cannot speak to God, then at least talk to Mikaela. She needs to be reminded she has a life out here. Now it is up to love to bring her back."

Liam turned to Rosa. "What if my love doesn't bring her back, Rosa?"

"It *will*."

Liam envied Rosa's simple faith. He searched deep inside himself for a matching certainty, but all he found was fear.

Rosa gazed up at him. "She needs you now . . . more than ever. She needs you to be the light that guides her home. This is all you should be thinking about now."

"You're right, Rosa." Then, stronger, "You're right."

"And what you talk about is *importante, sí*? Talk to her about the things that matter." She moved toward him. Her mouth was trembling as she said, "I have slept through my life, Dr. Liam. Do not let my daughter do the same thing."

Bret made it past lunchtime without screaming, but now he could feel the temper tantrum coming on, building inside him. At first he'd just been crabby, then he'd ripped the head off his action figure and thrown the brand-new *People* magazine in the garbage.

He was tired of being in this waiting room, tired of being ignored.

No one seemed to care that Bret was always by himself in this grody, disgusting room. *Jacey's* friends came at lunchtime—they had driver's licenses—and it didn't bother her one bit to leave her little brother alone while she went to the cafeteria with "the gang." Even Grandma and Daddy seemed to have forgotten all about him.

The only people who talked to Bret were the nurses, and whenever they looked at him, they had that *poor you* look in their eyes that made him want to puke.

Bret went to the sofa again and tried to interest himself in drawing, but he couldn't do it. There was that sick feeling in his stomach and it was getting bigger and bigger. He was pretty sure that he was going to start screaming.

Instead, he picked up the nearest crayon—black— and went to the wall. He didn't even bother looking around to see if he was alone. He didn't care. In fact, he *wanted* someone to see him. In bold, sweeping letters, he wrote *I hate this hospital* across the bumpy wall. When he finished, he felt better. Then he turned around and saw Sarah, the head nurse, standing in the doorway, holding a bunch of comic books.

"Oh, Bret," she said softly, giving him that *poor you* look.

He waited for her to say something else, maybe to come in and yell at him, but all she did was turn around and walk away. A few minutes later, he heard his dad's name ringing out through the hospital paging system.

He dropped the crayon on the floor and went back to the sofa. Picking up the headless action figure, he started playing.

"Bretster?"

Dad's voice.

Bret's cheeks burned. Slowly he turned.

Dad was standing there, holding a bucket and a sponge. He set the bucket down and crossed the room in a few big steps, then he sat down on the coffee table in front of Bret.

"I know, Daddy." He tried not to cry, but he couldn't help himself. Every time he sucked in a breath, he tasted his tears. "I'm sorry."

Dad wiped Bret's tears away. "I'm sorry we left you alone, Bretster. There's so much going on . . . I'm sorry."

Bret drew in a great, gulping breath. "I shouldn't've written on the walls, Daddy. I'm sorry."

Dad almost smiled. "I know you want to see your mom, kiddo. It's just . . . she doesn't look good. Her face is pretty bruised up. I thought it would give you bad dreams."

Bret thought about how she'd looked, with her eye open, staring at him, and he shuddered. He wiped his eyes and whispered, "When dead people have their eyes open, can they see you, Daddy?"

"She's *not* dead, Bret. I swear to you." He sighed heavily. "Do you want to see her?"

"The rules won't let me."

"We could break the rules. If you want."

Bret sniffed and wiped the snot away from his upper lip. That image of Mommy flashed through his mind again, and when he saw it, his heart did a little *ka-thump*. "No," he said quietly, "I don't wanna see her."

Dad pulled him into a hug, and Bret felt himself slowly, slowly relaxing. The hug felt so good. He felt almost safe. He clung to his dad for a long, long time.

Then, finally, Daddy said, "Well, pal, I guess you'd better start washing that wall. I don't think it's fair to make the custodians do it."

Bret scooted back. On wobbly legs, he got to his feet and went over to the bucket. When he picked it up, soapy water splashed over the rim and hit his pant legs. Holding on to the metal handle with both hands, he carried the bucket to the wall and set it down. He plunged the sponge into the water, squeezed it almost dry, and started cleaning up his mess.

It wasn't even a minute later that Dad was beside him, crouching down. He grabbed a second sponge, dunked it into the water, and wrung it out.

Dad smiled at him, right at eye level. "I guess this is sort of a family mess, don't you think?"

At dinnertime Rosa took the children home. Liam knew he should have gone with them, but he couldn't leave Mikaela. It was as simple as that.

He stared down at his wife. She was lying on her side now; the nurses had turned her. "I hired Judy Monk to take care of your horses," he told her. "They all seem to be doing great. Even that whacko mare— what's her name, Sweetpea? She's eaten through the top rail of the corral, but other than that, she's okay. And the vet said Scotty's colic is completely cleared up."

He reached for the box he'd brought from home. "I

brought you a few things." He lifted the cardboard box from the chair and brought it to the bedside table. He pulled out a beribboned bag of scented potpourri. "Myrtle down at the drugstore told me this brand was your favorite." He poured the multicolored clippings into a small glass bowl. The soft scent of vanilla wafted upward. Then he pulled out a collection of family photographs and layered them along the windowsill—just in case she opened her eyes when none of them were here.

He set a tape player on another table and popped a cassette in. Madonna's "Crazy for You"—to remind her of the old days. The last item was a sweater of Bret's, one he'd outgrown long ago. Liam smoothed it over her shoulders, tucking the tiny Shetland wool arms around her. If anything could reach her, it would be the never-to-be-forgotten smell of her little boy.

Memories tiptoed into this quiet room. He remembered the first time he'd seen Mikaela. It had been here, in this very hospital. He'd come home for his mother's funeral and found his father—the great Ian Campbell—suffering from Alzheimer's. The disease had slowly and methodically erased every larger-than-life aspect of Ian's personality.

When the inevitable slide to death began, Ian had been moved into the medical center that bore his name.

That was when Liam met Mikaela. She'd been young then—only twenty-five—and the most beautiful woman he'd ever seen.

"Did you know how much I longed to talk to you?"

he said softly, leaning toward her. "You were sitting by my dad's bedside. Do you remember that day? I didn't say anything. I just stood in the doorway, listening to the way you talked to my father."

He sat down in the chair by the bed and took her left hand in his, coiled his fingers around hers. "I still remember the first time you *looked* at me. You'd seen me, of course, but you never really noticed me until I told you that he was my father.

"It was springtime . . . remember that? You'd opened his window and brought him a small azalea plant that was a riot of pink flowers. I saw the sadness in you right away. Was it so close to the surface? I wonder about that now. Then, I thought I was special to see it, like we were soldiers of a similar war. The walking wounded. All I could think was how it would feel to be the one to make you smile. Do you remember what you said to me?

" 'Do you talk to him?' you asked me. I was so embarrassed. I said, 'No one really talks to my dad anymore.'

"And you said, 'Then you should. It doesn't matter what you say, just that you're here. He needs to know you care.' "

Care. It was such a little word. Like *love* or *hate.* There was so much packed into those four letters. Up until that moment, Liam and his father hadn't spent much time *caring.*

"You gave him back to me, you know. I never really knew him when he was strong and bold and sucking up all the sunlight, but when he was old and shrunken and afraid, he finally became mine. You taught me to talk to him, and in those last weeks, there were moments when he saw me, moments when he knew who I was and why I was there. The day before he died, he held my hand and told me he loved me for the first and only time in my life. You gave me that, Mikaela, and I don't know if I ever thanked you for it."

He stood and leaned over the bed rail. He slowly released her hand and touched her swollen cheek. "I love you, Mike, with everything inside me. I'll be here, waiting for you, for the rest of our lives. The kids and I . . . Come back to us, baby." His voice broke. He gave himself a minute, then kissed her forehead, whispering, "Forever," against her skin.

Then he sat back down in the chair, still holding her hand.

Part Two

Still do the stars impart their light
To those that travel in the night.

WILLIAM CARTWRIGHT

Part Two

Chapter Six

For four weeks, Mikaela had seen only darkness.

By the end of the first week, Liam and the children had learned the age-old truth that life went on. As much as they wanted the world to stop for them, it didn't. Day by day, ordinary life pushed into their sterile, grieving circle, demanding, prodding. Amazingly, the sun still rose in a world without Mikaela, and hours later, it set. Thanksgiving came and went, and in the last week in November, the first snow fell.

Liam had learned that it was possible to appear to move forward when you were really standing still. As the coma dragged on, he'd had no choice. The kids went back to school; Rosa knit enough sweaters and blankets to cover everyone in town. Liam hired people to care for the horses; he paid the bills. And eventually he began seeing patients again. At first he'd only seen a few, but now he was up to a half-day schedule. He left the office at two o'clock every afternoon and sat by Mike's bed until dinnertime. Some days Jacey showed up, some days she didn't. Bret hadn't yet found the courage to visit his mother, but Liam knew he would.

Liam's patients kept him busy a few hours a day, and he thanked God for it. Because when he wasn't working, he was waiting, watching his beautiful, cherished wife lie in a bed that had held someone else a month ago and would hold others again in the future.

He stood at his office window, staring out. Next door, the snow was beginning to stick to Mrs. Peterson's picket fence.

In a few hours, the last elementary-school bell would ring; children would begin to gather at Turnagain Hill, dragging their sleds and inner tubes along the snow-slicked street, careening down the hill on their breathless journey to the lip of Mr. Robbin's frog pond.

By tomorrow morning, Liam knew those same kids would wake early and race to their bedroom windows, hoping to find that their backyards were white. Parents would watch the morning news beside their shrieking children, praying silently that the buses could still make their routes. But their prayers would be drowned out by younger, more enthusiastic voices— and school would be canceled. By noon, Mrs. Sanman at the bakery would begin simmering pots of whole milk on her stove, offering free hot chocolate to anyone brave enough to venture to her street corner, and the firemen would blast water along the turnout at the end of Sasquatch Street, creating the best ice rink in the state.

Liam forgot for a second what his life had become. The urge swept through him to pick up the phone and call her, *Hey, Mike, come quick, it's snowing,* but he caught himself just in time.

She loved the snow, his Mikaela, loved the crisp, pure taste of a single snowflake and the tiny spray of icy water that was left on her face when she came inside. She loved mittens with fake fur trim and black angora cowled hoods that turned an ordinary housewife into Grace Kelly. She loved watching her children eat Cup-A-Soup at the kitchen table while snow melted from their bangs and slid down their pinkened cheeks.

He closed the curtains, went back to his desk, and sat down, stacking the last of the charts in a neat pile. He knew that in a matter of minutes, his nurse, Carol Audleman, would come to tell him what time it was. As if he didn't know, as if he hadn't been waiting for and dreading this exact minute all day.

A knock at the door. "Doctor?" Carol pushed the partially open door and stepped into the small, darkened room. "It's one o'clock. Marian was your last patient for the day. We scheduled a short day today, because . . ." She glanced away. "Well, you know why."

He smiled tiredly, knowing she would see the weariness in his face, wishing he could change it.

"Midge called around noon. She left a lasagna and salad on your kitchen table."

That was something else Liam had learned. People

didn't know how else to help—so they cooked. This town had banded together to help the Campbells through this terrible time, and they would remain at the ready for a long time. Liam was grateful for their help, but sometimes at night, as he wrote out thank-you notes, the pain was so flashing and deep that he had to put down his pen. Every baking dish and salad bowl reminded them all that Mikaela wasn't home . . . that she couldn't do the things she'd once done.

"Thanks, Carol." He pushed back in his chair, got up, and reached for his down parka, grabbing it off the hook on the wall. Shrugging out of his white coat, he carefully laid it over the chair-back and followed Carol out of the office, past the empty waiting room. At the door, he patted her shoulder, then went out into the cold.

As he drove toward the hospital, he passed the hand-painted, hand-carved wooden sign that read: GOOD-BYE FROM LAST BEND. HOME OF THE GRIZZLIES, 1982 STATE B-8 FOOTBALL CHAMPS. A banner hung suspended across the road, advertising Glacier Days, the annual winter festival.

Coming soon . . . don't forget . . .

He pulled into the hospital parking lot. The medical center was unusually quiet today. Snow covered everything now, turning the cars into white humps. He parked in his spot and reached under the seat for the two things he'd brought, a photo album and a small wrapped box. Without reaching for his coat, he flipped up the flannel collar of his shirt and headed for the hospital.

The center's electronically monitored glass doors whooshed open. Inside, a few candy stripers were putting up the first Christmas decorations.

He paused at the threshold, then forced himself to plunge into the antiseptic environment that used to be as welcoming to him as his own living room, but now brought him instantly to despair.

He nodded hellos to the familiar faces but never stopped, never slowed. Too many of the doctors and nurses wouldn't meet Liam's eyes.

They no longer believed that Mikaela would wake up . . . or if she did, they thought, whispering among themselves late at night in the midst of a surprisingly quiet shift, she wouldn't be *Mikaela* anymore. At best, they imagined a diminished imitation of what she had been, at worst . . . well, no one wanted to think about the worst possibilities.

He passed the nurses' station and waved briefly at Sarah, the head nurse. She smiled back, and in her eyes he saw a hope that mirrored his own. Ragged, a little worn at the edges, but there all the same.

He paused at the closed door to Mikaela's room, gathering his strength, then he turned the knob and went inside. The curtains were closed—no matter how often he opened them on his visits, he always found them closed when he returned. He walked past her bed and pulled back the blue fabric.

At last he turned to his wife. As always the first sight of her was difficult; it simultaneously made him breathe too hard and not at all. She lay as still as death on the metal-railed bed. A single strand of hair fell across one eye and stuck to her lip. Her chest rose and fell with deceptive regularity; she breathed. The only sign of life. He could see that her hair had been recently washed—it was still a little damp. The nurses took extra care of Mikaela; she'd been one of them. They'd even exchanged the utilitarian, hospital-issue gown for a soft, delicate, hand-sewn version.

He settled into the chair beside her bed. The hard, vomit-colored plastic had molded to his shape in the past weeks and was now almost comfortable.

"Heya, Mike," he said, putting new potpourri in the dish beside her bed. Bayberry this week, to remind her of the passing of time. To let her know that Christmas was on its way.

Bit by bit, he carried out his daily ritual—the potpourri, the careful placement of one of the kids' shirts on Mikaela's chest, the music that seeped softly from the tape player in the corner. *The Eagles' Greatest Hits* to remind her of high school. *The Phantom of the Opera* to remind her of the time they'd gone to Vancouver to see the show. Even the *Rocky Horror Picture Show* soundtrack . . . just to make her smile. He did anything and everything he could think of to engage her senses and remind her that life was still here, that *they* were still here, her loving family, waiting for her to open her eyes and join them once again.

In the corner, the small electric pond he'd placed on a wooden box pumped the music of falling water into the room.

"Hey, Mike . . ." He took hold of her foot and began gently manipulating it the way the physical therapists had taught him. When he'd run through all the exercises on both legs, her ankles, and all ten toes, he reached for a bottle of expensive, perfumed body lotion and began smoothing it on her calves.

Then he set to work on her left hand, starting with the thumb. A careful, precise movement, bend . . . extend . . . bend . . . extend.

He set his actions to the music of his voice. "It was a quiet day at the office," he said in a throaty voice, the only kind he seemed able to manage when he was beside her. "Jimmy McCracken came in again, this time with a marble stuck up his nose, and old Mrs. Jacobsen had another migraine. Of course, she really just wanted to talk. Since Robbie and Janine moved to Chelan, she's lonely. But she brought me some of her excellent cranberry rum cake. Remember how fast you used to sell out of that at the school bake sales?"

Across the room, the tape player clicked and changed. It was Barbra Streisand now, singing about people who needed people.

He squeezed Mike's hand. "Remember when we danced to this song, Mike? It was in the Center Hall at the Minors' fiftieth wedding anniversary, with that local band playing? Remember how the lead singer mangled the words and sang about peepers needing other peepers? We were laughing so hard we were crying—and you said if he said that word again, you were going to peeper in your pants?

"You were so beautiful that night, in your jeans skirt and Western blouse. I think every man in the place wished you were his. At the end of the song, I kissed you and it went on so long, you smacked me on the back and said, 'Jesus, Lee, we're not teenagers,' but I felt you shiver . . . and for a split second, we *were* kids again . . ."

This was how his evenings were spent now. In a gentle stream of words, he poured himself into her, his heart and soul. As if she were a dying flower that needed only a tiny taste of water to lend it the strength to reach again for the sun. He talked and talked and talked, all the while searching desperately for some movement, some blink of the eye or flutter in her hand that would tell him that the heat of his voice reached the cold darkness of her world.

"Heya, Mike, I'll bet you thought I forgot our anniversary." He started to reach for the photo album on the bedside table, but at the last second, he drew his hand back.

It was a collection of pictures from last year's Christmas in Schweitzer. Mike had chosen each photograph carefully to represent their vacation.

He'd been a fool to think that he could open it and look through the picture trail. Now he saw the album for what it was, a wound that, once torn open, would only seep infection and cause more pain. Instead, he glanced down at the thin, flat box beside the album.

It had been wrapped for almost two months and hidden deep in the sample drawer in his office. He'd been so damned excited on the day he'd decided what to give her for their tenth anniversary. He and Carol had scheduled a half day at the office, so Liam could spend this special day alone with his wife.

"I got us tickets on the Concorde, Mike. Paris . . ." *For New Year's.* His voice cracked. For years they'd talked about Paris, dreamed together about New Year's at the Ritz. Why had he taken so long to get tickets? It wasn't money, it wasn't even time. Plenty of friends had offered to watch the kids for two weeks at winter break. It was . . . life. Mike's saddle club activities and her horse training; Jacey's volleyball, skiing, and violin recitals; Bret's Little League and hockey practice; Liam's patients.

Just *life.* They'd blithely thrown their line of dreams out again and again, reeling in nothing but lost chances and missed opportunities. Why hadn't they realized how precious every moment was? Why hadn't they seen that one fall from an ordinarily gentle horse could take their future away?

He stood and grabbed the bed rail, lowering it. The railing fell with a clattering whine and clunked into the bottom position. Slowly he climbed into bed with her. Tucking one arm behind her head, he drew her close, being careful not to pull out her IVs. Her body was limp and seemed frail, though she'd lost only a pound or two.

He held on to her lifeless hand, squeezing gently so that she would know he was here. "Help me, Mike. Squeeze my hand, blink your eyes. Do *something.* Show me how to reach you . . ."

He lay there for almost an hour. When he next tried to speak, nothing came out except the broken, rusty moan that held her name.

"Dad?"

For a second, Liam thought his wife had spoken, but her hand was limp as death and her eyes were sealed. Slowly he turned to see Jacey standing in the open doorway. She was holding a cake.

"Hi, honey." He climbed awkwardly out of the bed and slumped into his chair.

She moved toward him, her long black hair swinging gently against the oversized flannel work shirt that swallowed her lithe, sixteen-year-old body. Her face was winter pale, and what little color her cheeks might have produced was sucked clean away by the sight of her mother. "It's your tenth anniversary. You and Mom always made such a big deal out of it . . ." Her words fell away, and he knew she was looking to him for reinforcement.

It was difficult, but he nodded and smiled. "You're right. She would have wanted us to celebrate."

Jacey set the cake on the table by the bed. It was a round, two-layered affair with pink butter-cream frosting, the same cake that Suzie Sanman at the Lazy Susan Bake Shop had concocted for them every year. Only this year, instead of the normal *Happy Anniversary Mike and Liam*, it was blank on top. Liam wondered how long Suzie had spent trying to think of something festive and hopeful to write before she gave up.

Jacey moved closer to the bed and leaned over her mother. "Happy anniversary, Mom." She reached out a shaking hand and brushed a lock of hair from Mikaela's face. "Can you believe it has been ten years since we married Liam?"

She turned and smiled at him, and in that instant, she was six years old again, a gap-toothed first grader who'd fallen off the jungle gym and sprained her finger. He ached to make everything better for her, but no amount of colored Band-Aids or knock-knock jokes would make her smile now.

"How is she today?"

"The same."

Jacey swiped a finger along the side of the cake, drawing up a big glob of pink frosting. She held it beneath Mikaela's nose. "Can you smell the cake, Mom? It's Suzie's best vanilla cream, with real Grand Marnier in the frosting. Just the way you liked . . . *like* it."

The tiny fissure in her voice was almost more than Liam could bear. "Here, pull up a chair. How was school today?"

Jacey tucked a long strand of hair behind her ear. "Good. I aced the math test."

"Of course you did."

She looked at him, then turned away. He noticed the quick, nervous way she bit down on her lip—a trait she'd inherited from her mother.

"What's the matter, Jace?"

It was a minute before she answered. "The winter

dance is coming up. Mark asked me if I wanted to go."

"You know it's okay. Whatever you want to do is fine."

"I know, but . . ."

He turned to her. "But what?"

She wouldn't meet his gaze. "Mom and I talked a lot about this dance. We were going to go into Bellingham to get a dress. She . . ." Her voice snagged on emotion and fell to a whisper. "She said she'd never been to a prom, and she wanted me to look like a princess."

Liam couldn't imagine his beautiful wife sitting at home on prom night. How come *he* didn't know that about her? It was another of his wife's many secrets. "Come on, Jace. It'll break her heart if she finds out you didn't go."

"No fair, Dad." She looked away, then, very softly, she said, "*If* she wakes up."

Liam wanted, just once, to hold Jacey and say, *I'm scared, too. What if this is it . . . or what if she wakes up and doesn't know us . . . or if she never wakes up at all?* But those were his fears, and it was his job to keep the lights on for his family.

"Jacey, your mother *is* going to wake up. We have to keep believing that. She needs us to keep believing. This is no time to go soft on her. We're a family of warriors, and we don't run from a fight. Do we?"

"It's getting . . . harder."

"It wouldn't be called a test of faith if it were easy."

She looked at him. "I heard you last night. You were talking to Grandma about Mom. You said no one knew why she didn't wake up. After Grandma left, I saw you go to the piano. I was going to say something, then I heard you crying."

"Oh." He sagged forward in his chair. There was no point in lying to her. It had been a bad night, the kind where his armor felt as if it were crafted of cellophane. Remembering their anniversary had done him in. He'd sat at the elegant Steinway in the living room, aching to play again, needing to recapture the music that had once lived inside him. But ever since the accident, he'd been empty; the music that had sustained him through so much of his life had simply vanished. Though he'd never said so to Jacey, she knew; perhaps she'd noticed even before he had. The house that once had been filled with Bach and Beethoven and Mozart was as silent these days as a hospital room.

Music had always been his release. In the Bronx, when he'd felt as if he was losing his soul, he'd played angry, pounding music that screamed that the world was unfair, and in the bleak days while his father was fading into a stranger, he'd played quiet, elegiac melodies that reminded him of the sweetness of life, of the fullness of promises made. But now, when he needed that solace most of all, there was only this aching emptiness inside him.

He gave Jacey the only truth he could. "Sometimes it catches up with me and grabs so hard I can't remember how to breathe. I sort of . . . fall through the floorboards of my fear, but I always land here, at her bedside, holding her hand and loving her."

Jacey looked at Liam with a sadness that wouldn't have been possible just a few short weeks ago. "I want to tell her I'm sorry for all the times she looked sad and I didn't care."

"She loves you and Bret with all her heart and soul, Jacey. You *know* that. And when she wakes up, she's going to want to see those dance photos. If you don't go, we'll be eating macaroni and cheese out of a box for months. No one can hold a grudge like your mother." He smiled gently. "Now, I may not know much about shopping for girl stuff in Bellingham, but I know about style because Mike has bucketloads. Remember the dress your mom wore to the Policemen's Ball last year? She went all the way to Seattle for that dress, and to be honest, it cost more than my first car. You'd look perfect in it."

"The Richard Tyler. I forgot all about it."

"She wore it with that pretty sparkly clip in her hair. You could do that. Grandma could help you. Or maybe Gertrude at the Sunny and Shear salon could help. I know I'm not as good at this as your mom, but—"

Jacey threw her arms around him. "She couldn't have done any better, Daddy. Honest."

He turned to his wife, forced a smile. "You see what's happening, Mike? You're forcing me to give fashion advice to our sixteen-year-old. Hell, the last time I picked out my own clothes, bell-bottoms were in fashion."

"Dad, they're in fashion again."

"See? If you don't wake up soon, honey, I might authorize that eyebrow piercing she's been asking for."

They sat together, talking to each other and to the woman lying motionless in the bed before them. They talked as if it were a normal day, hoping all the while that some snippet of their conversation, some word or sound or touch, would sneak through Mike's darkness and remind her that she wasn't alone.

At three o'clock, the bedside phone rang, jangling through one of Jacey's stories.

Liam reached for the phone and answered, "Hello."

"Hi, Liam. Sorry to bother you. It's Dawn at the school."

He listened for a minute, then said, "I'll be right down," and hung up. He turned to Jacey. "It's Bret. He's in trouble again. I've got to go down to the school. You want to come?"

"Nope. Grandma's going to pick me up here after her errands."

"Okay." Liam scooted back in his chair, hating the fingernail-on-chalkboard sound of the metal legs scraping across linoleum. As he stood up, he leaned over his wife. "I've got to go, Mike, but I'll be back as soon as I can. I love you, honey." He leaned closer and kissed her slack lips, whispering, "Forever."

Life sucks.

That's what Bret Campbell was thinking as he sat

on the hard bench in the nurse's room. His right eye, where Billy McAllister had punched him, hurt like crazy. He was doing his very best not to cry. Everyone knew that crying was for girls and for babies, and he wasn't either one.

Mrs. DeNormandie tapped Bret on the hand. "Hey, bruiser, why don't you lie down? I'll give you an ice pack for that eye. Mrs. Town just called your daddy at the hospital. He'll be right down." She turned to the small white fridge beneath the window and took out an ice pack. It was all floppy like a bag of peas and was the same color as the fluoride Dr. Edwards put on Bret's teeth at checkup time. "Here you go."

Bret leaned cautiously against the bumpy wall. He wasn't about to lie down. What if Miranda or Katie saw him? They'd be laughing at him forever, and they already made fun of him for eating ham sandwiches and carrying a *Goosebumps* lunchbox to school. This morning, he'd decided that the next time Katie said something about his sandwich, he was gonna pinch her right in the fat part of her arm. Of course, he'd decided that before the fight with Billy. Now Bret figured he was going to get such a talking-to from Daddy that he didn't dare add a girl-pinch on top of everything else.

He closed his eyes and pressed the ice pack to his throbbing eye. He could hear Mrs. D. moving around the small room, reorganizing stuff and shutting and opening doors. It sounded just like when Mommy was getting ready for dinner.

DON'T THINK ABOUT THAT.

It wasn't like Bret *wanted* to think about his mommy. When he did . . . when he accidentally remembered things like the way she used to scratch his back while they were watching TV or the way she yelled too loud when he caught a ball during Little League or how she cuddled with him every night for ten minutes before it was really bedtime . . . if he thought about those things too much, it was bad. He didn't cry so much anymore—not until night, anyway. He just sorta . . . froze. Sometimes whole minutes would go by and he wouldn't notice a thing until somebody smacked him on the back or yelled at him or something. Then he'd blink awake and feel totally stupid for spacing out.

That's what had happened at recess today.

He'd stepped out into the snowy yard, and that was all it took. It happened like that sometimes, the remembering.

All he could think about was his mom and how much she loved the snow. The next thing he knew, Billy McAllister was standing in front of him, yelling, "What's your damned problem, Brat?"

"Sorry, Billy," he'd mumbled, not sure what it was he'd done that made Billy mad.

"Come on, Billy," Sharie Lindley had said, "he didn't do anything. Besides, Mrs. Kurek told us to be nice to Bret. Remember?"

Billy's frown hadn't faded. "Oh, yeah. I forgot. His mom's a vegetable. Sorry, Brat."

All Bret remembered was the way he screamed, *My mom's no carrot,* and launched himself at Billy. The next thing he knew, Mr. Monie, the principal, was there, breaking up the fight, blowing his whistle. And now Bret was here, in the nurse's room, feeling like a geekozoid and wondering how he'd face his friends again.

"Bretster?"

Bret flinched at the familiar voice and slowly turned. "Hi, Dad."

Dad stood in the doorway. He was so tall, he had to kind of duck his head forward, and because of that he looked . . . bent. His silvery blond hair was too long now—Mommy used to cut it—and it fell across his wire-rimmed glasses a little. But Bret wasn't fooled by those bits of glass. He'd learned long ago that his daddy's green eyes saw everything.

Mrs. DeNormandie looked up from her work. She was organizing tongue depressors in a glass jar. "Oh. Hello, Dr. Campbell."

In the old days, Dad would have smiled at Mrs. DeNormandie and she would have smiled back, but now neither one of them smiled. "Hey, Barb," Dad said quietly, "could you give us a few minutes?"

"Of course." She put the tongue depressors away and quickly left the room, shutting the door behind her.

Quiet fell, the icky kind that spelled big trouble.

"How's the eye?" Dad said finally.

Bret turned to him, letting Daddy see for himself. He dropped the ice pack onto the floor. "It doesn't hurt."

Dad sat down beside Bret. "Really?" he said in that we-don't-lie-in-this-family voice.

"Okay, okay. It hurts worse than when Jacey's cow stepped on my foot at the fair." At his dad's soft look, Bret almost started to cry again. If Mommy were here—

DON'T THINK ABOUT THAT.

"I guess you've learned the first rule of fighting. It hurts. The second rule is: It doesn't change anything. Who started it?"

"I did."

Dad looked surprised. "That doesn't sound like you."

"I was mad." Bret braced himself for the horrible words: *I'm disappointed in you, son.*

He felt like crying already, and Dad hadn't said anything.

And he didn't say anything. Instead, he put his arm around Bret's shoulder and pulled him close. Bret climbed onto his dad's big, comfortable lap. For once, he didn't care if he looked like a baby.

Dad brushed the hair away from Bret's face. "That's going to be quite a shiner. Worse than the one Ian Allen got last Fourth of July. Why did you punch Billy?"

"He's a bully."

"But you're not."

Bret knew his dad would find out. Sharie's aunt Georgia was best friends with Ida Mae at the diner, who served lunch every day to Carol, who worked in

Dad's office. In a town like Last Bend, it would be big news that Bret Campbell punched out Billy McAllister and broke his front tooth. The only question would be why. "Billy said Mom was a vegetable."

It seemed to take Daddy a long time to answer. "We've talked and talked about this, Bret. Your mom is in a coma. She's sleeping. If you'd come down and see her—"

"I *don't* wanna see her!"

"I know." Dad sighed. "Well, come on, sport, let's go. They might need this bench for kids with serious injuries." He helped Bret into his puffy winter coat, then lifted him up. Bret hung on, burying his face in the warm crook of his dad's neck, as they headed out of the school and into the softly falling snow. At the car, Dad let Bret slide down to the icy sidewalk.

He stood next to the car, waiting for his daddy to get the car unlocked. His hands were cold, so he reached into his pockets for his gloves—but they weren't there.

It was Mommy who used to tuck mittens in Bret's pockets Just In Case, and now they were empty.

Dad got in his side of the car, then shoved the passenger door open, and Bret got inside. When the engine turned over, the radio came on. It was playing the first Christmas song of the season, "Silent Night."

Dad clicked the radio off, fast.

Snow pattered against the windshield, blurring the outside world. The windshield wipers came on and made two big humps through the snow. Bret stared at them—anything was better than looking at his dad right now. *Ka-thump*. *Ka-thump*. *Ka-thump*. The wipers moved right and left, right and left, making exactly the same sound as a heart beating.

Dad put the car in gear and drove slowly out of the school parking lot. He turned on Glacier Way, then again on Main Street, then again on Cascade Avenue. In silence they drove past the empty parking lot of the Bean There, Done That coffee shop, past the empty front window of the Sunny & Shear Beauty Salon, and past the crowded entrance to Zeke's Feed and Seed.

"I'll bet old Zeke is busier than a one-armed paper hanger right now," Dad said.

It was one of his dad's favorite expressions. No one could ever just be busy. They had to be busier than a one-armed paper hanger. Whatever that was. "Yep," Bret said.

"Lots of folks'll be caught by surprise with this weather. It's early for snow."

For the next few miles, Dad didn't say a thing. As they edged out of town, the paved road turned into snow-covered gravel, and there weren't any other tracks at all. Dad put the Explorer in four-wheel drive and lowered his speed.

Bret wished Daddy hadn't mentioned visiting Mommy. Just the thought made Bret feel sick. Usually he pretended that she was out of town, at a horse show in Canada.

He *hated* it when he was reminded that she was in the hospital. It was bad enough that he remembered THE DAY. He squeezed his eyes shut, but the memories came anyway, the ones he hated, the ones that lived curled in the wheels of his Corvette bed and came at him every night as soon as Daddy turned off the lights and shut the door.

Wait, Mommy. The jump is in the wrong place. Someone musta moved it . . .

Bret turned to look at Dad. "Do you *swear* Mom's gonna wake up?"

Dad didn't answer right away. When he finally did, it was in a quiet voice. "I can't *swear* she'll be fine, son. I can't even swear that she'll wake up. But I believe it with all my heart and soul, and she needs you to believe it, too."

"I believe it."

He said it too fast; his daddy knew he was lying.

After that, Bret leaned his head against the window and closed his eyes. He didn't want to see his mom lying in that hospital bed. He liked it better when he pretended she was still alive. Sometimes he could close his eyes and imagine her standing beside his bed, with her hair short and spiky around her face and her arms crossed. She'd be smiling at him, and she looked like she used to—no bruises or cuts at all. And she always said the same thing: *How's my favorite boy in the whole world?*

But it was just a silly old dream, and it didn't mean a thing. Bret might be little, and maybe sometimes he didn't know what to do with the remainder at the end of a long-division problem, but he wasn't stupid. He knew that fairy tales and cartoons weren't real. Everybody knew that Wile E. Coyote couldn't *really* fall from an airplane and live or that princesses who ate poisoned apples and slept in glass cases for years couldn't wake up.

And mommies who fell off horses and cracked their heads against the wooden post at the end of the arena were really dead.

Chapter Seven

Liam stared at the mail in his lap. Almost all of it was addressed to Mikaela. Bills from the Country Corner General Store and the feed store, stabling and lessons checks from the twelve families who paid to board their horses at the barn, postcards and leaflets and flyers. A postcard announcing Nordstrom's latest sale.

In ordinary times, he would have gone into the kitchen and tossed the postcard on the kitchen table and said, "Oh, no, the Christmas sale is starting. . . ." She would have laughed easily, turning away from the stove or the refrigerator or the washing machine as she said, "We'll just sell a few shares of Microsoft to get me through. . . ."

"Daddy, why are we sitting at the mailbox?"

"Oh. Sorry about that, Bretster. I was just thinking about something." Tossing the pile of mail into the well between them, he eased his foot off the brake pedal and pressed cautiously on the gas. The Explorer's tires spun on the mushy rim of the road, then grabbed on to the gravel and lurched forward. Ahead of them, the deserted road was a twisted river of fallen snow. Towering Douglas firs and cedar trees, their downslung branches dusted white, hemmed the thin strip of road that Ian Campbell had carved from the forest almost fifty years ago. There were a few other farmhouses along the way, their slanted, rock-dented mailboxes stuck at haphazard angles on spindly wooden legs.

"Maybe we could build a snowman after dinner," Liam said awkwardly, wondering where Mikaela kept the mittens and the extra woolen socks. He knew there was a box somewhere, probably marked *Winter clothes,* but he couldn't remember where they'd stashed it last year. Maybe behind the stack of Christmas decorations in the attic.

"Oh. Okay."

"Or maybe we could drive down to Turnagain Hill and go sledding. Mr. Robbin told us to come on down anytime for dinner."

"Oh. Okay."

Liam couldn't think of anything else to say. They both knew there would be no sledding, no ice-skating, no snowmen, and no hot cocoa. Not now. They would think of such things, perhaps even talk about doing them, but in the end, as they'd done for the past four weeks, they would come together in that big house in the middle of the snowy field and go their separate ways.

They would eat dinner together, each one in turn tossing out some inane, pointless bit of conversation.

After dinner they would do the dishes, the four of them. Then they would try to watch television together, *Wild Discovery* or maybe a sitcom, but gradually they would drift apart. Jacey would burrow into her room and talk on the phone. Bret would settle in front of his computer and play loud, fast-paced games that required his full attention, and Rosa would knit.

Liam would float from room to room, doing nothing, trying to keep his mind blank. More often than not, he ended up in front of the grand piano in the living room, staring down at the keyboard, wishing the music was still in his heart and in his fingers, but knowing that it was gone.

He downshifted and turned left, passing beneath the rough-hewn arch his dad had constructed years ago, onto the driveway that was lined with snow-dusted four-rail fencing. In some distant part of his mind, he heard the gentle clanking of the iron sign that hung suspended from the cross-beam of the cedar arch, the one that read ANGEL FALLS RANCH. Or maybe it was his imagination, that sound, and all he really heard was the tinny silence between himself and his son.

He pulled into the garage and turned off the engine. Bret immediately unbuckled his seat belt, grabbed his backpack, and hurried into the house.

Liam sat there, hands planted on the wheel. He didn't look at the album and present he'd tossed in the backseat, but he knew they were there.

Finally he got out of the car and headed into the

house, passing through the cluttered mudroom. At the end of the hallway, a light glowed faintly orange.

Thank God for Rosa.

He was still a little awkward around her, uncomfortable. She was so damned quiet, like one of those Cold War spies who'd learned to walk without making a sound. Sometimes he caught her staring at him, and in her dark eyes he saw a sadness that went clear to the bone. Sometimes he wished he were the kind of man who could go to her, smiling, and say, *So, Rosa, what happened to you?* But that's not how they were with each other. If Liam had asked the personal question, Rosa wouldn't have answered. And so, they moved around each other, close but not too close.

Now, as he moved through the house, he flicked on the lights. No matter how often he told Rosa that electricity was cheap, she turned on only the lights she needed.

Not like Mike, who hated a dark house.

When he reached the great room, he stood in the shadows, watching Rosa and Bret set up for Yahtzee. Within minutes they had a game going. He wished he didn't notice how quietly Bret played. There was none of the clapping or whistling or "All rights!" that used to be his son's natural soundtrack.

They were quite a pair, the silent little boy with the blackening eye and his equally solemn grandmother.

She was such a small woman, Rosa, only a hand's width taller than her grandson, and the way she moved—head down, shoulders hunched—made her appear even smaller. Tonight, as usual, she was dressed all in black. The somber fabric emphasized the snowy whiteness of her hair and skin. She was a woman of sharp contrasts. Black and white, cold and warm, spiritual and down-to-earth.

Rosa looked up and saw him. "*Hola,* Dr. Liam."

He'd told her a dozen times to please, please call him Liam, but she wouldn't do it. Smiling, he moved toward them. "Who's winning?"

"My grandson, of course. He takes advantage of my fading eyesight."

"Don't listen to her, Bret. Your grandma sees everything."

"You would like to join us, *sí*?"

"I don't think so." He ruffled Bret's hair—a substitute for time and intimacy, he knew—but it was all he could manage.

"You sure, Dad?" Bret's disappointment was obvious.

"I'm sure, buddy. Maybe later."

Bret sighed. "Yeah, right."

Liam headed toward the stairs.

"Dr. Liam, wait." Rosa stood up in a single, fluid motion and followed him into the dining room.

There, in the dark, quiet room, she stared up at him. Her eyes were as black as pools of ink, and as readable. "The children . . . they are much quiet today. I think something is—"

"It's our tenth wedding anniversary." He blurted the whole sentence out at once, then he slowed down. "The kids . . . knew I'd bought Mike tickets to Paris."

"Oh. *Lo siento.*" Something close to a smile breezed

across her mouth and disappeared. "She is lucky to have you, Dr. Liam. I do not know if I have ever told you this."

It touched him deeply, that simple sentiment from this woman who spoke so rarely. "Thanks, Rosa, I—" He started to say something else—what, he didn't know—but all at once his voice dried up.

"Dr. Liam." Her soft voice elongated the vowels in his name and turned it into music. "Come play a game of Yahtzee with us. It will help."

"No. I need . . ." A bad start. There were so many things he needed. "I have something to do upstairs. Jacey needs to borrow one of Mike's dresses for the winter dance."

She leaned closer. He had an odd sense that she wanted to say something more, but she turned away and headed back to the game.

Liam went into the kitchen and poured himself a drink. The Crown Royal burned down his throat and set his stomach on fire. Holding the drink tightly, he moved up the wide staircase to the second floor. He could hear music seeping from beneath Jacey's closed door. At least it was considered music by Jacey, some jarring, pounding batter of drums and electric guitars.

With a glance down the hallway, he turned into his bedroom and flicked on the light. The room, even in its current state of disarray—unmade bed, shoes and clothes and bath towels scattered across the floor— welcomed him as it always did. The creamy walls, stenciled with stars and moons, the gauzy drapery of the canopy, the creamy Berber carpet. If he closed his eyes, he could imagine Mike standing there at the French doors, looking out at the falling snow. She would be wearing the peach silk nightgown that fell in graceful folds down her lithe body.

He refused to close his eyes, but it was tempting, so tempting. Instead he stared straight ahead.

The door to Mike's walk-in closet seemed to magnify before his eyes. He hadn't ventured into it since the day of the accident, when he'd naively packed her a suitcase full of things she might need at the hospital.

He crossed the room and paused at the closet, then he reached for the knob and twisted. The oak door creaked and swung inward easily, as if it had been waiting for this moment for weeks.

A floor-length mirror along the end wall caught his image and threw it back, a tall, lanky man with unkempt hair and baggy clothes parenthesized by colorful fabrics. On either side of him, clothes were hung on specially ordered plastic hangers, the colors organized as precisely as an artist's wheel. The ivory plastic of Nordstrom's designer departments hung clustered in one area. Her evening clothes.

It took him a minute to get his feet to move. He began unzipping the bags, one at a time, looking for the dress Mike had worn to the Policemen's Ball. At about the sixth bag, he reached inside, and instead of finding a gown of silk or velvet as he'd expected, he found a pillowcase, carefully hung on a pants hanger.

Frowning, he eased it from the bag. It was an elegant white silk affair, not the kind of pillowcase they used at all. On one end was a monogram: *MLT.*

Mikaela Luna . . . Something.

His heart skipped a beat. This was from her life *before*.

He should turn away, zip up this bag, and forget its existence. He knew this because his hands had started to sweat and a tickling unease was working its way down his spine.

Over the years, he'd collected so many questions, stroked them in his mind every time she'd said, *Let's not go there, Liam. The past isn't something that matters now.* Every time he'd seen sadness darken her eyes or known that something had smoothed the edges of her laugh to a quiet mournful sound, he'd wondered *why*.

The past mattered, of course. Liam had been willing to pretend otherwise because he loved his wife, and because he was afraid of who or what had caused the deep well of her sorrow, but the moment he touched the pillowcase, made of a fabric so expensive he didn't know anyone who would know where to buy such a thing—certainly Mike wouldn't—and saw the tantalizing mystery of the *MLT* monogram, he was lost. The past they'd all ignored was here; it had lived with them all these years, hidden inside a Nordstrom bag in his wife's closet. And like Pandora, he simply had to look.

Once he had the pillowcase in his hand, he could see plainly that it was stuffed full of something. He felt strangely detached as he walked back into his bedroom and sat down on his big, king-sized four-poster bed, dragging the pillowcase up beside him. He stared down at it for a long time, weighing the danger, knowing that sometimes there was no way to undo what had been done, and that some secrets were composed of acid that, once spilled, could burn through the fragile layers of a relationship.

Still, the lure of finally *knowing* was too powerful to resist. For years he had longed to tear the lid off her jar of secrets. He'd always thought that if he knew her pain, he would understand. He would be able to help.

These were the lies he told himself as he turned the pillowcase upside down and watched as photographs, newspaper clippings, and official-looking documents, all bent and yellowed, fluttered onto the comforter. The last thing to fall out was a wedding ring with a diamond as big as a dime. Liam stared at it so long his vision blurred, and then he was seeing another ring, a thin gold band. *No diamonds, Liam,* she'd said softly, and though he'd heard the catch in her voice, he'd paid it no mind. He'd thought how nice it was that she didn't care about such things.

The truth was she'd already had diamonds.

Turning away from the diamond ring, he saw a photograph, an eight-by-ten full-color glossy print. It was half covered; all he could see was Mikaela in a wedding dress. The groom was hidden behind a carefully cut-out newspaper article. He wanted to pick it up, but his hands were shaking too badly. He thought, crazily, that if he didn't touch it, didn't brush away the newsprint, the man in the other half of the photo wouldn't exist.

He hardly recognized Mikaela. Her wavy black

hair was drawn up in a sleek, elaborate twist that glittered with diamonds, and makeup accentuated the catlike tilt of her brown eyes, turned her pale, puffy lips into the kind of mouth that fueled a thousand male fantasies. The sleeveless gown she wore was a soft, opalescent white—completely unlike the conservative cream-colored suit she'd worn for her second wedding. There were oceans of pearls and beads sewn into the silky sheath, so many that the dress appeared to be made of crushed diamonds and clouds. Not a thing of this earth at all.

She, his *wife*, was a woman he'd never seen before, and that hurt, but the pain of it was nothing compared to the way he felt when he looked at her smile. God help him; she'd never smiled at Liam like that, as if the world were a shining jewel that had just been placed in the palm of her hand.

Slowly he reached for the picture and picked it up. The newspaper clipping fell away and he saw at last the groom's face.

Julian True.

For a dizzying moment, Liam couldn't breathe. He could actually *feel* the breaking of his heart.

"Jesus Christ," he whispered, not knowing if the words were a curse or a prayer.

She'd been married to Julian True, one of the most famous movie stars in the world.

Chapter Eight

"Daaaaad! Dinner's ready!"

Liam rose unsteadily to his feet and walked away from the pictures on the bed. Closing the door behind him, he moved forward only when he heard the muffled click of the lock. There was no point in staying up here. The things he'd seen wouldn't change; he'd carry those burning images in his heart forever.

He clung to the slick oak banister and went down the stairs, drawing a heavy breath before he turned into the dining room.

Bret was already at the trestle table, looking dwarfed in the big oak chair that his grandfather had crafted by hand. Jacey sat beside him, just now putting the checkered red-and-blue napkin in her lap. "Hi, Dad," she said with a smile.

She looked so much like Mike that he almost stumbled.

Rosa came around the corner, carrying a glass bowl of salad, with a bottle of dressing tucked under her arm. She paused when she saw him, then she smiled softly. "Good, good, you are here. Have a seat, Dr. Liam," she said as she plunked the bowl onto the table and took her own place.

As usual, no one looked at the empty chair at the opposite end of the table.

Liam made it through dinner like one of those Disney robots. He forced his dry mouth to smile. He could feel the way Jacey and Rosa were staring at him. He tried to act as if this were a normal dinner— at least as normal as their meals had become in the past month—but he was weary and the veneer had worn thin.

"Dad?"

He looked up from the chicken enchiladas, realizing that he'd managed to push them around on his plate into an unappetizing pile of orange mush. "Yeah, Jace?"

"Did you find that dress for me?"

"Yeah, honey. I found it. I'll give it to you after dinner. Maybe you and Grandma can practice fixing up your hair."

She smiled. "Thanks, Dad."

Dad.

The word had a hook that drew blood.

Jacey had called him that almost from the start. She'd been a little bit of a thing back then, a baby-toothed four-year-old with jet-black pigtails and ears that seemed so big she'd never grow into them.

He could still remember the day Mike had shown

up in the clinic, carrying Jacey. It was only a few months after Liam's father had died, and he'd been trying to find an excuse to talk to Mikaela again.

Jacey had had a dangerously high fever; convulsions racked her body. One minute she was stretched taut and shaking, and the next, she was as limp as a rag doll, her brown eyes drowsy and unfocused.

"Help us," Mikaela had said softly.

Liam had canceled his nonemergency appointments for the day and rushed to the ER with them. He'd stood in the OR, watching as the surgeon gently sliced through Jacey's abdomen and removed her burst appendix. His was the last face she saw before the anesthesia took her, and the first one she saw when she woke up in Recovery. He transferred his patients to Dr. Granato and spent the next three days in the hospital with Mikaela and Jacey; together they watched the Fourth of July fireworks through the rectangular window of Room 320.

He'd sat in the hospital cafeteria for endless hours with Mike, listening to her ramble from topic to topic. At some point she'd looked up at the wall clock and started to cry. He'd reached across the table, past the remains of her uneaten meal, and taken hold of her hand. *She'll be all right,* he'd said. *Trust me . . .*

She'd looked up at him then, his Mike, with her brown eyes floating in tears and her mouth trembling. *I do trust you.*

That had been the beginning.

Jacey had called him Dad for so long, he'd forgotten

that there was another father out there, another man who could lay claim to both his wife's and daughter's hearts.

"Dad. DAD."

Bret stared at him. His little face looked unbalanced with the one black eye. "You're gonna take me to basketball tryouts aren't you?"

"Of course, Bretster."

Bret nodded and started talking to Jacey about something. Liam tried to pay attention, but he couldn't do it. A single sentence kept running through his mind. *She was married to Julian True.*

When he looked up again, he saw that Rosa was staring at him, her dark eyes narrowed and assessing.

"Do you have something you want to say to me, Rosa?"

She flinched, obviously surprised by his tone of voice. He knew he should have softened his tone, pretended that everything was okay, but he didn't have the strength.

"*Sí*, Dr. Liam. I would like to speak to you . . . privately."

He sighed. Perfect. "Sure. After the kids are in bed."

Liam knew that Rosa was waiting for their "talk," but he wasn't ready yet. He'd spent almost an hour reading to Bret, then kissed Jacey good night and taken a long, hot shower.

Jacey was bunkered in her room now, probably talking on the telephone to one of her many friends and trying on her mother's dress. Liam hadn't gone to her, afraid that if he saw her wearing that beautiful gown, looking like her mother, he'd lose it.

Right now he wanted to hole up in his own quiet space. Christ, he'd give almost anything to be able to go downstairs, sit at the piano, and play the hell out of some sad bit of music.

He wanted to be angry, to scream and rail and feel honest-to-God outrage. But he wasn't that kind of man. His love for Mikaela was more than just an emotion; it was the sum total of who he was.

This one thing he knew above everything else. He loved Mikaela too much. Which in its way was as bad as loving someone not enough.

Slowly he went downstairs.

The piano stood in the empty living room like a forgotten lover.

Liam closed his eyes and remembered a time when music swirled through this room every night . . . He could almost hear the squeaky joint of the bench as Mike sat down beside him.

Tips are welcome, he'd say, just as he'd said a thousand times on a thousand nights.

Here's a tip for you, piano man: Get your wife to bed or miss your chance.

When he opened his eyes, the room was empty and silent.

He'd never thought much about silence, but now he knew its every shape and contour. It was a cheap glass jar that trapped old voices and kept them fresh.

He went to the piano and sat on the antique bench

with its needlepoint seat. With one finger, he plunked at a single key. It made a dull, thudding sound.

Mrs. Julian True.

"Dr. Liam?"

He jumped, and his hand crashed on the keys in a blast of discordant sound.

Rosa stood in the archway that separated the great room from the dining room.

Liam didn't want to talk to his mother-in-law right now. If she opened the door to intimacy, he might ask the question that was killing him: *Did she ever love me, Rosa?*

And God help him, he wasn't ready for the answer.

"*Lo siento,* I do not mean to bother you."

He studied her, saw the nervous trembling in her hands, the almost invisible tapping of her right foot, and he was seized by a sudden fear that she knew what he'd found, that she'd talk about Mikaela's past now, tell him more than he wanted to know. He got slowly to his feet and moved toward her. In the pale, overhead light, she looked incredibly fragile, her wrinkled skin almost translucent. A tiny network of blue blood vessels crisscrossed her smooth cheeks. "Yes, Rosa?"

She gazed up at him, her dark eyes steeped in sorrow, and he knew that she understood the pain of a broken heart. "The anniversary . . . it must be very hard on you. I thought . . . maybe, if you do not think I am sticking my old woman's nose where it does not belong, that we could watch a movie together. Bret has loaned me his favorite: *Dumb and Dumber.* He says it will make me laugh."

The idea of Rosa watching *Dumb and Dumber* brought a smile. "Thank you, Rosa," he answered, touched by her thoughtfulness. "But not tonight."

"There is something else wrong," she said slowly, eyeing him.

He tried to smile again. "What else could be wrong? Love will reach my wife, won't it, Rosa? Isn't that what you're always telling me, that love will wake her up? But it's been four weeks and still she's asleep."

"Do not give up, please."

He looked at her for a long, desperate minute, then he said softly, "I'm falling apart."

It was true. His wife was hanging on to life by a strand as thin as a spider's web, and now suddenly it felt as if his whole life was hanging alongside her.

"No, Dr. Liam. You are the strongest man I have ever known."

He didn't feel strong. In fact, he'd never felt so close to breaking. He knew that if he stood here a moment longer, feeling Rosa's sympathy like a warm fire on a cold, cold night, he'd ask the question: *Did she ever love me, Rosa?*

"I can't do this now." He shoved past a chair, heard it squeaking and crashing across the floor. When he spun around, he found himself staring into the silvered plane of an antique mirror. The network of lines around his eyes had the ridged, shadowy look of felt-tipped etchings.

Laugh lines.

That's what Mike had called them. Only Liam couldn't now recall the last time he'd laughed.

The image blurred and twisted before his eyes, until for a flashing second, it wasn't himself he saw. It was a younger man, blindingly handsome, with a smile that could sell a million movie tickets. "I need to go to the hospital."

"But—"

He pushed past her. "Now," he said again, grabbing his coat off the hook on the wall. "I need to see to my wife."

The emergency room was bustling with people tonight; the bright hallways echoed with voices and footsteps. Liam hurried to Mike's room.

She lay there like a broken princess in someone else's bed, her chest steadily rising and falling.

"Ah, Mike," he murmured, moving toward her. It was beyond him now, the simple routine he'd constructed so carefully—the potpourri, the pillows, the music.

He stared down at her.

She was still beautiful. Some days he could pretend that she was simply sleeping, that it was an ordinary morning, and any moment she'd wake up and reach for him. Not tonight, however.

"I fell in love with you the first second I saw you," he said, curling his hand around hers, feeling the warmth of her flesh. Even then, he'd known she was running from something . . . or someone. It was obvious. But what did he care? He knew what he wanted: Mikaela and Jacey and a new life in Last Bend. A love that would last forever. He hadn't known who she was—who she'd once been. How could he? He'd never been one to read celebrity magazines, and even if he had, he would have read about Kayla True, a woman who meant nothing to him.

After Jacey had recovered from her surgery, Mike had begun to pull away from Liam. He'd seen how tired she was, how frightened and worn out, and he'd slipped in to stand beside her. *Let me be your buffer against the wind,* he'd whispered. *Let me keep you warm.*

He'd known why she reached for him, why she'd crawled into his bed and let him kiss her. She'd been a fragile, lonely little bird, and he'd built her a nest. Over time she'd learned to smile again. And every day that she stayed with him was a blessing.

He closed his eyes and culled memories, brushing some aside and savoring others. The first time he'd kissed her, on a bright and sunny day at Angel Falls . . . the way she snorted when she laughed really hard and cried at a good Hallmark commercial . . . the day Bret had been born and they'd put him in Liam's arms, and Mike had whispered softly that life was good. The day he'd asked her to marry him . . .

That was the one that hurt.

It had been the year *Batman* exploded across theater

multiplexes and the *Exxon Valdez* crashed in Prince William Sound.

They'd been at Angel Falls, stretched out on a blanket beside a still, green pool of water. There had been tears in her eyes when she told him she was pregnant.

He had known to tread carefully. It had been difficult, when all he wanted to do was throw back his head and laugh with joy, but he'd touched her cheek and asked her quietly to marry him.

I've been married before, she'd answered, a single tear sliding down her pink cheek.

Okay. That's what he'd said, all he'd said.

It's important.

He'd known that, of course.

I loved him with all my heart and soul, she'd said. *I'm afraid I'll love him until I die.*

I see.

But he'd known that she was the one who could see. She'd known she was breaking his heart. She turned and knelt beside him. *There are things I can't tell you . . . ever. Things I won't talk about.*

"I didn't care about all that, did I, Mike? I was forty years old and I'd seen things no human being should ever see.

"Until I met you, I had given up on love, did you know that? I had grown up in a great man's shadow; I knew that everyone I met compared me to the famous Ian Campbell, and beside him, I was an agate pushed up alongside a diamond.

"Then I met you, and you'd never really known my

father. I thought at last I'd found someone who wouldn't compare me all the time . . . but you'd already had a diamond, hadn't you, Mike? And I was still just an ordinary agate . . ."

But he hadn't told her any of this when he asked her to marry him, when she told him she'd already found—and lost—the love of her life. All he'd said was that he loved her, and that if she could return even a piece of his love, they'd be happy.

He'd known that she wanted it to be true, just as he'd known she didn't completely believe it. *I will never lie to you, Liam, and I'll never be unfaithful. I will be as good a wife as I can be.*

I love you, Mike, he'd said, watching her cry.

And I love you.

He'd thought that over the years, she'd learned to love him, but now he was seized by doubt. Maybe she cared for him. Only that.

"You should have told me, Mike," he said, but even as he said the words, he heard the lie echoing within them. She couldn't have told him. She was right in that, at least. The knowing was unbearable.

She had loved him that much, anyway.

"I found the pillowcase, Mike," he said, leaning close. "The pictures . . . the clippings. I know about . . . him."

He squeezed her hand. "I guess I know why you didn't tell me. But it hurts, Mike. Jesus, it hurts and I don't know what to do with all of it."

He leaned toward her. "Did you ever love me,

Mike? How can I go on without knowing the answer to that question?

"I guess I shouldn't even ask," he said. "I should have seen it in your eyes, should have known somehow that you were always comparing me to someone else. God knows I had the experience to see it, so why didn't I? And how could I ever measure up to Julian True?"

She blinked.

Liam gasped, squeezing her hand so hard it should have crushed the fragile bones. "Mike . . . can you hear me? Blink if you can hear me." With his other hand, he hit the nurses' button.

Within seconds, Sarah came bustling into the room, already out of breath. "Dr. Campbell, is she—"

"She blinked."

Sarah came closer to the bed, studying Mike first, and then Liam.

Mike lay perfectly still, her eyes sealed shut.

"Come on, Mike. Blink if you can hear me."

Sarah checked each machine, one by one, then she moved to stand by Liam. "I think it was a reflex. Or maybe—"

"It *wasn't* my imagination, damn it. She blinked."

"Maybe I should call for Dr. Penn."

"Do it," he said, without looking up.

He let go of Mike's hand for just long enough to hit the play button on the tape recorder. Music swept into the room, songs from the *Tapestry* album by Carole King.

Liam held her hands again, both of them this time, talking to her, saying the same thing over and over again. He was still talking, begging, when Stephen came into the room, examined Mike, and then quietly left.

Liam talked until his throat was dry and there were no more pleas left inside of him. Then he slumped back down into the chair and bowed his head. *Please God, help her.*

But deep inside he knew. It hadn't been God who'd helped Mikaela blink. It was a name, just that after all these weeks, just a simple name. When she heard it, she responded.

Julian True.

She is floating in a sea of gray and black . . . there is the smell of something . . . flowers . . . a music she can almost recognize.

She longs to touch the music, but she has no arms . . . no legs . . . no eyes. All she can feel is the thudding beat of her heart. Fast, like a baby bird's, and she can taste the metallic edge of fear.

"You should have told me."

It is the voice she's come to know, soft and soothing, and she knows that somewhere, sometime, she knew it, but here there is no before, there is no now. There is just the dark, the fear, the helpless longing for something. . . .

"Julian."

Julian. The word seems to sink deep, deep inside

her; it makes her heart beat faster, and she wants to reach for it, hold it against her chest.

Julian. In the black rubble of her life it is connected to another word, one she remembers.

Love.

Chapter Nine

The next morning, Rosa was finishing the last of the breakfast dishes when the phone rang . . . and rang . . . and rang. Frowning, she went to the bottom of the stairs and yelled up for Dr. Liam to answer it.

In the other room, the answering machine clicked on, and Rosa was momentarily stunned to hear her daughter's voice. For a split second, she felt hope . . . then she realized it was only the recorded message.

"Rosa? Are you there? Pick up the phone, damn it. It's me, Liam."

She threw the damp dishrag over her shoulder and raced back into the kitchen to answer. "*Hola,*" she said, a little out of breath.

"Have the kids left for school?" he asked.

"*Sí.* Bret's bus just left."

"Good. Come to the hospital."

"Is Mikaela—"

"The same. Just hurry." He paused, then said, "Please, Rosa. Hurry."

"I am leaving."

He didn't even say good-bye before she heard the dial tone buzzing in her ear.

Rosa snagged her car keys from the hook near the phone and grabbed her purse.

Outside it was snowing lightly; not much, but enough to make an old woman like her drive slowly. All the way through town and out to the hospital, she tried to be hopeful. But Dr. Liam had sounded upset. He was such a strong, silent man that such emotion from him was frightening. He had remained steady through much bad news already.

She parked in one of the vacant visitor spots and reached for her coat. It was then that she realized she was still wearing the wet dishrag across her shoulder . . . and that she hadn't braided her hair yet this morning. She would look like a demented scarecrow with all that snow-white hair flowing everywhere. A woman like her, old and unmarried, could not afford to look so bad.

As she crossed the parking lot, she braided her hair. Without a rubber band, it wouldn't stay, but it was better than nothing.

She hurried through the hospital. At the closed door to Mikaela's room, she paused and drew in a deep breath, offering a quick prayer to the Virgin, then she opened the door.

Everything looked the same. Mikaela lay in the bed, on her back this morning. A shaft of sunlight sneaked through the partially opened curtains and left a yellow streak on the linoleum floor.

Liam was sitting in the chair by the bed. He was wearing the same clothes from yesterday—khaki pants and a black sweater. Only now the clothes were so wrinkled it looked like they'd been stomped on. Shadows rimmed his tired eyes.

"You slept here last night," she said, frowning. "Why—" The look in his eyes was so cold and unfamiliar that she bit her sentence in half. "Dr. Liam?"

"Julian True."

Rosa gasped. She grabbed hold of the metal bed rail. If she hadn't held on to something, she would surely have fallen. Her legs felt like warming butter. *"Perdón?"*

"You heard me. I said his name."

She brought a trembling hand to her chest. "Why . . ." Her throat was dry as ashes; she couldn't force out another word. She let go of the bed rail and reached for the pitcher on the bedside table, pouring herself a glass of water. She drank it in three huge, unladylike gulps, then set the glass back down. At no time did she look at Liam. "Why do you say this name to me now?"

"Last night, when I was looking for Mike's dress, I found a pillowcase hidden in the closet. It was filled with pictures and newspaper clippings . . . and a huge diamond ring." He rose from the chair and moved toward her. "I knew his name, of course, everyone does, but I didn't know he meant anything to me."

She forced a smile. "Y-You must have loved a woman before Mikaela."

"Not Sharon Stone."

At last she looked at him. "Forget this, Dr. Liam. It is old news. You knew she had been married before."

"Watergate is old news, Rosa. This is something else—and you know how I know this?"

"How?"

"I said his name to Mikaela. That's all, just his name, and she blinked. Now, it could mean nothing, but after all these weeks, it'd be pretty damned coincidental, don't you think?"

"She blinked?"

"Yes."

And just that quickly, she saw the anger leave her son-in-law's eyes. Without it, he looked old and tired and afraid.

"All this time," he said quietly, "I've been talking to her, holding her hand, brushing her hair, and singing her love songs. Why? Because you made me *believe* that love would reach her. But it wasn't my love that reached her, Rosa. Or yours, either. It was just a man's name."

"*Madre de Dios.*" She clutched the bed rail again and stared down at her sleeping daughter. "Mikita, are you hearing us, *querida*? Blink if you can."

Liam sighed. "She's hearing us. We've just been saying the wrong things."

Rosa wanted to cover her ears. She didn't want to hear what Liam was going to say next, and yet she couldn't stop herself from asking the question. "What is it you think we should be telling her?"

Liam sidled in close beside her, so close she could feel the heat from his body. "Maybe it's not about our love for her. Maybe it's about her love . . . for him."

"Don't—"

"I want you to talk to her about Julian. Tell her everything you know about them. Remind her how much she loved him. Maybe that will help her come back to us."

She turned and gazed up at him. She could feel the way her mouth was trembling; it matched the shaking in her fingers, but she couldn't stop it. "That is very dangerous."

"Believe me, if she wakes up because of Julian . . ." He ran a hand through his shaggy hair and closed his eyes.

Rosa could only imagine how much this was hurting him, this good, good man who loved so deeply. She thought that if she listened closely enough, she would hear the sound of his heart breaking.

"It's her *life*," he said at last. "We have to do everything to reach her."

Rosa wished she could disagree. "I will try this, to tell her who she used to be and who she used to love, but only if you remember always that she married *you*."

He looked like he was going to say something; in the end, he turned and walked to the window.

She stared at him. "Y-You are not going to stay in the room for this, Dr. Liam? It will be most hurtful."

He didn't turn around. His voice, when he found it, was low and scratchy, not his sound at all. "I'm staying. I think it's time I got to know the woman I love."

Rosa stood beside the bed, clasping the silver St. Christopher's medallion at her throat.

Slowly she closed her eyes.

For fifteen years, she had not allowed herself to remember those days. That's how she thought of them—*those days*—when *he* had breezed into their airless life and changed everything.

It was only now that she realized how close the memories had always been. Some things could never be forgotten, some people were the same.

She pulled up an image of Mikaela—twenty-one years old, bright brown eyes, flowing black hair, a vibrant flower in a hot, desolate farming town where migrant workers lived eight to a room in shacks without indoor plumbing. A town where the line between the "good" folks and the Mexicans was drawn in cement. And Mikaela—a bastard half Mexican— wasn't fully welcomed in either world.

It had been the full heat of summer, that day he came into their lives. Mikaela had just finished her second and final year at the local junior college. She'd received an academic scholarship to Western Washington University in Bellingham, but Rosa had known that her daughter wanted something bigger.

Cambridge. Harvard. The Sorbonne. These were

the schools that called to Mikaela, but they both knew that girls like her didn't make it to schools like that.

It was Rosa's fault that Mikaela had felt so alone as a young girl. For years, Mikaela waited for her father to acknowledge her in public. Then had come the dark, angry years when she hated him and his perfect, white-bread children. The years when she wrote trash about him in girls' bathrooms all over town, when she prayed to God that just once his blue-eyed, blond-haired cheerleader daughter would know how it felt to *want*. In time that phase had passed, too, and left Mikaela with a deeper loneliness.

She dreamed of going someplace where she wouldn't be the Mexican waitress's bastard kid anymore. She used to say to Rosa that she was tired of staring through dirty windows at other people's lives.

They had been working in the diner, she and Mikaela, on the tail end of a slow, hot afternoon shift . . .

"Mikita, if you wash that table any more, it will disappear."

Mikaela tossed the rag down. It landed with a squishy thwack on the speckled yellow Formica. "You know how Mr. Gruber likes his table clean, Mama, and he should be here any second for lunch. I'll get Joe to start his meatloaf sandwich—"

Mikaela's words were drowned out by a loud, thundering noise, like the first rumble in an earthquake. Behind the counter, in the diner's small kitchen, Joe looked up from the grill. "What the hell is that?" he growled, wiping the back of his hand across his mouth.

Mikaela raced to the picture window that looked out on Brownlow Street. It was high noon in the first week of July, and the storefronts all wore the crackled, faded look of exhaustion. It was too hot for anyone to be outside.

The sound came closer, grew louder. Out in the deserted street, dust swirled up in a thick brown cloud that grabbed hold of black-tipped leaves and swept them into eddies in the air.

Three silver helicopters hurtled above the rooflines like bullets against the blue sky, then dropped out of sight behind Bennet's Drug Store. An eerie silence fell, the windows stilled.

A limousine pushed through the dust storm like something out of a dream, sleek and black and impossibly shiny in this dirty heat. No car could get to Sunville that clean, not if it drove on the back roads from Yakima. The blackened windows captured the town's tired reflection and threw it back.

Mikaela leaned forward, pressing closer to the glass. The orange polyester of her uniform stuck to her skin. Overhead, the wooden fan swirled slowly with a thwop-thwop-thwop that did little more than distribute the smell of burning bacon.

Three limousines pulled up in front of City Hall and parked. No one got out of the cars, and the engines kept running. Gray smoke seeped lazily from the tailpipes.

One by one, people came out of the stores and

stood on the sidewalks, drawing together, speculating among themselves, pointing at the cars that in this town were as foreign and unexpected as spaceships.

Rosa and Mikaela crowded into the diner's narrow doorway.

The click of a lock silenced the crowd, then the doors opened, all of them at once, like huge, enameled beetles unfurling their wings. Strangers in black suits and sunglasses emerged from the cars, one after another. And then he appeared.

A shiver of recognition moved through the crowd.

"Oh, my God, it's Julian True," someone whispered.

He stood with the casual, unaffected elegance of one who is used to the stares of strangers. Tall and lean, with long, sunstreaked hair that covered half his face, he looked like a rebellious angel cast down from the heavens. He wore a loose black pocket T-shirt and a pair of ragged Levi's that were tattered and ripped out at the knees. Whatever blue dye had once been woven into the denim had long ago bleached to a foamy white.

The crowd surged toward him, crying out. One sound, one name rose from the confusion.

Julian True . . . It's him . . . Julian True in Sunville.

Then came the requests: Here! Sign my shirt . . . my notebook . . . my napkin.

Rosa turned to whisper something to Mikaela, but the words caught in her throat. Her daughter looked . . . mesmerized. Mikaela stepped back into the diner and glanced around. Rosa knew that her daughter was noticing the cracked floor, the broken *light fixtures, the ever-present film of grease that coated everything. She was seeing the diner through this stranger's eyes, and she was ashamed.*

Rosa moved away from the door and went back to work. Mikaela headed for the lunch counter and began refilling the sugar jars.

Suddenly the bell above the front door jingled, and he was standing there, in Joe's Get-It-While-It's-Hot diner, beneath the lazily whirring overhead fan.

Mikaela dropped the half-empty sugar jars on the table. Her cheeks turned bright pink.

He gave Mikaela a smile the likes of which Rosa had never seen. It was the old cliché, sun erupting through the clouds. Eyes the color of shaved turquoise looked at Mikaela as if she were the only woman in the world.

"C-Can I help you?"

His smile held the tattered edge of exhaustion. "Well, darlin'," he said in that world-famous Texas drawl, as thick and sweet as corn syrup, "we've been travelin' for hours over the shittiest patch of road I've seen since I left Lubbock, and any minute that doorway's gonna fill up with every thirteen-year-old girl between here and Spokane. I was hopin' a pretty little thing like you could round me up a beer and a sandwich and show me where I could eat it in peace."

That had been the beginning.

Rosa opened her eyes. She could feel Liam behind her, hear his measured breathing, and she knew she'd been quiet too long.

"*Hola, Mikita,*" she said softly. "*Mama estoy aqui.*"

She took a deep breath and began. "You remember the first day you met him, *querida,* your Julian True?"

Mikaela sucked in a sharp breath; her eyelids fluttered.

Rosa felt a rush of hope, as pure and clean and cold as springwater. "We were at the diner, both of us working the lunch shift. There was a noise, one like I had never heard before. Helicopters, in our little town. And then *he* appeared. Ah, the way he looked at you, as if you were the only woman in the world. Even I could feel the lure of him. He was like no one we had ever seen before . . . like no one we would ever see again.

"You thought I was too old to understand what you were thinking, my Mikaela, but I could see it in your eyes. You thought you were Cinderella, all covered with soot and dirt, and here . . . here was a prince.

"He called you a pretty little thing, remember? *Dios,* I have never seen you smile so brightly. He started calling you Kayla almost from the start. Kayla of the midnight hair, that was his nickname for you, *recuerdes*? I hated that he would give you a *gringa* name and that you would take it . . . but it did not matter what I thought, not once you had met him.

"When he first kissed you, you told me it felt like you'd jumped off a skyscraper. I said that such a fall could kill a girl. Remember your answer? You said, 'Ah, Mama, but sometimes it is worth it to fly.' "

Rosa leaned down and touched Mikaela's still, white face. "I watched you fall in love with him, this man with the face of an angel. I knew there would be fireworks at the start of it—how could it be otherwise? I knew, too, that there would be pain at the end of it. Enough to last a lifetime.

"I told you that he was no good for you, but you laughed and told me not to worry. As if a mama could stop worrying so easily."

She let her fingertips linger on her daughter's cool, sunken cheek. "You thought I did not understand, but I was the only one who could."

Rosa gave her daughter a small, sad smile. "You promised that you would not make my mistake. But I knew, *querida*, I saw it in your eyes. You already had."

Chapter Ten

The pain of each new sentence was sharp and sudden, a rock thrown through a high glass window. Liam sat very still in his chair, trying to draw meaning out of every pause, trying to hear the story that wasn't being told as well.

It was no ordinary love that Mikaela had felt for Julian True. That came as no surprise. How could anything about that man be ordinary?

Diamonds and agates, once again.

He wondered why he had let Mikaela hold such secrets. It wasn't only Julian's identity; it was a hundred smaller things. The prom she hadn't gone to, the memories she hadn't shared. It was *her*. He'd been content with so damned little. He'd thought what mattered was that he loved her, that he made her smile and laugh again. Why had he never asked himself what fueled her dreams?

Probably, deep down, he'd been afraid of her answer. And so, afraid of the truth, he'd powered along in silence, comforted by the dull softness of words unspoken, questions unasked.

But what about now that he knew? He didn't know if he could believe in her love. Not now that he'd seen what she was hiding. He didn't know if the feel of her body next to his would generate any heat.

Rosa turned around suddenly, and Liam realized that she had stopped talking. The room was deathly quiet now; the only noise was the steady drone of the monitors. "She has not blinked again, Dr. Liam."

He stood and crossed the short distance to the bed. This time, when he looked down at his wife, he saw a stranger. *Kayla.* He picked up her hand, held it gently. "She never told me any of this, Rosa. Why did I let her keep such secrets?"

Rosa stood beside him, the snow-white cap of her head angled close to his shoulder. "You come from money," she said simply. "You are a doctor—from Harvard. You cannot understand what life is like for people like us. Mikaela had such big dreams, but no way to make them come true. Even her own *papa*, he did not show her any love at all." She turned to him. "I first came to Sunville to pick apples when I was a little girl. *Mi padre,* he died when I was eleven. Of a cold sore. There was no money to buy medicines, and no doctor to help him. I can still remember the pickers' camps—especially when the air smells of ripe fruit. I can smell the tin-roofed shack with no indoor plumbing, where we lived, ten people in a room this size. I remember the feel of old mattresses, and the heat. This I remember most of all, the heat.

"I found my way out with a man. He wasn't my man—that was my great sin—but I didn't care. I loved him. *Madre de Dios,* I loved him in the desperate way that women like me always love another woman's husband." She leaned over the bed rail and gazed down at Mikaela. "I am afraid I taught my daughter that a woman will wait forever for the man she loves."

Liam could tell by the sad end note of Rosa's sentence that she was finished. She turned slightly and looked up at him again.

"Lo siento," she said awkwardly, smoothing the hair away from her face. "I am sure this is more than you wish to know. Perhaps now you will think badly of me—"

"Ah, Rosa, don't you think I know how it feels to love someone who belongs to another?"

"She *married* you."

"Yes, and she stayed with me, and we built something. Over time I forgot . . . things that I should have remembered. But I always knew, deep down, I knew. There was a part of Mike's heart that was off-limits to me. But I loved her so damned much, and Jacey, and then Bret. And she seemed happy. Maybe she even was, in a I-lost-it-all-and-this-is-what-I-have-left sort of way."

"There was more to her happiness than that. This I know."

Liam gazed down at his beautiful wife. "I didn't even know her."

Rosa didn't say anything.

"Mike?" He said her name without the usual tenderness. This time he spoke to her as if she were a stranger. "Enough of this. Come back to us. You and I have a lot to talk about."

"*Nada,*" Rosa said, wringing her hands together. "Maybe we were wrong about the blinking. Maybe it was wishful thinking."

"Believe me, I *wish* she'd blinked when she heard my name." He leaned closer. "Julian True. Julian True. Julian True."

"*Nada.*"

"Keep talking to her, Rosa. You left off when she fell in love with him."

She frowned. "The rest of the story, it is filled with much pain for her. Maybe it will make the coma worse."

"Pain is a powerful stimulus. Maybe even stronger than love. We can't give up yet. Talk to her."

Rosa drew in a deep breath. It went against her every instinct to talk about these things—especially in front of Dr. Liam. But then she thought about the blinking of her daughter's eyes. Such a little thing, maybe it meant nothing at all, but maybe . . .

"You loved him so much, my Mikita. Loved him in the way that only young girls can. He swept you off your feet—it wasn't hard, not when you ached so badly to fly. He took your heart and your virginity . . . and then he left you."

Rosa brushed the hair from her daughter's forehead, letting her fingertips linger on the pale, cool flesh. "I watched you wait for him, day after day, night after night. You stood at the diner's cloudy window, waiting for a car to drive up."

Rosa remembered those days in brutal detail. Every time she'd looked in her daughter's eyes, she'd seen the sallow reflection of her own past. She had known what would happen; slowly, before Mikaela knew to guard against it, she would begin to shrink. Already her daughter had begun to keep her head down when she walked, already she moved silently aside when someone came too close. Rose knew it would go on, the slow chipping away of self-confidence, until only a shadow of Mikaela was left. Rosa had seen all this too clearly, but she hadn't known how to stop it.

She had tried to tell her. *This pain,* she'd said, *it will go away if you let it.*

Mikaela had turned to her, letting her gaze travel slowly over Rosa's tightly braided hair, across the wrinkles at her mouth that were anything but laugh lines, down the stained polyester of her waitress uniform. *Will it, Mama? Really?*

"When you asked me, I told you that it would go away, this love of yours, but we both knew it was a lie. I watched you fade into me, a little bit at a time. And then it happened. A *milagro*. He came back for you."

In later years, when Rosa looked back on it, she wondered how it was that there'd been no warning of such a thing, no salt thrown in Mikaela's path for good luck, no sun breaking through the clouds. Rosa had been in the diner, loading dishes into the dishwasher— Joe had already gone home and the place was closed for the night. Rosa was trying to keep her eyes open long enough to finish. She couldn't see Mikaela, but she could hear her in the dining room, pushing chairs into their places and stacking ashtrays.

Then she'd heard something completely out of place. The *clink-ka-ching* of money falling into the jukebox. It was such an odd sound; no one much played the music at Joe's. There came the buzzing blur of the machine skimming through forty-fives, then the music started. The love theme from *An Officer and a Gentleman*.

Rosa had put her soggy rag aside and closed the dishwasher with her hip. She edged past the big gas stove. At the closed door, she stopped again, head tilted, listening. Slowly she pushed the door open a crack. At first all she saw was darkness. The lights were turned off. There was only the electric blue haze from the outdoor neon sign.

Then she saw Julian, standing in the farthest corner of the room. Mikaela stood motionless in front of him.

Rosa knew then, as sure as she was standing there, in the diner that smelled of dreams left on a hot burner, that Mikaela would mortgage her soul for another day with him.

"I could not believe it when he asked you to marry him, *mi hija*. I knew you had hitched your heart to a star—or worse, the sun, and if you looked at it too long, you would be blinded. He took you out of Sunville and gave you the world. From that moment, you were someone who mattered.

"You were in every newspaper, on the television all the time; they turned you into a woman I'd never seen before, this Kayla of the midnight hair. When I went to California for your wedding, it was like being on the moon—people followed you everywhere. I wanted so badly to make your dress—we had dreamed of it for many years. But, of course, that could not be . . . not for Kayla."

Rosa's voice fell away. She turned to Liam. "After that come the years I do not know about. She kept secrets from me, too. I read in the tabloid newspapers about Julian's drinking, about his other women, but Mikaela told me none of this. All I remember is when she called me—it was the day after Jacey's first birthday party. She sounded tired and broken, my little girl, when she told me that it was over." Rosa sighed. "Mikaela was only twenty-three, but I heard in her voice that she was not young anymore. Loving Julian had broken something in her, and it was more than just her heart."

Liam made a sound, part sigh, part moan, and there was such a sadness in it . . .

Rosa wished she were the kind of woman who could go to him, hold him in this moment that was tearing at his heart. "I am sorry, Liam . . ." she said, curling her fingers around the bed rail so tightly her skin turned white.

He rose from the chair and went to the bed. "Help us, Mike," he said. "Let us know you're still there. We all miss you—me, Rosa, Jacey, Bret . . . Julian."

She sees something floating in the murky water. It's small and round and white. It bobs on the surface, peaking and sliding with the waves. The sound of the sea slapping against her body is so loud she can't hear anything else. Somewhere in the back of her mind drifts the thought that she should hear birds, seagulls or ducks, but the silence is endless and unbroken.

She knows that if she can relax, she can float on top of the water, and it can be peaceful. This she has learned in her months at sea.

Today she can smell cinnamon and pine trees— familiar, comforting—and now there is something else. She breathes deeply, and instead of the sea, she smells a woman's fragrance, one she can almost remember. She tries to concentrate on that, the concrete image of before, but the memory is unattached to anything.

"Helpus, Mike. Letusknow you're stillthere."

The voice, familiar and unfamiliar at the same time, keeps asking questions she can't answer, in words she doesn't truly understand.

But then there is that one sound again.

"Julian."

She tries desperately to extract a single perfect memory, just one, but the shallow, rocky soil of her mind gives up nothing.

If only she could open her eyes . . .

". . . Miss you . . ."

These are words she understands, and they hurt. Miss. It is about being alone and afraid . . . yes, she understands.

Please God, she prays, help me . . .

She can't remember if there is supposed to be an answer to these words, but when there is none, she feels as if she is sinking into the turbulent water. She is too tired to keep herself up, and she is missing . . . missing so much . . .

"She's crying. Jesus Christ." Liam reached for a tissue and gently wiped her eyes. "Mike, honey, can you hear me?"

She didn't respond, but those terrible silver tears kept falling. A tiny gray patch appeared on the pillow. Liam punched the nurses' button and ran for the door. When he saw Sarah, he yelled for her to go get Dr. Penn.

Then he went back into the room and bent over his wife, stroking her damp cheeks, whispering the same words to her over and over again. "Come on, baby, come on back to us."

Stephen Penn appeared in the doorway, out of breath. "What is it, Liam?"

He looked up at his friend. "She's crying, Steve."

Stephen went to the side of the bed and stared down at Mikaela. She was as still as death, her cheeks pale, but the trail of moisture glittered promiselike in the dim lighting. He produced a straight pin from his pocket. Gently lifting her bare foot in his palm, Stephen stuck the sharp tip in the tender flesh.

Mikaela jerked her foot back. A broken moan escaped her lips.

Stephen laid her foot down again and covered it back up with the blanket. Then he looked at Liam. "The coma's lightening. It doesn't necessarily mean . . ." He paused. "You know what it does and doesn't mean. But maybe . . . maybe something reached her. Whatever you're doing—keep doing it."

It was way past bedtime when Bret heard the knock on his door. He was sitting on the floor of his bedroom, playing Diddy Kong racing on his Nintendo 64.

He thought he said, "Come in," but he couldn't be sure, because he was concentrating on keeping Diddy on the track.

The door opened, and Dad poked his head in. "Heya, Bretster."

Bret looked up, just long enough. His guy hit the wall and started a free-form tumble across the multicolored screen. "Hi, Dad. You wanna play?"

Dad sat down beside him, picking up the second set of controls. "You know I'm terrible at this. I like the *Star Wars* one better."

Bret giggled. He loved watching his dad play Diddy Kong, because he couldn't ever keep his guy on the track, and Bret *always* kicked his butt. He started up another game, and for the next half hour they raced.

Finally Dad tossed the controls down. "That's it, Mario. You win. I give up."

"Mario's a different game, Dad."

Dad climbed awkwardly to his feet, hanging on to the fender of Bret's bed, as if he was going to fall at any minute. "Come on, kiddo. It's bedtime. Close up the game and get your fangs washed."

Bret turned off the television and hurried down the hall. In his bathroom, he brushed his teeth really good (Dad was *famous* for sending him back to do it again if he didn't do a good job) and peed. Then he went back into his room.

Dad was already in bed, stretched out under the covers, with a book open in his lap. The bedside lamp was on now.

Bret loved it when Daddy was in his bed. Then nothing seemed scary. He bounded over to the bed and started to get in.

"Hold it, pal. Put on your pajamas."

Bret made a face. "Aw, Dad—"

"Nope." He smiled. "I know you. You'll sleep in those clothes and then get up and wear them to school again tomorrow. And hey, when was the last time you took a shower?"

"Grandma made me take one yesterday."

"Okay. But no jeans in bed."

Bret pulled off his dirty jeans and tossed them in a heap in the corner—where he knew he'd just pick 'em up tomorrow and put 'em back on for school. Then he crawled over his dad and got into bed, snuggling up close. "Is that the lion book?"

"You bet."

Bret curled up next to his dad and listened to the story. It calmed him down, listening to his dad's deep, steady voice.

It felt like only a few minutes later that Dad shut the book and set it on the table by the lamp.

Dad took him in his big, strong arms and held Bret tightly. "I think you should visit Mommy. It's . . . important now."

Dad had never said that before—that it was *important* that Bret see her. All along, he'd thought he didn't matter . . .

Dad said quietly, "It's not a scary place. Just a plain old room with a plain old bed. I wouldn't lie to you, Bret. Your mom looks just like she used to . . . only she's sleeping."

"Why wouldn't you let me see her in the beginning?"

"Truth? Because of the bruises on her face. She didn't look very good, and the machines were scary. Now everything is fine. It won't scare you to see her, Bret. I promise. It might make you sad, might even make you cry, but sometimes when little boys are becoming big boys, they have to let themselves cry."

"You *swear* she's alive?"

"I swear it."

Bret wanted to believe his dad.

"She needs to hear your voice, Bretster. I know she has been missing her favorite boy in the whole world."

For the first time, Bret wondered if maybe *he* could wake her up. After all, he was her favorite boy and she loved him more than the whole world. She always told him that. Maybe all this time she'd been waiting to hear him. "I could sing to her," he said softly. "Maybe that song from *Annie* . . . Remember when she took me to see the show? That song, 'Tomorrow,' she always sang it to me when I couldn't sleep."

His dad started to sing, very softly, "The sun'll come up . . . tomorrow—"

"Bet your bottom dollar that tomorrow . . ."

Bret joined in and they sang the whole song together, and when it was over, he didn't feel so much like crying anymore. "I could go see her tomorrow—before school."

Dad's voice was quiet now, a little shaky. "That'd be great. Hey, you want to sleep in my bed tonight?"

"Could I?"

"You bet."

Together, hand in hand, they got out of bed and headed out of the room. All the time they were walking, Bret kept thinking about that song; it kept spinning through his head until he was smiling.

The next morning, Bret got up early and took a shower—without anyone even asking him to. He dressed carefully in his best clothes, a pair of black Levi's jeans and a plaid flannel shirt. Then he raced back into his dad's bedroom and stood by the bed.

"Daddy," he said, poking him in the arm. "Daddy, wake up."

Dad rolled onto his side and opened one eye. "Hey, Bretster," he said in a scratchy voice, "what—"

"Let's go see Mommy."

Dad gave him a smile. "Okay, kiddo. Give me five minutes to get ready."

Bret moved nervously from one foot to the other. He hurried downstairs and turned on all the lights. He snagged his backpack from the mudroom floor and slung it over his back.

True to his word, Dad was down in five minutes,

ready to go. They jumped into the Explorer and headed for town.

Bret bounced in his seat all the way to the hospital. Last night he'd dreamed of his mommy for the first time. In his dream, she woke up when he gave her the Mommy Kiss. *That's* what she'd been waiting for, all this time. The Mommy Kiss.

At the hospital, he held Daddy's hand and dragged him down the hallway to her room. But at the closed door, Bret felt all of his confidence disappear. Suddenly he was afraid.

"It's okay, Bretster. Remember, it's okay to be sad. She'll understand that. Just talk to her."

Bret pushed through the door. The first thing he saw was the baby bed, with the silver side rails. Not a grown-up bed at all. There were no lights on; the room was painted in dull gray shadows.

And there was Mommy, lying in the bed. Slowly he moved toward her.

She looked pretty, not broken at all. He could imagine her waking up . . . Just like that, she'd sit up in bed, open her eyes, and see Bret.

How's my favorite boy in the world? she'd say, opening her arms for a hug.

"You can talk to her, Bret."

He let go of his dad's hand and moved closer to the bed, climbing up the silver rails until he was leaning over his mom. Then, very slowly, he gave her the Mommy Kiss, exactly the way she always gave it to him. A kiss on the forehead, one on each cheek, then a butterfly kiss on the chin. At last he whispered, "No bad dreams," as he kissed the side of her nose.

She lay there, unmoving.

"Come on, Mommy, open your eyes. It's me. Bret." He took a deep breath and forced himself to sing, just like he'd promised himself he'd do. He sang "Tomorrow" three times.

Still, nothing.

He slid off the bed and turned, looking up at his dad through a blur of tears. "She didn't wake up, Daddy."

His dad looked like he was going to cry. It scared Bret. "I know," he said, "but we have to keep trying."

Chapter Eleven

The measure of a man comes down to moments, spread out like dots of paint on the canvas of a life. Everything you were, everything you'll someday be, resides in the small, seemingly ordinary choices of everyday life. It starts early, this random procession of decisions. Should I try out for Little League, should I study for this test, should I wear this seat belt, should I take this drink?

Each decision seems as insignificant as a left turn on an unfamiliar road when you have no destination in mind. But the decisions accumulate until you realize one day that they've made you the man that you are.

Liam had let himself be overshadowed by his father.

Decision.

He had gone all the way to Harvard, learned how many roads fanned out from where he stood . . . and he'd come home to Last Bend, where it was safe.

Decision.

He had fallen in love with Mikaela and settled his

whole world on the creaky foundation of that emotion. He'd known that their love was measured in unequal parts, but day by day, hour by hour, as their life together unfolded in a series of moments big and small— birthdays, anniversaries, family vacations, nights spent huddled on the sofa, watching television—he'd let himself fall into the sweet narcotic pool of forgetfulness.

Decision.

Today he faced another crucial choice. He had been grappling with it ever since Mike first blinked. He had no doubt that the decision he made would lay the groundwork for the rest of his life.

He pushed back from his desk. There was a pile of charts and messages, all needing his immediate attention. He didn't care. Not now. Instead, he grabbed his down jacket, put it on, and walked out of his office. Just before the reception desk, Carol popped out of the X-ray room and bumped into him.

"Oh, Doctor!" she said, giggling.

He smiled. It was the first normal moment they'd had in weeks. "I guess I should be glad you weren't carrying urine samples."

Carol's giggle graduated to a laugh. "Or scalpels."

"I'm going to sneak out early," Liam said.

"Good for you. Your mother-in-law called a few minutes ago. The elementary school lost electricity today, so they canceled classes. She said they'd be up at the pond, skating, if you wanted to join them." Carol pushed the glasses higher up on her nose and squinted up at him.

Liam tensed, knowing too well what was coming.

"How's she doing?" Carol asked.

Liam hoped he didn't look as irritated as he felt. "The same." God, he hated those words. When this was all over, he'd never say them again. Or *I'm sorry*.

"Give her my best."

"Sure, Carol. Thanks." He did his best to smile as he strode through the empty waiting room. He had a flashing memory of Mikaela redecorating this small space. *You can't expect your patients to sit on plastic . . . and what's that wall color—baby diarrhea brown?*

Now the waiting room was a cheerful blend of primary colors—yellow walls, complete with a sunflower mural painted by Mrs. Dreiling's second-grade class, bright cobalt blue overstuffed chairs, and a bold red Berber carpet.

He remembered Mike up on a ladder, her face and hair streaked with yellow paint, yelling down at him. *Hey, piano man, are your hands too precious to hold a paintbrush?* He'd gone to her then, pulled her off of the ladder, and held her in his arms, kissing her soft lips . . .

He strode out of the room.

Outside, the sudden plunge in temperature was exactly what Liam needed to clear his mind. He glanced down at his wristwatch: 1:38.

Suddenly he didn't want to go to the hospital and sit by his wife's bed. For three long days, he'd been beside her, holding her hand, saying Julian's name over and over again. Not once had she responded in any way.

He flicked his wool-lined collar up and headed

down the street. It was one of those moist winter days when the bloated, gray sky seemed to snag the rooftops and tangle in your hair. The mountains peaked above the mist, their snow-covered tips barely distinguishable from the clouds.

He ducked into the Bean There, Done That coffee shop and ordered a decaf latte. Irma made small talk as the milk whipped into a white froth, then didn't charge him for the drink. No amount of cajoling would get her to take his money. Finally he said thank you and went back outside.

Someone exited the Lazy Susan Bake Shop, and the scent of cinnamon wafted from the open doorway. He was tempted to get something for tomorrow's breakfast, but the thought of hearing "How's she doing?" and answering "The same" was more than he could bear.

The sound of children's laughter rode high in the still, clean mountain air. He followed it to Mr. Robbin's llama farm. His frog pond, settled comfortably in a flat patch of the pasture, had been turned by Mother Nature into a beautiful silver skating rink. There were already several cars parked around the perimeter of the pond, so that when it turned dark, they could use their headlights to cast tubes of light across the ice. A boom box was on. Garth Brooks was belting out "I've got friends in low places." Suzie Sanman was stationed at the picnic table, heating pots of milk on a camp stove, and Mayor Comfort was roasting hot dogs over an open fire pit.

Liam could see Bret. He was skating with a bunch

of his friends. Rosa was sitting on one of the benches near the pond, alone.

He greeted his friends and neighbors as he made his way through the crowd, pretending not to notice their surprise at seeing him here. Beside Rosa, he sat down. Wordlessly, she scooted sideways to make more room for him.

"Daddy, Daddy, look at me!" Bret waved his arms. When Liam looked up, Bret began furiously skating backward—until he ran smack into Sharie Lindley and they both fell down in a laughing heap.

"Life goes on, eh, Rosa?" Liam said softly, watching his son trying to master the skill of skating backward. Last winter that same boy had barely been able to skate forward.

"*Sí.*"

He curled his hands around the paper coffee cup; the moist heat felt good against his lips. He hadn't even realized how cold he was until he started to warm up. But then, maybe that pretty much summed up all of his life experiences. "She is not doing well, Rosa."

"*Sí. Yo sé.*"

"We've been talking to her for days now. I've said Julian's name to her so many times, I'm afraid I'll accidentally say it at dinner. I thought maybe Bret would be the key, but he's visited every day after school, and . . . nothing."

"She needs a little more time, maybe."

"Time isn't her friend right now. She's getting worse. Hell, I can *see* her fading into those gray sheets.

I've been doing a little soul searching and there's only one decision that feels right. I think—"

His pager went off, bleating from its place on his belt. He threw a quick, worried glance at Rosa, then reached down and pulled out the small black unit.

It was an emergency message from Stephen Penn. Nine-one-one. The code for call immediately.

"Oh, Jesus," he said. "It's Mike."

Rosa shoved her keys at him. "Take my car. It is right there."

He snatched the keys. "My car's in the office lot. The keys are in the visor. Get Bret and Jacey and get to the hospital. This could be—"

"We'll be right behind you."

"Cardiac arrest."

Liam slumped in his chair. He barely had the strength to lift his chin.

Stephen didn't look away. "I don't know what to tell you, Liam. Her heart just stopped. We got it going again in no time, but it could be an indicator. Her body may be giving out. I think . . . I think it might be time to prepare yourself and the kids for the end."

The End. He wished he'd never said that to a patient of his, but he knew that he had.

Stephen sighed. "It looked like she was getting better there for a few days."

Liam knew that Stephen was thinking of his own wife, Margaret, who was probably at home right now making snowmen with the kids. He could see it in his friend's eyes, the terrible understanding of what it would mean to lose the woman you loved. "How do you tell a nine-year-old that it's time to say good-bye to Mommy? And what if you don't tell him—how in God's name do you tell him tomorrow that it's too late to say anything?"

"Jesus, Lee." Stephen leaned forward, planted his forearms on the desk.

Liam could see that Stephen was searching for words that would honestly give comfort, rather than the standard platitudes. He saw, too, when Steve came up empty. Of course he would. This was a time for faith, for God and religion; science was hopelessly inadequate.

Before Stephen could say anything, Liam got to his feet and made his way out of the office.

The corridor was too bright; light stung his glazed eyes. In the waiting room, Jacey stood at the window with Mark beside her. Rosa sat perched on the very edge of the sofa. Bret—still in his skating coat and Gore-Tex bib overalls—stood pressed against the wall by the television. His little cheeks were candy-apple red. Water dripped from the frozen shelf of his bangs, plopping onto his upturned nose.

When Jacey saw Liam, she let go of Mark's hand and took a cautious step toward him. "Daddy?"

He couldn't tell them. Not here at least, not beneath these cold strips of fluorescent lighting. He'd tell the kids the truth tomorrow. Maybe he would find a miracle between now and then. And if Mikaela didn't make it through the night . . . he'd live with his decision.

It would become another of the many choices that formed the boundary of his soul.

He didn't look at Rosa as he spoke. "She's okay. Mom's okay. She had a little trouble with her heart, is all. It skipped a few beats, but everything is okay now."

"Can I see her?" Jacey asked.

"Of course, but only for a minute or two. Ironically, she needs her rest."

Jacey nodded and headed for the door. As she passed Liam, he reached out and grabbed her wrist. She stopped and turned to him.

"She doesn't look too good, sweetie."

Jacey paled. "Okay, Dad. I-I'll be back in a few minutes."

He forced a smile and let her go. What else could he do? She was old enough to find her own way along this desperate path.

Bret looked up at him. A drop of water snaked down his cheek and landed on his navy ski coat. His mouth trembled uncertainly and tears puddled in his eyes. "Is she awake?"

Liam touched his son's cold, cold cheek. "No, honey, she's not." He fought the urge to say *not yet*; he couldn't throw out hope as if it were penny candy. Not anymore.

Bret backed into the wall. "I don't wanna see her right now. Not . . . like that."

Liam didn't know what to do.

"Hey, Bretster," Mark said, moving toward them.

"I promised to get you an orange soda and some Gummi Bears. How about now?"

Bret's face broke into a relieved smile. "That'd be great. Can I, Dad?"

Liam felt like a coward for taking the easy road, but he nodded. There was no use pretending he wasn't relieved. He got to his feet, reached into his pocket, and pulled out a couple of dollar bills. "Here you go, but don't be too long. We've got to get home."

Bret snagged the money and fisted it. " 'Kay." Then he followed Mark out of the room.

At last Liam turned to Rosa. He could tell by the wary look in her dark eyes that she had been waiting for this moment.

She sat stiff as a fence post, her knees pressed together, her hands coiled in a ball in her lap. "It is bad, *sí*?"

He sat down beside her on the hard vinyl sofa. His bent knees cracked into the Formica coffee table. An old, dog-earred issue of *People* magazine slithered fanlike to the floor. Liam took a moment, trying to formulate his thoughts into words. In the end he said simply, "Her heart stopped."

Rosa drew in a sharp breath and crossed herself. *"Dios mio."*

"They revived her easily—and quickly, which is important—"

"There must be something you can do. Some medicine—"

He gave her a sad smile. "Faith in medicine, Rosa?" She couldn't smile back. "What do we do?"

He'd known they'd circle around to this question, which was, after all, the beginning. "The only moment of hope in this whole damned mess came when we said Julian's name." He was surprised that his voice sounded so ordinary.

"*Sí*. Perhaps it is coincidence."

"Once, maybe. Twice—no way. The crying was a response. I'm sure of it."

"But we have said his name many times. I have told her the story of her marriage to that man so often I could say it in my sleep. Still, there is *nada*."

Liam sighed. These were the issues that had kept him up all last night, tossing and turning sleeplessly in his lonely bed. They had followed him into the light, plaguing him all day.

The measure of a man. That was what it came down to. At least that was the cul-de-sac at the end of his thoughts. "We're going to have to try something else, Rosa. Something a little more extreme. She's not responding to our voices. And I don't think we have a lot of time."

He felt Rosa turn toward him, but he didn't look at her. He stared instead at the hands in his lap, at the small gold wedding band he'd worn for ten years.

"What are you thinking?" she asked.

He heard the worry in her voice, the tiny, halting hitch in the middle of the sentence, and he knew that she knew what he was going to say. "I'm going to call Julian True and ask him to come see her. Talk to her."

She gasped. "You cannot!"

He turned to her finally. Her cheeks were paper

white; her dark eyes looked like burn holes in a sheet. "You know I have no choice."

She laughed. It was a brittle sound like the breaking of an antique glass Christmas ornament. "He is . . . dangerous."

"You think he was physically violent to her?"

"No, no. Of course not. The danger is in how much she loves—*loved* him."

Liam pretended not to be wounded by her mistake. "Do you think he still loves her?"

"He never did, I think." She twisted around so they were face-to-face. "You do not have to do this. God will waken Mikaela if that is His plan. You need to take care of *su familia*. That man, he could ruin everything. Mikaela made her choice a long time ago. You do not have to do this, Liam."

He wondered if she realized that she'd used his name. Strangely, that little intimacy comforted him as no touch ever could. "You and I, Rosa, we're not kids. We know how easy it is to do the wrong thing. This is probably the clearest moment I've had in all my fifty years. I can call Julian and give my wife a chance at life. Or I can not call Julian and know that I was so afraid of losing Mikaela's love that I let her die."

Rosa's eyes filled with tears.

"I won't be able to look myself—or my children— in the eye if I let fear keep me from doing what's right. I am going to call Julian True. There's a phone number for his agent in the pillowcase."

Rosa reached out, placed her hands on top of his. "Does she know, I wonder?" she said softly, gazing at him through watery eyes. "Does my Mikita know how lucky she is to have you?"

Liam knew he shouldn't ask it, but he couldn't help himself. "Did she love me, Rosa?"

She squeezed his hands. "Of course."

"Like she loved him?"

Rosa paused, and in that heartbeat's hesitation, Liam saw the harrowing truth. "*Sí,*" she answered with a smile that was too bright, too fast.

Liam sighed. "Then I guess we have nothing to worry about."

Part Three

The fate of love is that it always seems
too little or too much.

AMELIA BARR, "THE BELLE OF BOWLING GREEN"

Part Three

Chapter Twelve

Beverly Hills. Two words, each unremarkable enough on its own, but like champagne and caviar, they combined to form the ultimate expression of the good life. In this pastel pocket of Los Angeles, everything was about fantasy; stardust from nearby Hollywood gilded even the mundane. Images of Beverly Hills were famous around the world: pink hotels with poolside phones, valet parking at the post offices, restaurant tables that couldn't be bought for any amount of money—ah, but a whisper of fame could get you seated in an instant. It was a city where last names were unnecessary among the chosen few. Harrison. Goldie. Brad. Julian.

Even in the rarefied perfection of this most trimmed and tucked and glamorized of cities, Julian True was special. Not just a star, but a superstar, a nova who showed no sign of burning out.

He'd come to Hollywood like thousands of young men before him, with nothing more than a handsome face and a dream. He'd wanted to be someone who mattered, and he knew it would happen. Things had always come easily to him—attention, women, invitations, everything—and he took what came easily.

Today he was flying high. That was the thing he loved most about fame: It gave a man wings. He eased off the accelerator. The Ferrari responded instantly, slowing down. He pulled up in front of a notoriously trendy new restaurant. Before he'd even reached for the door handle, a valet was there.

"Good afternoon, Mr. True," said the boy—no doubt an actor.

Julian flashed him a smile. "Thanks, kid." Without a backward glance, he headed for the front door, which also opened automatically at his arrival. "Good afternoon, Mr. True."

The maître d' was already there, smiling broadly. "Good afternoon, Mr. True. She is already at your table."

"Thanks, Jean Paul. When the bill comes, add fifty bucks apiece for the valet and doorman, and a hundred for yourself. *People* magazine can afford it."

"*Merci.*"

Julian followed Jean Paul to the table. He knew he was late, not that it mattered. People—especially reporters—were used to waiting for him.

He paused, looking around, searching for famous faces, power brokers, studio heads.

Unfortunately, it was that damn hinterland of time, after lunch but well before dinner. The place was almost deserted.

Too bad.

He was in the mood for a little schmoozing. Hell, he deserved it. Today's screening of his new film, *The Bad Boys of C Company,* had gone better than he'd hoped. Better than anyone had hoped. Julian had earned his twenty million. He'd given the studio a surefire hit.

A hit. Two of the sweetest words possible.

He saw the reporter from *People* magazine—a woman (good), sitting at the restaurant's best table. Clearly she'd told the maître d' that she was here to meet Julian.

He moved easily through the restaurant, hearing the few scattered whispers of recognition. At the table, he stopped, "Heya, Sara Sandler."

She stopped breathing, then started again, all at once, like a newborn baby. Color fanned up her cheeks. "Hi, Mr. True," she answered, making a clear attempt to compose herself. She tucked in a few fly-away hairs, resettled her eyeglasses. "Thanks for meeting me."

He gave her The Smile. "Call me Julian," he said, settling down into the seat across from her. He stretched out one leg, plunking his booted foot on the settee beside her hip. He ran a hand through his shoulder-length hair and lit up a cigarette, watching her through a haze of smoke. "So, Sara, what is America dying to know about me?"

"D-Do you remind . . . *mind* if I record this?"

He laughed. "'Course not, darlin'. But I'd appreciate it if you wouldn't mention the smoking. It used to be smokers were sexy and dangerous, but in the puritanical nineties, we just look stupid. Like we don't have the self-control to quit a habit that has killed millions." The smile he gave her was slow and intimate, designed to disarm. He'd learned a long time ago how to hook a woman and reel her in. It came as easily now as breathing. "Did you get a chance to see *Boys*?"

"It was *wonderful*." She leaned forward, all schoolgirl earnestness.

"Why, thanks. That really means something to me."

She struggled to tamp down a smile and reached into her briefcase, pulling out some papers and a notebook and pen. Then she took a deep breath and glanced up at him. "So, when did you know you wanted to be an actor?"

He laughed easily. It was a familiar question, one he answered all the time. This interview would be a breeze. He leaned toward her, gave her a conspiratorial look. "I'll tell you a secret, Sara. I *never* wanted to be an actor. Acting—that's a verb. It implies work. Actors spend the better part of their lives skulking around Broadway, learning their craft, and eating macaroni-and-cheese out of a box. But a movie star . . ." He settled back into the settee, gazing at her as if she were the most beautiful woman in the world. "Ah, now that's a different thing entirely. Lightning in a jar. Fame is the greatest drug in the world. Everybody wants to be your friend. That's what I wanted to be. I knew it the first time I saw how a star was treated."

She didn't seem to like that answer. "But you're a great actor. All the reviewers say so."

He was quiet for a moment, took a long drag off his cigarette, exhaled slowly. "I know what I am, darlin', and it ain't an actor. But you're sweet as hell to say so."

She glanced down at her notes. "Is Julian True your real name?"

Another familiar question. He gave her another Hollywood smile. "Nothing up on that movie screen is real, Sara," he said softly, using her name again to seduce her. "And at the same time it's as real as life. Everything I am, everything I've ever been is up there in Technicolor, forty feet wide. Nothing that came before matters."

"That's a nice way of saying 'No comment.'"

"Is it?"

She wrote something down, then looked back up at him. "What about love—does that matter?"

"I've been married four times. I'd say it matters to me."

"And divorced four times," she responded, maintaining a steady gaze.

The question rolled off him like warm water. "I'm an incurable romantic, I guess. Just haven't found the right woman. Maybe she'll be reading this article. Now, what do you say we talk about my movie? We can get back to all this personal stuff later on . . . maybe over drinks?" He smiled, knowing there would be no later, no cozy pair of cocktails. The truth was, he didn't have much to say about real life. It wasn't the world he lived in.

* * *

Julian sped down a residential street, going much too fast. As he approached the imposing entrance to Bel Air, he saw a couple standing on the side of the street.

The woman gasped, pointed. "Oh, my God, Sidney, it's—"

Julian flashed the lady his trademark grin, then hit the gas, following the winding, stop-and-go traffic into Century City. There, he pulled up in front of a grand high-rise building and parked at a metered spot.

A doorman rushed out, held the door open. "Good evening, Mr. True."

Julian patted his pocket, found it empty. *Damn.* He was so used to other people picking up the tab, he regularly left his wallet at home. "I don't have any money with me, kid. I'll tell Val to tip you, okay?"

"S-Sure, Mr. True . . . and thank you."

Julian followed the doorman through the ornate marble-paneled lobby and into the elevator.

At the penthouse, the doors opened. Julian's agent, Val Lightner, lounged in the open doorway of his condo.

No doubt he was waiting for his most famous client, waiting to pop the champagne.

"Hey, Juli," Val said, lifting his martini glass in a salute that upset his precarious balance. He staggered against the door frame. "How'd the interview go? I heard they sent you a baby reporter who couldn't talk for an hour after she got back to the office."

Julian grinned. "I think she wants to bear my children."

"The phones have been ringing off the hook since the screening. If you were any hotter, you'd need asbestos underwear."

They'd been friends forever, Julian and Val; they were cut from the same cloth. Val had made his bones in this business a long time ago, with the world-famous Angel DeMarco, an actor who, for years, had been called the young Robert De Niro, and who—at the peak of his game—had walked away from it all, creating in absentia a legend greater than anything he could have accomplished on screen. Val had wielded the power of Angel DeMarco to create a world-class career for Julian True.

Val grinned lazily and pushed a long, cornsilk-blond lock of hair away from his face. "Come on in, superstar. There's a babe with your name on her."

Julian followed Val into the condo, where a raucous party was in full swing. Movie stars mingled with wanna-bes; you could tell them apart by the eyes. The stars looked confident; the wanna-bes looked desperate, starvelings standing at a banquet table where they'd never be fed.

The place had the tasteful decor of a fraternity house. No paintings, no knickknacks, no rugs. Val had bought the unit, picked a few things to sit on, and called it home. But then, Val didn't need to decorate. In this town, failure to do what you could easily afford had a cachet all its own.

"I need a drink," Julian said to no one in particular, and within seconds someone handed him a drink. It didn't matter what was in the glass, as long as it had a kick. He downed it and glided into the room. He knew that every pair of eyes was on him. The men wanted to be him and the women wanted to sleep with him. And why not? He was on top of the world. There was no perfume like success. He moved through the crowd, laughing and talking, his gaze constantly searching the room.

He saw her on the sofa in the living room, a stunning blonde in a barely-there white dress. Perfect. He strode over and sat down beside her.

His hand slid familiarly along her thigh, and damn, she felt good. "Hiya, darlin'. You're the most beautiful woman in the room, but I guess you know that."

She giggled, and at the movement, her grapefruit breasts—the best that money could buy—threatened to pop out of her plunging neckline.

"I'm Margot," she purred. "Margot LaMere. You like that name? Val made it up for me." She sniffed and rubbed her runny, pink-tipped nose, then she leaned forward and grabbed her drink so fast that amber liquid sloshed over the rim and splashed on her dress. "I got *great* reviews in my high-school production of *Our Town*."

Julian felt an unexpected—and unwelcome—flash of pity for the girl. There were so many women like her in Los Angeles.

When he looked closely, he saw that she wasn't that pretty. Her hair had been bleached so many times it looked like straw, and she was dangerously thin. Her collarbone stood out in mountainous relief against her tanned, sunken flesh. And beneath a dozen layers

of mascara, her brown eyes held a lifetime's desperation. Girls like her landed in Hollyweird every day,
butterflies in search of fame's golden flower. In a few
years' time, she'd probably be broke and alone and
strung out on designer drugs.

It was not the sort of reality Julian liked to consider.
He yanked his hand back and lurched to his feet. "I'll
be right back, babe."

She sighed, and in the heaviness of her breath, he
heard that she'd understood. He wouldn't be coming back.

He turned away from her and made his way through
the crowd, past a couple having sex in the hallway.

He found Val in the bedroom, snorting a line of
coke off the table by the bed. There was a woman beside him, wearing nothing but a pair of lacy red
panties.

Val turned, grinning sleepily. "Hey, Jules, say hi to
May Sharona. She wanted to talk to you about a part
in—" He cupped the woman's perfect right breast in
his hand. "What movie were you interested in, doll?"

The woman was talking now. Julian could see her
painted lips moving, but he didn't listen. He'd heard it
all before.

"I'm going to another party. This one's dead."
Julian realized a second too late that he'd just stomped
all over the woman's litany of dreams.

Val didn't seem to notice that May Sharona—what a
name—had turned beet red and seemed to be gasping
for air. He angled up to a swaying sit. "Whassa matter?
I have more coke in the bathroom."

"No, thanks."

"No? *No?*" Val untangled himself from the woman and grabbed his martini glass from the end table. He sauntered unsteadily across the room. Looping an arm around Julian, he kind of hung there, swaying, smiling up through a fringe of blond hair. "Hey, before you go, I gotta message for you. Someone called the office, looking for you. A doctor. He said he needed to talk to you about Mikaela Luna. How's *that* for a blast from the past?" He lifted the martini glass to his lips and took a long, dribbling swallow.

"You're kidding?"

"No." Val frowned, as if he'd already forgotten what they were talking about.

"A doctor. Jesus, is she hurt?"

"I dunno. He just wanted you to call him."

Julian felt a strange fluttering in his chest. *Kayla.* Of all the women he'd known, he'd loved her the most. "Where's the number?"

Val waved a hand and almost fell over. "I told Susan to leave it on your answering machine."

"Thanks," Julian answered, distracted by a sudden onslaught of memories. His first love. Kayla. He hadn't heard from her in so long he'd almost forgotten her. Almost.

Val slid away from Julian and headed for the bed, collapsing in a heap on the edge. "It'd sure be something to find her. The missing Mrs. True. The press loved her." He paused, looked blearily at Julian. "And so did you."

*   *   *

At the gates to his home, Julian spoke into a small black intercom. Immediately the intricately wrought gates parted, revealing a short driveway that led to a sprawling Spanish bungalow. At least that's what the designer had called it. Five families could live here, and still, in this neck of the woods, it was a bungalow.

Julian had lived here for ten years, two of those with Priscilla-of-the-dessert, four with Dorothea-the-bitch, and one with Anastasia. None with Kayla.

Not one of his wives had added anything to the interior of the house, not a photograph or a lamp or a painting. They had each come here with nothing, added nothing, and left with a few million dollars of Julian's money. He supposed it was indicative of his problem. He cared more about this home than about the women he'd married and brought here to live.

No, that wasn't quite right. It wasn't a home. It was a house that wanted to be a home. He had never had time for a home.

Julian walked up the flagstone path. Bushy green trees in huge terra-cotta pots flanked the way, releasing—even at this dozing season of the year—a soft, citrusy scent. Spotlights cast golden, latticed shadows along the path. A riot of late-blooming pink bougainvillea arched above the front entrance. A dozen Japanese-style ceramic lanterns lit the path.

The door opened and Julian's housekeeper, Teresa, stood in the doorway. As always, her uniform was as starched and white as a brand-new sail, and not a single gray hair was out of place. "*Buenos noches, Señor True*. How did the movie go?"

Julian was too distracted to smile. "Another hit." Frowning, he moved past Teresa into the cool, airy house. It was a place of sharp contrasts—white stucco walls and dark walnut trim, white denim-covered, oversized chairs and dark, heavily carved wooden tables. The floor throughout was tile, huge terra-cotta squares and rectangles that forgave any spill.

In the spotless kitchen, he poured two shots of tequila into a Waterford tumbler and downed it, without bothering to reach for salt or a lime. Tucking the bottle under his arm, he began his search. Somewhere in this house there *had* to be a picture of Kayla. He went from room to room, lifting every photograph, until he found what he was looking for. There, tucked in the back of the music room, on a bookshelf too high to reach, he found a framed picture of her.

He dropped slowly to his knees on the thick Aubusson carpet, staring at the photograph. It was their wedding picture.

There had not been a photograph like this taken of Julian in many years. Now, he knew he looked handsome—better looking at forty than he'd been at twenty-four—but there was something more in this shot. He realized with a shock what it was: honesty. Here, in this picture, was the last true glimmer of the man Julian had once wanted to be.

He closed his eyes, remembering her. They had been on their honeymoon, on that yacht in the Caribbean . . .

"Tell me your real name," she'd whispered, smiling.

He'd grinned, but it was the Hollywood smile, and

he'd known that it hurt her. "Nope, I don't tell anyone that."

"You will. Someday . . . when you're ready."

He'd touched her face, brushed the flyaway hair from her eyes. "That boy is dead, Kay. He isn't coming back. I *like* being Julian True. It's who I want to be for you."

"Don't you see, Jules? You could be anyone, anywhere, and I'd love you till I die."

He'd opened his eyes and stared down at the photograph.

She had loved him like no one else ever had, before or since. Loved *him,* not the one-dimensional celluloid image of a man that was Julian True. She had said often that when Julian cut himself, she bled. Even in the blurred afterglow of a life half lived and fifteen years gone by, he knew that he was right in that one belief. She had loved him.

Chapter Thirteen

Liam sat at his desk. He didn't bother to turn on any of the lights, or to leaven the silence by playing one of the CDs stacked by the stereo.

The intercom buzzed. Carol's staticky voice came through the small black box. "Doctor? Are you in there?"

He pressed the button. "I'm here, Carol. You can go ahead and go home. We're done for the day."

"You're not going to believe this, Doctor. There's a man on the phone who says he's Julian True."

Liam's heart skipped a beat. "I'll take it."

"Do you think it's the real—"

"Patch him through, Carol, and go on home. We're done for the day."

"Yes, Doctor."

The red light on line one started flashing. Liam took a deep breath, stabbed the button, and picked up the phone. "This is Dr. Campbell."

There was a pause at the other end, then: "Dr. *Liam* Campbell?"

Even through the impersonal medium of the phone lines, Liam would have recognized the voice. "This is he."

"This is Julian True. You left a message with my agent, Val Lightner, regarding Mikaela Luna—"

"She's been injured."

"Oh, God. How bad?"

"She's in a coma."

Another pause crackled through the lines, and Liam realized that Julian was on a car phone. "A coma. Jesus . . . What can I do? I'll pay for her hospital bills, and for the best doctors in the country—not to say that you're not great, Dr. Campbell, but—"

"She doesn't need your money, Mr. True. I called you because . . . well, she shows some response to your name. I . . . *we* thought that maybe if she heard your voice—"

"You think she'll wake up for me?"

Liam was unprepared for the pain that came with that simple question. "We think there's a chance."

"I've got an interview this afternoon, but I can be there tomorrow. Where is she?"

"In the Ian Campbell Medical Center in Last Bend, Washington. About sixty miles east of Bellingham."

"Okay, I'll get Antoinette to set me up."

"When you get to the medical center, ask for me. I'll be in my office there."

"Okay."

Liam waited for Julian to end the conversation, but

he just hung on the line, breathing, not saying anything. Finally Liam said, "Is there something else?"

"Yeah. Uh . . . how does she look? I mean, I need to be prepared."

It was a perfectly human question, nothing wrong with it, so why did Liam feel suddenly angry? His answer was barely audible along the crackling line. "She looks as beautiful as you probably remember."

Val's office was a huge, open space tucked into the northeastern corner of a high-rise on Wilshire Boulevard. Huge glass windows paneled the corner, capturing a vista of other tall buildings. Behind them lay a filmy layer of brown smog.

A few sleek chairs were gathered around a glass coffee table. Movie posters and theater announcements graced the walls, each one representing a client. A huge television, flanked by fifteen smaller screens, dominated one corner. Currently a music video pulsed on every screen.

Val's desk was an immense, rectangular sheet of green glass. He was slouched over in his chair, holding his head in his hands.

Julian didn't need to be told to keep his voice down. He'd partied with Val enough over the years to know when his best friend was nursing an ugly hangover. He crossed the room and sat down in the cushiony black leather chair opposite the desk.

"Quieter," Val moaned.

"Look, Val, I know you feel like four kinds of shit, but I really need to talk to you."

"Whisper, please."

"I called that doctor in Podunk, Washington. It *was* about Kayla. She's had an accident. She's in a coma."

Slowly Val lifted his head. His eyes were puffy and bloodshot. "So, what, they need money for her hospital bills?"

"No. The doc said she responded to my name. They seem to think it would help if I talked to her."

Val ran a hand through his hair. The greasy blond locks fell right back in front of his ashen face. A slow-growing smile plucked one corner of Val's mouth. Julian recognized the look: It was Val's we-can-make-money-here look. "It's like one of those chick fairy tales. A kiss of true love to wake her up—get it? *True* love wakes her up. Now, there's a hell of a headline."

"This is serious, Val. She's pretty bad off. She could die."

"Oh." Val's smile faded.

Julian stared at his friend. Val was so goddamn transparent. Now he was thinking that it wouldn't do much good if the headline was TRUE LOVE KILLS.

"So, what are you going to do?" Val said at last.

Julian leaned back. The chair squeaked, rolled an inch backward. Images and memories drifted through his mind like clouds on a summer's day. "She was the one, Val. She really loved me."

"They all love you, Julian."

"Kay was different. I loved her, too."

"I've seen movies that run longer than your love."

That stung. "I'm going up there. Right after the *Rolling Stone* interview."

"*What?* This fucking movie's gonna be big, Juli. Big. We've got a shitload of press scheduled—"

Julian smiled. There was nothing he liked better than surprising Val; it was damned hard to do. "It's not like I'm vanishing. I'm just going out of town for a day or two. I pay you two and a half million a year. Make it work."

Val shook his head. "Okay, Jules. Go play Prince Charming. But be back in two days. I mean it."

"And no press. I want to do this alone."

Val looked at him hard. "Jesus, Juli, you never do anything alone."

"There's always a first time."

The kitchen lights were off, but Liam could see two blue spots of flame on the stove. The mouth-watering aroma of Rosa's arroz con pollo wafted up from the pots. In the dining room, the table was set for dinner. A vase of fern fronds and pine boughs made a graceful centerpiece.

In the great room, there were candles on every windowsill and tabletop. The candelabra on the grand piano was a blaze of flickering golden light.

He heard the soft, even patter of Rosa's slippered feet on the stairs.

"*Buenos noches,* Rosa," he said.

She reached the bottom of the stairs and turned toward him. "*Buenos noches,* Dr. Liam."

"What's with all the candles, Rosa?"

"It does not bother you, I hope? I know it is not my place . . ."

"*Mi casa es su casa,*" he answered. "I just wondered why . . . all of a sudden . . ."

She ducked into the great room, moving hurriedly toward the grand piano. The ebony surface captured her reflection, dotted it with candlelight.

He followed, came to a stand behind her. "Is this all for Mike?"

She shook her head. The tip of her white braid brushed against her hip. Slowly she turned around and looked up at him.

He could see the worry carved into her face. "It is for you also that I light these candles, Dr. Liam. For you and the children. I spoke to Carol today. She told me that Julian True called you. It is quite the fiery gossip in town."

"Hot," he said distractedly. "Hot gossip. And Julian will be here tomorrow."

Her mouth puckered with disapproval, but she didn't say anything.

"You think I shouldn't have called him."

"It does not matter what one old woman thinks."

He said, "Follow me," and led her to the sofa.

She sat stiffly, her knees and ankles clamped together, her gaze riveted on her lap.

He sat beside her, leaning forward in the hopes that it would make her look at him. "I'm afraid of him, too, Rosa. More afraid than I've ever been in my life. But I love her. I can't let her go without trying everything possible."

Rosa sighed heavily. "You cannot understand bad love. My poor Mikita, she grew up watching this kind of love . . . and I think I—what is the word?—infected her with my sorrow."

"Julian True married her, Rosa. He must have loved her."

"There is love . . . and *love*. The good love, like what you have for my Mikaela, it does not let a young girl run off alone with a tiny baby. It does not stay hidden for years and years. It does not leave you cold in the winter in bed all by yourself."

Liam looked away. Candlelight reflected all around the room, a thousand tiny golden drops hovering against the night-tarnished windowpanes. "When I asked Mike to marry me," he said quietly without looking at Rosa, "she told me she'd been married before . . . and that she was afraid she could never love anyone that way again."

"Of course she was afraid. Love for a woman like her is a terrifying thing. She knew only one kind of love then—the fiery kind that burns everything around it. And she had seen me, alone for so long, waiting for a man who would never come. How could my Mikita be anything but afraid when you said you loved her? But I remember when she first told me about you. 'A doctor, Mama,' she said. 'And he loves me something awful.' I tell her, 'You be smart, you love him back.' And she said to me that a broken heart doesn't love so good. I will always remember this, because it made me want to cry." She touched his face gently with her work-calloused hand. "I talked to her many, many times as the years went by. When Bret was born . . . I have never seen my Mikita so full of joy. I think she stopped thinking about the things that were gone. She loves you, Dr. Liam. I know this in my mother's heart."

"Enough?" he asked.

Rosa's gaze slid away from his. She made a soft, sighing sound, something like air leaking from an old, worn tire. "You have heard many of the words of Mikaela's story, but maybe they do not create the right picture. She was a young girl when she met Julian—only a few years older than Jacey. But she was nothing like Jacey. She had a mother who was weak and poor, and a father who would never speak to her in public. She lived in a bad part of town, in a house no one was supposed to see. One day she saw a god. She fell in love with him, in the way that only young girls can fall in love. They married . . . but he was not a god. He was just a young, selfish man who wanted nothing from life but to have fun. He wanted everything to be given to him, but love, it is not an easy road, *sí*? And the very heart that he once filled with love, he broke." She leaned over and touched Liam's hands. "When he comes here, you cannot tell Jacey who he is. This is *muy importante*. We cannot let him hurt our precious girl."

Liam knew it was the easy road, not telling Jacey the truth, but he told himself that Mikaela should be the one to reveal her secrets to Jacey. "You're right, Rosa. We won't say anything yet."

Yet even as he said the words, he knew it was the wrong thing to do.

Liam walked slowly up the stairs. He knew he shouldn't talk to Jacey right now. He figured his chance of saying the right thing to her was about equal to his chances of climbing Mt. Everest in a Speedo. But he had to sit with her, hold her hand, and look into her eyes. It was guilt, of course, but there was so much more. For the first time in his life, he was afraid of losing his daughter's love.

He paused at her bedroom door, then quietly knocked.

"Come in."

He opened the door and found her exactly as he'd expected: on the telephone. She said good-bye and hung up. "Hi, Dad."

Dad.

"Hey, kiddo."

"How is she?"

"The same." He sat down beside her and gently took hold of her hand. "How are you doing?"

She bravely hoisted a smile onto her pale face. "Okay."

He couldn't think of anything else to say. All he could think about was what would happen to all of them when Julian True came into their lives. Jacey, like Liam, had been told only that Mike had been married too young, to a man who wasn't ready to settle down. Two kids . . . a marriage that didn't work out. It was an ordinary story Mike had devised. There was no room in it for the possibility of Julian True.

Liam knew that in all the days and weeks and years

that lay ahead, he would divide his life into two neat pieces. Before the coma, and after.

Tragedy was like that, a razor that sliced through time, severing the now from the before, incising the what-might-have-been from reality as cleanly as any surgeon's blade. Even if Mikaela recovered, their lives would be changed. He was afraid that the secrets she'd kept would always be here, inside him, an ugly malignant thing lodged near enough to his heart to upset its rhythm, and though it could be removed, cut out, there would always be scars; bits and pieces of it would remain in his blood, making it wrong somehow, so that if he accidentally sliced his skin open, his blood would—for one heartbeat—flow as black as India ink before it remembered that it should be red.

Now, as he looked into Jacey's sad brown eyes, he knew he should tell her the truth about Julian. He knew, too, that he wouldn't do it. He would lay down his life before causing her such pain.

"Are you okay, Dad?"

A smile was beyond him. "Right as Seattle rain." He leaned toward her and pulled her into his arms. She clung to him, and for a brief and shining moment, everything was forgotten except that he loved her . . . and she loved him back.

When he pulled back, he could see it in her eyes, this mixture of grief and fear that had changed them all. "Dad?"

He felt fragile suddenly; one touch and he could shatter into a dozen pieces. "I love you, Jacey. That's all I came up here to say."

She smiled easily, relieved. "I love you, too, Dad. Remember when I had appendicitis?"

He stroked her hair. "Of course."

"You gave me a sucker and told me you'd take the pain away . . . and you did."

"I wish it were that simple now."

She lost her smile. "I wish I were little again."

He pulled her into his arms again.

If she wondered why he held her a bit too tightly, she never said a word.

Chapter Fourteen

The town looked like a damned movie set. Pleasantville at night.

Julian stared through the limousine's smoked-glass windows. He couldn't remember ever seeing a place this . . . cute. Any minute he expected to see Disney characters skipping along the sidewalks.

He lowered the privacy screen so he could talk to the driver. "We're looking for the Country Haus Bed and Breakfast. It's probably right next door to the Drift On Inn."

"I've got the address, sir."

"Thank God. In a town this size, we could miss it by what, a block? Two?"

The driver turned off Main Street onto Glacier. Halfway down the road, they came to a barricade. Several cars were parked in the center of the road, behind the orange dividers. The driver stopped and started to turn the car around.

"Wait." Julian hit the window control. The glass

descended silently. He poked his head out to see what the hell the barricade was for. The cold stung his eyes and nose.

Off to the right, there was a huge field, coated in white. In the middle of it was a large frozen pond. Cars ringed the perimeter of a makeshift skating rink; their golden headlights turned the place into an outdoor Madison Square Garden. There were people everywhere, kids and adults, all skating in the same direction.

He noticed a small concession stand set up just a few feet from the car. Some men were roasting hot dogs over an open pit fire.

"Jesus, the only thing missing is Jimmy Stewart." He drew his head back in and raised the window. "Go on, take me to the hotel."

The limousine turned around and reentered Main Street. "You don't see towns like this much anymore," the driver said, casting a nervous glance into the rearview mirror.

They pulled up alongside a huge Victorian house that sat on a corner lot, its roof covered in drifts of snow. A white picket fence cut the large lot into a pretty, bite-sized piece. Next to the open gate was an etched wooden sign that read WELCOME TO OUR COUNTRY HAUS.

Julian stepped out of the car. His breath clouded in front of his face. Christ, it was cold. He sure hoped Teresa had packed him a coat. He pulled his Ray-Bans out of his shirt pocket and put them on. "Bring the bags in," he said, already moving, his tennis shoes crunching through the hard crust of snow.

The door swung open before he even reached the porch. A gray-haired, heavyset woman in a floral dress and plaid apron stood in the doorway. "It *is* you! The girls and I didn't dare hope. In a town like this . . ." She dissolved into giggles.

At mention of "the girls," he pictured a herd of wildebeests, all dressed in flowered cotton. Even though he was tired, he flashed her The Smile. It never hurt to schmooze the fans. "Hello, darlin'."

She clapped her hands together; a little cloud of flour wafted upward. "Darling—ooh eee. Wait till I tell Gertrude. I made you shortbread, just in case. I read in the *Enquirer* that it's your favorite."

"You're an angel straight from heaven," he said, though in truth, he couldn't remember what in the hell shortbread was. "Now, if you wouldn't mind, I've had a long trip and I'm tired as hell. I'd sure appreciate it if you'd show me to my room."

"Of *course*." She scuttled around like a dung beetle and hopped up the narrow staircase. Julian could hear the driver, banging up behind them with his garment bag.

On the second floor, the woman waddled to the end of the hallway and opened a door, revealing a big, airy bedroom that exceeded the weight limit on ruffles. Laura Ashley on LSD couldn't find use for that many ruffles.

"It's the honeymoon suite," she said, beaming. She

offered her pudgy hand. "I'm Elizabeth, by the way, but you can call me Lizbet."

"Liz . . . bet. What a charming name." He poked his head into the room and frowned. "I'm sorry, Lizbet, but where's my bathroom?"

"Down the hall. Third door on the left."

He turned slowly to face her. "You're saying I have to *share* a bathroom with other people?"

"Ordinarily that would be true, but ski season hasn't started yet. You're our only guest. So, really, it's like a private bathroom."

"Except that I need to pack a lunch to get to it."

She puffed up. "Well, really—"

"I'm sorry. That was just a joke. The room is fine. Give my driver a room, too, would you? Preferably on another floor. Then I'll buy up all the rest. I'd like to have the place to myself."

"Of course." She flushed prettily and bobbed her head. Backing away from him, she smiled until the last possible moment, when she turned and disappeared.

He sat down on the end of the bed. The springs squeaked and moaned beneath his weight. "Unpack my bags, will you?" he said to the driver, flopping back on the bed.

A minor emergency kept Liam in the office until almost five o'clock. By the time he closed up the building and headed for the hospital, it was completely dark. As he stepped out into the night, he heard the high-pitched, faraway sounds of children laughing. They were skating tonight.

He got into his car and drove through the deserted town. In the hospital, he went to the small corner office that he shared with Tom Granato, a general practitioner from Deming.

He knew the instant that Julian True arrived. A flurry of sounds came through the door, footsteps sped up, whispers turned up in volume. He waited for his intercom to buzz.

Instead, Sarah appeared at the door, opening it without even a knock. Her face was flushed a bright pink, and she was grinning. "Dr. Campbell, there's a man here to see—"

"Julian True."

She sucked in a surprised breath. "How did you know?"

"Magic."

"He says he's here to see Mikaela."

"Send him in."

Sarah bobbed a quick nod and disappeared.

And so it began. Liam tried to steady his nerves. He had taken such care with himself this morning. Put on his best black pants and the blue flannel shirt Mike had given him for Christmas last year, but now he saw the pointlessness in it all. The white coat he wore would deflect only the measliest blow.

The door opened.

Liam turned.

The man standing in the open doorway smiled— just that—and Liam felt ill. The photographs didn't do Julian justice; no lens could capture the magnetic power of that face.

"I'm Julian True," he said unnecessarily, and Liam could tell that he enjoyed acting as if there were people on this planet who didn't know who he was.

Liam rose slowly to his feet. He pulled the glasses from his face—as if *that* would help—and tucked them in the pocket of his lab coat. "Hello, Julian. I'm glad you could come. I'm Liam Campbell. I wanted—"

"Can I see her now?"

Liam sighed. He didn't know why he'd wanted to put it off; it wasn't as if Julian was going to leave. Still, the thought of bringing them together made him feel sick. "Follow me."

He led Julian down the hallway toward Mikaela's room. Slowly he opened the door.

Julian pushed past him and went to the bed. He stared down at Mikaela for a long time. "What happened?"

"She fell off a horse and hit her head on a fence post."

"How long has she been like this?"

"A little more than a month."

Julian brushed a strand of hair from her eyes. "Heya, Kayla. It's Jules." Then he looked up. "Can she hear me?"

Liam stared down at Mikaela. "That's why you're here."

"What do I do?"

Liam felt like Grandpa Walton giving advice to Robert Redford about how to talk to a woman. "Just talk to her, Julian." His voice fell to a whisper. "She sometimes responds to . . . memories . . . stories from the past."

"And my name. She responded to my name, right?"

It took an incredible effort to answer. "Yes."

Julian dragged a chair over to the bed and sat down. "Leave us alone for a while, will you, Doc? Heya, Kayla. It's me. Jules."

She didn't respond.

Liam let out a shaky breath. He realized he'd been afraid she would simply wake up, just like that, when she heard Julian's voice.

Julian took her hand in his. "Kayla, honey?"

Liam couldn't stand the sight of Julian touching her, so he turned and walked out of the room. In the hall, he leaned back against the wall.

It wasn't until almost a full minute had passed that he realized what he'd done . . . or hadn't done.

He hadn't told Julian that he was Mike's husband.

Julian had never been any good at writing his own lines.

He thought about ringing the nurse to bring him something decent to sit on, and bagged the idea. He wasn't a complete idiot; he knew he was just fishing for something to think about, something except the woman lying before him.

She looked beautiful, like a sleeping princess. He half expected her to sit up, smiling, and say, *Hey, Jules, what took you so long?*

At the imagined sound of her voice, the years fell away. Julian hadn't thought about her in ages, but now, looking at her, he could recall clearly how it had felt to love her . . . and to be loved by her. Of all the women he'd known in his life, she alone had given him a safe harbor, a place that felt like home.

He closed his eyes; memories floated to the surface. "Remember the beginning, Kay? The first time I kissed you, I thought I'd die. Not in the 'I thought I'd die' way of teenagers, but in a truly frightening way. My heart was beating so fast, I couldn't breathe, and I thought, This is it, I'm going to die.

"You tasted like rainwater—did you know that?

"I fell so far in love with you it felt like I was drowning. Remember the first time we made love? We were out in some orchard, lying on a wool blanket. I had sent my assistant all the way to Yakima for a bottle of Dom Perignon. I wanted to be the first man to show you what starlight tasted like. I didn't know I'd be your first lover, too.

"When you tasted the champagne, you laughed. You tucked your hands beneath your head and stared up at the sky and asked me to tell you about myself.

"I tried to tell you the prefab story that Val had invented, but you said, 'The time we have is precious. I don't want to end up knowing nothing about you except what's in the *Enquirer*. I want to know that I touched *you*.' "

He tried to remember how they'd fallen out of love. It had been so deep, that well of their shared emotion, how had they drifted to the surface? Yet even as he wondered, he knew.

She'd wanted him to grow up. It sounded absurdly simple, but if he looked hard at the truth, that was the core of it. She had wanted him to make sacrifices for their family. But he'd been twenty-three years old. Barely ready to be a husband, completely unprepared to be a father. All he'd wanted was fun . . . and so he'd drawn back, taken the careless path he knew so well, the road lined with women whose names could never be remembered and parties that never died.

It felt as if a door had opened. Beyond it, he saw a glimpse into himself, past the golden boy, past the star, all the way back to the lonely boy he'd once been. In all the years between then and now, he'd never really loved anyone. This woman, Kayla, had been the closest. His love for her had been the best of him, and he'd turned his back on it.

He stared down at her face, studying the lovely half-moon curl of her black eyelashes, the pale puffiness of her lips. What could he say that would matter to this woman whom he knew so well and yet didn't really know at all, this woman whose heart he'd broken with the ease of a child smashing an out-of-favor toy?

Tears seared his eyes. He couldn't believe it. He hadn't cried in years. Except when they paid him to, of course.

"You'd love this, Kay. *Me,* crying." He leaned toward her, resting his chin on the cold silver bed rail. "Remember our first fight? It was at one of Val's parties, after some screening. He told me he had a part for me—a little picture called *Platoon.* I said, 'Who the hell cares about that war?' and you hit me—right in front of everyone. You told me to quit being such a damned *star* and try acting."

It had started there—the end that was all wrapped up in the beginning—and he'd been too selfish to notice. "You always asked so much of me, Kayla," he said softly, shaking his head. "I never had that kind of talent . . . Why didn't you realize that?"

He gazed down at her, noticing for the first time the plain gold band on the ring finger on her left hand.

"Jesus Christ," he whispered. "You're *married*?"

Chapter Fifteen

Liam drove through Last Bend. The town glittered like a diamond tiara set on white velvet. Behind it, a background of jagged blue peaks leaned toward the starlit sky.

He parked in front of the Country Haus Bed and Breakfast. In a silence broken only by the hushed moan of the car's heater, he took a minute to collect his thoughts.

The last thing in the world he wanted to do right now was talk to Julian True, but he had no choice. When he looked up again, Julian was standing beside the car. The idiot was wearing a black T-shirt and jeans. He had to be freezing.

Liam reached over and unlocked the door. Julian slid into the seat and leaned back. "Jesus H. Christ, it's cold out there." Smiling, he turned to Liam. "I'm glad you called. The thought of spending the evening in that bathroom-less room, watching one of three speckled television channels, was more than I could bear. What do you say we get a drink?"

Offhand, Liam could think of at least thirty-two hundred things he'd rather do. "Sure." He started the car again and drove through town. Liam couldn't think of anything to say and Julian didn't bother to speak.

Liam parked in front of Lou's Bowl-O-Rama and got out of the car. "Follow me."

Lou's Bowl-O-Rama was pre-dinner-hour quiet. No one was using any of the four bowling lanes. As always, the place smelled of burnt grease and cigarette smoke. The owner, Lou Padinsky, stood behind the counter, wiping it down with a soggy gray rag. When he saw Liam, he flashed a grin that made the cigarette in his mouth droop. Ashes fluttered to the countertop and were quickly wiped away.

"Howdy, Doc."

Liam nodded. "Get us a couple o' beers, willya, Lou?"

"Sure thing, Doc." Lou slapped the rag across his shoulder and turned toward the beer taps.

Liam led Julian to a red Naugahyde settee at the back of the bowling alley.

As they sat down across from each other, Liam was glad they'd come here. First off, the lighting was poor, and God knew he didn't need to see the younger man's face in good light. Second, there wouldn't be a bunch of look-e-loos wandering through the place and getting all hot and bothered about a genuine movie star in Last Bend. He hoped that Julian felt out of place in a joint like this, but truthfully, Liam figured that a man like Julian never felt out of place.

Liam knew it was childish, but he needed an edge, even one as feeble as poor lighting.

Liam stared at the younger man, remembering all the things he'd learned about him. The Internet was great for that sort of thing. He knew, for example, that Kayla True had "disappeared" one day. He'd learned, too, that Julian and Mike had been blessed in the beginning, a genuine Hollywood superstar couple, but something—some reports said drugs, some said other women, some said aliens—had tarnished their star. And that the four-times-married Julian True was one of the highest-paid actors in the world.

Lou waddled toward the table and set down two schooners. Beer sloshed over the glass rims.

Julian flashed the man a bright smile. "Thanks."

Lou started to answer, then stopped. "Hey, you look like that guy . . ."

Julian's smile was so bright, Liam wanted to reach for a pair of sunglasses. "Uh-huh."

"Julian True. You hear that a lot?"

"All the time."

Lou elbowed the actor. "Should help with the chicks, huh?" Then he turned to Liam. "And how's that beautiful wife of yours?"

"She's okay. Thanks, Lou."

Lou nodded and headed back toward the lunch counter, humming *Up against the wall, you redneck mother*, as he went.

Liam took a sip of beer.

Julian leaned back, sliding his arms across the top of the settee. Liam had the impression of a golden lion stretching in the sun. "I didn't expect . . . her to be so . . ." He didn't finish.

"She's better than she was."

"Jesus." Julian's eyes narrowed. He was looking at Liam for the first time.

"Earlier this week, she blinked."

"A blink, that's good, huh?"

"It's better than nothing."

"Well, it was awful damned good of you to call me. We sure as hell don't have doctors like you at Cedars-Sinai—well, maybe Liz and Michael do, but not the rest of us."

"I'm her husband."

"*You?*"

Liam refused to let the tone upset him. "We've been married for ten years. I'm sure you noticed the wedding ring . . ."

Julian rolled his eyes. "Fuck me."

Liam wouldn't touch *that* line with a ten-foot pole.

Julian's hand shot in the air. "Hey, Lou. Bring me a pack of Marlboros, willya?"

Lou grinned and grabbed a pack. Hurrying over to the table, he dropped them in front of Julian, with a book of matches. "It's nice to see a smoker in Last Bend. We're dying out."

"Nice imagery, Lou. Thanks." Julian opened the pack, extracted a cigarette, and lit it up. Smoke swirled across his face, but through the cloud, Liam could see those blue eyes studying him. Julian reached for his beer and took a long drink, then set it back down between them. "You must really love her. To call me, I mean."

"I do," Liam said quietly.

Julian leaned back again. "This place reminds me of that dump of a diner where Kayla used to work."

"Really?"

He smiled. "God, she was beautiful. And those good Christian folks in Sunville treated her like trash."

"She said she never fit in."

"Who the hell would want to? That town was a case of pinkeye on God's eyeball. But it hurt her, you know. She was so scared of ending up like her mom. Kay would have done *anything* to belong somewhere."

"You mean, like marry you?"

Julian didn't smile this time. "Or you. I can see why she came to this town. She probably needed someone like you, after . . . me."

Liam couldn't stop the question; it burned on his tongue, left a bitter taste. "What happened between you two?"

Julian sighed. "You know how it is. We were in love . . . and then we weren't. Hell, I was twenty-three years old. I didn't know who I wanted to be, but I knew it wasn't Mr. Cleaver." He looked away, took another long drag on the cigarette, then exhaled. "I wouldn't even try. When she left, she said she'd wait for me to come get her. Forever—that's how long she said she'd wait."

Liam wished he couldn't see it so clearly. He sipped

on his beer, studying Julian over the frosted rim. "What about your daughter? Why didn't you ever contact her?"

Julian flinched, and Liam thought, My God, he never even thought about Jacey. He got on a plane, rushed up here, and never once remembered that he had a child here.

"She was so little when I last saw her. To be honest, I don't know what I feel about her. I'm sure we'll work it all out when I meet her."

Liam knew the rich were different and that the rich and famous were more so, but he couldn't fathom the kind of man who could be so careless with a young girl's heart. He didn't look away from Julian. At least the man could *look* ashamed. "She doesn't know you're her father."

"What? Kay never told her? I would have thought she'd be proud of it . . ."

"You hurt her, Julian."

"Well, shit."

"Do you want to tell her yourself?"

"*Me?* No."

God help him, Liam was relieved. "It's a small town. I don't want her to find out—"

"I won't say anything. If word gets around, I'll say I'm here for the Make-a-Wish Foundation. Please, Liam, let's . . . wait and see what happens with Kayla, okay? I mean, if she doesn't wake up . . ."

"Okay," Liam said, watching Julian closely. "We'll wait."

Rosa was waiting up for Liam when he got home. She set her knitting aside and got to her feet, moving across the living room toward him. She started to say something.

"Sorry, Rosa, not now," he said, walking past her. Whatever she was going to say, he didn't want to hear it.

Instead, he went up the stairs and quietly entered Jacey's bedroom.

She was fast asleep, one arm flung out to the left, as if even in sleep she were reaching for the bedside phone.

"You'll always be my daughter," he murmured.

The next morning, Liam woke up early and rolled quietly out of bed, being careful not to waken Bret, who was sleeping peacefully beside him. He showered quickly, grabbed some clothes from his closet, jammed them in a duffel bag, and headed downstairs. On the empty kitchen table, he left a *Have a good day* note for Rosa and the kids.

Dawn crept through Last Bend like a slow reckoning. Thin bands of pink light crested the trees. The storefronts were all black.

He drove to the hospital, parked in his stall, and went to Mikaela's room. He flicked on the lights and went immediately to draw open the curtains.

Then, very slowly, he turned around.

She was as still as always, her pale face slack, her arms tucked gently along her sides. There wasn't a wrinkle in the blanket drawn up against her chest.

He hadn't realized until he exhaled a wobbling

breath that he hadn't been breathing. He'd been afraid Julian had already wakened her.

Now, for the first time, it felt important—essential even—that Liam be the one to reach her.

"Heya, Mike," he whispered, starting the music. Today he chose something by Andrea Bocelli, to remind her of the sad, aching sweetness of life.

At her bedside, he set down the duffel bag and unzipped it, extracting a navy cashmere sweater, the one she'd bought for him on their last trip to Vancouver. Very gently, he placed it on her chest.

"Can you smell me, Mike? *Me?*" He knew that if he closed his eyes, he would remember that last day of their trip. They'd driven across the Canadian border to see a road show performance of *Rent*, and in that darkened theater, amid a crowd of strangers, they'd held hands like a couple of school kids.

"You bought me the sweater the next day, remember? I tried to tell you that it was too expensive, that a cotton sweater from Eddie Bauer was good enough for me." His voice broke. "And you said nothing was too good for me."

He took hold of her hand. "But that's not what I came here to say, is it?"

He lowered the bed rail. Slowly he climbed into bed beside her. "I don't know why I never thought to bring one of my own sweaters before. Last night I woke up in a cold sweat, thinking that very question. I thought of everyone but me . . . everyone you loved except me. You always said that was my greatest strength—that I thought of everyone before I thought of myself. But it's my weakness, too, and we both know that."

He brought her arm up, hating the lack of resistance in her limb, and kissed the back of her hand. "I let everyone else feed you memories because I was afraid of the power they held. I was afraid of . . . breaking. I still am, I guess, but I can't let another day pass without going through that fear. It seems that all I can think about is you and Julian. He fell in love with a young girl who had big dreams and seemed at home in the fast lane, a girl who charmed the whole country. I can't imagine that woman at all. I fell in love with a nurse with haunted eyes and a heart that was tender to the touch.

"There's a whole part of you I never knew, and knowing that makes me feel . . . lost. Like our life together wasn't real."

He took a deep breath. "When I think of us, I think of little things. Like last Christmas, when we all went skiing at Schweitzer Mountain, and you said the only thing to look forward to in a sport that froze your nose hairs was quitting it."

He smiled at the memory. For the first time, his words had brought *her* to him. Not the wife who was frozen in sleep, but the laughing, vibrant woman he'd married.

"When we got home, it was just in time for Glacier Days. As usual, you were the big kahuna, organizing everyone."

An unexpected memory hit him hard and he laughed out loud. "Remember what happened in the gym? I was the last one in there, trying to figure out how to get into that damn hairy suit. Everyone else was outside, gearing up for the sled race."

He grinned. "You came looking for me. You were wearing that ridiculous ice princess costume for the horse rescue float, and you said, 'I've always loved a man in a Bigfoot costume.' I grabbed your hand and dragged you into the boys' locker room. You locked the door."

She had laughed along with him. *Liam, not here . . .*

He'd swept her into his arms, lifting her up until her feet didn't even touch the floor. The kiss she gave him was deep and sexy, and seemed to draw every bit of air from his lungs.

He'd torn off her gauzy white polyester dress and the white silk long johns she wore underneath . . .

"You were as crazy as I was. You unzipped my costume and pulled it off of me . . ."

Liam laughed, a deep throaty sound that he hadn't heard in weeks. "Jesus, I feel like one of those 1-900 operators. Remember what happened next, Mike? Remember?"

"We made love right there—us, a married couple with two kids and a whole town waiting for us outside, and we went at it like a couple of horny teenagers. In the middle of it all, Myrtle knocked on the locker room door.

"There we were, lying on the floor of the boys' locker room, all naked and sweaty, our bodies twisted together like a licorice whip. I had to put a hand over your mouth to keep you quiet. But you were laughing so hard, your shoulders were shaking and there were tears in your eyes."

He sighed. "Jesus, you were beautiful. I'll never forget how beautiful you were right then and how it felt to have you in my arms, with nothing between us.

"When Myrtle left, you laughed so loud, I thought the whole damn town would hear you. You said, 'There goes our reputation.' And I laughed along with you. 'Speak for yourself,' I said. 'This is going to do my reputation a world of good.' "

He stroked her hair, noticing the trembling in his hand. "That's who we were, Mike. Who we can be again if you'll just open your eyes and look at me. I love you. Always. I love you."

Very slowly he leaned down and kissed her forehead, murmuring, "Forever."

Chapter Sixteen

Julian woke up with a deadly hangover. It was inevitable, of course. There was nothing to do in this Norman Rockwell town except sit in your room, watch one of three channels, and drink. Last night he'd spent at least two hours trying to get Val on the phone. At every busy signal, he'd taken a swig of Scotch.

Groggily, he turned onto his side and reached for the phone, punching in Val's office number. Susan answered on the second ring: "Lightner and Associates."

At last. Julian angled to a sit. "Is Val in?"

"Hi, Julian. Just a second."

Val came on the line. "Juli, how goes it in the great white north?"

"Where the hell have you been? I tried calling you all last night."

"Whoa, big guy. If I wanted to hear talk like that, I'd have gotten married." He laughed at his own joke. "We screened *On Mystic Lake* last night—the new

211

Annette Bening, Richard Gere tearjerker. Afterward
we all . . . well, you know how those things go. I
didn't make it home until about four. So, what's up?"

"I saw Kayla."

"I sorta figured that. How is she?"

He tried to put into words how he'd felt yesterday,
but as always, this kind of honesty was difficult. "It
was weird, Val. There she was, unconscious. I didn't
know what to do. They said she'd responded to
memories, and so I started talking about us." He
laughed. "You know me, I can't remember yesterday,
and there I was remembering the first time I kissed her.
I felt . . . something."

"Juli, I feel honorbound to point out the dis-
turbingly necrophilic overtones here."

"Very funny."

"So, what's the deal? You want to stay longer, is
that it?"

Julian was vaguely disappointed. He wished they
could talk, just this once, about something that mattered. "She really loved me, Val. I guess that's what I
remembered most. How it felt to be loved."

"Every woman you meet adores you."

"That's not the same thing, is it?" he asked softly.

Val was quiet, and Julian wondered if his agent had
really listened this time. "No, I guess it's not. So, what
are you going to do with all this rampant emotion?"

That wasn't something Julian had thought about.
He'd been so busy *feeling*, he hadn't bothered to think
much. "Well, nothing, I guess. She's married."

"She's *what*?"

Julian jerked the phone away from his ear. Val's tone of voice was so high that dogs were probably barking all over town. "You heard me. She's married . . . to the doctor who called me."

Through the lines came the unmistakable sound of a cigarette firing up, then a whoosh of smoke exhaled into the receiver. "Does he love her?"

"Yes. Her hospital room is a shrine to their life together, and the nurse told me yesterday that he sits by her side for hours—every day since the accident. Sometimes he even sleeps with her."

"So, he's the real deal, cape and all. A goddamn superhero who loves his wife enough to call *you*—her first husband—to help wake her up. Jesus, the press'd have a field day." Val fell quiet for a minute, an uncharacteristic display of thoughtfulness. "You'd better be very careful here, Jules."

Julian knew Val was right. Kayla was a part of his past. She had a new life now, one that didn't include him, but when he'd touched her, he'd remembered their love, and the remembering had made him feel . . . lonely.

"Julian? You're coming back now, right? I mean, tomorrow you're scheduled for Leno—"

Julian hung up. Hollywood and his career felt far away suddenly, a sepia-toned photograph next to the Technicolor memories of his first love.

He closed his eyes. Though it was the last thing he wanted to do, he found himself trolling through the pain of his youth . . .

His mother, Margaret Jameson Atwood Coddington, had said from the beginning that he was cursed, and it had appeared to be true. Eight months after Julian's birth, his father had died. Margaret had wasted no time reminding her son that she had never wanted a child. She'd taught him to call her ma'am and to be seen but not heard. As soon as he was old enough, she'd shipped him away to boarding school in Switzerland, where he stayed while she worked her way through husbands and plastic surgeons and dinner parties. She sent him checks, but never letters.

At sixteen, he'd packed up what he needed in a backpack and headed to America, following a string of pointless jobs to Lubbock, Texas.

He had just turned nineteen when he glimpsed his future. Of course, it came in the form of a woman. He could still remember her stunning beauty. She picked him out as if he were a handbag she couldn't pass up. *I'll take him,* she said. He'd found out later that she was a famous actress in town to shoot a movie. Before he knew it, he was in the movie and then in Hollywood. He became an overnight sensation. He changed his name and changed his life. Val took him on as a client and constructed an elaborate fictional background that included two dead parents. It was Val who'd named him Julian True.

Julian had waited years for someone to find out the truth about him, but no one had.

Kayla was the only one who'd insisted on knowing him, the man behind the wrapping paper of fame. He'd told her everything except his real name.

"Jesus, now I'm thinking about my *mother*. Enough." He swung his legs over the side of the bed and stood, making his unsteady way down the hallway to the bathroom.

He showered in the world's smallest white fiberglass shower stall (it could have doubled as a coffin), then dressed in faded Levi's and a black T-shirt. He grabbed the coat he'd bought yesterday—at that lightning rod of fashion, Zeke's Feed and Seed. Shrugging into it, he flipped up the collar and left his room, hurrying downstairs. He pounded on his driver's door. "Come on, let's go!"

Lizbet popped out of the kitchen and met him in the foyer. She looked like she'd been dipped in flour and was ready for the fryer. "Good-bye, Mr. True. Will we see you for lunch?"

"I don't know. Bye, Lizbet." He opened the front door—and saw a dozen teenage girls standing on the sidewalk beyond the white picket fence. The second he appeared, they screamed his name.

It seemed that gossip spread pretty damned fast in Pleasantville.

He grinned lazily. "Well, hello, ladies. It's good to see y'all."

They crammed together, a centipede in cheerleader outfits and bare legs. Giggling.

He bounded down the steps. "What have we here, the Last Bend welcomin' committee? Such pretty gals, too. I'm honored."

"Will you sign my autograph book, Mr. True?"

asked one of the girls. Her saucer-round cheeks were bright red.

"It'd be my great honor." He pulled a pen out of his pocket and started signing autographs. The girls talked all at once, giggling, pushing one another toward him.

"Tonight's the winter prom, Mr. True . . . I don't suppose you'd like to stop by?" one of the girls asked, dissolving into a fit of laughter before she finished the sentence.

He planted a hand against his heart. God, he loved this. "Why, I'll bet a girl as pretty as you already has a date."

"Yeah, Serena," someone yelled, "you've already got a date. How about going with me, Mr. True?"

He was about to answer the silly question when he saw her, off in the back of the group, smiling but not giggling, not asking for his autograph.

His jaded heart skipped a beat. Maybe two.

She was beautiful—Hollywood beautiful—this tall, thin, black-haired girl with eyes as soft as melted bittersweet chocolate. Midnight-black hair fell like a waterfall of ink down her back. It had to be her . . .

He spelled his name wrong and handed the piece of paper back to a red-haired girl who was grinning up at him, showing a mouthful of multicolored braces.

He pushed easily through the crowd and sidled up to the dark-haired girl. His heart was beating hard. "And who are you, darlin'?"

"I'm Jacey."

Juliana Celeste. J.C.

His daughter. He was too stunned to speak. For the first time, she was real; not a faded image of a baby in a crib, but a young girl who'd grown up without him.

He didn't mean to close his eyes, but somehow they slid shut. In the darkness, he saw an image from long ago, him and Kayla in bed together, a squawking bundle of baby tucked gently between them.

Isn't she perfect? Kayla had said . . .

He opened his eyes and gazed down at his daughter.

"Mr. True?" She blushed prettily. "W-What are you doing in Last Bend?"

"I'm . . . uh . . . here . . . for the Make-a-Wish Foundation, visitin' sick folks at the hospital."

"My mom is sick. She's in a coma. Maybe . . . maybe you could visit her."

"I'd be happy to. Why, I'll do it right now."

"I'm here, Mr. True!" The driver's buoyant voice lifted above the giggling.

The girls instantly drew back, showing a respect he hadn't seen in Hollywood in a long time. All except Jacey. She stood there, staring up at him through eyes that were suddenly sad.

He looked down at her, trying to memorize her face for a moment longer, then he went to the limo. He refused to look back, but when he was in the car, he finally turned, gazing at her through the smoked glass.

A new and alien emotion unfolded in Julian's chest, made it difficult to breathe.

Shame.

*   *   *

Night fell like sudden blindness, obliterating the last pink rays of the setting sun. Liam turned away from the window and stared at his daughter.

Jacey stood in front of a full-length mirror, staring at her reflection. Her hair had been swept back from her face and coiled into a thick black mass, accented with four glittering pink crystal butterflies. The sleek, lavender gown fit her perfectly.

She looked so grown-up. He couldn't help feeling a brush of sadness, as if he'd already lost his little girl.

Tears glazed her dark eyes, and he knew she was thinking of her mother.

"She would be so proud of you," he said. "You look beautiful."

"Thanks, Dad."

"You know what I remember? Your first Halloween in Last Bend. You were five years old, and you dressed as the tooth fairy. Mike went all the way to Bellingham for the perfect pink satin. She sewed a thousand pink sequins on your gown." He moved toward her; for a second, he saw her as she'd once been, a little princess in a glittering dime-store tiara. "Mike and I weren't married then, but that was the night . . ." He swallowed hard. "You asked if you could call me Daddy."

"I remember."

"If your mom were here right now . . ."

She took his hand, squeezed it. "I know."

He forced a smile. "Well, m'lady, it's time."

Holding hands, they went downstairs. A few minutes later, Rosa ushered Mark into the living room.

He was wearing a navy blue tuxedo with a ruffled white shirt and a lavender bow tie. His jet-black hair was slicked back from his face.

"Oh, Jacey," Mark said, moving toward her, "you look great."

She smiled. "Thanks, Mark."

Upstairs, Bret poked his head over the railing and started singing at the top of his lungs, "Here comes the bride, all fat and wide—"

"Bret!" Liam yelled, biting back a laugh. "Stop it."

Bret dissolved into laughter and scampered down the stairs, skidding into place beside his sister. She elbowed him in the shoulder. "Thanks a lot, rugrat."

Bret looked up at her. Rosa had scrubbed his little face to a mop-and-glow shine. "Really, you look pretty."

"Thanks, kiddo."

Mark handed Jacey a clear plastic box. Inside it lay a white orchid wrist corsage with tiny lavender ribbons. "This is for you. Norma at the nursery said it was the very best kind." He stumbled around, trying to open it for a minute, then gave up and shoved the box at her.

Jacey removed the flower and slipped the elastic band on her wrist. "Thanks. Grandma—would you get Mark's boutonniere out of the fridge?"

Rosa bobbed her head and scurried into the kitchen. She came back a moment later with a small white carnation, its tips dyed lavender. "Here you go."

After that an awkward silence fell. Liam wanted to

break it, but his throat felt swollen and tight. He kept turning to his wife to say *Look at her, honey*, but there was no one beside him. He hoped Jacey didn't hear the serration in his voice when he croaked, "Okay, kiddos, photo op."

Mark groaned.

Jacey shoved his shoulder. "Very funny." She took Mark's hand and led him to the piano. He slipped an arm around her waist and pulled her close.

"Think sex!" Bret said, darting behind the sofa. Giggles rose up from his hiding place.

Liam snapped enough pictures for a *Town & Country* layout. He knew he was prolonging the moment—as if Mikaela would magically walk through that door if only he could extend this scene a little longer.

"Enough, Dad," Jacey said, laughing. "The band is probably on their second set." She disentangled herself from Mark's arm and went to Liam.

"I know," she said softly, "she'll want to see all the pictures. Every angle, every pose. That's why I'm bringing my camera in my purse. I'll take pictures of everything."

He pulled her into his arms and held her close. Then he drew back and smiled down at her. "Now go and have a good time."

Jacey kissed Rosa and Bret good-bye, then hurried out the door.

Liam stood at the kitchen window, watching her drive away. *There she goes, Mike.* In ordinary times, he would have turned to his wife now and taken her in his arms. She would have been crying. Liam would have gone to the piano, sat down and played something sad and sweet, something that gave her the room she needed to grieve for the little girl who was crossing the bridge to womanhood.

Only right now he was the one who felt like crying, who had glimpsed the emptier nest of the future and seen how much quieter this house would be when Jacey left.

And there was no one there to hold him.

With a sigh, he went into the living room and turned on the television.

Julian knew it was the wrong thing to do. Dangerous, even, but he couldn't help himself. In truth he didn't even try. Self-control had never been his strong suit. He couldn't have said exactly why he wanted to go to the prom, but he'd never been one to get caught up in reasons. He wanted to go. That's all that mattered. He had spent a long, depressingly quiet day at the hospital, sitting by Kayla's bedside, and he needed some action.

In his overdecorated bedroom, he dressed carefully, as if he were headed to the Oscars, instead of some backwoods high-school dance. A black silk T-shirt and black pleated Armani pants. Instead of bothering his driver, he walked the three blocks to Angel Falls High School. When he got there, his cheeks were numb from the cold, his eyes were watering, and he desperately needed a smoke.

He walked through the empty hallways, stopping

now and then to look at the trophies displayed in glass cases between rows of gray metal lockers.

At the auditorium, he paused, took a deep breath, and opened the double doors. It took his eyes a second to adjust to the darkness, but gradually he saw that the gym had been turned into a cheesy tropical paradise. False palm trees clustered around a patch of gold shag carpeting; beside it, a dozen tuxedoed boys and ball-gowned girls formed a line for pictures. Against the far wall, a band played some hard-edged song that was almost familiar.

He knew the moment he'd been recognized. A hush fell across the room. Dancing stopped. The kids eased away from him, forming a whispering, pointing funnel toward the dance floor.

He looked around, smiling his big, overpracticed smile until he saw her. She was on the dance floor with her date. Even from this distance, Julian could see that they were staring at him.

He moved through the crowd in the way he'd learned long ago: head up, smile planted, making eye contact with no one.

The song ended and another began. The love theme from *Titanic*, the movie. That damned heart was still going on.

He stopped beside Juliana—J.C., he reminded himself—and held out his hand. "May I have this dance?"

The crowd gasped. Her date—a big, good-looking kid in a ridiculously cheap tux—looked confused.

Jacey turned to the boy. "Do you mind?"

"Uh . . . no."

Julian swept her into his arms and began dancing. The crowd closed in on them, whispering and talking so loudly, it was hard to hear the music.

"Why me?" she whispered.

He smiled. "Why not? So, J.C. of the midnight hair, tell me about yourself. Do you get good grades? Have lots of friends? Practice safe sex?"

She laughed, a throaty, barroom sound that was exactly like Kayla's. "You sound like my dad—not that he'd ask about my sex life."

Something about the way she said it—*dad*—while she was smiling up at him . . . well, it pinched his heart.

It seemed odd, but he'd never thought about that word until today. *Dad.* Such a solid, dependable, grown-up word. Even now, with his daughter in his arms, Julian couldn't really imagine being someone's dad.

"Mr. True? Did you hear me?"

He laughed easily. "Sorry, I was thinking about something. So, what do kids in this town do for fun?"

She shrugged. "The usual stuff. Skiing, ice-skating, bowling, horseback riding. In the summer we hang out at Angel Lake. There's a cool rope swing off a big madrona tree at Currigan Point."

It sure as hell wasn't "the usual" in Los Angeles, not for a celebrity's kid, anyway. If J.C. had grown up with Julian, she'd have spent her life behind iron gates and sheltered by bodyguards. She wouldn't have known what it was like to ride her bike to town for a drug-store soda.

For the first time, he understood what Kayla had asked of him all those years ago. She'd used words like *rehab* and *safety*, but that wasn't right. What she'd wanted was a normal life for their daughter.

Just that. A normal life.

It was something Julian had never wanted. But now, as he held this daughter who was and wasn't his, he wondered about the price he'd paid for his fame.

It struck him hard, left him breathless, the sudden realization of how deeply he'd failed his daughter. As if he'd just walked into a room as familiar as his own bedroom and suddenly found it empty.

He should have known it all along, of course, but he hadn't thought about it until now.

He wasn't J.C.'s father. She had a man at home who'd loved her, who knew if she'd worn braces or snored in her sleep, who'd been there to pick her up when she fell down.

Julian had planted the seed of her, but he hadn't chosen to nurture it; he could never have helped her grow into the vibrant, beautiful flower he now held in his arms. How could he help another person grow when he needed so much sunlight for himself?

Even though he was smart enough to know the truth—that he wasn't this girl's father and never would be—he couldn't help wishing, dreaming, that things could be different.

The song came to an end. Sadly he leaned down and

kissed her cheek. Then he did what he did best: He walked away.

Liam was in the living room, nursing a watered-down Scotch, when he heard the car drive up.

Immediately he tensed. He'd been sitting here for hours, by the light of a single lamp, thinking about the decision he and Julian had made. The more he considered it, the more he saw how reckless and dangerous it was to withhold the truth from Jacey. This was a small town; gossip moved like bees from one backyard flower to the next, over picket fences and through telephone lines. The Make-a-Wish ruse would work for a while, but Liam didn't really trust Julian to understand the stakes. Anyone who said, "You know how it is—we were in love and then we weren't," had a pretty hazy understanding of love and heartache.

The bottom line was this: Liam hated deceiving Jacey. He couldn't quite believe that deceit was ever really in a person's best interest. Now, every time he looked at her, he felt the heavy, ugly curtain of this lie between them.

The front door swung open suddenly, and she breezed into the room. Her cheeks were flushed a deep, rosy pink and her espresso-dark eyes were shining.

He couldn't tell her now, not on this night that should hold only magical memories.

"Hi, Dad," she said dreamily, twirling around, her arms poised like a ballerina's.

He grabbed the camera beside him and snapped a few shots—for Mike. "How was it?"

She swept over to the couch and dipped down like a hummingbird, planting a feather-light kiss on his cheek. "Totally awesome. Perfect. I took *tons* of pictures for Mom." She stifled a yawn.

He gazed up at her, loving her so much, it was an ache in his heart. "She'll want to see each one."

Smiling, she spun around and floated toward the stairs. He followed along behind her, turning off lights as he went.

At her bedroom door, she stopped and grinned up at him. "Guess what happened."

He brushed a lock of hair from her eyes. "What?"

"Julian True showed up at the prom. He asked me to dance. *Me*. He called me Jacey of the midnight hair. I'll remember this night forever."

Liam's hand froze against her cheek. "But—"

"Good night, Dad."

Before he could answer, she kissed his cheek and went into her room, closing the door.

He stood there a long, long time. Then, slowly, he knocked on her door. When she answered, he tried to find a smile. "I . . . uh . . . just got an emergency call— don't worry, it's not about Mom—but I have to run to the hospital. I'll be right back."

She smiled dreamily; he could tell that she was barely listening. "Okay. Drive safely."

He nodded and closed the door. Anger seeped through him, rising steadily. It fit uncomfortably on him, this dark and stinging emotion, like a cheap wool sweater that was a size too small. He raced down to the garage and jumped into his car.

He found Julian on the front steps of the bed-and-breakfast, smoking a cigarette. He was wearing a T-shirt and jeans—the fool—and his whole body was shaking.

Liam skidded to a stop and jumped out of the car. "What in the hell were you thinking?"

Julian looked up. The cold was cruel to his face, leeched the color from his cheeks. "I had to see her."

Liam lost his hold on anger. Without it, he felt drained. There was a wealth of sadness in Julian's blue eyes, a look of pure defeat. *Of course* he'd had to see her.

"She's beautiful, Liam. The spitting image of Kayla, and when I looked at her . . . I couldn't see anything of me."

Liam didn't know what to say. He could tell that Julian had never really considered his daughter before, what it meant to have fathered a child. A young girl.

Julian took a last drag on his cigarette, then stabbed it out in a cushion of new snow. It hissed and sent up a thread of smoke. "I didn't tell her. I can't imagine I ever could."

Liam took a step forward. "Why not?"

"How could I make a man like you understand?" He sighed; a cloud of breath puddled in front of his face. "I break everything I touch." He tried to smile. "I think I've only just realized that. I don't want to hurt J.C."

Liam felt as if he'd finally glimpsed something real in Julian, and he couldn't help pitying the younger man.

Julian got slowly to his feet. "Don't tell her, Liam. Please, don't . . ."

Later Liam would wonder what had gotten to him, the sad regret in Julian's eyes or his own fear of wounding Jacey's tender heart. Whatever it was, he found himself saying, "Okay, Julian."

Chapter Seventeen

Julian sat by Kayla's bedside, spoon-feeding her the stories of their life together. Finally he understood how momentous a blink would be—right now, he'd take *any* sign of life.

Her skin seemed to have gotten paler in the past twenty-four hours.

"Hey, Kay," he said softly, scooting toward her. The chair legs made a horrific squeaking sound on the linoleum, and he was glad for the noise. Anything was better than this godawful silence.

He closed his eyes. It made it easier to slide into the past. In darkness he could remember the girl he'd fallen in love with. "I was thinking about the day I asked you to marry me. Do you remember that?"

It had been late in the autumn. The air in Sunville had been crisp and cold, and with every indrawn breath came the pungent scent of ripening apples. He hadn't really meant to return to Kayla. When he had left her, after the movie finished shooting, he'd thought she was simply another notch in his bedpost, not unlike the French gymnast he'd slept with while he was in Paris shooting *Bone Deep*. But every hour away from Kayla had felt like a day, every day a month. To his shock, he'd found that he missed her.

And so he'd returned to that flea-bitten spot on God's ass. He'd waited until it was closing time at the diner, until she was alone, and then, very quietly, he'd gone inside and stood by the jukebox . . .

"I'll always remember the look of you, standing by the lunch counter, the way that ugly orange uniform clung to your body. The way my name sounded wrapped up in your voice . . .

"I could tell you were afraid to hope that I'd come back for you. I knew you were thinking about the price tag that came with a man like me. You said, 'I'm not pregnant, if that's what you came to find out.' "

He almost smiled. "I remember wishing I was the kind of guy who would have come back to ask that question. I knew I should turn around and walk away, but I could feel it sparking between us again, that passion. I'd never been so scared, and somehow you knew that.

"I tried to tell you the truth about me. I told you I was no good for you, that I'd never been faithful to a woman in my life, but all you did was smile. So I told you everything, that I'd gone back to Hollywood and started reading scripts and doing interviews and talking to people . . . but I woke up in the morning and I thought of you. I went to bed at night, and I thought of you. I screwed other women, and I thought of you.

"I knew it would hurt you, but I told you anyway. I thought maybe it would keep me from saying the rest of it, that maybe you would throw me out and I'd have to leave you again. But you just stood there, smiling up at me, waiting.

"Do you remember what I said next?

" 'I don't want to love you, Kayla.'

"I knew you heard the word that mattered—*don't*—but next to love, it seemed to have no power at all. I pulled the small velvet box out of my pocket and handed it to you. When you saw the diamond ring, you started to cry.

"I knelt down on one knee—remember that? It was the only time I've ever done that in my life. I knelt down and begged you to marry me. You took the ring and slipped it on your finger.

"I meant to say something romantic, but what I said was 'If you're smart, you'll say no.' "

He touched her hand. "I knew I would hurt you, Kay. Sooner or later. And I'm so damned sorry . . ."

The door creaked open.

He heard the familiar cadence of Liam's footsteps. "How is she today?"

Julian shrugged. "The same."

Liam popped a tape into the player—Air Supply's "Lost in Love"—then took his usual place on Kayla's other side, standing close to the bed. "Heya, Mike."

Julian envied Liam, who was able to sit here for

hours, talking to his wife, holding her hand, believing in a happy ending, even as they saw how she was fading into the sheets.

Julian gazed down at Kayla, his thoughts turning again to the day he'd asked her to marry him. "I hurt her," he said softly, realizing a second too late that he'd spoken aloud.

"Why?"

After last night, Julian felt a strange kinship with Kayla's husband. Liam was the only one in the world who knew how it felt to sit here, hour after hour, praying for a miracle. "There's something wrong with me. I don't love for long. I wanted Kayla, wanted her like I've never wanted a woman before or since. I was so goddamned in love with her . . ."

"I think maybe 'in love' has the shelf life of whipping cream. No matter how you handle it, it goes sour. But if you're lucky, you get past 'in love' and end up just loving someone."

"That's how you love her."

"Yes."

Julian knew his next question would wound Liam, but he had to ask it. "Did she love you that way?"

Julian saw that Liam wanted to lie to him, to say certainly, absolutely, with all her heart; he saw, too, the moment Liam lost that battle.

He gave a lopsided, half smile. "Ironically, I think she loves me . . . but I don't know now if she was ever in love with me." Liam paused, then asked, "Have you ever had a family, Julian? I mean, a real family that lasts through good times and bad . . . the kind that keeps you out of the deep end?"

The question stung. He'd always wanted a family, but a family was give-and-take. He had always specialized in take-and-take. His only chance had been Kayla; if he'd held on to her, he might have known what it felt like to belong to a group of people who loved you no matter what, who cried when you failed and cheered when you won.

Julian patted his pocket, looking for a pack of cigarettes, then remembered he was in the hospital. Liam was staring at him now, *seeing* him. Julian felt as if his insides were splayed out on an operating table for Liam to see, and like a smoker's lungs, they were black and ruined.

Julian didn't answer. Finally, Liam pulled up a chair and sat down. For the next hour, they took turns talking quietly to Kayla.

After a while, Liam looked up at the clock. "Well, I have to get going. The kids'll be home soon." He stood up and stroked Kayla's cheek. "Heya, babe. I'll be back tomorrow." Then he leaned down and kissed her forehead, murmuring a word that Julian couldn't make out.

Liam was almost to the door when Julian asked, "How do you do it?"

Liam glanced back at him, his hand on the door handle. "Do what?"

"How do you keep believing she'll wake up?"

"I love her."

Julian frowned. "I know. But how do you do it?"

Liam's gaze flicked over to his wife. "I have to."

Julian watched Liam leave the room. Without Liam there, the silence felt awkward. He moved closer to the bed, picked up Kayla's limp hand, and squeezed it hard. "How is it I can remember falling in love with you, and have so little memory of the end? Our love affair is clear as glass, but our marriage, our *life* is . . . gone. All I remember is the day you left. I don't even remember trying to stop you. Did I? Did I ever say, 'Don't leave me'? Did I know what I would become without you?" He sighed. "Jesus, Kayla, did I even care?"

She hears him call her name.

She tries to reach for him, but there is nothing beside her. She feels the panic building again, swirling around her.

Pictures twirl through her mind like images in a child's viewfinder, and when they stop, she is somewhere else. A house.

She tries to say something, to call out, but there is something wrong with her throat. In the distance she can hear a moan. It is her . . . or maybe not . . .

She is in Hollywood now, in their home, waiting for Julian. She is staring out the window; all she can see is gray. Gray trees, gray flowers, gray sky; the only color is a black crow sitting on a branch, cawing down at her.

No, it isn't a crow. It is her baby's cry. She instinctively turns to go to her daughter, but she hears the nanny's footsteps. She hesitates, afraid to intrude on the older, sour-faced woman who seems to know everything about taking care of baby girls.

She is tired of this life filled with laughter and drugs and sex that happens in other people's beds. Tired of thin, beautiful women with vacant eyes who never carry photos of children in their wallets. She is lonely, more now than ever. Since Jacey's birth, Julian is distant. He never holds his daughter or talks to her. Instead he hires other women to do the chores that Kayla longs to do herself.

How can it not have changed him, this bringing of a child into their lives? It has transformed her every cell.

She stands in the shadows of the living room, beside the ornate gas fireplace that holds the sounds and color of fire, but none of the heat.

When Julian gets home—late, as usual, and smelling of another woman's perfume—she sees how old and tired he looks, and she wonders how long he has looked this way, how long she has overlooked his deterioration. The drugs and alcohol have left marks on his skin, on everything, even the way he moves, all slow motion.

"Jules?"

He turns to her, smiling before he even sees her. "Hey, baby."

As he gets closer, she can see the red cast to his eyes, the way his nose is running from too much cocaine. He moves unsteadily, a marionette with broken strings, and it breaks her heart, seeing this so clearly.

She takes his hands in hers, trying not to notice the

way his fingers are shaking, the dampness in his palms. "We have to talk, Jules."

She sees the flash of irritation in his eyes. Even though he tries to hide it, she sees. "Not again, Kay. Jesus, not again . . . I know I missed the kid's birthday party. Let's not rehash it forever." He pulls free and goes to the bar, making himself a cocktail, drinking it too fast. Then he reaches into his pocket and pulls out a Baggie of cocaine.

She watches him snort the drug, and there is no word to describe the depth of her sadness. She turns away from him. "We have to change our lives, Julian."

"I know, baby," he whispers, kissing her cheeks, her eyelids, cupping her face in his hands. "And we will."

It is the answer he's given her a dozen times, but it's not good enough anymore.

"I can't watch you kill yourself, Jules. I . . . love you too much for that. And I can't let Juliana grow up in this world. I want her to know how it feels to be safe."

He frowns. "You mean it this time."

She turns away from him and goes back to the big picture window. It is funny, she thinks, how fast a life can change. One minute, one set of words that really say nothing at all, and you see what you hadn't seen before.

She feels him come up behind her. The window reflects his faded image. "You meant what you said in Sunville," she says dully. "You didn't really want to marry me."

"I didn't want to lose you."

She wonders if he sees the continent that separates her question from his answer.

She can't raise Juliana in this world. No matter how much she loves Julian, she can't do this to her daughter. If there's one thing Kayla knows, it's the pain of a father who can't be bothered to spend time with his child. "I'm sorry, Julian," she whispers, feeling the tears fall down her cheeks.

His arms circle her, holding tightly. "I love you, Kayla, but I can't give all this up. It's who I am."

She touches his face. "I love you, Julian, more than . . ." She can't finish. There is nothing big enough to compare to her love for this man. "I wish we were old and gray and all of this was behind us," she says at last. "I wish we were sixty years old and we could sit together by the fire with pictures of our grandchildren between us . . . and laugh about these times. I wish . . ." Her voice gets caught in the ache spreading through her insides, and she can't say more.

It is too much for her, these memories. She closes her eyes and sinks again into the sweet, blessed darkness . . .

At dinner that night, Liam tried to smile and make conversation with his beloved children, but all he could really hear were the tinny silences that collected between his sentences. As he helped himself to another serving of rice, he caught a glimpse of his reflection in the hollowed silver surface of an oversized spoon.

The fear hit him then; it was like plunging into Angel Lake on winter's deepest night.

His hand started shaking. The silver spoon rattled against his pewter plate.

"Daddy?" Bret said, wide-eyed. "Are you okay?"

Liam dropped his spoon and held his hands out. If anyone was surprised by the suddenness of his action, there was no sign of it. "Let's hold hands," he said.

Around the table, they reached out for one another. Liam felt Bret's small hand slip into his; then Jacey took hold of his other hand. Rosa reached out at the other end.

In their gentle, trusting touch, Liam felt it return, the faith he needed.

"Let's pray. Rosa, will you do the honors?"

Across the table, she was watching him. He could tell that she understood. She nodded briefly and closed her eyes, bowing her head. Her lovely, lyrical voice was like music in the silence. "Heavenly Father, we thank You for the four of us at this table, for the love we share and the strength we find in each other. We thank You for Mikaela's continued life, still as it may be. We know You are watching out for her and protecting her and blessing her with Your presence in the darkness of her sleep. Once again, we offer You our humble prayers that she will soon come back into the loving arms of her family. In the name of the Father, the Son, and the Holy Ghost, Amen."

Liam opened his eyes and looked at his children. "I love you," he said softly.

It was like that these days. The best of times were

quiet moments like this one, tucked into the corners of what passed for everyday life. They were learning, each of them, to notice the things they'd once taken for granted.

And to be thankful for the life that was left.

Part Four

Life can only be understood backwards,
but it must be lived forward.

Søren Kierkegaard

Chapter Eighteen

The water is now a beautiful aqua blue. She is at the bottom of a swimming pool, staring up. Her limbs feel heavy; the water resists her movements, but she has learned that if she really concentrates, focuses all of her will, she can lift her fingers and wiggle her toes. She knows that at some time, long ago, this would have been next to nothing, something the tiniest newborn can do, but to her, in this pool of endless clear blue water, it is everything.

She is floating up through the water, rising, rising, her body weightless. The water moves easily aside for her and buoys her.

As she reaches the surface, the water slides away from her face. She gasps, breathing in the sweet, pine-scented air, then sucking greedily. Her fingers twitch, and she is reaching for something . . . the shadow in front of her.

She opens her eyes and immediately cries out. The light is so bright, she cannot stand the brightness.

"She opened her eyes. Jesus Christ, Mike . . . we're here . . ."

She takes a deep, calming breath and opens her eyes again. At first the world is a confusing, jarring mixture of white-hot light and black, slanting shadows. She can feel something warm against her palm. She tries to grasp hold, but her fingers are weighted down again, unresponsive.

She blinks; it takes all her concentration to turn her head. Something stops the movement, a swell of cottony fabric.

The shadows spin in front of her, waving like mirages on a desert highway, then, slowly, slowly, they begin to take shape.

There are three people around her, men.

Julian. She sees him, sees those beloved blue eyes staring down at her. She reaches out for him, meaning to touch his face in the gentlest caress, but her control is shot, and she slaps him hard across the cheek. She means to laugh at the surprise on his face, but instead she bursts into tears. More water, sliding down her cheeks now, tasting salty, like the black sea that held her captive, and she is afraid. She can't stop crying.

She tries to talk. It hurts, burns. Still, she pushes a sound up her cracked, broken throat, and when the word comes out, mangled and unfamiliar, she weeps even harder. "Ju . . . li . . . an."

"I'm here, baby," he says in the voice she remembers so well, the voice that seems connected to the tender cords in her heart.

"Kayla, baby, are you there? Squeeze my hand."

She opens her eyes again, blinking slowly.

It seemed to take her hours to focus, but when she did, she saw him standing beside her, staring down at her, and she felt a rush of joy. "You came . . . back."

Another man leaned toward her. On the front of his white coat, it read *Dr. Liam Campbell*. "Hi, Mike."

She frowned and tried to turn her head to look for Mike. It tired her and she gave up. She tried to remember how she got here, but there was nothing. She remembered every moment of her life up to when she said good-bye to Julian. After that, there was a complete and utter blankness. It terrified her. "I . . . don't . . . where . . ."

"You're in the hospital," someone says.

"Juliana," she croaked. "Where's my baby?"

"Baby?" Julian turned to the other man. "What the hell is going on?"

Something was wrong. She'd been hurt, she realized suddenly. Hurt. And they wouldn't answer her question about Juliana. Oh, God . . .

The other man touched her face, and there was a gentleness in him that calmed her. She blinked up at his watery, out-of-focus face. He blotted her tears with a tissue. "Don't cry, Mike. Your daughter is fine. She's okay."

She trusted him. *Juliana's okay.* "Who . . ."

"Don't rush it, sweetheart. Take it slowly."

"Who . . . are you?" she asked at last.

Before he answered, she lost interest. Her head felt so heavy, so . . . broken. All that mattered was that her baby was okay.

She closed her eyes and sank back into the cool, blue water, back to the place where it was calm and warm and she was unafraid.

"Retrograde amnesia."

Liam and Julian were seated in front of Stephen Penn's massive oak desk. Stephen looked worn and tired.

Liam leaned forward, rested his arms on his thighs. "In posttraumatic—"

"Goddamn it, wait a sec." Julian shot to his feet. He prowled the small office like a caged lion, repeatedly running his hand through his hair. "I haven't had twenty years of college and I don't know what you two are talking about. What in the hell is retrograde amnesia?"

Stephen removed the small, circular spectacles from his face, carefully setting them down on the cluttered surface of the desk. He didn't look at Liam as he spoke. "At the moment of serious trauma, the brain stops accumulating memories. That's why a victim of serious brain injury rarely remembers the actual incident itself. More often than not, the last clear memory is one that happened days or weeks . . . or even years before. These are often powerful, significant memories—weddings, births, that sort of thing. It appears that Mikaela's mind is . . . trapped, if you will, some years ago. She seems to believe that Jacey is still a baby." He paused. "Clearly she doesn't remember her life with Liam at all."

"How long do you think the amnesia will last?" Liam asked, even though he knew the answer.

"There is no way of knowing," Stephen said slowly. "Although chances are that she *will* remember. Long-term retrograde amnesia is rare." His voice softened. "But it does happen."

"How can we help her?" Liam asked quietly.

"Right now she's afraid and confused. We want to tread very, very carefully. The mind is a fragile thing, much more delicate than the brain. We don't want to overwhelm her with frightening information." At last he looked at Liam. "I think it's best if we let it come back naturally."

Liam sighed tiredly. "You're saying that the kids and I should stay away."

"I'm sorry, Liam. I can only imagine how hard this is for you. But I think she needs some time to let her mind heal. Can you imagine realizing that you'd lost fifteen years of your life?"

"Yes," Liam said, "I can imagine it." He leaned forward and hung his head, staring down at the Oriental carpet so long, the colors smeared into one big bruise.

What in God's name was he going to tell his children?

Julian went to a pay phone and called Val. "She woke up today," he said when Val answered.

"No shit. How is she?"

"She's got amnesia. She doesn't remember anything of the last fifteen years. She thinks we're still married."

"Are you saying—"

"She's still in love with me, Val. With none of the bad memories of our breakup."

Val made a low, whistling sound. "Jesus Christ, what did you do—script this? It's a goddamn fairy tale and you're the prince. The press'll *love* this."

Julian sagged against the wall. "You don't get it. How am I going to tell her that I never came back for her. Val? Val?"

His answer was a dial tone.

With a curse, Julian hung up the phone. For the first time since he'd gotten here, he was afraid.

She was alive. That was the miracle Liam needed to focus on. Over the past weeks, he had asked God to heal her, to help her open her eyes. All the while, he'd prepared himself for the physical impairments that could come with an extended coma. Paralysis, brain damage, even death—these he'd readied himself to handle. He'd never asked God to return her memories.

Now, as he drove home, he reminded himself that retrograde amnesia was a common short-term side effect of severe brain injury.

Short term. Those words were the ledge he tried to hold on to, but they kept crumbling beneath the weight of his fear.

What if she never remembered him or the kids?

He concentrated on breathing; it didn't seem like much, but if he didn't think about it, he stumbled into a place where panic was inches from his face, where he had to draw in great, sucking breaths just to survive.

Who are you?

Would he ever forget those words? Forget the pain that knifed through him in that single, horrifying moment when she'd said Julian's name . . . and then asked Liam who he was.

He knew that her condition was purely medical in nature, a lapse in the function of her traumatized brain. But he was a man as well as a doctor, and the man in him felt like any man would feel. As if in twelve years of life together, of moments big and small, of a love that was enacted in errands and dinners and bedtime conversations, Liam had left no mark on her at all.

As if his love were like the waves that shifted and shaped, but never really changed the shore.

He was being foolish. She loved her children with every strand of her soul, and she had forgotten them, too—

No, that wasn't right. She'd only forgotten Bret; Liam's son. She remembered Jacey. And Julian.

He couldn't shake a terrible, rising panic that in the end, his love would count for nothing. And what would he tell his children? They'd been through so much pain already, so much fear. Poor Bret had courageously visited her day after day, singing her favorite songs to her, waiting for a smile. It would crush him to discover that his mom didn't remember him. One blank look and Bret would crumble.

Jacey would try to handle this like an adult, but inside, where it mattered, she would break like a little girl. She would understand that everything she and

Mike had shared was gone. Every talk, every memory that entwined their lives would be Jacey's alone now.

Liam couldn't even think about his own fear right now; it was too overwhelming. "Please, God," he whispered, "we can't take this, too. It's too much . . ."

The windshield wipers thumped in front of him, punctuating the silence in the car. A light snow began to fall, patterning the glass, piling up on the edges of the wiper's sweep.

He flipped on the radio. "Memories" by Barbra Streisand blared from the speakers.

He snapped it off. Christ, what was next—"As Time Goes By"?

The snow was coming faster now. He didn't see his own driveway until he was practically on top of it.

He put the car in four-wheel drive and lowered his speed, maneuvering carefully over the bumpy gravel road and into his own garage.

At the mudroom door, he paused, taking a moment to collect himself, then he pushed into the house. "Hello," he called out. "I'm home."

He heard the scurrying sound of slippered feet on the hardwood floor. Rosa appeared, wearing one of Mike's old saddle club aprons over a black house-dress. "*Buenos noches,*" she said, wiping a hand across her brow, leaving a snowy trail of flour across her skin. "I am making the . . . biscuits for dinner. You would like a cup of coffee, *sí*? Or a glass of wine?"

"Where are the kids?"

"Jacey will be home any *momento*. Bret is upstairs in the shower. Would you like—"

"Mike woke up today."

She gasped. Her hand flew to her mouth. "*Dios mio,* it is a miracle. How is she?"

Liam didn't know how to take all the information of this day and mold it into an ordinary sentence. In the end he simply said it: "She didn't recognize me, Rosa." He could hear the terrible ache at the edge of his voice; it didn't sound like him at all. "Julian . . . she recognized Julian."

Rosa's hand fell slowly, slowly to her side, where her fingers curled into a tight fist. "What does this mean?"

"I could give you a bunch of technical explanations, but the bottom line is that her memory has failed. She seems to think she's twenty-four and still married to Julian. She thinks Jacey is still a baby."

Rosa was staring at him with a familiar look; it was the look of a patient who'd just received devastating news. She desperately wanted him to grant her hope. "This will get better, though. *¿Sí?*"

"We *hope* it's temporary." He put the tiniest emphasis on the word *hope*. "Usually people get their memories back."

"So she does not remember you or the children or all the years she's been away from him."

Each word was a brick, and when they piled one on top of the other, he broke. It was as simple as that, as anticlimactic. He'd been afraid of this moment for weeks—this time when his heart and his mind said simply *no more*—and yet now that it was here, it was nothing. No screaming agony, no crying jag that couldn't be stopped. Just a narcotic weariness, an emptiness that ate through his bones. "No."

Rosa closed her eyes and let her head drop forward. It was almost as if she were praying. "This pain for you . . . I can barely imagine it."

His throat felt tight. "Yes."

Finally she looked up, and her brown eyes—so like Mike's—were glazed with tears. "What will you tell the children?"

There it was. Liam sighed. "I can hardly think of it, Rosa."

"*Sí.* They have been praying for this for so long. It will break their hearts to learn that she does not remember them."

"I know. But it's a small town. Not a place where secrets keep."

Secrets. Like a famous father a girl knew nothing about.

Rosa took a step toward him. "Do not tell them yet. At least for this night. Give Mikita until tomorrow. Maybe then we will never have to tell the *niños* this terrible thing, *sí*?" She gazed at him. "You had faith in Mikaela, Dr. Liam, from the start of this, you believed in God and in her. Don't you stop. She will need you still . . . maybe even more now."

"She has always needed me, Rosa. That's why she married me. But before this thing is over, it will be about something else."

Rosa flinched.

He knew that she understood what he was going to say before he spoke. "It will be about love."

Chapter Nineteen

That night, after dinner, Liam tried to think of something that would take his mind off Mikaela. They were all in the living room now, ostensibly watching a TV movie, but no one seemed to be paying much attention.

At a commercial, Jacey hit the remote control and muted the television. "So," she said suddenly, "how's Mom?"

Liam dropped his medical journal. "Uh . . . the same," he said into the awkward, sudden silence. "Hey, I have an idea. How about if we have one of our camp-out nights?"

Jacey frowned. "It's freezing outside."

Liam's laugh had a forced, brittle edge. "I know, I know. I meant a pretend one. Like we used to when Bret was little. We'll unplug the phones and bring our sleeping bags into the living room. Roast marshmallows and make s'mores. And I'll tell you the story of Sam McGee."

"That'd be *great*!" Bret said.

Jacey looked scared. "We haven't done that in years. And we need the phone. If Mom—"

"I've got my pager. If something . . . happens, we'll plug the phones back in."

Jacey looked unconvinced. "I told Mark I'd call him tonight."

Liam smiled at her. "You can live a few hours without talking to him."

"No, she can't," Bret piped up. He planted a hand on his chest and rolled his eyes dramatically. "She'll *die* if she doesn't talk to her boyfriend."

Jacey smacked her brother playfully on the head. "Very funny. Just wait till you stop thinking that girls have cooties."

"Come on," Liam said, smiling, "it'll be fun. Your grandma's never done it."

Bret twisted around to face Rosa. "It's *totally* rad, Grandma. Dad's the best poem-teller."

Rosa was smiling. "He is good at telling stories, *si*?"

Liam clapped his hands together. "Let's get started."

An hour later they were ready.

Night turned the living room into a huge, rectangular cave. A fire crackled in the stone fireplace, casting a dancing, golden glow across the room. They'd thrown green and brown afghans over all the furniture, a disguise as fine as any. A navy blue king-sized sheet draped the piano, turning it into the mysterious Piano Lake, where swimmers were often lost even in the dog days of summer.

Jacey's voice was quiet as she spun out the legend their family had created long ago: "And the townspeople swear that on a night like this—in the snowiest, blackest winter, when a full moon rises into the cloudless sky—that they hear the screams of souls drowned long ago."

Bret made a face. "She's not saying it right—"

Jacey gave a spooky laugh and turned on a flashlight, holding it beneath her chin. "Ah, but there's more . . . about the little boy who wandered away from his campsite and ended up on the banks of Piano Lake . . ."

Bret leaned forward. This was a new and interesting detail. "What happened to him?"

Liam closed his eyes. The room smelled of popcorn and wood smoke, of melting chocolate and oozing marshmallows. He imagined Mike beside him, her head resting on his shoulder, her arm looped around his waist.

The sadness was like that. Sometimes he went whole minutes in blissful ignorance—a dad enjoying the sound of his children's voices—then he'd remember *Who are you?* and the pain would hit so hard he couldn't breathe. In those moments, he'd see his whole life stretching before him, an endless, lonely highway. At the end of it was the fear, however irrational, that he would lose her to Julian.

It was a buoyant fear; there was no way to drown it.

"Daddy. *Daddy!*" Bret was yelling now.

Liam pushed the thoughts aside and looked up—right into Rosa's frowning, watchful brown eyes.

"Daddy, do the shooting of Dan McGrew. That's my favorite."

Liam scooted back and leaned against the sofa (now the dormant volcano, Mt. Mikaela), then opened his arms. Bret crawled through the broken graham cracker crumbs, spilled popcorn, and bunched-up goose-down sleeping bags, and cuddled beside Liam. Jacey and Rosa moved in closer, sitting side by side in front of the warm fire.

The poem, though he hadn't recited it in years, came back to him with a surprising ease. It was the tale of men in the Yukon gold fields who'd—

Fought over a woman.

Liam bit back a curse. "Hey, Bretster, how about I do Sam McGee instead?"

"No way. Dan McGrew."

Liam sighed. He closed his eyes and began quietly, "A bunch of the boys were whooping it up at the Malamute Saloon . . ."

It took concentration to keep going. When he finished the last sentence, he managed a smile.

"This is not a good story," Rosa said, frowning.

Liam ignored her. "Come on, kids, go brush your teeth. It's midnight."

"On a camp-out? No way I'm brushing my teeth," Bret whined.

"Come on, foot-breath," Jacey said, taking her brother's hand.

Within minutes, the kids were back, crawling into

their sleeping bags. Liam gave them each a kiss good night, then he got to his feet.

Bret jackknifed upright. "Where are you going?"

"I'm going to walk Grandma back to the cottage. I'll be right back."

"You're gonna sleep down here, right?"

"Of course."

Bret grinned. "'Night, Grandma."

"'Night, Grandma," Jacey added.

Rosa kissed them both, then followed Liam out of the room. At the mudroom, they put on their coats and boots. Liam hit the garage door opener and together they headed outside.

A beautiful moon glazed the snowy pastures and backlit the black trees. The whole farm held an ethereal glow, all blues and blacks and glistening whites.

"Mike would love this night," Liam said. "If she were here right now, she'd be racing ahead of us, scooping snow up in her mittens to make snowballs . . . or she'd fall backward without warning to make an angel. I hope the snow is still here when she gets out of the hospital."

They came to the cottage's two-rail gate. Through the sparkling layer of new snow, you could just make out the knobby brown rose vines that, in the summer, were a wall of bright green and shocking pink.

The gate made a high-squeaking sound in the silence. Rosa went ahead and opened the front door, flicking on the kitchen light. She took off her coat and hung it up in the antique armoire by the door. Liam laid his over the back of a chair at the kitchen table.

Rosa turned to him. "What did she say, my Mikita, when you told her about your marriage?"

He was caught off guard. "We didn't tell her."

"What? This is madness not to tell her—"

"Steve thinks the truth might frighten her. We don't want her to suffer a relapse."

Rosa seemed to think about that for a minute, then she shook her head. "You men—you doctors—you do what you think is best. But I am her mama, no? I have always taken care of my Mikaela. I will not stop now. I will need the *fotografías* you found."

Liam tried to imagine what it must be like to have a mother like this. What a power it must grant a person in life to have a place where you could always land softly, even after the hardest hit. "Rosa," he said quietly, touching her hand. "I'm glad you're here. I don't know how I would have made it through this without you."

Rosa grabbed his hands and held them tightly. "You are stronger than you think, Liam. This I have seen in you over these past weeks. Now you are thinking that Mikaela does not need you, that she has forgotten you because she does not love you, but you are wrong. Her eyes may be open, but *mi hija* is still asleep. Give her time."

She woke easily this time. No floating at the bottom of a swimming pool, no black and angry sea slapping around her. She just . . . opened her eyes.

Strangers surrounded her bed. Some she'd seen before, some she hadn't. They were talking to her and to one another. She could see their mouths opening and closing, opening and closing, but nothing made any sense.

Do you know where you are . . . who you are . . . what happened . . .

She wished they would shut up. One by one, their faces came into focus, and the questions they were asking began to make sense. Dr. Penn—the nice-looking man with the gray hair and white coat—smiled at her.

"Good morning, Mikaela. Do you remember me?"

"Penn," she answered, her voice as cracked as old porcelain and nearly as fragile. Her throat still hurt. "What . . . happened me?"

"You fell off your horse and hit your head. You suffered quite a head injury. You've been in a coma."

She wanted to ask questions, but she couldn't remember any of the words she needed.

"Don't worry, Mikaela. It'll all come back to you." Stephen turned to the strangers. "Let's go. She needs to rest."

Wait. She tried to sit up. It was hard; her right side felt weighted down, too weak to move easily. Her heart started beating too fast, her breathing broke into gasping bits. Before she could remember the right words to make them stay, they were gone.

The door to her room squeaked open, and a new stranger appeared. She was a heavyset woman in a blue polyester pantsuit. Her fleshy face was creased into a bright smile. "Good morning, Mikaela. How are we feeling today?"

She frowned. Her name was Kayla now. Everyone knew that. *Everyone.* So why did they all keep calling her Mikaela? She hadn't used that name in years—not since Sunville.

She tried to push a question past her disobedient tongue. The word she was searching for—*hello*—was bouncing around in her mind, but it disappeared before reaching her mouth.

"We removed the catheter last night—do you remember that? I thought you might like to try going to the bathroom by yourself. Doctor will be here in a few minutes."

Kayla gazed up at the woman, trying to make her mouth work. "Who . . . where?"

"I'm Sarah Fielding, honey," she answered the unasked question. The nurse bustled around the bed and pulled the sheets back.

Kayla stared down at her skinny, hairy legs. They *looked* okay. So why wouldn't they work right?

Sarah eased a plump arm behind Kayla's head and gently tilted her upright. In spare, economical movements, she maneuvered Kayla to a sit, then helped her to a shaky stand. She clung to Sarah and tried to walk. She had to kind of drag her heavy right leg as they made their slow, shuffling way to the door across the room.

"Do you think you can use the toilet by yourself, honey?"

Toilet. The word fluttered around for a second, then landed on the white porcelain seat beside her. *Toilet.* "Yes," she answered, gripping the counter unsteadily.

She was shaking and breathing hard, but she could stand on her own.

"I'll be just outside if you need me." Sarah backed away and half-closed the door behind her.

Kayla sank onto the cold seat. It burned when she urinated, so badly that she had to clamp a hand over her mouth to keep from crying out. When she was finished, she leaned forward and grabbed the counter again, dragging her reluctant body to an awkward stand.

That's when she saw herself in the mirror. Her face was chalky pale. And her hair was short; it looked as if it had been cut with children's scissors.

But her hair was long—down to her waist. Julian wouldn't let her cut it.

Shaking, she leaned closer to the mirror, pressed her damp palms to the cold glass. There were tiny lines around her eyes and mouth. Lines she'd never seen before . . . the kind of lines that Mama had, and there were more than a few gray hairs threaded through all that black . . .

She screamed.

The door burst open and Sarah was there. "What happened?"

Kayla tottered around, her hands on her face. "I'm . . . old. Oh, God . . . what happened?"

"I'll get the doctor."

Kayla grabbed the woman's sleeve. "I'm old . . . what happened?"

Sarah wrenched away. "I'll be right back." She ran from the room. The door slammed shut behind her.

Kayla grabbed a handful of her hair—so short now—and stared at the gray strands. She couldn't breathe; her knees felt weak. "Oh . . . God . . ."

How long had she been lying in that bed? How long—

Dr. Penn rushed into the room. A breathless, flushed Sarah waddled along behind him.

Kayla looked at him and started to cry. "How old am I?" In her mind, she screamed the question, but in truth it came out as a hacked-up whisper.

Dr. Penn took her hand and held it. "Calm down, Mike."

"I'm *Kayla*." This time she did scream.

"Do you want a sedative, Doctor?" Sarah asked.

"No! Don't put me back to sleep. I'll . . . be quiet." Kayla gulped in a great, wheezing breath of air. She clung to the doctor's hand, staring at him through a stinging veil of tears. "I'm . . . scared . . ."

He touched her face gently, as if he were a friend, and she wondered how it was possible to sleep so long that you woke up old. "Remember what I told you? You've been in a coma, Mike. I thought with your nursing background you'd remember. I forgot that . . . oh, never mind."

This time she remembered the word—*coma*. It came with a picture of that girl, Karen Ann Quinlan, curled into a ball, weighing nothing . . .

Dr. Penn was still talking. He didn't know that there was a roaring white noise in her head. "It'll come back to you . . . Kayla. If you just relax."

Her mouth trembled. Tears found their way into the

corners of her mouth, leaving a wet, salty taste on her tongue. "How long . . . asleep?"

"A little more than a month."

The relief she felt at that was so stunning she laughed out loud. She meant to wipe her eyes, but she had no control. She smacked herself in the nose and laughed harder.

"It's okay," Dr. Penn said in a nice, even voice. "Your emotions are off track right now, along with your motor skills. But there's no permanent damage. It'll all come back."

She was still grinning as tears rolled down her cheeks and plopped onto her bare arm. She felt like an idiot, laughing and crying at the same time. She didn't care about her motor skills; she cared about her *life*. "How old . . . am I?"

He paused, glanced at Sarah, and then sighed as he looked back at Kayla.

They wanted to lie to her; she could see it in their eyes. "Don't . . . please . . . don't lie," she whispered.

Dr. Penn sighed. "You're thirty-nine."

She couldn't breathe. Focusing on his gray eyes, she shook her head. "No . . . no . . . I'm almost twenty-four. I got married two and a half years ago. Juliana just had her first birthday. I remember all this perfectly."

"There are other things—other times—you can't remember yet. But it'll come back. It's best if you let it come back naturally. Just give yourself a little time."

It took all her strength of will to formulate one little sentence. "I want . . . to see my husband now."

Dr. Penn looked at Sarah again, then he nodded. "Just a minute."

Kayla tried to keep breathing evenly as they left the room. She climbed back into bed, where she felt safe. Julian would tell her the truth. He would tell her—

The door opened again. Only it wasn't Julian; it was another stranger. She shook her head. "No . . . more . . ."

Slowly he came up to the bed.

She frowned. She couldn't marshal her scattered thoughts into a sentence. She wanted to tell him to go away.

He touched her, grabbed her shoulders, and pulled her gently toward him. She felt like a rag doll, sagging in his arms.

He stared at her, and his eyes were so green. She'd never seen eyes so filled with comfort. It calmed her, the way he looked at her. "Forever," he whispered.

The word struck a chord deep, deep inside her. She felt her body go still, her heartbeat even out. Even the air in her lungs seemed to refill itself. The word—*forever*—drifted through her, swirling, meaning something that she couldn't grasp on to; it found no perch and fluttered away.

"Remember me," he said, gently shaking her.

And all at once, she did. "I do . . . remember you," she said quietly. "You're the other doctor."

He let go of her; it was so unexpected that she fell back into the mound of pillows. She had the strangest thought that she had wounded him. Those green eyes looked so sad . . .

"I'm sorry . . ." she whispered, though she had no idea what she'd done to wound this man. "I just . . . want to see my husband."

As he turned away, she almost called out for him. She wanted him to look at her again, to touch her and make her feel safe, but she knew it was ridiculous.

"Okay," he said softly. "I'll go get Julian."

Chapter Twenty

Julian sat in the waiting room. He tried to remain calm but couldn't stop his foot from tapping. There were only two people in the room—him and Stephen—but still it felt airless and crowded. Liam had left a few minutes ago to see Kayla.

He'd spent most of last night trying to figure out how and when to tell her the truth of their past. Now, here it was, nearly noon, and he was no closer to an answer.

Liam walked into the room. He looked . . . beaten. He pushed a hand through his hair and sighed heavily. Even from this distance, Julian could see that Liam's hand was shaking.

He looked at Julian. "She wants to see her husband."

Julian turned to Dr. Penn. "What now? You told her she was thirty-nine years old, and then you bolted. What am I supposed to tell her when she asks where she's been for fifteen years?"

"Tell her where *you've* been." It was Liam's voice.

Julian spun to face him. "Yeah, you'd like that."

"*Like* that? I don't like you even being in the same room with her." He moved toward Julian. "If she asks you a direct question, I want you to answer truthfully. You can evade—but don't lie. Steve said that she left him no room to weasel out of her questions."

"Maybe I shouldn't go see her."

"How could they let such a coward play Lizard Man?"

"I was the Green Menace," he answered automatically, "and a stand-in did all the dangerous stuff." Julian's voice fell to a whisper that only Liam could hear. "I'm . . . afraid of hurting her."

"That's the best news I've heard today."

Julian waited, but Liam didn't say anything else. "Well," he said at last, "I'll go see her."

He ducked out of the room and walked slowly down the hallway. Really slowly.

At her door he paused. Forcing a bright smile, he opened the door.

She was asleep.

He shut the door quietly and went to her bedside. She looked so peaceful, so beautiful . . .

Slowly she blinked awake. "Jules? Is that you?"

He leaned over her. It took an act of pure will to force a smile. "Heya, Kay."

She worked herself up to a sit, and by the time she was finished, she was breathing heavily. There was a fine sheen of perspiration on her forehead. "Where's Juliana? I want to see my baby—"

"She'll be here soon, I promise."

"I missed you." She smiled, reaching for him in a jerky, uncontrolled movement. "I knew you'd come back for us."

He grabbed her hand and held it tightly. "I missed you, too." It surprised him, the truth of that simple statement. He *had* missed Kayla; he'd missed the man he'd once been—the man he could have been with her at his side.

Her gaze focused on his face, caressing it with equal measures of wonder and confusion. "You're older, too."

"Nice of you to notice. Hey, do you remember—"

"Why are we old?"

He smiled uneasily. "You're not even forty yet. Young."

"Julian, no one will tell me the truth. But I know you wouldn't lie to me. Please . . . I need to understand."

He wanted to lie to her, wanted it with a fierce desperation, but there was no way out.

"You have a few gaps in your memory, that's all. The docs say it's nothing to worry about."

"Fifteen years is hardly nothing."

"It'll all come back. Don't rush it." He leaned down and kissed her. She tasted just like he remembered, all sweet compliance and homecoming. When he kissed her, he felt . . . complete.

"How could I forget fifteen years of loving you and Juliana? Tell me about us, Jules. Help me remember."

"Ah, baby . . ." He would have done anything to erase the sorrow in her eyes. "She's beautiful, Kay. The spitting image of you."

She gazed up at him, her pale face as serious as he'd ever seen it. "I remember when I left. Do you remember that, Jules?"

"I remember."

"I remember packing my bags, buying a car—that green station wagon with the wood-grain side panels—and loading it up. I hardly took anything from our life together, not even your money. I was so sure you'd come for us quickly . . . I can remember waiting and waiting, but I can't remember ever seeing you again."

He actually thought he might cry; that's how fucking awful he felt. "I'm sorry, baby. Jesus, I'm sorry."

"How long, Jules?"

"H-How long what?"

"How long?"

He touched her soft, soft cheek. He was cornered; there was no way out of this except to lie—and that was pointless. She might remember it all in ten seconds. "Now," he answered in a tired, broken voice. "Just now."

She frowned. "Just now what? I'm thirty-nine years old, that means my—*our* baby is sixteen. You don't mean . . ."

"Just now," he repeated quietly.

Tears filled her eyes, magnified her pain until it seemed to suck the air from the room. "You mean . . . you *never* came back for me? In all those years, never?"

He felt the sting of tears in his own eyes. "I was

young and stupid. I didn't know how special it was between us. It took me a long time to grow up."

"Never." The single word slipped from her mouth, toneless and dead. "Oh, my God."

"Kayla, I'm sorry."

"No wonder I forgot."

"Don't look at me like that."

"Like what?"

"Like . . . I've broken your heart."

She tried to wipe her eyes, but her effort was a failure; she slapped her own cheek. "I guess you did that a long time ago—and lucky me, I get to experience it twice. Oh, Jules." She sagged into the pillows. "I love you so much. But it's not enough, is it?" She turned her head and closed her eyes. "I wish I'd forgotten you."

"Don't say that. Please . . ." He wanted to kiss her tears away, but he had no right. He had hurt her again, as he'd known he would, and he regretted it more deeply than he would have thought possible. Suddenly he saw all the chances he'd lost. For the first time, he wanted the years back, wanted to have become the kind of man who knew how to love.

She rolled awkwardly onto her side. "Go away."

"Kayla, don't—"

"Go away, Julian. *Please.*"

If he'd had Liam's courage, he would have known what to say, but as it was, he was empty. He turned away from her and headed for the door.

"I want to see my daughter," she said.

He nodded, saying nothing, not knowing if she even knew he'd answered. Then he left.

She wanted to curl into a small, safe ball and close out the world again.

He never came back.

She couldn't seem to grasp that. It broke her, pure and simple. For a long, long time, she lay in her lonely bed, trying to wrap her arms around a truth that was too big to hold.

What had she been doing all these years? If things were normal, if *she* were normal, would she have laughed at him and told him to run along, that her love for him had died a long time ago?

That was the hell of it. She didn't know who she'd become in the years after their parting. Everything she'd learned or touched or believed in was gone, along with all the memories that, when sewn together, scrap by scrap, made up a life.

And what about her daughter, her baby girl who hadn't been a baby in years? She remembered a pudgy, brown-eyed toddler with a halo of jet-black curls, a little girl who could go from hysterical sobbing to laughter in a heartbeat. She remembered the feel of that baby in her arms, but after that, nothing. No images came to her of frilly Easter bonnets or lunch boxes or loose teeth. Fifteen blank years, as unknown as tomorrow.

She wished she could be angry; it was so much better than this aching, overwhelming sorrow.

In her heart, she was twenty-four years old and

deeply in love with her husband. Only he wasn't her husband and she'd had fifteen long years to heal the wounds he'd inflicted.

Fifteen years that had been wiped out.

Without memories, there was no passage of time, no change, no growth. There was just this love for Julian, this runaway train of emotion that she could do nothing but ride.

He must have nearly killed her with his betrayal. She knew that because when she'd said the word *never*, she'd felt it in her heart and soul. She'd loved him too much—and it would destroy her, that bad and dangerous love. But knowing a thing didn't change it.

The door opened. "Mikita, you are awake?"

"Mama!"

Rosa stood in the doorway, smiling brightly.

Mikaela gasped, brought a shaking hand to her mouth. "Oh, Mama . . ."

The years had been hard on Rosa. Her hair was snow-white now, her dark skin creased heavily around the eyes and mouth. Mikaela wanted to ask "What happened?" but before the question was even formed, she knew the answer. Bad love.

Rosa came up to her bedside. She touched Mikaela's cheek, said softly, "A *milagro*." Then she bent down and scooped Mikaela into a hug. "I never think to see you smile again, *hija*." She drew back.

Mikaela's throat constricted. "*Hola, Mama.*"

"I have missed you very much." Rosa held on to Mikaela's hand.

"What happened to me, Mama? No one will tell me."

Rosa picked up a brush from the bedside table and began brushing Mikaela's short hair. "You fell from a horse."

"So they tell me. What in the hell was I doing on a horse?"

Rosa smiled. "You remember the bad language, I am not happy to say. In the past years, you have become the good horse rider. It is something you love."

Mikaela grabbed her mother's thin wrist. "Tell me about Juliana, Mama."

Rosa carefully set down the brush. Her bony fingers curled around the bed rail. "We call her Jacey now, and she is everything you would wish for in a daughter." She gazed down at Mikaela, her eyes glistening. "She is beautiful and gifted and loving and *muy intelligente*. And popular—I have never heard the phone ring so much. Look around this room, Mikita, and tell me what you see."

For the first time, Mikaela looked around the room. There were flowers and balloons everywhere; cards lined the tables and the windowsill. "Are they all from Julian?"

Rosa made a sweeping gesture with her hand. "Not from that one. They are from your friends. This is your home now, Mikaela. It is a wonderful place, not like Sunville at all. Every shop I go in, someone asks about you. The women, they bring food to the house every day. Here, *mi hija,* you are much loved."

Mikaela couldn't imagine that she'd found a real

home, a place to belong, and not to remember that, it wasn't fair . . .

She looked up at her mother. "He never came for me, Mama."

"I know. This was hard on you before. Maybe it is even harder now. Then, you remembered why you left him. Now, I think maybe you forget."

"I want to see my daughter."

Rosa didn't answer for a moment. Then, softly, she said, "It will . . . wound her heart . . . this forgetfulness. Dr. Liam wishes for you to have another day to remember, *sí*? You do not want to hurt her."

Mikaela didn't know how she could survive the heartache seeping through her. "I remember how it feels when a parent doesn't know you. I remember this from . . . my father."

"You have never called him this before."

"I know." She sighed tiredly. "But calling him something else doesn't make him someone else, does it?"

"No." Rosa reached into her pocket, pulling out a photograph. "Here."

Mikaela's fingers didn't work right. It took her several tries to grasp the picture, and even then, Rosa had to gently guide her daughter's fingers. She stared down at the picture—it was of Mikaela and Rosa and a beautiful young girl. They were standing in an unfamiliar room, beside a gorgeous, wonderfully decorated Christmas tree.

Mikaela's hungry gaze took in every detail about the girl—the brown eyes, the easy smile, the waist-length black hair. "This is my Juliana . . . No, my *Jacey*."

"*Sí.* The memories, they are in you, Mikaela. Place this *fotografía* next to your heart and sleep well. Your heart will remember what your mind forgets."

Mikaela stared down into the eyes so like her own. Try as she might, she couldn't remember holding this little girl, or stroking her hair, or kissing her cheek. "Oh, Mama," she whispered, and at last she cried.

Chapter Twenty-one

Not long after lunch, Mikaela fell asleep.

She knew she was dreaming now. It was the first dream she'd had since waking up, and there was a comforting familiarity in the sensation. In her dream, the world was a hazy smear of blues and greens. A gentle summer breeze fluttered through the towering evergreen trees.

She was walking along a deserted road. Her body was working perfectly, no right leg dragging along behind her, no fingers that wouldn't close. She came around a bend in the gravel road and saw an imposing wooden barn set on the crest of a hill. In the fields around it, there were horses standing in a group, munching contentedly on sweet green grass that came up to their hocks.

She kept moving, floating almost, past the barn, toward a beautiful log house.

A bank of gray clouds moved in suddenly, obliterating the lemon sunshine, casting the log house in shadow. It began to rain, spits of cold water that landed on her upturned cheeks like God's own teardrops.

The front door opened for her.

She stumbled on the porch steps. Crying out, she grasped the railing and a splinter drove deep into the tender flesh of her palm. When she lifted her hand, she saw the bright, ruby-red trail of blood snaking down her wrist.

"No," she tried to say, but the wind snatched her words away, and she was still walking, across the porch, into the house.

The door slammed shut behind her. She felt her way down the smooth wooden wall toward a staircase she somehow knew was there.

At the bottom, she paused, listening. Somewhere in this cold, dark house, a child was crying.

I'm coming. The words played across Mikaela's mind but didn't quite reach her mouth. She was moving again, running this time.

The cries became louder, more insistent. Mikaela had a fleeting, heartbreaking image of a little boy, red-haired, sucking his thumb. He was tucked back in a corner, waiting for his mommy to come for him.

But there were a hundred doors in front of her, and the hallway stretched for miles, fading out of focus at its end. She ran down the corridor, yanking open doors. Behind those doors lay nothing, yawning black rectangles spangled with starlight, breathing a cold winter wind.

All at once, the crying stopped. The silence terrified her. She was too late . . . too late . . .

She woke with a start. The ceiling above her was made of white acoustical tiles, their pattern sharp and bright after the hazy quality of her dream.

The hospital.

There was a man standing by her window. Her first thought was *Julian*—but then she noticed that he was wearing a white coat.

He turned toward her, and she saw that it wasn't Dr. Penn. It was the other one—what was his name? He was a tall man, with longish blond hair and a nice face. He reminded her of an aged version of that actor from *Thunderbolt and Lightfoot*. Jeff Bridges, that was his name. It disgusted her that she could remember an actor's name, and practically none of her own life.

"You need a haircut." The words just popped out of her mouth, and she winced. What on earth had made her say that to this man?

He ran a hand through his shaggy hair and smiled, but it was a sad smile, and she wondered why he looked so . . . forlorn. "Yeah, I suppose I do. My . . . wife cuts my hair."

When he spoke, it sent a shiver through her. "You're the voice," she said softly.

He pulled up a chair and sat down beside her bed. He stared at her boldly, without apology, and there was something in his eyes—a yearning, maybe—that made her want to touch him. But that was crazy; she didn't even know him.

"What voice?" he said at last.

"When I was asleep, I heard you."

He smiled again. "I didn't know if you'd be able to. It seemed like I talked forever."

Forever. That word again. It teased her, tickled some forgotten chord. "Who are you?" she asked.

He studied her for a minute. "Dr. Liam Campbell."

Somehow she knew that wasn't right. She looked around the room, at the photographs along the window that she hadn't bothered to look at, and the bottles of fragrant spices, at the lovely pond filled with slick black rocks. She knew without knowing that this was the man who'd played the endless stream of her favorite songs. He was the one who'd given her something to hang on to through all that darkness.

And it was this man—this stranger with the sad, familiar eyes—who'd been here at her bedside for all those days, talking, touching, waiting. She could *remember* the feel of his hand stroking her hair while she slept, and the sound of his laugh. Somehow she knew that, too. She knew that he had a booming, throaty laugh that filled a room and begged you to join in.

"I remember how you laugh," she said, amazed.

That seemed to please him. He smiled. "The memories will come like that, in bits and pieces."

"Who are you?"

"Dr. Li—"

"No. Who are you to me?"

His whole body seemed to deflate, to sink into that ugly chair. Slowly he stood up and reached for her left hand. He caressed her fingers, so tenderly that her breath caught in her throat. She couldn't remember ever being touched in just such a way, and then something came to her, some half-formed memory that couldn't quite be reached. "This ring," he said quietly. "I put it on your finger ten years ago."

She stared down at the ring. A wedding ring. "You're . . ." She couldn't seem to form the word.

"I'm your husband."

It was incomprehensible. "But . . . Julian . . ."

"Julian was your first husband."

She panicked. First a child, now a husband. How much had she forgotten? How much more was out there?

She stared at him, shaking her head in denial. She wanted to say *It can't be*, but in the last few days, she knew that anything could be. "How could I forget such a thing? How could I have . . . no feeling for you at all?"

He flinched, and in that tiny expression of pain, she knew it was true. "Don't worry about it, babe," he said. "It's okay not to remember."

"I—I don't know what to say to you . . . Liam." She tried out the name on her tongue, but nothing came with it. It was just a collection of vowels and consonants that had no meaning.

He touched her face. "It's okay."

But it wasn't okay. It was a long, long way from okay. This man was her husband, her *husband*, and she had no feelings for him whatsoever. He was her family now, what she'd done for the past ten years.

At some point she must have stopped loving Julian and started loving this gentle, quiet man. But what would happen now that she only remembered the love for Julian?

She tried to smile at him, but it was a trembling failure. "Tell me about our life together." These were the words that slipped from her lips, but what she meant was *Make me love you again* . . .

He smiled, and she knew he was recalling a memory that was now his alone. "You were a nurse then. I first met you when you cared for my father . . ." He looked at her. "Do you mind if I hold your hand?"

It surprised her, that request. There was something so . . . gentle and old-fashioned about it. She couldn't help thinking how different he was from Julian. Jules would never ask; it would never occur to him that his touch might not be welcomed. "Okay, sure," she said.

Their gazes met and held. She felt awkward suddenly, confused by this man who was both a stranger and her husband.

Husband.

"Kinda weird, huh?" he said with a crooked, nervous grin.

She smiled in return and leaned toward him, studying his face, searching for *something*, some vagrant memory. But there was nothing. Still, he had the kindest eyes she'd ever seen. "This must be hard on you," she said softly.

"The coma was harder."

Somehow she didn't think so. "Are you the one . . . did you call Julian?"

"Yes."

"I don't understand. If you and I are married now, why would you do that?"

"I couldn't . . . wake you up. I sat here every day, holding your hand, talking to you, playing your favorite music. I did everything I could think of to reach you, but . . . day after day, you just lay there." His voice fell to a throaty whisper. "I knew I was losing you."

"Why Julian?"

He let out a long, sighing breath. "Because, Mikaela, I knew."

She felt her heart skip a beat. "Knew what?"

"That you never completely stopped . . . loving him."

For a heartbeat, she forgot to breathe. "You loved me very much." She couldn't keep the wonder from her voice. She could never remember feeling this way before, this awesome mixture of joy and sadness, this feeling of being . . . loved deeply and completely. Julian's love wasn't like that. It was a blast of red-hot fireworks that exploded in Technicolor around you, but when it died, it left a cold, black sky behind.

"I still do," he said, smiling down at her with a sadness that wrenched her heart.

"I must have loved you, too."

He paused a moment too long before answering. "Yes."

And she knew. "I stayed in love with Julian, didn't I?" Somehow it hurt, that realization. "I hurt you," she said softly, sadly. "Did I know it?"

"I hope not."

She gazed up at him. "I'm sorry."

There was more to say, and no way she could think of to say it all. How could you apologize for what you couldn't remember?

Or worse, for what you were afraid you were going to do all over again?

It began simply enough, with the whooshing sound of the electronic doors opening. Julian sat in the lobby, staring at the wall clock. The slim black hands seemed to be stuck at 2:45. Liam was in with Kayla now, and he'd asked Julian to wait for him.

"Hey, Juli."

Julian looked up and saw Val sauntering toward him. Instead of his usual faded jeans and movie T-shirt, his agent was wearing a black Hilfiger suit with a dyed-to-match silk shirt and tie. His blond hair had been recently styled and cut; only a fringe of curls lay against his shoulders. He hadn't bothered to remove the Ray-Bans that shielded his eyes.

Julian would have smiled if he hadn't felt so damned bad. "This is Last Bend, you idiot, not Cannes. The only designer they know around here is L.L. Bean." He got to his feet and turned.

That's when he saw them. Outside, beyond the wall of windows that flanked the front doors, the vans and rental cars were already lining up. People in rumpled black clothes streamed out of those cars like locusts, gathering in a semicircle.

He'd seen it enough times to know the sequence by

heart. The media circus coming to town. "Jesus, Val, what did you do?"

Val lifted his hands, Christ-like. "You're white-hot, Juli. A few words whispered in a few ears and the story spread like wildfire. I have to admit, I didn't expect this kind of turnout."

"Goddamn it, Val, I *told* you not to—" He stopped. It was too late. They'd seen him.

Reporters swarmed through the doorway, microphones at the ready, cameras stationed on their shoulders. Within seconds, Julian and Val were engulfed. Val winked at him. "Too late to hide now, Juli."

Julian had to get them out of here. He pushed through the crowd and headed outside, into the freezing cold. The locusts followed, firing questions.

"Julian? Is it true? Have you found your Cinderella?"

"How badly is she hurt?"

"Is she still beautiful?"

"How come there's no Kayla True registered in this hospital? Is this a hoax?"

Julian held up his hands, forcing his trademark smile. Flashbulbs popped like gum in a whore's mouth, cords slithered across his feet. "There's no story here, boys and girls. I'm here for the Make-a-Wish Foundation. That's all."

Val thumped him on the back. Hard. "He's too shy to tell you the truth. You all know that Juli's first wife, Kayla, was the love of his life. Unfortunately, they were too young . . ." He paused and glanced around.

Val had them—hook, line, and sinker. Julian could

see it in the reporters' feverish eyes, hear it in the sudden, indrawn silence.

Julian's best intentions cracked under the strain. God help him, he couldn't let Val hog the spotlight. "You can imagine how I felt when I heard that she'd had an accident. I rushed up here to be at her bedside—"

"Why did they call you?" someone shouted out.

"I was told that Kayla had suffered a serious head injury—"

"Is she brain damaged?"

"Maybe that's why she asked for Julian!"

Val touched Julian's shoulder lightly, taking the reins of the story again. "She was in a coma for a month. For a while it looked hopeless . . ." He hesitated, shaking his head sadly. "Then the doctors discovered that Kayla responded to only one thing—the sound of Julian's name."

A gasp rippled through the crowd; they recognized the taste and feel of it, the *story* that had just been handed to them. Several reporters glanced at their watches, trying to figure out how to get to their editors before the rest of the crowd.

"Naturally, Julian raced up here," Val said. "He sat with her, day after day, talking to her, holding her hand, reminding her that there was a man who loved her and was waiting for her to waken." He gave them a brilliant, here-comes-the-good-part smile. "Yesterday she woke up. Julian was beside her. The first person she saw."

One of the female reporters sighed. "What were her first words?"

Julian started to answer; no one was listening.
"She—"

"Is she brain damaged?"

"Is she still in love with you, Julian?"

Julian sighed. They didn't care about the miracle of
Kayla's awakening. All they wanted was "the story,"
the gilt-edged fairy tale—or, better yet, a scandal. A
death. Anything sensational.

He looked around, at the faces. A few he recognized. They came and went, these low-rent reporters
from the tabloids. It wasn't a job that any normal
human being could stomach for long.

They were a reflection of his life. Funny, but he'd
never realized that before. He'd always dismissed the
media as a necessary evil; you couldn't get famous
without them. But now he saw the empty black space
that ringed the spotlight. Nothing captured in a glass
lens was real.

But Julian had no life except that which was filmed,
and that made him the blankest spot of all. He'd
traded everything real for the split-second brightness
of a camera's flash.

"That's enough for today," he said, wishing he'd
never talked to them.

Val grinned. "You've got your headline, kids. The
kiss of True love wakes up Sleeping Beauty."

As Liam walked out of Stephen's office, he heard his
name paged over the hospital's system. He grabbed the
nearest phone and punched in his code. The message

was from Rosa. She was waiting for him in the lobby.
It was an emergency.

He saw Rosa before she saw him. She was standing
in the center of the room—unusual for a woman who
always sat in a corner with her head down—with her
arms crossed. Even from this distance, he could see the
way her mouth was drawn into an angry line.

Something was wrong.

Up close, he could see the worry lines etched
around her eyes and mouth. "Rosa?"

"You see what he has done?"

"What are you talking about?"

She took a deep breath. "I am *muy* upset. I am listening to the radio at home while I make the tortillas
for tonight's supper, *sí*? And I hear the local news."
She cocked her head toward the hospital's front doors,
where a crowd was gathered around Julian. "It is the
big story, Dr. Liam. They are saying that Julian brought
his true love out of a coma."

"Damn it." Liam ran down the hall and into the
lobby. He saw the crowd gathered outside, and
headed for the doors.

Reporters circled Julian, angled toward him like sup-
plicants, microphones instead of prayer books in their
outstretched hands. They all talked at once, their questions climbing over each other in a frenzied outburst.

"When will we get to interview Kayla?"

"When will we get a shot of the two of you?"

"What has she been doing all of these years?"

"Are you two going to get married again?"

Liam grabbed Julian by the arm and spun him

around. Trying not to look at the reporters, he said in a quiet voice, "I need to speak to you. Now."

Julian had the grace to look embarrassed. "Sure thing, Doc." He threw the crowd a false smile. "This here is Liam Campbell. He's Kayla's . . . doctor."

The crowd had a dozen simultaneous questions. Liam ignored them. Hanging on to Julian's arm, he dragged him into the lobby, past Rosa, and into an empty examining room.

An instant later, the door opened and Rosa walked in.

"Hi, Rosa," Julian said, then turned to Liam. "I'm so sorry, Liam. I told my agent to keep the press away, but he ignored me. Really, I'm sorry. And believe me, they're like termites—once they infest your house, you have to deal with them. If I didn't talk to them, God knows what story they'd come up with. At least this way it's the truth."

Liam looked at him. "*Your* truth, maybe."

"What do you mean?"

"You've spoon-fed them a romance, haven't you, with you as the hero of the piece, the white knight who arrived in a black limousine and pulled her back from the brink of death."

"You have not heard the worst of it, Dr. Liam," Rosa said, shuffling toward the two men. "When I was walking into the hospital, I heard the questions. The reporters were asking about his daughter."

"Jesus *Christ*." Liam grabbed Julian by the shoulders and shook him. "Tell me you protected her. Tell me you didn't say a goddamn word about your daughter."

Julian winced. "I protected her—honestly, but

Val . . . he told them that she was a cheerleader at the high school."

For the first time in his life, Liam punched a man. He drew back his fist and slammed it into Julian's pretty-boy jaw. Pain radiated all the way up his arm. "There are only eight cheerleaders at the high school."

He turned to his mother-in-law. "You stay here with Mike. Keep the press away from her. I'll get the kids and be back as soon as I can. We'll come in through the back way."

Chapter Twenty-two

Please let me get to her in time.

Liam glanced at the clock on the Explorer's dashboard: 3:05. Cheerleader practice ended five minutes ago . . .

He pressed harder on the gas. At the entrance to the high school, he knew he was going too fast. When he turned the wheel, the tires skidded sideways. For a split second, he lost control of the car. Then the tires grabbed hold. The car hurtled down the driveway and into the parking lot.

He was too late. Already there was a crowd of reporters outside the school's front doors. Klieg lights stood on their perimeter like black insects. They were all talking at once; their combined voices sounded like the start-up of a buzz saw.

Liam lurched out of the car and ran toward them. The ground was slick and mushy with old snow, and twice he almost fell. By the time he reached the sidewalk, his heart was hammering.

"Jacey!" His voice was lost in the din.

Reporters circled the small group of cheerleaders like a pack of wolves, jockeying for position, making it impossible for Liam to get through. They were shouting out questions, one after another.

"Which one of you is Juliana?"

He heard Mrs. Kurek, the cheerleader adviser, answer, "There's no Juliana here, now go away."

Liam tried to see above the crowd, but there were lights and cameras everywhere, and the reporters knew how to close access.

He screamed his daughter's name, trying to push through the sardine-packed bodies. It was impossible.

"Which one of you has a mother in a coma?"

He knew that all it would take is a look at Jacey . . .

"There she is!"

The mob shifted, separated, and came back together around Jacey, cutting her off from everyone else with practiced ease. Wolves separating a baby lamb from the herd.

"Are you Kayla's daughter?"

"Are you Juliana?"

He could see that Jacey was breathing heavily. She was afraid. "I'm Jacey," she answered softly. "My mom's in a coma. . . ."

A microphone flew at her face, almost hit her in the nose. "How does it feel to be his daughter?"

Liam screamed her name. He grabbed hold of the cameraman in front of him and shoved. The camera fell to the ground, the man stumbled sideways.

Liam surged through the opening. "Jace—come here!"

Above the crowd, their gazes met. Liam saw the fear in his daughter's eyes. He saw when she gave way to panic; not all at once, but in little breaths. He plowed through the crush of bodies. She held out her hands toward him.

He pushed and shoved his way forward, his hands outstretched, fingertips straining to touch hers.

"How does it feel to be Julian True's daughter?" someone yelled out.

A hush fell. Jacey looked at Liam, her mouth open, her eyes widening in shock.

"Jesus Christ, she doesn't know—"

"Move in, Bert, get a shot of her face—*now*—"

"GET AWAY FROM HER!" Liam screamed the words. He threw himself forward, knocking people aside, ramming them with his elbows.

At last he was at her side. He slipped an arm around Jacey and pulled her close. He could feel her trembling. "It's okay, honey," he whispered in her ear, even though he knew it wasn't true.

"Who are you?" someone shouted at him.

"It's the doctor," someone else said. "What are you—"

"She has no comment." Liam heard the snarl in his voice; it was an unfamiliar sound that came from a dark place deep inside him. He dragged a dazed Jacey through the crowd and helped her into the Explorer.

The reporters followed them all the way, still shouting out questions and popping photographs. The last thing

Liam heard as he slammed the car door was "Get the license plate number."

He started the engine and hit the gas. The car surged forward, tires spinning on the slushy snow, and spun out of the parking lot.

His heart was hammering, and there was a coppery fear taste in his mouth. He'd never felt so ashamed and defeated in his life. He had failed to protect her. It was his fault. The daughter he loved more than his own life had been hurt.

Jacey twisted around in her seat, watching the road behind them. "They're not following us," she said in a watered-down version of her ordinary voice.

Liam veered left onto the snowy, unmaintained forest service road that led to Angel Falls State Park. He chose this road because it only appeared on the most detailed maps of the area. No one would follow them here.

When they reached the end of the road, they found the empty parking lot as pristine as a new sheet of paper. In the late afternoon it was dark in these deep woods.

He parked near the information board, a rough-hewn wooden pyramid that told the story of these falls, discovered and named by Ian Campbell in honor of his beloved wife.

Liam took a deep breath and turned at last to his daughter. "I couldn't get to you fast enough."

She looked at him, her dark eyes confused and afraid. "Is it true, Dad?"

He wanted to be angry with Mike right now, but as

it was, all he felt was cold and hollow. "It's true. Your mom was married to Julian True."

The color faded from her cheeks. She looked impossibly young and vulnerable. "He's my father?"

Father. The word hit Liam like a blow to the larynx. For a moment he couldn't speak, and when he did find his voice, it was dull and flat. "Yes."

Her eyes rounded. "Oh, my *God* . . ."

He waited for her to say more, but she remained silent. It felt to Liam as if seawater were rising between them, rising, becoming a rippling wall that distorted their images. He tried to think of what it was that he should say, but that emptiness was inside him again, bleeding into the silence. Finally he told her the only truth that mattered. "I should have told you—"

"Is that why he's really in town? To see Mom?"

"Yes."

"Did you know he was my father?"

He understood the question. She didn't want to believe that he had lied to her all these years, and as much as he wanted to protect Mike, he wouldn't deceive Jacey. That's why she was so hurt now. "I heard the same stories you did. Mike told me that she'd been married too young, to a man who only wanted to party and have fun. I didn't know it was Julian. I found out the truth when I went looking for that dress you wore to the dance."

"The way she wouldn't ever talk about my other dad . . . I figured he was a bum or a bad guy. Some loser she met in college." She paused, looking at him.

"When I was little, she used to cry every time I asked about him, so I stopped asking. Jeez . . . Julian True."

Liam tried not to be hurt by the tiny, hitching smile that tugged at her mouth. What teenager wouldn't be thrilled to find out that a famous movie star was her father? It didn't mean she'd turn away from the father who'd always been there for her, holding her hand, kissing away her little girl's tears. At least that's what he told himself as the silence between them stretched on and on.

"When was she going to tell me? When we colonize Mars?"

It had come faster than he'd expected, the anger, and he didn't know how to assuage it. There was no way to excuse what Mike had done to her. It was selfish and hurtful, and now, these many years later, they would all pay for the lie that had lain between them, curled silently in a silk pillowcase.

"I don't know when she was going to tell you," he said at last.

He could see that she was close to crying. She seemed to be holding the tears back one shallow breath at a time. "That's why he came to the prom— to dance with me—but he didn't say anything that mattered. How did he know Mom was hurt?"

"I called him. I . . . discovered that your mom responded to his name. I thought that if he talked to her, she might wake up, and it worked. She woke up yesterday."

"Julian woke her up—after all the hours we all spent talking to her?"

Liam winced. He felt hemmed in by all the times he'd told Jacey that love would reach Mikaela in her darkness. "Well—"

"Oh, my *God*, what if . . ." This time she couldn't hold back the tears. She launched herself at Liam, landing in his arms as if she were a child again. She cried on his shoulder. The warm moisture of her tears seeped through his flannel shirt. When she drew back, she looked different somehow, changed, as if the tears had washed away the last, sticky traces of the little girl she'd been and made room for a young woman.

"I hate her." At the confession, she started crying again.

He touched her face. "No. You're hurt and angry— and you have every right to be. But you could never hate your mom. She loves you, Jace—"

"What about you? She lied to you all these years, too."

He sighed. "Sometimes people lie to protect their loved ones. Maybe she thought . . . we couldn't handle the truth."

Jacey sniffed, wiped her nose with the back of her hand. Her eyes were glazed with tears as she looked at him, her mouth quavered. "He didn't want me, did he? That's why he never called or wrote."

Liam wanted to lie to her, but it was lies that had brought them to this sorry, painful place in their lives. "I don't know Julian well enough to answer that."

He could see that she was shocked and confused and angry. The truth had pushed her out on a twisting, narrow road, and only she could find her way. "I'm sorry, Jace. For all of it."

She gazed at him, tears sliding down her cheeks. "I love you . . . Dad."

He heard the tiny hesitation, the way her voice snagged on the hook of new information, before she called him Dad. "I love you, too, Jace."

"We're still a family," he whispered. "You remember that. Your mom loves you and Bret—oh, shit, *Bret*." He jerked back so hard his head hit the window.

"The reporters." Jacey slid back into her seat and clamped the seat belt in place. "It's three-thirty. He's in music class."

Bret was getting cranky. They'd been practicing for the Christmas assembly for more than an hour, and he, like most of the boys, hated standing still. They were all in rows, all the fourth and fifth graders, standing side by side on three risers. The music teacher, Mrs. Barnett, had organized them by height, which meant that the girls were next to the boys, and that was *always* a problem.

Mrs. B. rapped her wooden pointer on the metal music stand. "Come on, children, pay attention. Now, let's try the last verse again." Mrs. B. raised her poker and nodded at Mr. Adam, who was sitting at the piano in the corner. At the cue, he started playing "Silent Night."

Bret couldn't remember a single word.

Katie elbowed him, hard. "Sing."

He hit her back. "Shut up."

She pinched him, right in the fat part of his upper arm. "I'm gonna tell."

"Bite me."

Katie slammed her arms down and stomped one foot so hard the whole riser shuddered. "Mrs. Barnett," she yelled in a shrill, gloating voice, "Bret Campbell isn't singing."

Mr. Adam's fingers stumbled on the keys. There was a confused jangle of notes, and then silence.

Katie flashed Bret a satisfied smile.

He rolled his eyes. *Like he cared.*

Slowly Mrs. B. lowered her pointer. "Now, Katherine, that's not really your concern, is it?"

"She thinks everything is her concern," someone said, laughing.

Katie blushed. It was totally cool the way her whole face turned red. "B-But you said we all—"

Mrs. B. smiled at Bret, but it was a weird smile, sorta wiggly and sad. "Let's not pick on Bret. We all know—"

Bret stuck his tongue out at Katie.

"—that his mom just woke up, and that it's been a hard time for the family."

We all know his mom woke up.

Bret couldn't breathe. It couldn't be true. Dad would have told him if Mommy woke up. But Mrs. B. said it . . .

He clutched Katie's arm to steady himself.

She let out a little squeal, then opened her mouth to tell on him again. Only nothing came out. Instead, she frowned at Bret. "You look gross. Are you gonna puke?"

"My daddy wouldn't do that," he said to her.

Suddenly the door to the music room banged open and Jacey stood in the opening. Her face was all red and streaked, as if she'd been crying. "Mrs. Barnett," she said, "I need to take Bret home now."

Mrs. B. nodded. "Go along, Bret."

Bret wrenched away from Katie so hard that four kids fell backward off the risers. He could hear everyone whispering, and he knew they were talking about him. Something else he didn't care about.

He walked around the curious circle of his friends. Now he didn't care if everyone saw that he was almost crying. He just wanted Mrs. B. to say that it was a mistake. Daddy would *definitely* have told Bret if Mom was awake.

He went to his sister. He felt very small all of a sudden, like a broken-legged action figure staring up at G.I. Joe, and his heart was beating so fast he felt dizzy. "Is Mommy—"

"Come on, Bretster." She grabbed his arm and dragged him out of the music room and down the hall. Outside, the Explorer was parked in the bus loading zone—a complete and total no-no at this time of day. The buses would be pulling up any minute. He saw that his dad was in the driver's seat.

This is bad.

Bret allowed himself to be loaded into the backseat like a bag of grain. Jacey strapped him into his seat, then jumped into the front seat. Before Bret could even think of what to say, they were speeding through town. People were all over the streets, putting up decorations for the Glacier Days Festival this weekend, but Dad didn't wave to a single person. And he was driving *way* too fast.

Bret wanted to ask something, to scream something, but it felt like Superman was squeezing his throat.

Dad pulled the car up to the back door of the hospital. He didn't even look at Bret, just at Jacey. "Stay with your brother. Stay *away* from the lobby. I have to talk to Sam in Administration. I'll meet you in the cafeteria in ten minutes, okay?"

Jacey nodded.

Then Daddy was gone, running off ahead of them, and Jacey and Bret were walking down the empty hallway in the back of the hospital. Their footsteps echoed, and it was creepy. At every noise, Bret flinched.

She was dead. He was sure of it this time. When he got to his mommy's room, the bed would be empty, and it would be too late for him to see her . . .

He yanked away from his sister and ran toward his mother's room.

"Bret—come back!"

He ignored her and kept running. At his mom's room, he skidded to a stop and pulled the door open.

There was Mommy, lying in that old bed just like always. Asleep.

He stumbled. It was only because he was clutching the doorknob that he didn't fall.

He didn't know which emotion was stronger: relief

that Dad hadn't lied, or disappointment that she wasn't awake.

He shut the door quietly and went to Mommy's bed.

It still scared him, to see her like this. Even though she was still pretty, and Daddy had shown Bret the important things—like the rosy pink on her cheeks and the way her chest rose and fell with every breath—

All good signs, Daddy always said.

But to Bret, she looked like she was dead. He had to keep telling himself that she was alive.

It's still her, Bretster. You remember that.

He tried to take strength from Dad's words. His dad, who wouldn't lie, said Mommy was alive . . . somewhere.

Bret moved in closer and climbed up the bed rail, leaning over her. He was so close, he could feel the softness of her breath against his eyelashes. Then he closed his eyes and tried to think of a happy memory of her.

Well, I guess any boy big enough to saddle his own horse is old enough to go on an overnight ride . . . I'm proud of you, Bretster.

He knew the memory would make him cry, and it did. All he could think about was the way she'd dropped to her knees on the cold cement floor and hugged him. He missed her hugs most of all . . . maybe even more than her kisses.

He heard the door open behind him, then the soft sound of his sister's footsteps. "Come on, Bret. Dad told us to meet him in the cafeteria."

"Just a sec." He leaned a little closer and gave her

the Mommy Kiss, just exactly how she always did it to him: a quick kiss on the forehead, one on each cheek and a butterfly kiss on the chin, then a longer kiss on the right side of the nose. While his lips were brushed against her nose, he whispered the magic words: "No bad dreams."

When he drew back, his heart was hurting. A tear leaked down his cheek and splashed on Mommy's lip.

And, very slowly, she opened her eyes.

Bret almost fell off the bed.

She eased up to a sit and stared at him. He waited and waited, but she didn't smile. "Well, hello, little boy."

At last she smiled, but it was all wrong.

It wasn't his mommy.

Bret opened his mouth; nothing came out. All this time, he'd waited and prayed, and in every dream he had, his mom said the same thing when she woke up. *How's my favorite boy in the whole world?* And then she'd sweep him into her arms and hold him like she always did . . .

Tears burned his eyes.

The lady who wore his mommy's face frowned. "Is something wrong?"

They were the wrong words. His real mommy would have said, *Those can't be tears in my big boy's eyes . . .*

No, he meant to say, even if it was a lie, but when he opened his mouth, nothing came out except his own breath.

The fake mommy looked around the room. Her

gaze caught on Jacey, who was standing by the door, hugging herself and crying. "How's my favorite girl in the world?"

A tiny sound escaped Bret then. He couldn't hold it all in. Those were *his* words, *his,* but she'd given them to Jacey.

RUN.

That was all he could think. He tore out of the building and plunged into the darkening afternoon.

By the time he got to the highway, he was freezing, but he didn't care. He kept running.

Chapter Twenty-three

We call her Jacey now.

It was like looking in a mirror that reflected the past. Instinctively she wanted to reach out. She thought of all the things she'd forgotten. Her daughter's first word—what had it been? What had she done on the first day of kindergarten—had Jacey climbed onto that big yellow bus all by herself and waved good-bye, or had she clung to her mother's arm, crying, begging to stay home just one more day?

"Mom?"

The sweet fullness of that word made the memory loss almost unendurable. That she could be a stranger to this child of hers . . .

"Jacey," she whispered, holding out her arms.

Jacey moved slowly toward her. Mikaela felt an odd reluctance in her daughter, but at last Jacey leaned over the bed rail. Mikaela wrapped her arms around Jacey, pulling her close. She breathed in the sweet, forgotten scent of her little girl—not the baby powder she remembered, but something citrusy and adolescent.

When she drew back, Jacey was crying.

Mikaela touched her cheek. "Don't cry. It'll be okay."

A tear slid down Jacey's cheek. "How? How will it be okay?"

"I'll get my memory back. You'll see."

Jacey's eyes rounded. "You lost your memory? That's why . . ." She glanced at the open door.

"I'm sorry. I have some gaps is all—"

"Why didn't Dad tell me?"

"I think they asked Julian to hold off on that."

"Juli— You don't remember Dad?" Jacey's voice was barely audible.

"Oh, I remember Julian . . . up to a point, anyway. Everything after I left him is kind of a blank. I think—"

"Oh, *perfect*!" Jacey stared at Mikaela as if she'd grown horns. "I can't believe this."

Mikaela frowned. "You're mad at me."

"My *dad* is Liam Campbell." Jacey clutched Mikaela's flimsy hospital gown. "We fell in love with him a long time ago, when I was only four years old. He's been your husband for ten years. And you don't remember him. You only remember Julian, who never, *ever* called me or sent a birthday card or wanted to see me."

Mikaela was confused. "But Julian is your father . . ."

Jacey backed away. She seemed to be hanging on to composure by the thinnest thread. "Oh, he's my father, all right. And thanks to your lies, I didn't know that until today."

Mikaela felt like she'd been punched in the stomach. "I never told you?"

"No."

"Oh, Jacey . . ." Mikaela didn't know what to say. What kind of woman had she become that she would do this to her daughter? "Jacey, I—"

The door swung open. Sarah bustled into the room, rosy-cheeked and out of breath. "Jacey, I was hoping to find you here. The receptionist just called. She saw Bret run out of the hospital. He wouldn't stop—"

"Bret! Oh, my God. It's my fault!" Jacey spun around the heavyset nurse and ran out of the room.

Mikaela looked helplessly at Sarah. "Who's Bret?"

Sarah gave her a sad, knowing look. "Get your rest, honey."

Mikaela's heart beat too fast. Any second, she expected one of the machines to sound an alarm. The room spun around her, making her sick and dizzy. She grabbed Sarah's arm, yanked her so hard the nurse hit the bed rail. "Sarah . . . did you know me . . . before?"

"Of course. I hired you right out of nursing school."

Mikaela released Sarah and sank into the mound of pillows. These facts of her life were meaningless; she wanted the truth of it. "Was I a good person?"

Sarah gazed down at her, smiling softly. "You have the pure heart of an angel, Mikaela. You were—and are—a good person. Believe me."

She wanted to believe it, but she couldn't. She'd lied to her daughter for all these years, and obviously she'd broken Liam's heart. For the first time, she wondered if this amnesia was a gift from God. A momentary respite that allowed a sinner to feel like a saint.

Julian sat in the familiar cocoon of the limousine, staring at the reporters clustered beyond the smoked glass.

He'd really screwed up today. There was no way around that fact. He'd set the hounds on his own daughter. It hadn't been broadcast yet, that footage from outside the high school, but he'd heard about it in excruciating detail, the way they'd caught her off guard and thrown questions at her.

How does it feel to be Julian True's daughter? And the way they'd sniffed out the ugly truth: *She doesn't know.*

Outside, he saw Liam push through the crowd of reporters.

Julian couldn't help himself; he sank deeper into the seat, rubbing his tender jaw. The last person he wanted to talk to right now was Liam Campbell.

Julian was deeply ashamed of what he'd done. Usually when he screwed up, he paid for it. Literally. People who worked for him ran along in his wake, throwing money at anyone whose life or property had been damaged in a brush with Julian True.

Now, for once, he wanted to be a better man than that. He wanted to do the right thing.

He pulled his Ray Bans out of his pocket and slid

them onto his face. Then, after running a comb through his tangled hair, he got out of the limo.

It was snowing. Again.

"He's out!"

Reporters surged toward him, microphones at the ready. They looked as bad as he felt. This weather was too damned cold. He knew that if they were going to stand outside for a story, they'd rather be in Los Angeles, where the elements gave you cancer instead of frostbite.

He barely heard the questions hurled at him. Wordlessly, unsmiling, he pushed through the crowd, knowing they wouldn't follow him into the hospital. They were like vampires—they had to be invited in.

He was halfway to Kayla's room when he saw his daughter. She was in the waiting room, standing still as stone, with her back to him.

"Juliana." He remembered a second too late that it was the wrong name. "J.C."

Slowly she turned around. For a disorienting moment, the past slammed into the present. Her eyes were red and puffy, and her mouth was trembling. She looked exactly like Kayla on the day she left him. "Hi," was all she said.

"I . . . was hoping we could talk. I know . . . you know the truth about me . . . about us."

"Not now." She took a step toward him, hugging herself. "My brother ran away."

Julian frowned. "What do you mean? I don't have any other children."

"Okay, my *half* brother."

"Jesus," he whispered. "No one told me there was another one. He's Kayla's . . . and Liam's?"

She nodded. "His name is Bret. We saw Mom today for the first time since she woke up. She didn't recognize us. It was bad. Bret . . . ran away."

Julian wanted to help her, say something that would ease her sadness, but he didn't even know her, couldn't possibly understand what she needed. No, that wasn't true. He knew she needed her father.

Liam would know what to do. This moment, and a thousand others like it, had made Liam this girl's father. There was no way now to turn Julian into that which he was not. "It's not your fault. Your dad will find him."

"Yeah . . ." She gazed up at him, saying nothing else.

Julian wished he could look into J.C.'s sad eyes and see his own future, but all he saw was a screwed-up past. "Your dad's the real thing. He'll find your brother. Trust me."

"Trust you?" Slowly she moved toward him. "Did you ever think about me?"

He knew when a lie was called for, and though he knew a better man would take the high road, he lied. "All the time." He flashed her a nervous smile. "You look exactly like your mom when I first met her. You are the two most beautiful women I've ever seen."

He could see that she didn't believe him, and worse, that the lie had hurt her, and so he gave her the only gift he could. For once he told the truth: "No, not really. When your mom left me, I . . . moved on. I loved her—and I could have loved you—but I moved on instead. I'm sorry, but your mom . . . and your dad love you. And boy, when Kayla loves, it's one of those out-of-the-ballpark kind of things."

She turned away from him and went to stand at the window.

He followed her. He wanted to touch her shoulders, but he didn't dare. Instead he stared at their reflections, side by side in the tarnished windowpanes. "I'm sorry. For all of it. The reporters, the years I stayed away, the letters I didn't write. I'm sorry."

Then, with his daughter's silent tears glittering in the windowpane between them, Julian caught a glimpse of his own empty soul. It happened fast, came and went as quickly as a breath taken and released, but he knew he'd never forget.

Liam tried not to think of everything that could go wrong on this dark, December night when God had seen fit to drop the temperature four degrees in the last thirty minutes. Or that Bret was alone out there, his precious nine-year-old son, still more baby than young man, out there all alone, on this coldest of evenings. Did Bret know how dangerous it was to walk along the side of the road when the streets were icy . . . when visibility was cut in half by the falling snow?

These were lessons Liam didn't remember passing down to his son, and now his not having done so preyed on his fraying nerves.

He kept glancing at the outside temperature gauge he'd had installed on the dashboard. It was thirty degrees outside, as cold as it got in this part of the world. And he was out there—

Stop it.

He's all right. He's just hiding somewhere, sitting someplace where it's warm and dry—

Thinking about why his mom didn't recognize him, wondering why his daddy hadn't told him the truth.

"Hang on, Bretster," Liam whispered aloud. His hands were curled so tightly around the steering wheel, he wouldn't have been surprised to see ten indentations when he let go. He leaned forward, peering through the obscured windshield. It was snowing so hard now, the wipers were having trouble keeping up.

The highway was empty, just as the medical building parking lot had been. Liam had wasted precious minutes searching the hospital—he'd been unable to believe that Bret would leave—but eventually he'd been forced to accept the fact that his son had been so hurt and afraid that he'd run. Without thinking, probably without even feeling the stinging bite of cold as he pushed through the double doors.

At first, anyway.

By now Bret would be freezing. He'd run off without his coat.

The car phone rang.

Liam's heart skipped a beat as he punched the "Send" button. "Did you find him?" he asked whoever was calling.

"No." It was Jacey's soft, quavering voice. "Everyone

is looking, though. Grandma's at home, waiting for a call. I'm waiting at the hospital, in case he comes back here. I thought—"

"I know, honey, but we'd better stay off the line."

"Dad?" She paused, and he knew everything she was feeling. "I'm sorry."

"It's not your fault. It's mine. I should have told you guys the truth. We'll talk about it later, okay? When . . . we've got him home safely."

"Yeah. When he's home."

Disconnecting the line, he focused on the road again. He had to do that, focus on ordinary things—the road, the streetlights, the hiding places along the way— because when he did that, he kept himself together.

He cut the enormity of his fear into little pieces. Details. These he could handle.

He slowed the car speed, from eight miles per hour to five. He had gone less than a quarter of a mile from the hospital. The distance to town stretched out before him, an endless, twisting path of darkness.

Details.

He forced his gaze to the right, into the black fields along the side of the highway. Bret wouldn't have crossed the road; he knew better than that. Liam was certain. His son wouldn't cross the road at night alone . . . but would he take a ride with a stranger?

Liam suppressed a horrified shudder. *Please tell me he learned that rule.*

The temperature gauge indicated that, outside, it had dropped another degree.

Liam concentrated on the little things—his foot on

the gas, his hands on the wheel, his gaze on the side of the road, where there were no footprints. Just a layer of newfallen snow.

Up ahead, on the right side of the road, the county fairgrounds were a cluster of big metal buildings, barns, arenas, and pavilions. The barn was awash in light; it stood out like a beacon against the blackness all around it.

The lights were on . . . in the middle of a winter's night.

Liam felt an electrifying strand of hope. It was one of Mike's favorite places, that barn. She and Jacey had spent countless summer days there for horse shows and county fairs and riding clinics. Only a few months ago, Bret had earned his first 4-H ribbon there.

At the turnoff, he slowed. Perspiration itched across his brow, turned his hands cold and slick.

Any wrong choice would hurt. He glanced at the temperature gauge again; it was holding steady at twenty-nine. He turned onto the road and floored the accelerator. The wheels screeched for a second before grabbing hold. He sped down the bumpy road, his face pressed so close to the windshield that his nose was almost touching glass. In the parking lot, he slammed on the brakes. The car fishtailed, then came to a shuddering stop.

He left the engine running and jumped out of the car, racing through the downy, ankle-deep snow. "Bret?" he yelled. His cry echoed off the unseen mountains and bounced back at him, thin as a sheet of ice.

He flung the metal doors open. The well-lit barn was cavernous, a row of empty stalls. *"Bret?"* he yelled.

He ran from stall to stall, peering in each one.

He found Bret in the very last stall—the one Mike had used at last summer's Last Bend Classic horse show. Shivering and curled into a tiny ball, Bret was sucking his thumb.

Liam had never known a relief this big; it made it hard to move, to speak, to do anything except sweep down and pull his son into his arms. "Oh, Bret," he whispered brokenly, "you scared me."

Bret drew back. His cheeks were bright red and streaked with tears, his eyes were bloodshot. "I knew you'd find me, Daddy. I'm—" He burst into chattering, shivering tears again.

"It's okay, baby," he said, stroking his son's hair.

Bret blinked up at him. "D-D-Daddy, she didn't even h-hug me."

He touched Bret's cheek. "I'm sorry, Bret. I should have told you the truth."

"Sh-She's n-not my mommy, is she?"

"Yes," he answered softly. "She's your mom, but the accident . . . it broke something in her brain and she can't remember some really important things."

"L-Like me?"

"Or me. Or Jacey."

"She remembered Jacey!"

"No. She'd heard about Jacey, and so she was able to figure out who she was. But she doesn't really remember."

Bret wiped his eyes. "So how come no one tole her about me? I'm as important as Jace."

Liam sighed. "You're *everything* to her, Bret. You and Jacey are her whole world, and it hurt her so much to hear about Jacey. She cried and cried. I just . . . couldn't tell her about you, too. I was hoping she'd remember on her own and then . . . everything would be fine."

Bret drew in a great, shuddering breath. Liam could tell he was trying to be a big boy. "Will her memory get unbroken?"

Liam wanted to say *Of course*, but in the last weeks, he'd learned a thing or two about his children and himself. They were all strong enough to handle the truth. The only wound that festered was a lie. "The doctors think she'll remember most things. Not every little thing, but the big things—like us—we think she'll get those back."

"But you don't know for sure?"

"No. We don't know. But you know what?"

"What?"

"The love . . . I believe she'll remember all of that."

Bret seemed to think about that for a long time. "Okay, Daddy."

Liam smiled. Thank God for the resilience of a little boy's heart.

"Daddy? I love you."

The simple words sifted through Liam, soft as a summer rain. "I love you, too, Bret." He held him tightly. "And I'm proud of you. This is a hard thing for a little boy to understand."

Slowly they got to their feet. Liam picked Bret up and carried him out of the barn. When he flicked off the lights, a crashing darkness descended, and he followed the Explorer's headlights through the falling snow. As soon as they were in the car, Liam called Rosa and Jacey and gave them the good news. Rosa offered to pick Jacey up from the hospital and meet Liam and Bret at home.

Bret leaned back in his seat. Even with the heat roaring through the vents, he was shivering. "I'm sorry, Daddy."

"It's okay. Sometimes a man has to get away to think." He glanced at Bret. "But next time, how about if you go into a room and slam the door shut?"

Bret almost smiled. "Okay. But I'm gonna slam it *really* hard."

Chapter Twenty-four

Liam couldn't let go of Bret's hand. All the way home in the car, he held on to those cold little fingers.

When they pulled into the garage, Liam clicked the engine off and turned to his son. He would have given anything in that moment to say the perfect thing.

If wishes were horses, all beggars would ride.

It was one of Mike's favorite expressions, and it brought her back to him. He knew what she would say if she were here right now: *Come on, piano man, face the music.*

It gave him the shot of strength he needed.

"Bret, there's something else we need to talk about."

Bret turned to him, his face still red from the biting cold. "Do we hafta?"

Already his son had learned to expect the worst. He'd learned to be afraid. "Come on, I'll make us some hot chocolate and we'll sit by the fire and talk."

"Chocolate *and* sugar. This is gonna be good."

Liam smiled. "Move it, Jim Carrey."

Bret blinked up at him, owl-like. "That's what Mommy said to me . . . on the day . . . you know . . . just before she fell."

Liam tousled his son's still-damp hair. "The memories will be like that, pal-o-mine. They'll come out of nowhere—for you, and for Mommy. And Bretster, it's easier if you let them come, along with any emotion they happen to bring with 'em. You can't be afraid of what you feel. Not ever."

"Okay, Daddy." Bret got out of the car and went into the house, flipping on every light switch along the way. Liam followed along behind him, turning off the ones they didn't need. In the great room, he knelt in front of the fireplace and arranged the wood and paper. When the fire was cracking and popping, he went into the kitchen and made two cups of instant cocoa. He added a generous amount of milk to Bret's, then carefully carried the two mugs into the living room, where his son was already playing with an action figure, sound effects and all.

Liam stopped, took a deep breath . . . and went on. That's what parents did. This was a conversation that had to happen. Tomorrow Bret would go to school and some kid in some class would ask about Julian True. Bret deserved to learn the truth from his dad.

"Hey, pal," he said, handing Bret a cup.

Bret peered into the mug and scrunched his face. "You put milk in it. It looks like a bunch of floating toilet paper in there."

"Mom doesn't add milk—to cool it down?"

"Ice cubes when it's instant; milk when its the real thing. It's okay, Dad." He bravely took a sip. "Yum."

Liam smiled. "I love you, Bret."

Bret set down the mug. Liam knew that was it for the cocoa. "I love you, too, Dad."

"Come here."

Liam sat down in the huge, overstuffed chair by the sofa, the one they'd picked up at a garage sale outside of LaConner. Mike had spent more money refinishing and re-upholstering it than it would have cost to buy a new one, but as she always said, this chair was as comfortable as fifty years together. It easily held a man and his nine-year-old son.

Bret climbed up onto his lap.

Liam touched his son's face. Come this summer, there would be a dusting of freckles across this little nose.

"Is this more about Mommy?"

"You remember we told you a long time ago that Mommy had been married before?"

"Yeah. That's Jacey's other daddy."

Liam swallowed hard. "And did you know that Julian True was in town?"

"Lizard Man? Hel-*lo*, Dad, everyone knows that."

Liam held back a smile. "Actually, he prefers to be remembered as the Green Menace, but that's neither here nor there. The point is, he's in town to visit Mom."

"Lizard Man knows Mommy?"

Liam took a deep breath and jumped into the deep end. "More than that. Mommy used to be married to him."

Bret made a disbelieving sound—half snort, half giggle. "Yeah, right."

"It's true, Bretster."

Bret frowned. It was a long minute before he asked, "But you're my daddy—and she's my mommy, right?"

"That's right."

Bret seemed to turn it all over in his mind, this way and that. Sometimes he was frowning; sometimes he wasn't. At last he said, "Okay."

"Okay?" Liam had expected tears, anger, something more . . . traumatic than this quiet okay. Maybe Bret didn't understand—

"Yeah, okay. Sally Kramer's mom used to be married to Lonnie Harris down at the feed store, and Billy McAllister's dad used to be married to Gertrude at Sunny and Shear. *My* mom's ex-husband is way cooler than that. Hey, do you think he could get me a Lizard Man poster for my room?"

"You amaze me, Bret," he answered softly.

The mudroom door crashed open. Jacey and Rosa rushed into the house. Jacey was screaming her brother's name. She raced over to them and dropped to her knees beside the chair.

"Oh, Bret . . ." Crying, she ran her hands across Bret's face like a blind person hoping to memorize every shape. "Don't you *ever* do that again."

Bret shoved his sister's hand away. "No kisses. Gross. Hey, Jace, did you know that Mommy used to be married to Julian True—and he's your other dad?"

Jacey wiped her eyes and dropped her mouth open. "No *way*!"

Bret grinned from ear to ear. He leaned toward Liam and whispered in his ear, "You told me first?"

Liam clamped down on a smile. "You're a big boy now."

Bret giggled. "Yeah," he said to his sister, puffing up his narrow chest, "but we're still a family."

Jacey's arms embraced both of them. She pressed her tear-stained cheek against her brother's back. "A family," she said softly. "All we need now is Mom."

That evening the story broke. Pictures of "Kayla" and Julian were splashed across television, each one scrutinized and commented upon, their life together cut up into bite-sized pieces for mass consumption. At eight o'clock—right after *Entertainment Tonight*—the phone rang for the first time. Liam made the mistake of answering it. Some woman from the saddle club was screeching about how it couldn't be true.

After that, the phone began ringing nonstop. Liam yanked the plug out of the wall.

He went through the motions of ordinary life—he ate dinner, washed the dishes, watched a little television with the kids, then he tucked Bret into bed and read him a bedtime story.

When Bret was finally asleep, Liam carefully crawled out of the bed and padded out of the room. He was about to head downstairs when he noticed the slat of light beneath Jacey's bedroom door. With a sigh, he headed down the hallway toward her room.

After a long pause, he knocked. "Hey, honey, it's me."

"Oh. Come in."

He opened the door and found her exactly as he'd expected: sitting on her bed, wearing headphones, and crying. The television was on.

"Hey, kiddo."

She pulled off the headphones and tossed them on the pile of sheets and blankets beside her.

He grabbed her pink beanbag chair and dragged it closer to the bed, then plopped down into its cushy center.

"I yelled at her," Jacey said. "Mom wakes up after a month in a coma and I yelled at her."

"Don't worry about it, honey. You just go back tomorrow and tell her you love her."

"I *do* love her, but I'm mad at her, and I'm afraid she'll never remember us. That she'll only remember . . . him."

"I wish you were still a little girl right now," he answered in a quiet voice. "If you were, I'd make up a story or tickle you or offer you an ice-cream cone."

She smiled. "Something to change the subject."

"You bet. But you're almost grown up, and I can't protect you from all the hurts in life anymore. The truth is, love comes in a million colors and shades. Some are so clear they're almost see-through; others are black as pencil lead." He stopped, unable to think of anything to say that didn't sound lame or pathetic.

So he took a deep breath and told her what he believed. "Jacey, I don't know what your mom's past means to this family, but I know this: We will *always* be a family, the four of us. Somehow we'll get each other through it. That's what families do best."

"I love you, Daddy."

His heart constricted. A little girl's word: *Daddy.* It reminded him of all they'd been through together. They *would* get each other through this, one way or the other, and when it was all over, they would know how and where the love came to rest among them. "I love you, too, Jace. Now, come here, give your old man a hug."

She slid off the bed and dropped onto his lap, twining her arms around his neck.

The beanbag chair was too little, and together they slid off its slick surface and landed in a heap on the floor. Laughing, they separated and crawled awkwardly to their feet.

"Good night, Dad."

"Good night, Jace."

He left her room and closed the door behind him, then went downstairs. He drifted from room to room aimlessly. It wasn't until he found himself in the living room, standing beside the grand piano, that he realized he must have been coming here all along.

He sat down. The piano keys were dark. Not that he needed light to play; he didn't need anything—not sheet music, not light, not an audience. All he needed was Mikaela . . .

He plunked a single key with his forefinger. The

note—B flat—reverberated in the room, reminded him of the times he'd sat here, his family clustered around him, his wife seated close beside, and played his heart out. The lone note died.

He drew his hands back from the keys. He couldn't play yet.

Julian sat in one of the back booths at Lou's Bowl-O-Rama, staring down into his fourth schooner of beer. It was almost ten o'clock—apparently prime bowling time in Pleasantville.

He could hear the commotion going on behind him—people clustering together, pointing at him and whispering. The word that most often rose above the static hum was *Mikaela.*

They were easy to ignore. Part of being a star was learning to be alone in a mob of people, all of whom were looking at you. You learned to look without seeing, peruse a crowd without making eye contact. Celebrity 101. Unfortunately, at some point you realized that being alone in a crowd was hardly a skill you wanted to perfect.

He took another sip of beer.

He couldn't forget the emptiness he'd seen in himself today. He should have known it was there all along, of course, but he'd never been the kind of man who really thought about things like that.

Love was a word he'd used carelessly over the years. So often, he'd told people—reporters, friends, other women—that Kayla had been his one true love.

He could never say that now that he'd seen Liam, glimpsed into the heart of a man who truly loved.

Julian realized he liked the *idea* of love. That's why he'd married so often. But what he really wanted was something else—like that movie (or had it been a book first?) *The Bridges of Madison County.*

The perfect male fantasy: a few days of passionate, reckless sex that didn't change your life, then ripened into a bittersweet regret. Sure, you'd lost that one true love, but there was something inestimably romantic in loss. And why not? That love hadn't been tested by time or boredom or infidelity. It remained caught in a shining web of timelessness, and as the years went on, it grew brighter and brighter.

Regret, Julian now understood, was the only true emotion he'd retained from his marriage to Kayla. It tasted like fine port, that regret; over time, it had mellowed into a sweet, full-bodied wine that could intoxicate.

It was better than the truth: that he'd loved her, married her, watched her leave him, and moved on. That his love for her had been a fleeting emotion.

Or worse, that there was a hole in his soul that could never be filled, that real love was beyond him.

Someone clapped him on the shoulder. "Hey, Juli, I've been looking all over town for you. Are you *bowling?*"

Julian didn't smile. "You know me, Val. I love a sport where you wear other people's shoes."

Val grinned and sat down. "What's next, steer roping?"

Julian turned to him. "Val, do you ever think about what happens to guys like us when we get old?"

"My personal role model is Sean Connery. Sixty-eight years old and the babes still go for me. You can be Jack or Warren, but the God—Connery—he's mine."

Julian stared into his beer. "I think we end up alone, sitting in some expensive chair in an expensive house, looking through photo albums of who we used to be, what we used to have. I think we lose our hair and our looks and no one comes to visit us."

Val raised his hand. "Bring me a Scotch, will you?" he yelled to Lou, then he turned back to Julian. "You're as much fun as detox."

How could he make Val understand? Julian had always craved the glitz and glamour of Hollywood; he'd thought he'd die if he didn't become someone who *mattered*, and he'd gotten his wish. But the years had strung together like broken Christmas lights, and not until now—in Last Bend—had he realized what he'd given up for fame. He could see clearly how he would end up—an aging, arrogant movie star who showed up at every party, drinking too much, smoking too much, screwing any woman who got close enough. Looking, he'd always be looking . . .

Until one day he'd realize that he'd given up on finding what he was looking for, and that the ache in his heart was permanent.

Kayla had loved him, and in loving him so deeply, she'd seen the empty place in his heart. She had known that a true and lasting love couldn't grow in such shallow, rocky soil. No doubt, she'd hoped that he would come for her, a changed and better man, but deep down, she must have known. That's why she'd never told Jacey the truth about him. Why spin romantic tales about a man you'd never see again?

Lou set a glass of Scotch in front of Val. "There ye' be. Anything for you, Julian?"

"No, thanks, Lou," Julian answered.

"You're *thanking* someone? Jesus, Juli, what the hell's going on?"

Julian turned to his friend. "Kayla's made me . . . see my life, Val, and it isn't much."

Val looked thoughtful. "You're like one of those teenage girls who see the supermodels in the magazines and think they really look like that. You and me, we know about the airbrushing and the bingeing and the drug use and the Auschwitz rib cages. You're thinking that maybe you want a different life, filled with lawn mowers and block parties and Little League. But that's not who you are. Don't you know that all those real guys out there working seven-to-seven to support their snot-nosed kids and heavy-duty wives would kill to have your life for one day?"

"They can have it."

Val's eyes held an abiding sadness. "Julian, she's married."

"I know," he answered. "But what if I love her?"

The falling apart of a man's life should make noise. It should startle passersby with its Sturm und Drang. It ought to sound like the Parthenon crashing down. Not this ordinary, everyday kind of quiet.

His wife was in love with another man. There was simply no way around that; no matter how often he tried to push the thought away, it came creeping back.

Liam lay back in bed, staring up at the gauzy mosquito netting that canopied their bed. It was almost midnight, but he couldn't sleep.

He couldn't forget the images he'd seen on television tonight, or the quippy headlines that accompanied them.

True Love, after all these years.

Sleeping Beauty awakens to Prince Charming's kiss.

Every program had had photographs of Kayla, all of them showing a young, vibrant woman who was clearly in love.

It was a woman he'd never seen. Until today—this second—he'd had this hope that he would catch a glimpse, however fleeting, of his wife. But all he'd seen was image after image of *Kayla*.

Now she was neither Kayla nor Mikaela. Without memories, she was a leaf, caught up in the swirling current of a dream, but soon she would land on earth. She would remember the fifteen years they'd spent together. He had to believe that.

But what then?

She would reach out for something solid, and the thing that would steady her, her anchor, would be her love for her children. That love was the cornerstone of her soul, and nothing—not even Julian—could separate her from Jacey and Bret.

When she came back to herself, Mike would put her

kids' needs first. She always had. She'd left Julian because of Jacey and she'd married Liam because of Bret.

In the end, she would stay married to Liam. Of this, he was certain. When push came to shove, she would again sacrifice her passion for her children's welfare.

The realization brought no solace; instead it weighed him down.

Julian wasn't a threat to their marriage; Liam knew that. It was Mikaela's love for Julian that threatened everything. Before, Liam had been able to tell himself that she loved him enough. But now that he'd seen the way she looked at Julian . . .

He closed his eyes.

And still it was quiet, this falling apart of his life, as silent as the last beat of an old man's heart. A quiet, echoing thud, and then . . . nothing.

Chapter Twenty-five

Mikaela dreamt she was in the big log house.

She could hear the child crying again, and this time she was more afraid. She climbed the stairs and crossed the empty porch. Beside her, a rocking chair squeaked and moved, pushed by unseen hands.

She grabbed the doorknob and twisted, swinging the door open so hard, it cracked against the interior wall.

"Hello?" Her voice was a reedy whisper, beaten by the heaviness of her breathing.

The crying came again, louder this time.

She felt along the wall; this time she knew there was a light switch there, and when her fingers brushed it, she cried out in relief. The lights came on—an overhead chandelier crafted of deer antlers that threw a soft, golden net across a deserted dining room table. She had a quick, flashing image of herself sitting at that table, at a certain chair; she heard a voice saying, *So, kids, tell me about your day . . .*

But there was no one there, just a trio of ghostly images, the sound of forks on china, the thump of a glass hitting the planked table.

"Where are you?" she called out.

The crying came again. She felt her way past the table, up the long, wide staircase made of split logs. It felt as if there were people behind her, a crowd whispering among themselves, pushing her deeper and deeper into the darkness above, but every time she spun around, she was alone. Only her own shadow snaked out behind her as she reached the second floor.

"Mo . . . mmmy . . . Mo . . . mmmy . . ."

"Where are you?" she screamed.

Only silence.

She started to run, but this time there were no doors, no windows . . . just the child's cry.

She ran and ran, until the hallway ended in a blank wall.

"Where are you?"

She spun around. There was no hallway behind her anymore. When she looked down, she saw that she was standing on a tiny patch of carpet.

A door appeared in front of her.

Her hand was shaking as she reached for the brass knob. It turned easily. Inch by inch, she pushed the door open. Behind it lay a box of perfect blackness.

And the quiet sound of a child crying.

She touched the rough-hewn wall and a light came on.

The child was tucked in the corner, his skinny white

legs bent at an awkward angle. He was wearing flannel boxers—*like Daddy's*—and a Seattle Super-Sonics T-shirt.

He looked up at her, his pale face streaked with tears, his blue eyes magnified into pools of watery pain.

The boy from the hospital.

"Mommy?" he said.

"Bret," she cried out, falling to her knees and taking him into her arms.

Then she woke up. Memories washed over and through and around her.

She said that one simple name over and over again.

Bret. Bret. Bret. The child she'd turned away from, said nothing to when he leaned down and kissed her forehead with all the gentleness of a butterfly's landing.

Her baby boy.

She reached for the phone, but before she dialed a number, she noticed the wall clock. It was three o'clock in the morning.

She couldn't call yet. She closed her eyes and leaned back into the pillows, letting the memories come again.

Mikaela woke with a start. She glanced at the clock. Nine-thirty.

"Damn it." The kids were already at school.

She saw the tray of food by her bed. It looked disgusting. She couldn't imagine how anyone was supposed to actually recuperate if they ate this garbage.

With a sigh, she pushed the tray away.

She closed her eyes and thought of all the things she'd remembered last night.

Bret. Jacey. Her precious children. She couldn't remember every single thing, but she remembered most of it.

Julian. She remembered all the days and nights she'd waited by the phone for his call, the countless times she'd cried herself to sleep, waiting. Waiting . . .

And Liam. She remembered the hows and whys of her love for him . . . and how it had never been enough for her.

She'd spent years waiting for Julian to come back to her, but at some point, she'd had to go on with her life. She'd enrolled in school and become a nurse, and taken a job in this very building.

She'd first met Liam in his father's hospital room. She'd been so lonely then, so lost. She'd read about Julian's new marriage and it had broken her spirit. When Liam finally asked her out, she'd said yes.

She'd known that Liam fell in love with her almost instantly, and though she hadn't felt the same, she'd needed someone to love her, someone to care about her. Day by day, Liam had shown her how it felt to be truly wanted.

Still, when she found out she was pregnant, she'd felt trapped. She could remember every nuance of the day she'd told him.

They'd been out at Angel Falls, their favorite spot, stretched out on a blanket. When she told him about the baby, he stifled a laugh of joy, and then, quietly, asked her to marry him.

She'd told him some of her past. She'd said, *I've been married before. I loved him with all my heart and soul. I'm afraid I'll love him until I die.*

I see, he'd said. But she was the one who could see. She was breaking his heart, this gentle, caring man who loved her the way she loved Julian. She'd wanted to believe that they could be happy. And in many ways they had been. She had grown to love Liam, but never had she fallen head over heels in love. In truth, she'd never allowed herself to; she saw that now.

She'd always been secretly waiting for Julian. Down deep, in that place reserved for true love, she'd kept a single candle burning for his return. Because of that, her love for Liam had been thin and brittle, a layer of ice on a bottomless blue lake. How could it be more when Julian was already there, taking up too much space in her heart?

She didn't know if she'd regretted it then—that was something she couldn't seem to remember—or if she'd ever let herself look closely enough to see it. But she regretted it now, regretted it with a ferocity that was nearly desperation.

Her past felt like a huge and tangled fishing net, filled with debris, and she wondered if she could ever untangle it enough to find the pearls that had to be hidden in the mess.

Now, whenever she closed her eyes—and sometimes even when she didn't—she saw the flickering reel of her whole life. It was everywhere, in the dozens of floral arrangements and green plants that filled this tiny room, in the accordion of get-well cards that lined her windowsill, in the pad of phone messages that the nurses brought in to her each day.

In Last Bend, she'd found a place where she *belonged*. And the saddest part was, she was certain that she hadn't recognized that. For years, she'd thought that she was an outsider here. Even as she'd volunteered for a dozen different charitable events and organized the Bits-n-Spurs 4-H club, as she'd sat down to dinner at friends' houses and sipped punch with people after church, she'd always believed that she didn't belong. It was, she realized, an ugly bit of baggage that she'd carried here from her youth, and she'd been so damned busy hanging on to it that she'd failed to notice that the bags were empty.

She was so deep in thought, she didn't hear the knock at the door.

Rosa stood in the doorway. She looked old and tired, and for once, her white hair wasn't held hostage in a tight braid. She wore a pair of crisply creased black pants and a red turtleneck sweater. In her arms, she held a big, square book.

Mikaela maneuvered herself to a sit. "*Recuerdo mi vida, Mama,*" she said softly, not even bothering with hello.

Rosa stumbled, then went still, her wide brown eyes focused on Mikaela's face. "You remember? All of it?"

"How's Bret . . . after yesterday?"

"A *milagro*." Rosa moved again, taking shuffling steps toward the bed. Her smile was gentle. "He is fine. This boy of yours, he has a hardy heart. And, of course, Dr. Liam was there."

Mikaela swallowed hard. "Can I see the kids now?"

"Bret is on a field trip today. His class went eagle watching at Rockport—it is the migration time. Jacey has a social studies presentation to give at noon. It is half of her grade."

Mikaela sagged back, disappointed. "Oh. I guess life goes on, eh, Mama?"

"It is for a short time, only. I will bring them to your room this afternoon, *si*?" Rosa handed Mikaela the big leather book she was holding. "This is for you."

Mikaela touched the fine leather. "*Muy caro, eh, Mama?*"

"Sometimes it is good to spend the money. Myrtle—your friend at the drugstore—she told me that you have wanted this for a long time."

That was something Mikaela couldn't remember, but she did know that she'd been meaning to put together a family scrapbook for years. Another entry in her endless stack of somedays. "*Gracias,* Mama. It's beautiful."

"Ah, you did not used to be so *stupido*. Open it."

Mikaela's mouth fell open. "*Stupido? Stupido?*" Her mother never talked like that. "A little respect for the recently brain damaged, if you don't mind."

Rosa shrugged. "*Lo siento.* Lately I have spent much time with a little boy, and he has changed me. Yesterday I actually said that a cartoon was *rad.*"

"That's my Bretster. Last year everything was either awesome or puke-o-rama. Now it's rad." Mikaela opened the book. The first page was a sheer piece of crinkled tissue, inset with dried violets. On a panel in the middle, in Rosa's careful hand, were the words *Mikaela Conchita Luna True Campbell.*

It made her sound like she belonged on a throne. Slowly she turned the page, and there, alone against a sea of white paper, was a dog-eared old black-and-white Kodak print.

It was a picture of her and her mother. In the background was the shack they'd lived in during apple harvest, twelve to a room with no working bathroom.

The memories of that time were still buried in Mikaela's heart, as jagged and sharp as bits of glass. Those were the days that had shaped Mikaela's spirit, snipped the edges off her dreams.

For all of her life, Mikaela had been running away from these memories, as if with enough speed she could distance herself from the truth. Now, she was standing still at last and she saw the past for what it had been. She saw these photographs not as a child, rather as a mother. Rosa had had no choices. Without an education, a poor Hispanic woman who barely spoke the language had no way out, except—

She looked up at her mother. "I would have done it, too, Mama."

"Done what?"

"William . . . the house . . . If Jacey had crawled into my arms and looked at me with sad, hungry eyes, I would have done it, too."

It was the first time Mikaela had ever seen her mother cry. "I would give anything to have loved him less and myself more, but I cannot regret that my sin gave you a chance for something better."

"I'm sorry it took me so long to say."

Impatiently, Rosa wiped her eyes. "Keep looking."

Mikaela turned the next page, then the next, and saw the few photographs of her childhood.

Then came the wedding picture. Julian and Kayla.

Mikaela gasped. *This* she had hidden. She remembered that; this photograph had been in a pillowcase in her—

"Liam found these while I was in the coma," she said in a dull voice.

Softly, sadly, *"Sí."*

She could hardly imagine the pain it must have caused Liam to see her life in such vivid shots. She'd kept Julian hidden, both because no man could live up to such competition, and—if she was honest—because she couldn't give up this secret obsession she called true love. She'd wanted the piece of herself that loved Julian to be hers alone. Not even Jacey was allowed to share him.

Maybe she'd been afraid that if she exposed her true feelings, if she talked about him as if he were someone ordinary, just a first husband, she'd fall out of love with him. And the thought of not loving Julian was more than she could bear. It had defined her for so long.

Mikaela turned the pages slowly, mesmerized by the images of the life she'd led.

She had forgotten how young she was when she married Julian.

At first, in the pictures, she was bright and beautiful and always smiling, but as the photos accumulated, she saw how thin she'd grown, how jaded her look had become.

In all the photographs of Mike with Jacey, it was just the two of them, alone. No smiling father. And later, as they waited for Julian, the pictures of them had been taken by strangers.

She sighed. "Oh, Mama."

Rosa flipped through a few pages, until she found the first pictures with Liam. "You see it?"

"See what?"

"Your smile. It is coming back here. I notice this the first time you send me pictures of you and Liam."

An aching sadness spread through Mikaela. "Why didn't I love him, Mama? What's wrong with me?"

"You know the answer to this question."

"I've made a mess of my life."

Rosa laughed. "You are young. It takes many years to truly make a mess of your life. This I know about."

Mikaela turned to her. "How will I fix it?"

Rosa's smile faded. "Let me tell you something else I know. When you hide things away, and keep them secret, they have a . . . power. Take your life apart, Mikita, look at it for once . . . and maybe you will be surprised at what you see."

Chapter Twenty-six

Mikaela counted the moments until she could see her children. After Rosa left, Mike had spent an hour with the physical therapist, trying to relearn how to gracefully use a spoon. Who would have thought it would be so damned *complicated* to stick a spoon in a bowl of oatmeal and get the gruel to your own mouth? At one point, she'd wanted to hurl the whole breakfast at the wall. Then she'd remember why it was that men had temper tantrums and women didn't: cleanup.

Now it was nearly noon. She stood at the small window of her room, staring out at the parking lot below. The outdoor Christmas decorations were in place. Multicolored bulbs twined around the street-lamps. At night, she knew, the sparkly lights transformed even this ordinary parking lot into a winter wonderland.

It saddened her, this evidence of the coming holidays. Usually she was a Christmas addict, a whirling dervish who maniacally put up decorations and gathered her children around her on the sofa for the yearly viewings of *It's a Wonderful Life* and *Miracle on 34th Street*. This year all she felt was a yawning, aching sense of loss. She couldn't get a true sense of where she belonged anymore, and somehow, at Christmas, that sense of being lost was even worse.

There was a knock at the door.

Mikaela turned so fast she stumbled. Her right leg was still weak, and it couldn't keep up with such quick movements. She clutched the windowsill and hung on to avoid falling onto that ugly speckled linoleum floor.

Liam stood in the doorway. He looked awkward and uncertain, his tall, lanky body tilted to one side, his too-long hair falling across one eye. Quietly he closed the door behind him. He moved into the room but stopped short of her.

She could see the uncertainty in his eyes; he didn't know where he stood with her. And how could he, now that he knew everything she'd hidden from him? She felt an overwhelming shame. She'd hurt him so much . . .

"Hello, Liam." She wanted to say more, but she didn't know where to start; she didn't know if there even *was* a beginning that could take them where they needed to go.

He looked at her, still unsmiling. "Rosa tells me that you've regained a huge chunk of your memories."

She let go of the windowsill and limped toward him, holding her weakened right arm against her suddenly upset stomach. "Yes. There are still a few blank spots, but a lot of it's back."

"That's great." There was no enthusiasm in his voice, just a dull flatness that didn't sound like him at all.

She gazed up at him, noticing the network of lines that had gathered around his eyes. They were new lines, etched on by the trauma of her injury.

I love you, Liam. Those were the words he needed to hear. She could have said it, easily in fact. She did love him; she always had. But it was a watery version that had more to do with comfort and friendship than passion.

If only Julian were simply the first man she'd loved. That would have left room in her heart for falling in love with Liam. Hardly anyone stayed with their first lover anymore.

But Julian was more than that. She'd always called it love, what she felt for him; now, standing here with her husband, she saw what it truly was: obsession.

First love was like a sweet song that turned you weepy and nostalgic. Obsession, she knew, was different; a dark and secret need that never mellowed into something pretty. A first love could someday let you go. An obsession, she was afraid, held on to your throat until you died.

"I don't want to hurt you, Liam," she said softly.

He smiled. It was sad and tired, that smile, worn as thin as ancient blacktop. "I don't know what to say to you anymore, Mike. It's like . . . treading water in the deep end."

"Liam—"

He held up a hand. "Let me finish. I've got some things that have to be said. You could have told me more of the truth, you know. We might have had a chance if you had."

Mikaela turned away from him and limped toward her bed, climbing in, pulling the sheets up to her chin—as if a little layer of cotton and acrylic could shield her from the emotional punch of his words. "I know."

A flash of anger darkened his green eyes, but was gone almost before it began, replaced by a resignation that tore at her heart. "Don't you know what it was like for me . . . loving you all those years, *knowing* it wasn't enough for you, and needing so goddamn badly for you to love me back?" He sighed. "I love you, Mike. I've loved you from the moment I first saw you . . ."

"I only did it because I knew you," she said. "I knew what it had been like for you, growing up in Ian's shade. I didn't want you to always wonder about Julian. I thought . . . if you didn't know who he was, you'd be able to forget I'd been married. Same with Jacey—I thought Julian would be too . . . big for a child to ever forget, and she needed you as a father so much."

"I know all that, Mike." He said her name softly, on a sigh. "I just want to say this: no more lies. That's all I'm asking. While you were sleeping, I woke up. Before, I could hold on to the illusion that someday it would change. I kept thinking I could love enough for both of us, but I couldn't, could I?" He touched her face with a gentleness that made her want to weep. "Maybe you were right to hide the past from me. When I didn't know, I could pretend not to see the little things. I let you have your secrets and your silences and your sadnesses. Can you imagine what those silences would do to me now? I'd constantly be wondering, Is she thinking of *him*?"

She could feel the tearing of her heart, and the pain of it was worse than anything she'd ever imagined.

She'd planted the seeds of that pain herself and fertilized them over the years with her own obsession.

He leaned toward her and held her face in his strong, steady hands, and very slowly, he kissed her. In that one, tender touching of lips was all the heartache and desperation and joy of a deep and lasting love.

While she was still gasping for an even breath, he turned and left the room.

It was three o'clock. An hour until the kids would be here.

Mikaela lay in bed, staring dully at the television tucked up into the corner of the ceiling. In beautiful black-and-white images, *It's a Wonderful Life* unfolded.

It was nearing the end now. George Bailey—Jimmy Stewart—had just realized what the world was without him, and everything he'd always wanted and longed for had changed. He was tearing into that drafty old house now, breaking off the banister . . .

As always, Mikaela was crying, but this time she

wasn't crying for George Bailey; she was crying for herself. When the townspeople started showing up with their money to save the savings and loan, she automatically looked for Liam, to tell him that his favorite scene was on.

But there was no Liam beside her, no Christmas tree in the corner, no children rattling packages under the tree and whining that they'd seen this movie a billion times.

She threw the covers back, got up, and walked to the closet. There, sitting forlornly beneath a row of empty hangers, was a small brown leather suitcase. She reached down and picked it up with her left hand—the right one was still too weak to use—and dragged it to the bed, flipping it onto the mattress. Then she unlatched the small brass closures; the suitcase twanged open.

She ran her fingers across the clothing. It had to be Liam's doing, this artful arrangement of her favorite things. A black broomstick skirt and white turtleneck, with a matching tapestry vest. The silver concho belt she always wore with the skirt. A pair of black riding boots. Bra and panties. He'd even remembered her favorite gold hoop earrings—the ones that dangled a pair of cherub angels. And all of her makeup, even her hairbrush and perfume.

She couldn't help thinking how it must have been for him as he'd stood in her huge, walk-in closet, choosing clothing to go in a suitcase that might never be opened . . .

She would have grabbed anything to get out of

that closet, stuffed mismatched clothing in a brown paper bag.

But not Liam. No matter how much it hurt, he would have stood there, thinking, choosing, touching. She imagined that if she looked closely enough, there would be tiny gray tear spots on the white cotton of the turtleneck.

She stripped out of the flimsy hospital gown and tossed it onto the molded pink chair. It was difficult to dress herself—her right hand was barely any help at all—but she kept at it, pulling and tugging and strapping and buttoning until it was done.

Then she went into the bathroom and wet down her hair, combing it back from her face. There was no way she could put on makeup with her left hand, so she settled for pinching her cheeks.

She walked down the hall, with no idea where she was going. When she ended up at the hospital chapel, she realized she must have been heading there all along.

Kneeling in front of the utilitarian Formica altar, she stared up at the brass cross, then closed her eyes and imagined the altar at St. Michael's.

"Please, God, help me. Show me the way home."

At first there was only darkness. Then a small, yellow ray of piercing sunlight. She heard voices as if from far away, a child's high-pitched giggle, a man speaking to her softly.

She saw herself at a funeral, standing back, away from the group of mourners at the grave site. *Ian's funeral*. The melancholy strains of a lone bagpipe filled the cold winter's air. Liam turned and saw her. She barely knew him, and yet she was moving toward him. She took his hand and walked him back to the car. They didn't say a word. He got into the limousine, and she watched him drive away . . .

The image shifted, went in and out of focus. After that, the memories came one after another, unconnected by time or space, just the random moments of life. She and Liam dancing at last year's Tex-Mex hoedown . . . him drying the dishes while she washed them . . . him driving her to the feed store in that rickety red truck they called "the heapster."

She'd remembered her marriage to Liam, but this was the first time she'd *felt* it.

She was afraid to open her eyes. "More," she pleaded, "show me more . . ."

Midnight Mass. Last year. They were in the front row, all four of them wearing their Sunday best. Bret's hair was still wet, and all through the service, he kept wiping droplets away from his cheeks. It made her smile, remembering that even then, on Christmas Eve, they'd fought about him taking a shower. He'd put it off until the last minute, and so he'd gone to church with wet hair.

She saw the four of them clearly, like strands of a rope, twisted together; they strengthened one another.

Slowly she opened her eyes. The cross blurred in front of her; the silk flowers on the altar became a smear of faded colors. She stared down at the wedding ring on her left hand.

"I hurt Liam," she whispered, whether to herself or

to God, she didn't know. All she knew was that it was almost unbearable, this knowledge of how much she had hurt him over the years. How much she was hurting him at this very moment.

She closed her eyes again and bowed her head. This time she didn't want a memory—each one seemed to cut clear through to her bones—but it came anyway. She and Liam were in this hospital, in the waiting room. Bret was in surgery. The doctors had spoken of screws and plates and a hand that might never be able to make a fist again.

She and Liam had stood apart from each other, he at the window, she by the sofa. The fear between them was so dense, it made the walls and furniture look black. She was desperate to find a way to comfort her husband, this quiet, loving man who asked for so little. Slowly she got up from her chair and went to him. When she touched his shoulder, he seemed to crumble. He turned and said, *I shouldn't have let him go.* She took him in her arms and held him. All she said to him was, *It's not your fault.* At those simple words, the strongest man she'd ever met buried his face in the crook of her neck and cried like a little boy.

She felt as if she were looking at the moment from far, far away, through another woman's eyes. From a distance, she knew exactly what she was seeing. Love. Pure and simple.

See? You know what love is, Mikaela.

She heard the words as clearly as the ringing of a church bell. She opened her eyes and looked around. There was no one there.

Slowly she smiled. The Virgin had spoken to her at last, after all these years of prayer.

Surprisingly, the Blessed Mother sounded exactly like Rosa.

Chapter Twenty-seven

Mikaela was back in her room, pacing, when the knock came.

Suddenly she was nervous. She had hurt them all so badly . . . what if her family didn't forgive her?

She shuffled away from the window and went to stand by the bed. She gripped the bed rail with her right hand; in her anxiety, she barely noticed that her fingers were working better.

The door opened and Jacey stood in the doorway, looking as nervous as Mikaela felt.

Mikaela limped toward her daughter. With her weakened right hand, she reached out and touched Jacey's cheek. "Hello, Jace."

"I'm . . . sorry, Mom. I shouldn't have yelled at you."

"Oh, baby . . ." Mikaela swallowed hard. "Don't ever apologize for your feelings." She moved closer. "There are still a lot of gaps in my memory. I don't remember your first day of school, or how old you were when you lost your first tooth. I've driven myself crazy trying to find these moments in my messed-up brain, but I can't. But I remember that I love you. I love you more than my own life, and I can't believe how I've hurt you."

Jacey's eyes filled with tears.

"You know what I do remember? Our last girls' day out, when we drove down to the Guild 45th theater in Seattle and watched *Gone With the Wind.* I remember sitting in all that darkness, holding your hand." She took a deep breath. She knew she was stalling; this was not what Jacey had come to hear, and it wasn't what Mikaela needed to say. "That night we had dinner at Canlis, remember? The Christmas ships were on Lake Washington. That was one of a dozen times in the last few years when I tried to tell you about Julian."

Jacey looked unconvinced, a little afraid, a little angry, a little sad. Mikaela had watched her daughter's face for so many years that no nuance of emotion was missed. "Why didn't you tell me?" Jacey asked.

Mikaela had answered this question in her head so many times. Still, she was uncertain. Even now, after all that had happened, she didn't want to tell Jacey the whole truth.

"No more lies, Mom," Jacey said.

"I know, *querida*. But I don't want to hurt you. All the lies were for that reason."

"Tell me all of it."

"I loved Julian too much. When I married him and moved to California, I became someone else, a *gringa* named Kayla True who had no past at all. It was what I'd always wanted. Your *abuela* tried to tell me that he was no good for me, but I wouldn't listen. I loved him so . . .

"In Hollywood I . . . lost myself. Not just the poor Hispanic girl I'd been, but more. *Me.* I did many things of which I am ashamed." She tried to smile and failed. "But then I got pregnant. You brought me back to me. I knew what I wanted for you, even if I'd lost track of what I wanted for me. I knew the life I wanted to give you. And Julian . . . well, he wasn't ready to be a father."

Tears beaded Jacey's eyes. "He didn't want me."

Mikaela took a deep breath. There was nowhere to go now except forward. "No." She took Jacey's hands, held them tightly. "But I wanted you and I wanted to give you the kind of childhood I hadn't known. So I left Julian."

"But you loved him."

"Yes."

A tear streaked down Jacey's cheek and Mikaela forced herself not to wipe it away. Some tears were meant to fall, had to fall. This was one of the many truths she'd failed to see in her life.

"You know what I remember?" Jacey said in a soft, fluttery voice. "When I was little, I used to ask you about my daddy. Every time I did, you cried, until I stopped asking. I ruined it for you, didn't I?"

"No. Don't ever say that." Mikaela squeezed her daughter's hand so tightly, she felt the thin bones shift. "I ruined it for me . . . for a while. Then I met

Liam . . . and I found myself again. I know I've been dishonest with you and Liam, and I'll have to find a way to make that right. Together we are a family, and that's what we need to remember. We'll get through this hard time."

"Are you coming home?"

Home. The word elicited a memory so clear, Mikaela could have pressed it under glass and framed it.

Liam is sitting at the piano, wearing cut-off shorts and that ridiculous T-shirt he got at last year's doctors' convention. It reads: VIAGRA—KEEP YOUR SUPPLY UP. *There are two wineglasses on the shining ebony surface of the piano. He is playing her favorite song: "A Time for Us."*

She comes up behind him, touches his shoulder. "Hey, piano man, get your wife to bed or lose your chance."

He turns, smiles up at her, and it is there, in his eyes, the love, the welcome, the need she's seen so many times and—until now—always taken for granted.

Mikaela laughed. She knew it was an inappropriate response, but she couldn't help herself. The joy inside her was so big, so dizzyingly unexpected, that she wouldn't have been surprised to look down and see that she was floating. "Come here, Jacey." She opened her arms for a hug.

Mikaela clung to her daughter. God, it felt so good.

"Oh, Mom . . . I missed you. I was afraid—"

"Shhh. I know." She stroked Jacey's hair. "I know, baby . . ."

It came to her then, wrapped in the scent of her

daughter's hair, caught in the sticky dampness of tears, and Mikaela laughed and cried at the same time. "Oh . . . there it is! I remember your first day of school. You wore a black corduroy jumper and carried a Fraggle Rock lunch box. You wouldn't get on the bus without me, so I went with you. I was the only mom there."

Jacey drew back and smiled up at her. "I love you, Mom."

"Oh, Jace, I love you, too, and I'm so sorry for ev—"

The door burst open. Bret and Rosa stood in the doorway. Rosa shrugged. "He thought that Jacey had enough time."

Mikaela kissed Jacey's damp cheek and drew back.

Bret stood motionless, his arms belted to his sides, his little hands curled into fists. His mouth was trembling and there was a look of fear in his eyes. This fear and uncertainty, he'd learned recently. The boy she'd raised was fearless . . . not this hesitant child.

The smile she gave him was weak and watery, and she could see that it scared him more. It wasn't her smile at all.

She started to cry; there was no way to stop it. She knelt in front of him and opened her arms. "So, how's my favorite boy in the whole world?"

He screamed "Mommy!" and flung himself into her waiting arms so hard that they toppled backward.

She lay there on the ugly linoleum floor, squeezing her son until neither one of them could breathe.

"I love you, Bretster," she whispered against his small, pink ear. He buried his face in the crook of her neck. She felt, more than heard, his broken voice when he whispered back, "I love you, too, Mommy."

At last they drew apart and climbed awkwardly to their knees. Mikaela's weak right leg was trembling so badly, she couldn't get to her feet. She stayed kneeling, unable to let go of Bret's hand.

Over his head, she looked at Rosa, who was crying now, too.

Mikaela sniffled. "Too bad we can't sell all this water to the Californians."

Bret giggled. It was what Liam always said when Mikaela cried over a stupid movie.

She smiled at her son. "So, kiddo, what's new with you?"

"Sally May Randle has a crush on me. She smells bad, but she's sorta pretty."

Mikaela laughed, mesmerized by the ordinariness of it, seized by a sudden hope. Maybe, with time, they could all find their way out of the woods and back onto the main road. "Where's Daddy?" she asked Bret.

Bret bit his lip and didn't answer.

Rosa looked down at Mikaela. "He did not come."

"He's at home," Bret said. "I think he's sad 'cause you didn't remember him."

Mikaela grabbed the bed rail and dragged herself to a stand. She looked at Rosa. "Take the kids home, Mama. I'm going to check out of the hospital and meet you there."

Rosa frowned. "The doctors say—"

"I don't care." She started to say more, then

changed her mind. "Please, Mama, take them home. I'll be right there."

Rosa swallowed hard. "What are you going to do, Mikita?"

"Please, Mama."

Rosa sighed. "*Sí*. But, Mikaela, stay away from the front doors. The reporters, they are waiting for you."

Jacey moved toward Mikaela. "I don't want to leave you, Mom."

"There's nothing to be afraid of anymore, honey. I'll be home soon."

"You promise?"

Mikaela smiled. "I promise."

After they left, Mikaela decided not to bother checking out of the hospital right now. There would be time enough for technicalities tomorrow. She called for a cab, then carefully packed up all the photographs from the bedside tables and windowsills. At the last minute, she folded up her hospital gown and placed it gently on top of the things in the suitcase—to remind her always of this time. She didn't ever want to forget any part of it. It was the coma that had saved her life. She prayed only that she had not awakened too late. That was one thing she knew now. Some chances came and went, and if you missed them, you could spend the rest of your life standing alone, waiting for an opportunity that had already passed you by.

She'd been unconscious for over a month. In reality, she had slept through the last fifteen years of her life.

Someone knocked at her door.

She froze, her heart thumping in her chest. Her gaze darted to the packed suitcase and empty table. *Please don't let it be a nurse*—

Julian strode into the room as if he belonged there. "I started sneezing this morning. I think I'm developing an allergy to this Podunk town." He grinned. "You should see the hoopla goin' on on Main Street. Grown men are walking around in Sasquatch costumes."

Glacier Days. She'd forgotten all about it.

In ordinary times, Liam would have been dressed in one of the Bigfoot costumes Mikaela spent hours putting together. Every year he grumbled about his dignity, and every year he ran in the race for charity.

"Kayla?"

She limped toward Julian. When she was close enough to touch him, she stopped. Finally she saw him, the man and not the myth. He was still devastatingly handsome, still a shooting star in a dark sky that wasn't quite big enough to contain his magic. But when she looked past that, she saw what had been there all along, what had swept her up and then broken her to bits. She didn't need to see Julian and Liam side by side to recognize the difference between tinfoil and sterling silver.

"Oh, Julian." She said his name in a soft and tender voice that held a lifetime's regret.

"I don't like the way you're looking at me."

"Of course you don't. You want to be watched, not seen." It was true, she realized. His was the magician's life, full of illusion and sleight of hand, where only one man saw what was behind the curtain.

"Kayla, I've been doing a lot of thinking lately. I realized how much I've missed you."

"Oh, Jules." She sighed. It saddened her that she'd given up so much of her life waiting for this cubic zirconia moment. As if they could simply ride off into the sunset together. She'd forgotten that they'd already gone that direction once. It had taken them to a place so bright and hot that everything they were burned down to ash.

He flashed her the grin she'd seen a million times, the one that used to curl her toes and make her heart lurch into overdrive. "I know you've missed me, too."

At her look, his smile faded.

"What?" he asked, his voice uncharacteristically uncertain.

How did you tell a man that at last you'd grown up, that you'd learned true love wasn't a night of passionate sex under a sky lit up by fireworks, but an ordinary Sunday morning when your husband brought you a glass of water, two aspirins, and a heating pad for your cramps?

"I used to have a dream," she began, gazing up at him. "It started right after I left you. It changed a little over the years, but the point of it was always the same. In the dream, I'm an old woman with flowing white hair. My children have grown up and moved on and had children of their own. Liam is gone; he's been dead for many, many years.

"I imagine myself on a pink-sand beach. There is a

white cottage behind me, and I know it is my home, where I live alone. I am sitting on the beach in a portable chair, as I do every day, all day. And one day I look up and an old man is coming for me. It's you, Jules. I realize then that I've waited fifty years for you to show up. You tell me that you've given it all up for me. You're not Julian True anymore. You're the other man, an ordinary man, the one whose name you never gave me."

"Mel," he answered softly. "My name is Melvin Atwood Coddington the Third." He tried to smile, as if anything about this moment were funny. "Who would have guessed that Gibson would do so well with it?"

She touched his face. "You should have been Melvin."

"What are you saying?"

"Last night I had the dream again—only I wasn't alone on the beach anymore. I was sitting with Liam, watching our grandchildren play in the water." She gazed up at him. "I love him more than you can imagine, Jules. I only hope it's not too late to tell him that."

"I know he loves you, Kayla."

She felt an aching sadness for all the things that could have been, for all the things she'd lost while waiting for what could never be. "There is no Kayla, Jules. There never was. And you were never Melvin."

His voice was thick. "It sounds like you're saying good-bye."

"Oh, Jules, we said good-bye a long, long time ago. I'm only just now getting around to leaving." She caressed his cheek, let her fingers linger there for a moment, then slowly she drew back her hand and headed for the door.

"Wait! You can't just walk out of here. The press is waiting at the front door. I'll go make a statement, then I'll pick you up at the back door and take you . . ." He paused, said softly, "Home."

She turned back to him. "What will you tell them?"

He looked sad. "I'll tell them the story's over. That Sleeping Beauty found her Prince. They might . . . follow you for a while."

She smiled. "And cover my glamorous life? After ten minutes, they'll realize that the ordinary life of a small-town doctor's wife is hardly front-page news."

"I'll be right back with the limo. I'll meet you around back." He gave her a last, heavy look, then turned and left.

Mikaela reached for her suitcase, then decided to leave it in the closet. It was too unwieldy for her to carry, and it would only arouse suspicion. She called and canceled the cab. Empty-handed, she left her room. She kept her head down, and her side brushed against the wall as she made her slow, limping way down the hospital corridors.

When she opened the door, the first thing she noticed was the evergreen smell of Christmas. Green pine needles and fresh snow. A dark purple sky filled with the first few evening stars made her feel small. She smiled; that was what she expected from the sky. All her life, she'd gone out at night and stood beneath all that blue velvet darkness. It was her temple, the

true house of her God, and it never failed to remind
her of her place.

She liked feeling small. It had been the wanting to
feel big that had led her to Julian.

The limousine pulled up, the door opened, and she
got inside.

Chapter Twenty-eight

The limo crawled through town at the posted speed limit of ten miles per hour. Outside, there were people everywhere, moving in gray clouds of exhaled breath, walking beneath banners that read: WELCOME TO GLACIER DAYS.

Julian couldn't take his eyes off Mikaela, although she rarely looked at him. She directed the driver out of town, onto a back road where trees outnumbered houses a thousand to one. They turned into a driveway, passed beneath an arch announcing ANGEL FALLS RANCH.

Acres of white pastures rolled away from the road on either side, bracketed by four-rail fencing. Beneath a huge old tree, a dozen horses stood, their big butts turned into the wind.

Mikaela touched the smoked-glass windows. "Hi, babies," she murmured to the horses. "I missed you."

At last the house came into view; it was a beautiful log structure set against the serrated black mountains.

White icicle Christmas lights hung from the eaves and made the house look like a princess's castle.

The car pulled up in front of the house and stopped. The driver—Julian could never remember his name—hurried around to their door.

"Thank you," she said to the young man as she got out.

Julian realized that not once in all these weeks had he offered the driver those simple words. He got out of the car and stood beside Kayla. She shivered with cold and he put an arm around her.

"It's beautiful, isn't it?" she said, speaking of the house.

He looked down at her, only her. "The most beautiful thing I've ever seen."

The driver got back into the car and shut the door, giving them privacy.

Kayla turned to him. "Come in with me, Jules. Meet your daughter."

He saw the sorrow in her eyes, and he knew that she understood what hadn't yet been said. Still, as always, she expected the best of him. It was, he knew now, one of the things he loved most about her. In all the world, she was the only one who had ever wanted him to reach for the man he could be.

He hated to hurt her again, to remind her of the painful truth. "You know I can't."

"Oh, Julian . . ." She said his name on a sigh of disappointment, a sound more intimate and knowing than any kiss they ever shared.

"If I walked through those doors, it would be a lie. We both know that. I don't want to do to Jacey what I did to you."

She looked at him and tried to smile.

It broke his heart, that soft realization in her beautiful eyes. "Tell me you'll always love me," he whispered.

She touched his cheek. In the coldness, her touch was a brand that burned his flesh. "I'll always love who we were."

He felt and heard the continent that lay between his question and her answer. He knew as certainly as he'd ever known anything that this time he would miss her forever. When his fans had died and the women no longer followed him, he would sit in a leather chair in his lonely house and dream of this woman who had once and truly loved him.

He reached down for her left hand. The plain gold band glittered in the pale glow of the limo's headlights. "Do you still have the wedding ring I gave you?"

"Of course."

"Give it to Jacey. Tell her . . ."

"What, Jules?"

"Tell her that out here, somewhere, is a man who wishes he were different."

"*Be* different, Jules. Come in with me. You know Liam, he'll make a place for you."

"Liam's not the problem. I wish . . ." He couldn't say it.

"What do you wish?"

Somewhere a branch snapped in the breeze, and it sounded dangerously like the breaking of his own brittle heart. "I wish I could love you the way he does."

He didn't want her to answer, so he pulled her into his arms and kissed her for the last time. "Good-bye . . . Mikaela."

She turned away from him and limped through the snow. One last time, she stopped at looked at him. "Good-bye, Julian True." It was spoken so softly, he wondered later if he'd imagined it.

The house smelled of evergreen boughs and baking apple pie, of hollyberry candles and a newly stoked fire. Mikaela paused in the doorway, breathing in the welcoming scent of *home*. She could see her mother in the kitchen, alone, wiping down the tile countertops. Rose looked up suddenly. Mikaela pressed a finger to her lips and moved silently forward. As she passed the living room, she saw Liam sitting at the piano. Last year's Sasquatch costume lay heaped on the floor by his feet.

"Where are the kids?" Mike whispered to her mother.

Rosa pointed upstairs. "They are cleaning their bedrooms for you."

Mike nodded. She could imagine how their bedrooms must look. No doubt Bret had at least a thousand chewy-bar wrappers strung across his desk. He'd probably talked Rosa into buying him Twinkies and

Ding Dongs. "Keep them busy for a few minutes, will you?"

"*Si.*" Rosa started to turn away.

Mikaela touched her mother's arm. "*Gracias,* Mama. For everything."

"*De nada, mi hija.*" With a quick smile, Rosa headed out of the kitchen and hurried upstairs.

Mikaela took a deep breath. It disconcerted her to see Liam at the piano, with his hands in his lap. She'd missed his music. She hadn't realized until this moment how much a part of her it had become. Every moment and memory in her life seemed to be accompanied by some piece of music drawn from her husband's heart.

She tiptoed into the living room. A brightly lit Christmas tree stood in the corner, a thousand sparkling lights reflected in the black picture window. It was the first year ever that she hadn't chosen the tree and directed the placement of each ornament; it saddened her, this evidence that somehow her family had . . . gone on.

When she was directly behind Liam, she paused and closed her eyes. *Please, God, don't let it be too late.*

"Liam?"

He spun around so fast his knees cracked into the piano bench. When he saw her, he frowned, running a hand through his too-long hair. "You should be at the hospital," he said, looking awkward and uncertain.

"Tell me it's not too late."

He looked confused. "What do you mean?"

She sat down beside him, laid her hand on his

forearm. She needed to be touching him, and yet she was afraid to do more. "I wish I were smarter. I know there are words I need right now and I can't find them. For twelve years, you loved the woman I wanted to be. I used to look at you sometimes, especially when you were with the kids, and the ache in my heart . . . I *wanted* to be the kind of wife you deserved. I just . . . couldn't."

He stroked her hair, and she knew that the tenderness of his touch was as natural as breathing. "I know that, Mike, but—"

"I love you." She flung the words at him, wincing at the high, tinny edge of desperation in her voice.

He yanked his hand back. "Mike, please . . ."

"I love you," she said, softer this time. "I want to grow old with you, Liam Campbell. I want to sit on our porch and sip lemonade and watch our children grow up and go on and have children of their own. I want to fix holiday dinners for all of us, and watch our grandchildren learn to walk and talk and have them fall asleep in our arms." She gazed up at him.

For the first time, she knew it was in her eyes, all the bits and pieces and scraps of love she'd collected over the years. Love, as pure and clean as rainwater, as complex as memories themselves. It was all for him, for this gentle, steady man who'd always been there for her, whose heart she had so carelessly broken in a thousand little ways, in the things she hadn't said. Hadn't felt.

"What about Julian?" he asked quietly.

For once, the beloved name hit the hard shell of her

rib cage and clattered away. No piece of it reached the tender walls of her heart. "He will always be a part of me . . . but now, I can put him where he belongs—in the past. Part of my wayward youth that was lived too hard and too fast and in a world that wasn't real." She caressed his cheek; it was a soft, fleeting touch. She hadn't the courage for more. "It was real, what I felt for Jules; I'll never deny that. No more lying to myself or to you or the kids. I loved Julian True. But it was a fragile love that didn't pass the test of time. When it broke apart, I never let it go. I held the pieces together, thinking—dreaming—that they'd magically fuse again. I was so busy holding them, I never noticed the emptiness in my hands." Tears stung her eyes. "I was a fool, Liam. And it took a smack upside the head to make me see the truth. *You're* the one I love, and if you'll give me another chance, I'll love you until the day I die. You'll never, ever wonder again."

"I've always loved you, Mike," he said simply.

Tears blurred her vision. "I know."

Slowly he smiled, and now it was in his eyes, too, that love they'd built together over all these years. She could see it, feel it warming her. "I missed you. God, for twelve years, I missed you."

How was it that the profound simplicity of those words had the power to rock her world? Never again would she lose sight of what mattered, not for a day or an hour or even a minute. She would treasure every instant of her life from now on, for she knew something now, a deep truth that had eluded her all of her life. Love wasn't a great, burning brushfire that swept across your soul and charred you beyond recognition. It was being there, simply that. It was a few people, standing together in a living room, trimming a Christmas tree with the decorations that represented the sum total of who they were, where they'd been, what they believed in.

It was simple, everyday moments that laid like bricks, one atop another, until they formed a foundation so solid that nothing could make them fall. Not wind, not rain . . . not even the faded, watercolor memories of a once-brushfire passion.

Nothing.

"Play me a song."

Something passed through his eyes; it almost looked like fear. Then, slowly, he faced the piano and lifted his hands. For a split second, his fingers floated hesitantly above the keys, and absurdly, she thought *he doesn't play anymore*—

Gently, he began to play. He chose their song, "A Time for Us," and the sweet, familiar music filled the room. She thought she heard him breathe a soft sigh, as if in relief, and when he finished the song, he turned to her.

"Hey, piano man," she said in a throaty voice, "take your wife to bed."

He laughed and stood up, drawing her up alongside him. "I know, I know, or lose my chance."

She held onto him, unable to stop touching him, even for a moment. "You already lost your chance, Liam Campbell. You should have run when I was in a coma. Now you're stuck with me." She pressed up onto her tiptoes and kissed him with fifteen years of pent-up passion. When she drew back, she whispered the word that had brought her through the darkness: "Forever."

For a sneak peek at
Kristin Hannah's
next wonderful novel,

The Things We Do for Love,

please read on.

Available in hardcover in summer 2004.
Published by Ballantine Books.

ONE

THE STREETS OF WEST END WERE CROWDED ON THIS UNEX-pectedly sunny day. All across town mothers stood in open doorways, with hands tented across their eyes, watching their children play. Everyone knew that soon—probably tomor-row—a soapy haze would creep across the sky, covering the blue, obliterating the delicate sun, and once more the rain would fall.

It was May, after all, in the Pacific Northwest. Rain came to this month as surely as ghosts took to the streets on the thirty-first of October and salmon came home from the sea.

"It sure is hot," Conlan said from the driver's seat of the sleek black BMW convertible. It was the first thing he'd said in almost an hour.

He was trying to make conversation; that was all. Angie should return the volley, perhaps mention the beautiful hawthorn trees that were in bloom. But even as she had the thought, she was exhausted by it. In a few short months, those tiny green leaves would curl and blacken; the color would be drawn out of them by cold nights, and they would fall to the ground, unnoticed.

When you looked at it that way, what was the point in noticing so fleeting a moment?

She stared out the window at her hometown. It was the first time she'd been back in months. Although West End was only one hundred twenty miles from Seattle, that distance had seemed to swell lately in her mind. As much as she loved her family, she'd found it difficult to leave her own house. Out in the world, there were babies everywhere.

They drove into the old part of town, where Victorian houses had been built one after another on tiny patches of lawn. Huge, leafy maple trees shaded the street, cast an intricate lacework pattern of light on the asphalt. In the seventies, this neighborhood had been the town's heart. Kids had been everywhere back then, riding their Big Wheels and Schwinn bicycles from one house to the next. There had been block parties every Sunday after church, and games of Red Rover played in every backyard.

In the years between then and now, this part of the state had changed, and the old neighborhoods had fallen into silence and disrepair. Salmon runs had diminished and the timber industry had been hit hard. People who had once made their living from the land and the sea had been pushed aside, forgotten; new residents built their houses in clusters, in subdivisions named after the very trees they cut down.

But here, on this small patch of Maple Drive, time had stood still. The last house on the block looked exactly as it had for forty years. The white paint was pure and perfect; the emerald green trim glistened. No weed had ever been allowed to flourish in the lawn. Angie's father had tended to this house for four decades; it had been his pride and joy. Every Monday, after a weekend of hard work at the family's restaurant, he'd devoted a full twelve-hour day to home and garden maintenance. Since his death, Angie's mother had tried to follow that routine. It had become her solace, her way of connecting with the man she'd loved for almost fifty years, and when she tired of the hard work, someone was always ready to lend a hand. Such help, Mama often reminded them, was the advantage to having three daughters. Her payoff, she claimed, for surviving their teen years.

Conlan pulled up to the curb and parked. As the convertible top shushed mechanically into place, he turned to Angie. "Are you sure you're okay with this?"

"I'm here, aren't I?" She turned to look at him finally. He was exhausted; she saw the glint of it in his blue eyes but knew he wouldn't say more, wouldn't say anything that might remind her of the baby they'd lost a few months ago.

They sat there, side by side in silence. The air-conditioner made a soft whooshing noise.

The old Conlan would have leaned over and kissed her now, would have told her he loved her, and those few and tender words would have saved her, but they were past such comfort these days. The love they'd once shared felt far, far away, as faded and lost as her childhood.

"We could leave right now. Say the car broke down," he said, trying to be the man he used to be, the man who could tease his wife into smiling.

She didn't look at him. "Are you kidding? They all think we paid too much for this car. Besides, Mama already knows we're here. She might talk to dead people, but she has the hearing of a bat."

"She's in the kitchen making ten thousand cannoli for twenty people. And your sisters haven't stopped talking since they walked in the door. We could escape in the confusion." He smiled. For a moment everything felt normal between them, as if there were no ghosts in the car. She wished it were an ease that could last.

"Livvy cooked three casseroles," she muttered. "Mira probably crocheted a new tablecloth and made us all matching aprons."

"Last week you had two pitch meetings and a commercial shoot. It's hardly worth your time to cook."

Poor Conlan. Fourteen years of marriage and he still didn't

understand the dynamics of the DeSaria family. Cooking was more than a job or a hobby; it was a kind of currency, and Angie was broke. Her papa, whom she'd idolized, had loved that she couldn't cook. He took it as a badge of success. An immigrant who'd come to this country with four dollars in his pocket and made a living feeding other immigrant families, he'd been proud that his youngest daughter made money using her head, rather than her hands.

"Let's go," she said, not wanting to think about Papa.

Angie got out of the car and went around to the trunk. It opened silently, revealing a narrow cardboard box. Inside was an extravagantly rich chocolate cake made by the Pacific Dessert Company and a to-die-for lemon tart. She reached down for it, knowing some comment would be made about her inability to cook. As the youngest daughter—"the princess"—she'd been allowed to color or talk on the phone or watch TV while her sisters worked in the kitchen. None of her sisters ever let her forget that Papa had spoiled her mercilessly. As adults, her sisters still worked in the family restaurant. That was real work, they always said, unlike Angie's career in advertising.

"Come on," Conlan said, taking her arm.

They walked up the concrete walkway, past the fountain of the Virgin Mary, and up the steps. A statue of Christ stood by the door, his hands outstretched in greeting. Someone had hung an umbrella from his wrist.

Conlan knocked perfunctorily and opened the door.

The house rattled with noise—loud voices, kids running up and down the stairs, ice buckets being refilled, laughter. Every piece of furniture in the foyer was buried beneath a layer of coats and shoes and empty food boxes.

The family room was full of children playing games. Candy Land for the younger kids; crazy eights for the older. Her eldest nephew, Jason, and her niece Sarah were playing Nintendo on the television. At Angie's entrance, the kids squealed and flocked to her, all talking at once, vying for her attention.

From their earliest memories, she was the aunt who would get down on the floor and play with whatever toy was "in" at the moment. She never turned down their music or said that a movie was unsuitable. When asked, they all said Aunt Angie was "way cool."

She heard Conlan behind her, talking to Mira's husband, Vince. A drink was being poured. She eased through the crowd of kids and walked down the hallway toward the kitchen.

In the doorway, she paused. Mama stood at the oversized butcher block in the center of the room, rolling out the sweet dough. Flour obscured half of her face and dusted her hair. Her eyeglasses—a holdover from the seventies—had lenses the size of saucers and magnified her brown eyes. Tiny beads of sweat collected along her brow and slid down her floury cheeks, landing on her bosom in little blobs of dough. In the five months since Papa's passing, she'd lost too much weight and stopped dyeing her hair. It was snow white now.

Mira stood at the stove, dropping gnocchi into a pot of boiling water. From behind, she looked like a girl. Even after bearing four children, she was still tiny, almost birdlike, and since she often wore her teenage daughter's clothes, she appeared ten years younger than her forty-one years. Tonight, her long black hair was held back in a braid that snaked almost to her waist. She wore a pair of low-rise, flare-legged black pants and a cable-knit red sweater. She was talking now—there was no surprise in that; she was always talking. Papa had always joked that his eldest daughter sounded like a blender on high speed.

Livvy was standing off to the left, slicing fresh mozzarella. She looked like a Bic pen in her black silk sheath. The only thing higher than her heels was the puffiness of her teased hair. Long ago, Livvy had left West End in a rush, certain that she could become a model. She'd stayed in Los Angeles until the sentence "Could you please undress now?" started to accompany every job interview. Five years ago, just after her thirty-fourth birthday, she'd come home, bitter at her lack of success, defeated by the effort, dragging with her two young sons who had been fathered by a man none of the family had ever seen or met. She'd gone to work at the family restaurant, but she didn't like it. She saw herself as a big-city girl trapped in a small town. Now she was married—again; it had been a quickie ceremony last week at the Chapel of Love in Las Vegas. Everyone hoped that Salvatore Traina—lucky choice number three—would finally make her happy.

Angie smiled. So much of her time had been spent in this kitchen with these three women; no matter how old she got or what direction her life took, this would always be home. In Mama's kitchen, you were safe and warm and well loved. Though she and her sisters had chosen different lives and tended to meddle too often in one another's choices, they were like strands of a single rope. When they came together, they were unbreakable. She needed to be a part of that again; she'd been grieving alone for too long.

She stepped into the kitchen and put the box down on the table. "Hey, guys."

Livvy and Mira surged forward, enfolded her in a hug that smelled of Italian spices and drugstore perfume. They held her tightly; Angie felt the wetness of tears on her neck, but nothing was said except "It's good to have you home."

"Thanks." She gave her sisters one last tight hug, then went to Mama, who opened her arms. Angie stepped into the warmth of that embrace. As always, Mama smelled of thyme, Tabu perfume, and Aqua Net hair spray. The scents of Angie's youth.

Mama hugged her so tightly that Angie had to draw in a gulp of air. Laughing, she tried to step back, but Mama held on.

Angie stiffened instinctively. The last time Mama had held Angie this tightly, Mama had whispered, *You'll try again. God will give you another baby.*

Angie pulled out of the embrace. "Don't," she said, trying to smile.

That did it—just that quietly voiced plea. Mama reached for the Parmesan grater and said, "Dinner's ready. Mira, get the kids to the table."

The dining room held fourteen people comfortably and fifteen tonight. An ancient mahogany table, brought here from the old country, held center stage in a big, windowless room papered in rose and burgundy. An ornate wooden crucifix hung on the wall beside a portrait of Jesus. Adults and children were crammed around the table. Dean Martin sang in the other room.

"Let us pray," Mama said as soon as everyone was seated. When silence didn't fall instantly, she reached over and thwopped Uncle Francis on the head.

Francis dropped his chin and closed his eyes. Everyone followed suit and began the prayer. Their voices joined as one: "Bless us, O Lord, and these thy gifts which we are about to receive from thy bounty through Christ our Lord. Amen."

When the prayer ended, Mama stood up quickly, raised her wineglass. "We drink a toast now to Sal and Olivia." Her voice vibrated; her mouth trembled. "I do not know what to say. Toasting is a man's job." She abruptly sat down.

Mira touched Mama's shoulder and stood up. "We welcome Sal to our family. May you two find the kind of love that Mama and Papa had. May you have full cupboards and warm bedrooms and—" She paused. Her voice softened. "—many healthy babies."

Instead of laughter and clapping and clanking glasses, there was silence.

Angie drew a sharp breath and looked up at her sisters.

"I'm not pregnant," Livvy said quickly. "But . . . we're trying."

Angie managed to smile, although it was wobbly and weak and fooled no one. Everyone was looking at her, wondering how she would handle another baby in the family. They all tried so hard not to bruise her.

She raised her glass. "To Sal and Livvy." She spoke quickly, hoping her tears would pass for joy. "May you have many healthy babies."

Conversations started up again. The table became a frenzy of clanging forks and knives scratching on porcelain and laughter. Although this family gathered for every holiday and two Monday nights a month, they never ran out of things to say.

Angie glanced around the table. Mira was talking animatedly to Mama about a school fund-raiser that needed to be catered; Vince and Uncle Francis were arguing about last week's Huskies–Ducks game; Sal and Livvy were kissing every now and then; the younger kids were spitting peas at one another; and the older ones were arguing about whether Xbox or PlayStation was better. Conlan was asking Aunt Giulia about her upcoming hip replacement surgery.

Angie couldn't concentrate on any of it. She certainly couldn't make idle conversation. Her sister wanted a baby, and so it would happen. Livvy would probably get pregnant between Leno and the news. *Oops, I forgot my diaphragm.* That was how it happened for her sisters.

After dinner, as Angie washed the dishes, no one spoke to her, but everyone who walked past the sink squeezed her shoulder or kissed her cheek. Everyone knew there were no more words to say. Hopes and prayers had been offered so many times over the years they'd lost their sheen. Mama had kept a candle burning at St. Cecilia's for almost a decade now, and . . . still it would be Angie and Conlan alone in the car tonight, a couple who'd never multiplied into a family.

Finally, she couldn't stand it anymore. She tossed the dishrag on the table and went up to her old bedroom. The pretty little room, still wallpapered in roses and white baskets, held twin beds ruffled in pink bedding. She sat down on the end of her bed.

Ironically, she'd once knelt on this very floor and prayed not to be pregnant. She'd been seventeen at the time, dating Tommy Matucci. Her first love.

The door opened and Conlan walked in. Her big, black-haired Irishman husband looked ridiculously out of place in her little girl's room.

"I'm fine," she said.

"Yeah, right."

She heard the bitterness in his voice, felt stung by it. There was nothing she could do, though. He couldn't comfort her; God knew that had been proven often enough.

"You need help." He said it tiredly, and no wonder. The words were old.

"I'm fine."

He stared at her for a long time. The blue eyes that had once looked at her with adoration now held an almost unbearable defeat. With a sigh, he turned and left the room, closing the door behind him.

A few moments later it opened again. Mama stood in the doorway, her fists planted on her narrow hips. The shoulder pads on her Sunday dress were *Blade Runner* big and practically touched the door frame on either side. "You always did run to your room when you were sad. Or angry."

Angie scooted sideways to make room. "And you always came running up after me."

"Your father made me. You never knew that, did you?" Mama sat down beside Angie. The old mattress sagged beneath their weight. "He could not stand to see you cry. Poor Livvy could shriek her lungs out and he never noticed. But you . . . you were his princess. One tear could break his heart." She sighed. It was a heavy sound, full of disappointment and empathy. "You're thirty-eight years old, Angela," Mama said. "It's time to grow up. Your papa—God rest his soul—would have agreed with me on this."

"I don't even know what that means."

Mama slipped an arm around her, pulled her close. "God has given you an answer to your prayers, Angela. It is not the answer you wanted, so you don't hear. It's time to listen."

* * *

Angie woke with a start. The coolness on her cheeks was from tears.

She'd had the baby dream again; the one in which she and Conlan stood on opposite shores. Between them, on the shimmering expanse of blue sea, was a tiny pink-swaddled bundle. Inch by inch, it floated away and disappeared. When it was gone, they were left alone, she and Conlan, standing too far apart.

It was the same dream she'd been having for years, as she and her husband trudged from doctor's office to doctor's office, trying one procedure after another. Supposedly she was one of the lucky ones; in eight years, she'd conceived three children. Two had ended in miscarriage; one—her daughter, Sophia—had lived for only a few short days. That had been the end of it. Neither she nor Conlan had the heart to try again.

She eased away from her husband, grabbed her pink chenille robe off the floor, and left the bedroom.

The shadowy hallway waited for her. To her right, dozens of family photographs, all framed in thick mahogany, covered the wall. Portraits of five generations of DeSarias and Malones.

She looked down the long hallway at the last, closed door. The brass knob glinted in moonlight from the nearby window.

When was the last time she'd dared to enter that room?

God has given you an answer. . . . It's time to listen.

She walked slowly past the stairs and the vacant guest room to the final door.

There she drew in a deep breath and exhaled it. Her hands were trembling as she opened the door and went inside. The air felt heavy in here, old and musty.

She turned on the light and closed the door behind her.

The room was so perfect.

She closed her eyes, as if darkness could help. The sweet notes of *Beauty and the Beast* filled her mind, took her back in time to the first time she'd closed the door on this room, so many years ago. It was after they'd decided on adoption.

We have a baby, Mrs. Malone. The mother—a teenager—chose you and Conlan. Come down to my office and meet her.

It had taken Angie the full four hours until their appointment to choose the outfit and do her makeup. When she and Conlan finally met Sarah Dekker in the lawyer's office, the three of them had bonded instantly. *We'll love your child,* Angie had promised the girl. *You can trust us.*

For six wonderful months Angie and Conlan had given up trying to get pregnant. Sex had become fun again; they'd fallen effortlessly back in love. Life had been good. There had been hope in this house. They'd celebrated with their families. They'd brought Sarah into their home and shared their hearts with her. They'd accompanied her to every OB appointment. Two weeks before her due date, Sarah had come home with some stencils and paint. She and Angie had decorated this room. A sky blue ceiling and walls, crowded by puffy white clouds. White picket fencing entwined with bright flowers, their colorful faces attended to by bees and butterflies and fairies.

The first sign of disaster had come on the day Sarah went into labor. Angie and Conlan had been at work. They'd come home to an empty, too-quiet house, with no message on the answering machine and no note on the kitchen table. They'd been home less than an hour when the phone rang.

They'd huddled by the phone together, holding hands, crying with happiness when they heard of the birth. It had taken a moment for the other words to register. Even now, Angie only remembered bits and pieces of the conversation.

I'm sorry—
changed her mind
back with her boyfriend
keeping the baby

They'd shut the door to this room and kept it closed. Once a week, their cleaning woman ventured inside, but Angie and Conlan never did. For well over a year, this room had stood empty, a shrine to their dream of someday. They'd given up on all of it—the doctors, the treatments, the injections, and the procedures. Then, miraculously, Angie had conceived again. By the time she was five months pregnant, they'd dared once more to enter this room and fill it with their dreams. They should have known better.

She went to the closet and pulled out a big cardboard box. One by one, she began to put things into it, trying not to attach memories to every piece she touched.

"Hey."

She hadn't even heard the door open, and yet here he was, in the room with her.

She knew how crazy it must seem to him, to find his wife sitting in the middle of the room, with a big cardboard box beside her. Inside it were all of her precious knickknacks—the Winnie-the-Pooh bedside lamp, the Aladdin picture frame, the crisp new collection of Dr. Seuss books. The only piece of furniture left was the crib. The bedding was on the floor beside it, a neat little stack of pale pink flannel.

She turned to look up at him. There were tears in her eyes, blurring her vision, but she hadn't noticed until now. She wanted to tell him how sorry she was; it had all gone wrong between them. She picked up a small pink stack of sheets, stroking the fabric. "It made me crazy" was all she could say.

He sat down beside her.

She waited for him to speak, but he just sat there, watching her. She understood. The past had taught him caution. He was like an animal that had adapted to its dangerous environment by being still and quiet. Between the fertility drugs and the broken dreams, Angie's emotions were unpredictable. "I forgot about us," she said.

"There is no us, Angie." The gentle way he said it broke her heart.

Finally. One of them had dared to say it. "I know."

"I wanted a baby, too."

She swallowed hard, trying to keep her tears under control. She'd forgotten that in the last few years; Conlan had dreamed of fatherhood just as she wanted motherhood. Somewhere along the way, it had all become about her. She'd focused so much on her own grief that his had become incidental. It was one of those realizations that would haunt her, she knew. She had always been dedicated to success in her life—her family called her obsessive—and becoming a mother had been one more goal to attain. She should have remembered that it was a team sport.

"I'm sorry," she said again.

He took her in his arms and kissed her. It was the kind of kiss they hadn't shared in years.

They sat that way, entwined, for a long time.

She wished his love could have been enough for her. It should have been. But her need for a child had been like a high tide, an overwhelming force that had drowned them. Maybe a year ago she could have kicked to the surface. Not now. "I loved you. . . ."

"I know."

"We should have been more careful."

Later that night, when she was alone in the bed they'd bought together, she tried to remember the hows and whys of it, the things they'd said to each other at the end of their love, but none of it came back to her. All she could really remember was the smell of baby powder and the sound of his voice when he said good-bye.

TWO

IT WAS AMAZING HOW MUCH TIME IT TOOK TO DISMANTLE A life. Once Angie and Conlan had decided to end their marriage, details became what mattered. How to divide everything in half, especially the indivisible things like houses and cars and hearts. They spent months on the details of divorce, and by late September it was done.

Her house—no, it was the Pedersons' house now—was empty. Instead of bedrooms and a designer living room and a granite-layered kitchen, she had a sizeable amount of money in the bank, a storage facility filled with fifty percent of their furniture, and a car trunk full of suitcases.

Angie sat on the brick hearth, staring out across the gleaming gold of her hardwood floors.

There had been blue carpeting in here on the day she and Conlan had moved in.

Hardwood, they'd said to each other, smiling at the ease of their agreement and the power of their dream. *Kids are so hard on carpet.*

So long ago . . .

Ten years in this house. It felt like a lifetime.

The doorbell rang.

She immediately tensed.

But it couldn't be Con. He'd have a key. Besides, he wasn't scheduled to come by today. This was her day to pack up the last of her things. After fourteen years of marriage, they now had to schedule separate time in the house they'd shared.

She got to her feet and crossed the living room, opening the door.

Mama, Mira, and Livvy stood there, huddled together beneath the entry roof, trying to keep out of the rain. They were trying to smile, too; neither effort was entirely successful.

"A day like this," Mama said, "is for family." They surged forward in a pack. The aroma of garlic wafted up from a picnic basket on Mira's arm.

"Focaccia," Mira said at Angie's look. "You know that food eases every trouble."

Angie found herself smiling. How many times in her life had she come home from school, devastated by some social slight, only to hear Mama say, *Eat something. You'll feel better.*

Livvy sidled up to her. In a black sweater and skintight jeans she looked like Lara Flynn Boyle on Big Hair Day. "I've been through two divorces. Food *so* doesn't help. I tried to get her to put tequila in the basket, but you know Mama." She leaned closer. "I have some Zoloft in my purse if you need it."

"Come, come," Mama said, taking charge. She herded her chicks to the empty living room.

Angie felt the full weight of it then: failure. Here was her family, looking for places to sit in an empty house that yesterday had been a home.

Angie sat down on the hard, cold floor. The room was quiet now. They were waiting for her to start talking. They'd follow her lead. That was what family did. The problem was, Angie had nowhere to go and nothing to say. Her sisters would have laughed about that on any other day. Now it was hardly funny.

Mira was the first to actually move. She sat down beside Angie and scooted close. The rivets on her faded jeans made a scraping noise on the floor. Mama followed, sat down on the brick hearth; Livvy sat beside her.

Angie looked around at their sad, knowing faces, wanting to explain it for them. "If Sophie had lived—"

"Don't go there," Livvy said sharply. "It can't help."

Angie's eyes stung. She almost gave in to her pain right there, let it overwhelm her. Then she rallied. It wouldn't do any good to cry. Hell, she'd spent most of the last year in tears and where had it gotten her? "You're right," she said.

Mira took her in her arms.

It was exactly what Angie needed. When she drew back, feeling somehow shakier and steadier at the same time, all three women were looking at her.

"Can I be honest here?" Livvy said, opening the basket and pulling out a bottle of red wine.

"Absolutely not," Angie said.

Livvy ignored her. "You and Con have been at odds too long. Believe me, I know about love that goes bad. It was time to give up." She began pouring the wine into glasses. "Now you should go somewhere. Take some time off."

"Running away won't help," Mira said.

"Bullshit," Livvy responded, offering Angie a glass of wine. "You've got money. Go to Rio de Janeiro. The beaches are supposed to be great. And practically nude."

Angie smiled. The pinched feeling in her chest eased a little. "So I should buy a thong and show off my rapidly dropping ass?"

Livvy laughed. "Honey, it wouldn't hurt."

For the next hour, they sat in the empty living room, drinking red wine and eating, talking about ordinary things. The weather. Life in West End. Aunt Giulia's recent surgery.

Angie tried to follow the conversation, but she kept wondering how she'd ended up here, alone and childless at thirty-eight. The early years of her marriage had been so good. . . .

"That's because business is bad," Livvy said, pouring herself another glass of wine. "What else can we do?"

Angie drifted back to the here and now, surprised to realize that she'd left for a few minutes. She looked up. "What are you guys talking about?"

"Mama wants to sell the restaurant," Mira said.

Angie straightened. "*What?*" The restaurant was the hub of their family, the center of everything.

"We were not going to speak of it today," Mama said, shooting Mira an angry look.

Angie looked from face to face. "What in the hell is going on?"

"Don't you swear, Angela," Mama said. She sounded tired. "Business at the restaurant is bad. I don't see how we can keep going."

"But . . . Papa loved it," Angie said.

Tears sprang into her mother's dark eyes. "You hardly need to tell me this."

Angie looked at Livvy. "What's wrong with the business?"

Livvy shrugged. "The economy is bad."

"DeSaria's has been doing well for thirty years. It can't be—"

"I can't *believe* you're going to tell us how to run a restaurant," Livvy snapped, lighting up a cigarette. "What would a copywriter know about it?"

"Creative director. And it's running a restaurant, not performing brain surgery. You just give people good food at good prices. How hard can—"

"Stop it, you two," Mira said. "Mama doesn't need this."

Angie looked at her mother, but didn't know what to say. A family that only moments before had been the bedrock of her life felt suddenly cracked.

They fell into silence. Angie was thinking about the restaurant . . . about her papa, who had always been able to make her laugh, even when her heart had felt close to rending . . . and about the safe world where they'd all grown up together.

The restaurant was the anchor of their family; without it, they might drift away from one another. And that, the floating on one's own tide, was a lonely way to live. Angie knew.

"Angie could help," Mama said.

Livvy made a sound of disbelief. "She doesn't know anything about the business. Papa's princess never had—"

"Hush, Livvy," Mama said, staring at Angie.

Angie understood everything in that one look. Mama was offering her a place to hide out away from the painful memories in this city. To Mama, *coming home* was the answer to every question. "Livvy is right," Angie said slowly. "I don't know anything about the business."

"You helped that restaurant in Olympia. The success of your

campaign made the newspapers," Mira said, studying her. "Papa made us read all the clippings."

"Which Angie mailed to him," Livvy said, exhaling smoke.

Angie *had* helped put that restaurant back on the map. But all it had taken was a good ad campaign and some money for marketing.

"Maybe you *could* help us," Mira said at last.

"I don't know," Angie said. She'd left West End so long ago, certain that the whole world awaited her. How would it feel to be back?

"You could live in the beach house," Mama said.

The beach house.

Angie thought about the tiny cottage on the wild, windswept coast, and a dozen treasured memories came to her, one after another.

She'd always felt safe and loved there. Protected.

Maybe she could learn to smile again there, in that place where, as a girl, she'd laughed easily and often.

She looked around her, at this too-empty house that was so full of sadness; it sat on a block in a city that held too many bad memories. Maybe going home was the answer, for a while at least, until she figured out where she belonged now.

She wouldn't feel alone at the cottage; not like she did in Seattle.

"Yeah," she said slowly, looking up. "I could help out for a little while." She didn't know which emotion was sharper just then—relief or disappointment. All she knew was this: She wouldn't be alone.

Mama smiled. "Papa told me you would come back to us someday."

Livvy rolled her eyes. "Oh, great. The princess is coming back to help us poor country bumpkins run the restaurant."

A week later Angie was on her way. She'd set off for West End in the way she started every project—full speed ahead.

First, she'd called her boss at the advertising agency and asked for a leave of absence.

Her boss had stumbled around a bit, sputtering in surprise. There had been no indication at all that she was unhappy, none at all. *If it's a promotion you want—*

She'd laughed at that, explaining simply that she was tired. *Tired?*

She needed time off. And she had no idea how much. By the time the conversation had wound around to its end, she had simply quit. Why not? She needed to find a new life, and she could hardly do that clinging to the hemline of the old one. She had plenty of money in the bank and lots of marketable skills. When she was ready to merge back into the traffic of real life, she could always find another job.

She tried not to think about how often Conlan had begged her to do this very thing. *It's killing you,* he always said. *How can we relax if you're always in overdrive? The doctors say . . .*

She cranked up the music—something old and sweet—and pressed her foot down on the accelerator.

The miles sped past, each one taking her farther from Seattle and closer to the town of her youth.

Finally, she turned off the interstate and followed the green *Washington Beaches* signs to West End.

The tiny town welcomed her. Light glinted off streets and leaves that were still wet with rain. The storefronts, long ago painted in bright blues and greens and pale pinks to reflect the Victorian fishing village theme, had, in time, weathered to a silvery softness. As she drove down Front Street, she remembered the Fourth of July parades. Every year the family had dressed up and carried a *DeSaria's Restaurant* banner. They'd tossed candies to the crowd. Angie had hated every moment, but now . . . now it made her smile sadly and remember her father's booming laugh. *You are part of this family, Angela. You march.*

She rolled down her window and immediately smelled the salty tang of sea air mixed with pine. Somewhere a bakery had opened its doors. There was the merest hint of cinnamon on the breeze.

The street was busy but not crowded on this late September afternoon. No matter where she looked, people were talking animatedly to one another. She saw Mr. Peterson, the local pharmacist, standing on the street outside his store. He waved at her, and she waved back. She knew that within minutes he would walk next door to the hardware store and tell Mr. Tannen that Angie DeSaria was back. He'd lower his voice when he'd say, *Poor thing. Divorce, you know.*

She came to a stoplight—one of four in town—and slowed. She was about to turn left, toward her parents' house, but the ocean sang its siren call and she found herself answering. Besides, she wasn't ready for the family thing yet.

She turned right and followed the long, winding road out of town. To her left, the Pacific Ocean was a windblown gray sail that stretched to forever. Dunes and sea grass waved and fluttered in the wind.

Only a mile or so from town it became a different world. There were very few houses out here. Every now and then there were signs for a so-called resort or a collection of rental cabins perched above the sea, but even then there was nothing to be seen from the road. This stretch of shoreline, hidden amid the towering trees in an out-of-the-way town between Seattle and Portland, hadn't been "discovered" yet by the yuppies, and most of the locals couldn't afford beach property. And so it was wild here. Primitive. The ocean roared its presence and reminded passersby that once, not so very long ago, people believed dragons lived in the uncharted waters. It could be quiet sometimes, deceptively so, and in those times tourists were lulled into a false sense of safety. They took their rented kayaks out into the rolling water and paddled back and forth. Every year some of those tourists were simply lost; only the bright borrowed kayaks returned.

Finally she came to an old, rusted mailbox that read: *DeSaria.*

She turned onto the rutted dirt driveway. Giant trees hemmed her in on either side, blocked out most of the sky and all of the sun. The property was covered in fallen pine needles and oversized ferns. Mist coated the ground and rose upward, gave the world an impossibly softened look. She'd forgotten the mist, how it came every morning in the autumn, breathing up from the earth like a sigh made visible. Sometimes, on early morning walks, you could look down and not see your own feet. As children, they'd gone in search of that mist in the mornings, made a game out of kicking through it.

She pulled up to the cottage and parked.

The homecoming was so sweet and sharp she swallowed a sudden lump in her throat. The house her father had built by hand sat in a tiny clearing, surrounded by trees that had been old when Lewis and Clark passed through this territory.

The shingles, once a cedar red, had aged to the color of driftwood, silvery soft. The white trim was barely a contrast at all.

When she got out of the car, she heard the symphony of her childhood summers—the sound of surf below, the whistling of the wind through the trees. Someone somewhere was flying a kite. The fluttery thwop-thwop sent her back in time.

Come on over here, princess. Help Papa trim these bushes back. . . .

Hey, Livvy, wait up! I can't run that fast. . . .

Mama, tell Mira to give me my marshmallows back. . . .

It was here, all those funny, angry, bittersweet moments that made up their family's history. She stood there in the watery sunlight, surrounded by trees, and soaked them all in, the memories she'd forgotten.

Over there by the giant nurse log that sprouted a dozen smaller plants was where Tommy had first kissed Angie . . . and tried to feel her up. There by the well house was the best ever hiding place for hide-and-go-seek.

And there, hidden in the dark shade of two gigantic cedar trees, was the fern grotto. Two summers ago, she and Conlan had brought all the nieces and nephews out here for a campout. They'd built a fort amid the huge ferns and pretended to be pirates. They'd told elaborate ghost stories that night, all of them gathered around a bonfire, roasting marshmallows and making s'mores.

Back then, she'd still believed that someday she'd bring her own children here. . . .

With a sigh, she carried her luggage into the house. The downstairs was one big room—a kitchen off to the left, with butter yellow cabinets and white tile countertops; a small dining area tucked into the corner (somehow all five of them had eaten at that tiny table); and a living room that took up the rest of the space. A giant river rock fireplace dominated the north-facing wall. Around it were clustered a pair of overstuffed blue sofas, a battered pine coffee table, and Papa's worn leather chair. There was no television at the cottage. Never had been.

We talk, Papa had always said when his daughters complained.

"Hey, Papa," she whispered.

The only answer was wind on the windowpanes.

Tap. Tap. Tap.

It was the sound a rocking chair made, on a hardwood floor, in an unused room. . . .

She tried to outrun the memories, but they were too fast. She felt her control slipping away. With every breath she took, it seemed that time marched on, moved away from her. Her youth was leaving her, as impossible to grasp as the air she breathed in her lonely bed at night.

She let out a heavy breath. She'd been a fool to think things would be different here. Why would they? Memories didn't live on streets or in cities. They flowed in the blood, pulsed with your heartbeat. She'd brought it all with her, every loss and heartache. The weight of it bowed her back, exhausted her.

She climbed the stairs and went into her parents' old bedroom. The sheets and blankets were off the bed, of course, no doubt stored in a box in the closet, and the mattress was dusty, but Angie didn't care. She crawled up onto the bed and curled into a ball.

This hadn't been a good idea, after all, coming home. She closed her eyes, listening to the bees buzzing outside her window, and tried to fall asleep.

The next morning, Angie woke with the sun. She stared up at the ceiling, watching a fat black wolf spider spinning its web.

Her eyes felt gritty and swollen.

Once again she'd watered her mattress with memories.

Enough was enough.

It was a decision she'd made hundreds of times in the last year. This time she was determined to mean it.

She opened the suitcase, found a change of clothes, and headed for the bathroom. After a hot shower, she felt human again. She brushed her hair into a ponytail, dressed in a pair of faded jeans and a red turtleneck sweater, and grabbed her purse off the kitchen table. She was just about to leave for town when she happened to glance out the window.

Outside, Mama sat on a fallen log at the edge of the property. She was talking to someone, moving her hands in those wild gestures that had so embarrassed Angie in her youth.

No doubt the whole family was arguing about whether Angie could be of any use at the restaurant. After last night, she questioned it herself.

She knew that when she stepped out onto the porch, all those voices raised in disagreement would sound like a lawn mower. They would spend an hour arguing over the pros and cons of Angie's return.

Her opinion would hardly matter.

She paused at the back door, gathering courage. Forcing a

smile, she opened the door and went outside, looking for the crowd.

There was no one here except Mama.

Angie crossed the yard and sat down on the log.

"We knew you'd come out sooner or later," Mama said.

"We?"

"Your papa and me."

Angie sighed. So her mother was still talking to Papa. Grief was something Angie knew well. She could hardly blame her mother for refusing to let go. Still, she couldn't help wondering if this was something to worry about. She touched her mother's hand. The skin was loose and soft. "So what does he have to say about my being home?"

Mama sighed in obvious relief. "Your sisters ask me to see a doctor. You ask me what Papa has to say. Oh, Angela, I'm glad you're home." She pulled Angie into a hug.

For the first time, Mama wasn't dressed to the nines and layered in clothes. She wore only a cable-knit sweater and an old pair of Jordache jeans. Angie could feel how thin she'd gotten and it worried her. "You've lost more weight," she said, drawing back.

"Of course. For forty-seven years I eat dinner with my husband. Alone is hard."

"Then you and I will eat together. I'm alone, too."

"Are you staying?"

"What do you mean?"

"Mira thinks you need someone to take care of you and a place to hide out for a few days. Running a restaurant in trouble is not easy. She thinks you'll be gone in a day or two."

Angie could tell that Mira spoke for others in the family, and she wasn't surprised. Her sister didn't understand the kind of dreams that sent a girl in search of a different life . . . or the heartache that could turn her around and send her home again. The family had always worried that Angie's ambition was too sharp somehow, that it would cut her. "What do you think?"

Mama bit down on her lip, worried it in a gesture as familiar as the sound of the sea. "Papa says he's waited twenty years for you to take over his baby—his restaurant—and he doesn't want anyone to get in your way."

Angie smiled. That sounded so much like Papa. For a second, she almost believed he was here with them, standing in the shadows of his beloved trees.

She sighed, wishing she could hear his voice again, but there was only the sound of the ocean, roaring up to the sand. She couldn't help thinking about last night and all the tears she'd shed. "I don't know if I'm strong enough yet to help you."

"He loved to sit here and watch the ocean," Mama said, leaning against her. "*We have to fix those stairs, Maria.* That's what he said first thing every summer."

"Did you hear me? Last night . . . was hard."

"We made a lot of changes every summer. This place never looked the same two years in a row."

"I know, but—"

"It always started with the one thing. Just fixing the stairs."

"Just the stairs, huh?" Angie said, finally smiling. "The longest journey begins with a single step and all that."

"Some sayings are simply true."

"But what if I don't know where to start?"

"You will."

Mama put an arm around her. They sat that way a long time, leaning against each other, staring out to sea. Finally, Angie said, "How did you know I was here, by the way?"

"Mr. Peterson saw you drive through town."

"And so it begins." Angie smiled, remembering the web that connected the residents in this town. Once, at the homecoming dance, she'd let Tommy Matucci put his hands on her butt; the news had reached Mama before the dance was over. As a girl, Angie had hated that small-town feeling. Now, it felt good to know that people were looking out for her.

She heard a car drive up. She glanced back at the house. A forest green minivan pulled into the yard.

Mira got out of the car. She was wearing a faded pair of denim overalls and an old Metallica T-shirt. In her arms were a pile of account books. "No time like the present to get started," she said. "But you better read 'em fast—before Livvy realizes they're gone."

"You see?" Mama said, smiling at Angie. "Family will always show you where to begin."

THE THINGS WE DO FOR LOVE $5.00 REBATE

Buy one copy of
THE THINGS WE DO FOR LOVE
by Kristin Hannah and receive a
$5.00 rebate!

Name: _____

Address: _____

City: _____

State or Canadian Province: _____ Zip: _____

Country: _____

Consumer: To receive your $5.00 rebate, simply purchase a copy of THE THINGS WE DO FOR LOVE, by Kristin Hannah, and send this completed form with the original, dated cash register receipt for the book to: Ballantine Books, Marketing Department, 1745 Broadway, New York, NY 10019. Offer ends on August 15th, 2004, and coupon with store receipt must be received by that date. Limit one coupon per customer. Not valid with any other offers. Multiple requests, mechanical reproductions, or facsimiles will not be honored. Reproduction, sale, or purchase of this coupon is prohibited. 18 U.S.C. Section 1341 and other mail fraud statutes apply to all redemptions. Ballantine Books reserves the right to reject any proofs or forms not deemed genuine. Offer valid in the United States and Canada (excluding the province of Quebec). Please allow 6-8 weeks for delivery.

MAIL-IN OFFER/MANUFACTURER'S COUPON EXPIRES: 8/15/04

Subscribe to the new Pillow Talk e-newsletter—and receive all these fabulous online features directly in your e-mail inbox:

♥ Exclusive essays and other features by major romance writers like Linda Howard, Kristin Hannah, Julie Garwood, and Suzanne Brockmann

♥ Exciting behind-the-scenes news from our romance editors

♥ Special offers, including contests to win signed romance books and other prizes

♥ Author tour information, and monthly announcements about the newest books on sale

♥ A Pillow Talk readers forum, featuring feedback from romance fans...like you!

Two easy ways to subscribe:
Go to **www.ballantinebooks.com/PillowTalk**
or send a blank e-mail to
join-PillowTalk@list.randomhouse.com.

Pillow Talk—
the romance e-newsletter brought to you by
Ballantine Books